A Cozy Fantasy Novel

DISTILLED MAGIC

ALEX PEACHY

In Light Syrup LLC

Copyright © 2025 Alex Peachy
All rights reserved.
Published by In Light Syrup LLC
Mill Creek, WA
e-book ISBN: 978-1-966930-00-6
print ISBN: 978-1-966930-01-3

No part of this book may be reproduced in any form or by any electronic or mechanical means, including information storage and retrieval systems, without written permission from the author, except for the use of brief quotations in a book review.

Generative AI was not used in the creation of this book.

NO AI TRAINING: Without in any way limiting the author's [and publisher's] exclusive rights under copyright, any use of this publication to "train" generative artificial intelligence (AI) technologies to generate text is expressly prohibited. The author reserves all rights to license uses of this work for generative AI training and development of machine learning language models.

This is a work of fiction. Names, characters, places, and incidents either are the products of the author's imagination or used fictitiously. Any resemblance to actual persons, living or dead, businesses, events, or locales is entirely coincidental.

Content Warnings

This novel includes instances of transphobia, body shaming, gender dysphoria, misgendering, dead naming, unaccepting family, and mentions of physical abuse. They are not overly prevalent but may trigger some readers. The novel also contains themes of adoption, infertility, and substance abuse. There are small sections involving experimentation on animals and people (goblins) which may be disconcerting to some readers.

Acknowledgements

Many people have encouraged and supported me as I've found my way as a writer. However, none have done so as much as my wife. Thank you for everything, Rebecca.

Before starting this story in earnest, I reached out to an old friend. Thank you, Justine, for your early consult, feedback, and ideas.

The editors I worked with helped make this something worthy of your time, dear readers. Thank you to Laura for their early developmental eyes. Thank you to Emeric, whose expert eyes hopefully kept my foot out of my mouth when talking about experiences I have not personally lived. Thank you to K.F., who leveled up my prose.

Finally, I want to acknowledge all transgender people and anyone who identifies as a member of the LGBTQ+ community. I am not a member of your community, but I consider myself an ally and do what I can to advocate for you. I have friends and family who are transgender and care deeply for everyone.

Chapter 1

The Raid

"Watch it, runt!" Grooble, the goblin, snapped when Traz ran right into him, oblivious to the fact that the marching squads had all slowed and stopped. The annoyed warrior adjusted his boot and brushed at his clothes as if the collision had soiled him or infested him with bugs. Grooble had earned a leather chest piece and routinely made a show of his importance.

"Sorry," Traz mumbled, taking a few paces back until he almost collided with another raider.

He turned, apologizing to the goblin he narrowly missed before settling into a ready stance. As usual, he wished he could disappear. It was clear being a warrior was not his calling. He wasn't even cut out to be a goblin.

He had yet to gain enough status to earn any armor. The wind plastered his cotton tunic and trousers against his slender form. Anyone could see he was no hob, but even compared to other goblins, his muscles had never bulked up. Which was fine by Traz. He didn't want a large, hairy, muscular body.

The squad leader had assigned him a basic wooden club.

Simple weapons like this were standard issues to recruits with little training. Explaining how to use a cudgel is fairly straight-forward. Pick a target. Bonk it on the head. Traz had taken to it naturally and had whacked three guards on his last raid. It should be easy enough to bop a few more skulls today. Their unit and several others hunted a caravan of three wagons laden with untold goodies and riches.

"Quiet up, you dunderheads!" yelled Grax, a large hob in the front. "The scouts report the caravan is just over the next rise. I know it's hard, but try not to prove you are a bunch of stupid grunts. On my signal, charge and take out as many guards as you can."

He looked over the rag-tag mess of warriors and recruits. Nodding to his seconds, he raised his hand, holding a wicked curved blade with jagged serrated teeth. He slashed his sword down and belted, "Now! Move it. Attack!"

The sea of goblin raiders swept Traz up with their momentum, propelling him up and over the hill. He stumbled down the slope with his club held high. Below him, the three wagons halted abruptly, and guards poured from the sides. Those posted on top strung their bows and nocked arrows.

The goblins' sheer numbers were their only advantage. All the sentries wore better armor and held finely crafted weapons. Traz, along with several other raiders, barreled through an opening between two wagons. He whacked a guard in the shin with his club. The man fell to his knees, and vicious green attackers promptly swarmed him while Traz backed away, wrinkling his nose at their brutality.

The rooftop archers rained arrows down into the war band. A shaft pierced right through Traz's left arm, and he cried out, pain racing through his veins like lightning. Composing himself with a small whimper, he mustered the courage to fight on. After smacking the nearest guard with his club, he dove under a nearby wagon. He found courage much easier to come by sheltered and out of sight. Letting his cudgel roll to the side, he pulled a knife from his belt and sliced at the guards' legs as they rushed past, the blade barely scratching the tough leather of their boots.

The arrow stuck through his arm, a barbed head on one side, the feathered fletching on the other. Pulling it out would not be easy, and he didn't have bandages to bind it. Leaving it in hurt, but the shaft allowed a mere trickle of blood to leak from the wound. Traz did what he could to keep stabbing and slashing with his good hand. Occasionally, the blade would slice through clothing or skin.

As fewer and fewer legs offered themselves up as targets and the sounds of the battle dulled and eventually silenced, Traz could see dead goblins strewn about the road. There were dead guards as well, but only a few.

The guard leaders called out wagon assignments to the remaining defenders, and boards creaked as men hoisted themselves up onto outboards. Traz lay as still as he could, hoping they would write him off as dead.

The wagons rolled forward, uncovering him, but Traz's limp form garnered no attention. Instead, the guards scanned the surrounding hills for signs of additional raiders. They likely were afraid this was the first of several attack waves, but no more goblins descended, and the sound of the horses' hooves on the dirt road faded away.

He waited ten more minutes. Each felt double the length of the last as his arm throbbed. Finally, he deemed it should be safe and dragged himself up to his feet to look around at the aftermath. Searching some bodies, he found a stash of bandages. This was not the greatest spot to treat his wounds, but Traz noticed what could be the mouth of a cave two hills over.

The caravan was unlikely to come back; however, other travelers on this road would not be out of the ordinary. Resting up and tending to his wound sounded like a much better idea than trudging home to the clan den. With that decided, he headed toward the spot.

Traz approached the alcove and found a wooden door recessed into the opening. Happy not to find a bear or other dangerous beast, he couldn't help but wonder who would live out here. It was too small to be a proper goblin warren, and closer to the Chubug clan than any rival would comfortably settle.

He cautiously approached the door and gave a knock. A gruff but muffled voice said something unintelligible on the other side. Traz waited.

The area around the entrance looked freshly swept. The door itself appeared to have been prized from a carriage. Someone had fitted it into a rough wooden frame held in the rock alcove with pressure against the stone.

Traz knocked again and heard jostling, then a harrumph. A long-drawn-out moment later, the door pulled open, a soft whine emanating from the hinges.

A large hobgoblin stood looking down at him. The hob had dark forest-green skin and long black hair streaked with strands of gray and silver.

She? Must be. She had eggplant-purple eyeshadow applied thickly on her eyelids, flaring away from the eyes into a point outlined with charcoal. Her cheeks had stubble from a day or two of growth. She wore a long dress, and the bodice portion of the garment held what appeared to be a large bosom.

The staring contest continued. Traz tried to determine who exactly he was looking at. Finally, the owner of the cave broke the silence with a gruff voice. "Got yourself poked too hard, I see. That arrow needs to come out. It'll be tough to do on your own. Don't just stand there. Get in here."

She stepped aside, and not knowing what else to do, and at a complete loss for words, Traz obediently shuffled past the hob into the cavern. The huge goblin closed the door and led him to a stool positioned at a simple wooden table. A fire crackled and popped in a hearth carved into the wall. The updraft pulled the smoke through a vent to the outside that must have been hidden in the alcove. A candle burned slowly on the table, and others were spaced strategically in the large room.

As Traz sat down, the hob said, "You can call me Zigla."

Zigla? So that confirmed it. She had some features that suggested she may be a woman, but also, no. This seemed to be a hobgoblin, but he had never heard of a female hob. He didn't want to be rude and instead kept those thoughts inside his head. She had, after all, been willing to bring him in and help him.

"I–" Traz's voice cracked. "I found these bandages. I planned on wrapping the wound."

"Gotta get the arrow out first. No point wrapping around it. Here, bite on this," Zigla said, shoving a piece of leather in his mouth.

Before he could say or do anything about it, she broke the fletching off and pulled on the arrowhead, yanking what remained of the shaft through the hole in his arm. Blood immediately flowed from the open puncture.

"Unnngg," Traz let a moan escape and spat out the wad of leather. "Ow! That stings. I can handle it, though."

"Shh, shhh. I'll get you fixed up. Just sit still."

The old hob poured water over his arm to clean away the filth and grime from the battle. She placed two pads on either side of the wound and wrapped a length of bandage around, securing them against his arm. He could see a blossom of red spread and seep through, but it should heal with time.

She put a kettle on the fire to heat water and dug around in a cupboard before triumphantly holding up a pouch.

"Found some Whispering Willow. This should ease the pain and boost your system."

Once the tea finished brewing, she handed him a mug, and Traz carefully sipped, the heat from the mug comforting in his hands. Zigla sat across from him. She had pulled up a large stump of a log from the firewood pile to use as a makeshift stool.

"Thank you," he said. "It was real kind of you to fix me up, and this tea is already numbing some of the pain. My name is Traz." He idly pulled the half of the arrow with the feathers on it toward him.

"Well, couldn't have you bleeding out there all over my front entry. It's a hike back to Chubug. Assuming that's where you're from. Better to rest and heal up for a bit. You want to tell me about what happened?" Zigla asked with a toothy smile.

Traz picked at the feathers. He separated the barbules from a barb. "Um, yeah. I'm from Chubug. We were on a raid. Rumors said a lightly guarded caravan was passing through. The rumors were right about the caravan but wrong about how guarded it was."

"Rumors tend to act like that. Full of half-truths and omissions," Zigla said, nodding along with his tale. "What about the rest of your unit or the squad? How is it one lone bloody goblin ends up at my door?"

"All wiped out," Traz said. "Far as I could tell, anyway. Doesn't matter, though. Probably better off without some of them. Not exactly the most popular goblin. They all think I'm weak and worthless. None of them are my friends."

Zigla cocked an eyebrow. "I'm sure they aren't all that bad. Are they? You must have some friends."

He shook his head. "No, no. I'm pretty sure they are that bad. My best friends are women. They don't go raiding. I don't even want to join the raids. Was pretty much pushed into it by my dad. Think maybe he thought raiding might drive out my odd habits. Mom didn't do anything to stop it. She knew better than to stand up to him. I did too, I suppose."

Zigla merely nodded knowingly, sipping on a cup she had poured herself.

"What about you?" Traz asked. "Why are you out here all alone? Did you leave Chubug?"

"My mama thought that to be for the best," Zigla said, then chuckled. "You're a good kid. I know I must look a sight and you just sit there ignoring it. I wasn't planning on visitors. Tend to let myself go a bit when I'm all alone."

He cleared his throat and, still picking at the feather, said, "You are pretty large for a woman?" His voice turned the last word into a question. "I don't think I've heard of a female hob before."

The immense goblin barked a harsh laugh. "There have been such hobs, but they are rare and not welcome. And yes, I consider myself a woman. I hope you will, too. Can't say everyone back in Chubug would."

"Sorry," Traz said. Having destroyed one feather, he picked at another. "I shouldn't pry. Sometimes the words just fall out of my head. My friend, Quilka, she would always tell me to *read the room*." He wiggled his fingers, making air quotes. "She always wanted me to be less awkward. I knew she was teasing. I could only be me. Quilka is great, actually."

"Oh, please." Zigla waved her hand. "You're right. You can only be you. I can only be me. And you aren't wrong. I am pretty large." She barked another laugh.

They continued to sip their tea and chat. It was easy to talk to her. She may have looked odd, but he had no trouble looking past that. By the time the tea and conversation finished, he had picked the shaft clean and left a pile of feather detritus.

Zigla stood up and walked over to a chest. "I've got some blankets and pillows. You're welcome to stay and heal up. That way, I can make sure that wound doesn't fester. We'll keep the dressing fresh."

"That's kind of you, ma'am," he said, waving his hands. "I shouldn't impose. You've done enough. I can just head back to the warren."

She chuckled and continued pulling bedding from the chest. "No. I won't hear of it. You'll stay at least tonight. But stay as long as you want. I haven't had a visitor for a long spell."

And so Traz stayed.

Chapter 2

Rebirth

The next morning, Traz woke to find Zigla already up, sitting in the corner, working on something with her hands.

"I should head to the warren today," he said. "I appreciate all your hospitality, but I should head home. Find some fresh clothes. Let my parents know I'm not dead on the road with the rest of the raiding party."

Zigla looked up from a small wood carving she had been working on with a knife. "Keep an open mind and hear me out; I'd like to look after your arm some more. I don't want to send you off with such a terrible wound that's still bleeding. It could get infected during a strenuous hike back to the clan. But I know you'd like some fresh clothes and I have little like what you've been wearing. Have you ever worn a dress? I have some in smaller sizes I found down the hill, left behind from a successful caravan raid."

"Wear a dress? Like a girl?" Traz paused. He had often looked at some of the dresses his mother wore and wondered what it would be like to wear one. "No. I haven't. I don't think dresses fit boys, do they?"

"Of course they can!" Zigla barked her now familiar harsh laugh. She was already digging in a chest. "There aren't any rules. You can always choose to do whatever you want. Here, this one should fit you."

He took the dress. "I don't know if my dad would agree with that. He isn't here, though."

Traz went behind a changing screen and emerged soon after, wearing the simple navy blue dress. It was soft and comfortable. Zigla had a mirror on one wall, and he looked at himself. The dress hung well on him, even if his chest was flat.

"So..." Zigla said as she came up behind him. "What do you think? It seems to me like that could work for clean clothes. You can stay longer if you're up for it. It's been great getting to know you. I'm almost done with the piece I've been carving for you."

"Yeah," he said. "It feels great. I can wear this for a while. I'll stay longer. Never knew a dress could be so nice."

Traz pulled himself away from the mirror and sat at the table, picking up a cup of dragonroot tea with milk she had set out for him. The aroma filled his nostrils, and when he took a sip, he found the milk added sweetness, cutting through the intense spicy tea.

"What are you carving? You said it's for me? Why?"

"It's just a small trinket," Zigla said. "I noticed your fingers like to have something to keep them occupied. Truth be told, it's why I do things like my wood working. Some folks have hands or feet with a mind of their own. Need something to grab the attention. Stick around, at least until I finish it."

Traz nodded and sipped at his tea. He ripped small bits off a scrap of paper while they chatted.

"I suppose I get fidgety," he said, realizing that's exactly what he had been doing with the paper. He pushed it aside, trying to keep his focus on the tea and conversation.

Hopefully, she would finish the carving tomorrow. Yes, he would probably leave for home tomorrow.

He did not leave the next day. Instead, he tried on another dress. This one was a delicious chocolate brown. The soft fabric wrapped around him comfortingly. His arm still oozed some blood under the bandages despite the evening cups of Whispering Willow tea. It wouldn't hurt to stay a while longer—at least until his arm didn't actively seep blood.

A week after he arrived, his arm had healed enough to no longer need bandages, and he had switched to fiddling with the beads on the wooden carving during his chats with Zigla. The small toy had a spine that fit nicely in the palm of his hand, with three wooden beads threaded over a dowel. Flicking the beads with his fingers, they would slide up and down the rod, spinning and clacking lightly.

With his arm in better shape, he gathered his trousers and tunic. She had taught him how to mend his shirt with a needle and thread, and he had washed the outfit.

He changed behind the dressing screen. The clothes itched, and he shifted in them uncomfortably.

"I should probably head back home today," he said. "Maybe I can find another outfit. This one isn't fitting quite right. Maybe I mended it poorly."

She chuckled and sat down, setting out two cups of dragonroot with milk.

"You should have a cup of tea with me before you go."

And so, he sat and sipped tea and fiddled with the wooden beads. "I do love the dragoonroot tea. Especially when you add just the right splosh of milk."

She pulled her mug from her lips and said, "I don't think

you mended the tunic poorly. Maybe you got used to the dresses. They are comfortable, don't you think? That's why I wear one."

He nodded. "Yes. They are, actually. But it's different for you. My dad would blow his top if he saw me in a dress."

She leaned over and whispered conspiratorially, "Let you in on a secret. Between you and me. My dad felt the same way. He wouldn't accept a son of his wearing a dress. But sometimes, sometimes, a father's son is actually his daughter, and he just doesn't understand—sometimes can't understand."

Traz choked on a sip of tea. A cloud of thoughts he didn't understand tripped and tumbled over each other.

"What do you mean? Are you saying you were his son? But then his daughter? Was there a curse or poison? Some kind of magic?"

"Did I strike something with that?" Zigla asked with a chuckle. "A bit too much informeation? It wasn't magic. Wish it was, though. Lots of folks would probably say I'm still not a woman. Seemed that way back in the warren. Curious if you'll humor me with some questions? And I'll answer some of yours. I imagine you have some."

"But why? It wasn't magic? Why did your mama send you away? Why are you out here in this cave wearing makeup and a dress?"

"Short answer?" she asked and paused. "Makes me feel better. When I look in the mirror, it calms my mind. I think, maybe, you feel a little something similar. Longer answer? Well, it's complicated. But I'm happy to talk it over with some back and forth."

Traz stared at her a moment before answering. He tried to get a feel for how well he could trust her. The past week had been great, and the dresses had fit fantastically.

"Okay. Sure. What kinds of questions do you have?"

"You look good for a young gob," she said. "A bit light on the beard, and your eyes are maybe larger than they should be. Not bad, though. Can you picture in your head what an ideal goblin would look like to you?"

The beads spun faster in his fingers. "Dunno," Traz mumbled. "Um. I mean, I guess I never thought of it. I'm not sure I ever felt attracted to anyone. I never saw anyone I wanted to woo. I guess I have quite a few friends that are girls. I get along well with them."

"Hokay then," she said. "What if we aren't talking about attraction? I was just asking what you thought the ideal goblin might be. Let's not talk about the goblins you want to have a relationship with; I never said that to start with. You just went there with it. Backing up. You are, as I said, a decent-looking gob. Most folks feel some features could be better, though. If you could wave a magic wand or drink a potion, what would you see in the mirror as the ideal goblin man?"

Traz sat silently. He took a sip of the tea, letting the creamy, spiced liquid linger on his tongue. It was strange. He felt he could talk but didn't know the right words.

"I didn't mean—I just meant—I don't know. That's a weird question. I don't think I look good. I never have. I think you are wrong there. I can't even imagine what would make me look better. If I try. I dunno. It's hazy. Or fuzzy. Like a smeared charcoal drawing. I can't firm it up."

"Interesting," she said. "What about the other side of the coin? Let's not talk about a woman you might be attracted to. I want to know if you can imagine a goblin outside of a relationship interest. What would the ideal woman look like?"

He gazed up at the shadows dancing on the ceiling. "She would have large ochre eyes. Pouty lips with the tips of her sharp fangs poking out. Olive-green skin. Round cheeks. Wide, pointed ears, but not droopy. Long, blue-black hair. Maybe braids? Yes. Braids would look great. Some color streaks in the hair as well. My friend Tendella has streaks of color in her hair. It looks fantastic. She'd be thin, but athletic. A round bosom, but not too large."

"Interesting," she said again. "Now, look at her face closer. Really firm up the picture. Do you recognize her? Does she remind you of anyone?"

Traz's fingers furiously spun the wooden beads with one hand. The other tapped on the table while he thought. His fingers froze. He pulled his eyes from the dancing forms on the ceiling and gazed at Zigla.

"She looks a lot like me. But not. She looks better than me. I wish I could look as good as she does."

She let him sit in silence. Thoughts ran this way and that in his head.

Eventually, she said, "You know. You could. You could look as good as she does. We all have the power to create change. You just have to choose to make the change you desire. I could help you. I'm sure we could get you fixed up. That is. If you are interested?"

Zigla pulled out a segmented box with tubes, brushes, and powders.

And Traz stayed. He experimented. He learned about what comforted him as well as what did not. Zigla had a myriad of dresses to try. He found he looked cute in them and rotated through different ones each day. She taught him to apply eyeshadow and tint to his lips. This expanded into other forms of makeup. The more he used it, the more things clicked and felt right. Some days, he looked at the goblin in the mirror and thought she looked beautiful.

While Traz looked in the mirror, Zigla came up from behind. "Does she look like you imagined she might?"

Traz nodded and said, "Yes. The woman in the mirror looks very much like I imagined. I wish I could be her."

"What's stopping you?" Zigla asked. "You look like her to me. I've already started to think of you as her. Though, your name tends to cause friction there."

"My mama always said if she had a girl, she would name her Trinx," Traz said. "Could I just become Trinx?"

"I became Zigla, didn't I?" She laughed. "You don't think my mama named her son Zigla, do you? From now on, I'll think of you as Trinx."

Months slipped by as Trinx got to know herself. Thinking of herself as Trinx and not Traz and as her and not him, was a strange experience. She enjoyed the journey, though, and Zigla was excellent company.

Trinx's hair grew long and straight, and Zigla taught her how to craft her smooth hair into two braids, which she loved. They had talks covering this and that. Zigla knew a ridiculous amount about dyes. She used the knowledge to dye clothes, hair, powders, and pastes.

Trinx talked of Serenya Dawnwhisper. She loved her music and knew all of her songs. This was something she had had in common with several of her female friends. Most of her buddies in the raiding group hadn't understood.

Wait, she thought, *she hadn't had buddies in the raiding group.* He had.

One day Zigla set down two cups of dragonroot tea on the table. Trinx picked up the bead spinner, as she often did. She enjoyed fiddling and fidgeting with it when they talked. It made her fingers feel they had something to do and kept her mind on the conversation.

Zigla took a sip of the strong tea and said, "You seem much more comfortable now than when you first knocked on my door. It's been close to a year now. You're too young to spend your life in this cave. Have you thought much about going back to the clan?"

Trinx sipped at her tea, her left hand spinning the beads with her nimble fingers.

"I have. I miss the hustle and bustle. But I don't think I can. I'm not sure I could go back to my old life. This is me now. I feel like Traz died from that arrow, back in the raid."

"Well," she said with a sly grin. "Who says you have to go back to your old life? Maybe Traz did die from that arrow. I haven't seen him in a long time."

"What do you mean?" she asked.

"I mean," Zigla said, "you've been gone for months. You told me the caravan wiped out your whole raiding party. I'm sure they think you died with them. But what if? What if it was your brother who died?"

"My brother?" Trinx asked, fiddling with her toy, still not catching on to her point.

"Yes," she said with a sigh. "Traz. Your brother. You, his sister, could return to the clan. Obviously, you would have to avoid your parents. I understand if that would be too hard. But if you could, would you?"

"Oh!" Comprehension flashed in her eyes. "I could. I could just be Trinx in the warren. It's probably best if I don't see my parents. But my friends? Quilka? I'm not sure I could go back and not see her."

"Then see her," Zigla said. "If she is really as good a friend as you've told me, she'll understand. She'll accept you for who you really are."

"I bet she will," Trinx agreed. "You're right. I'm being silly. Quilka might even be able to help me get a job at the tavern where she works. I could get a place over on that side of the warren. That would make it easy to avoid my parents."

Trinx stood up and tossed her two braids over her shoulders

to drape down her back. Zigla had helped add streaks of color to them.

"Thank you, Zigla. Thank you for the past few months. Thank you for helping me find Trinx. I'll head to the clan tomorrow if that's okay? I'll come back and visit and check up on you. I promise. Tonight, we should have a feast to celebrate. A farewell dinner."

Chapter 3

The Barmaid

Trinx sat in front of the chipped, cracked mirror, brushing her long blue-black hair. The candlelight reflected off her silky tresses with the vibrant streaks of cerulean and magenta adding fun highlights. The goblin crafted two separate braids, each holding all three colors. Braids always brought generous tips from the patrons of the Arsonist's Tender.

Now, for the makeup. Trinx applied an olive-green foundation liberally over her entire face. The concealer blended in well with her skin. While Trinx worked on her transformation, music from a box spelled with the latest hits played via an amplification rune. Her favorite song from the elven artist Serenya Dawnwhisper filled the room.

Whispers of the woodland, echoes in the night,
Tales of love and legends, shining in the light.

Yes, Trinx was a Whispie. Both she and her friend Quilka adored Serenya. They had never been to a concert, but both desperately wanted to. Serenya only played in large venues in or near the biggest cities. Neither had the extra funds to make a trip like that. But they could both dream, and until then, they could share their love of her music.

While the tune played, she brushed dusky rose eyeshadow on her eyelids. An elixir, Vash's Extreme Lashes, added the perfect length. The goblin grabbed a vial of ruby-red lip tint and used an applicator to brush it over her pouty lips. Lip tint solutions were popular among the races with fangs and tusks as they actually dyed her lips, fading over time. This design was perfect for a goblin like her since her protruding fangs on both the upper and lower jaws would make a mess out of the glosses humans and elves wore. With an audible smack, Trinx blew a kiss to the mirror and stood up.

She smoothed out the chocolate-brown dress. It was stylish and complemented the goblin's olive-green skin. Male goblins were well known across all the races of the world for excessive body hair, much like the dwarves. Dwarven women were often just as hairy, but goblin women rarely had any hair other than that on their heads. Full sleeves for her arms and dark tights on her legs covered the black hair that grew thick on her limbs. She enjoyed the feeling of smooth skin when she shaved away the hair, but it was much too difficult to keep up with.

Trinx adjusted the pouches she had tucked in a simple black bra. Zigla had first made them for her while she had spent time in the cave nearly two years before. It turns out that scoops from a recently deceased gelatinous cube mimic breasts with just the right amount of gravity-induced droop to look believable. As long as Trinx kept any probing hands above the clothing, most wouldn't notice the difference. The would-be breasts even bounced slightly with her steps as she walked.

The daily transformation was complete. Deciding she looked bombastic, she glanced at the clock and cursed. She'd done it again. All wrapped up in the music and daydreaming, time had lost all meaning like it often does. How is it that minutes and hours could slip through her fingers without notice? Trinx tapped the music box to silence it and raced out the door of her pocket-sized room.

She flung herself into the network of tunnels that made up the home warren of the Chubug extended clan. The cavernous system spanned a large area, and while it held a healthy population, it was small compared to the larger cities. Most cities were above ground; however, settlements primarily inhabited by goblins or dwarves tended to be below, but just because they were below ground didn't mean they were filthy. In fact, most such towns prided themselves on the diligent upkeep of the tunnels they called their homes.

The stone walkway Trinx hustled along this morning was free of debris and swept clean of dirt. The six-centimeter heels on her pumps clicked frantically, nearly drowned out by the buzz of the surrounding crowd. After calling on three different cobblers, she had managed to find one willing to craft her shoes. She'd had to go out of the way to get to his shop, but it was worth it.

While the warren was large, with a population to fit, most would consider it a rural settlement. The larger cities often had a much broader demographic with a wide range of races. This was a goblin settlement, and most of those in the tunnels were goblins and hobgoblins. Of course, you could also see the occasional orc or troll, as they had rural settlements nearby with reciprocal peace treaties.

Various royal families ruled the larger metropolises, and their influence spanned miles outward from the cities. Chubug, like many other rural settlements, fell outside of these spheres of power. A warlord led Chubug, which, besides the typical industries, gained much of its wealth from raiding and warring.

Some would argue the High Council of Goblin Grandmas led the clan, and they were probably right. While the official story held that they were advisors to the warlord, the council had outlived many warlords over the years.

The goblins of the clan were always busy. Sometimes it seemed like the entire population crowded into the tunnels every time Trinx left home. They surrounded her and made it a chore to travel any distance. She did not need this that day.

She pulled the iron-reinforced door open and entered the Arsonist's Tender, an aptly named tavern. On more than one occasion, a powder keg of aggression would explode as heated arguments erupted between drunken patrons. The gruff, but kind-hearted proprietor Gristle, would put an end to things before they became too out of hand. At this hour, few goblins filled the seats of the currently calm room. Trinx had no trouble spotting the scowl Gristle shot her from behind the counter. The door to the kitchen opened, and Quilka popped her head out, waving her arms to beckon Trinx to the back-of-house.

Needing no further excuse to duck out of Gristle's glare, she hustled into the kitchen.

Quilka rolled her eyes in exasperation and asked, "How can you be late again? Here, I made you some tea. Just the way you like it." A steaming mug of dragonroot, with the perfect amount of milk, landed in her hands.

"I–" Trinx started to answer.

"No," Quilka said, cutting her off. "It's not like I didn't know you would be late. You almost always are. That's why the tea is still pretty hot. Drink up, and then let's get to work."

Trinx took a sip and put it on the counter. She'd nurse on it throughout her shift. At least until she forgot about it, and it became the first of several cups in her daily beverage graveyard.

Flashing a shameful grin, she said, "Thanks! You're the best."

The chronically late goblin noted the special scrawled on the chalkboard above the prep stations, gave a friendly wave to Brizla, the old cook, and slipped back out to the main room to check on the patrons. Trinx didn't notice Quilka's flushed cheeks as she left. There would be time for gossiping and catching up on the latest over their pre-dinner-rush meal break.

"Not so fast," Gristle said, stopping her before she could pass the bar.

The older hob sat on a stool, waving her to him with his sole remaining arm. Losing the left in a raid led him down the path to running this tavern.

"Ye can't keep doin' this, Trinxy. Granted. 'Tis usually slow in the mornin'. Not fair to Q, though, is it? She's yer friend. Gonna hafta dock yer pay."

Breath rushed through her slightly parted lips, and she waved her hand, swatting the issue away like an annoying fly. "I know. I know. Feel bad enough as it is without the pay cut. She even made me tea. Now let me just see what folks need."

She left him looking after her with a shake of his head.

Gristle's bark was worse than his bite. He might not even dock her like he had threatened. When Quilka asked him to take her on as a barmaid, he had no problem with it all, which surprised Trinx at the time. She had known Gristle from before, having spent some time in the tavern on occasion while waiting for Quilka to get off work. He had quirked an eyebrow and then simply agreed to hire her. That had been close to a year ago, and it had made her transition back into the warren much easier than she had feared it might be. She was still grateful for it.

Scanning the room, she found most of the tables empty—only a couple of smaller ones had guests. The space was warm, though, with the crackling fire in the corner hearth and the frosted lanterns hanging from the ceiling by chains. At the end of each day, everyone tidied up. Gristle never let the staff leave until the room looked immaculate.

Trinx breezed through the quiet tavern. This early, it was always calm. Even if a bard planned on playing today, they wouldn't be here until the dinner rush or later when people would do more drinking than eating. It made it easy to hear the snippets of conversation as she approached the first table. Two goblins sat talking and stuffing their mouths with roasted root vegetables.

"You notice the moon last night? Bigger than I've seen in a while. Bright, too," one of them said.

"I'm not blind. Course I saw it. I's in the same hunt group you were. Word is the grammas are sayin' we been pleasing the forest spirits. Figure s'why we landed that rockhorn last night," the other answered and crammed another wedge of potato in his mouth, despite his puffy cheeks.

Trinx seized the pause in the conversation and asked with a smile, "Everything good? Either of you need anything else right now?"

The goblin with slightly less food in his mouth nodded and said, "Yeah. We good. Right?" He directed the question at his companion, who waved a finger at his mug. "Oh yeah. Good point. Couple more beers. Drinking the house ale."

"Of course," she said, flashing two fingers to Gristle before moving to the next table.

A goblin at the next two-top looked away from his buddy and asked, "Settle a bet for us, Trinx?"

She smirked and said, "Sure, why not? What's the prop?"

This gob's name was probably Glink. She remembered it rhymed with sink because he was a plumber. He grinned from ear-to-ear.

"Which of us?" He motioned, waving his hand back and forth between him and his companion. "Which of us you tink Quilka is more likely to say yes to a date?" He looked expectantly for an answer, failing to suppress a sharp snort of laughter.

Trinx took a moment to step back and made an exaggerated show of appraising them. She ran her eyes up and down, head to toe, one after the other.

"It's a tough call," she finally said to probably-Glink. "If I had to guess, it's a toss-up between your buddy there and the dire rat that's been skulking in the cellar. Honestly, I'd say the rat's in the lead."

The goblins at the prior table burst into laughter. Over their snorts, cackles, and whoops, his buddy excitedly clapped his hands and said, "See, Glink! I told ya! Course she wants me more'n you."

Glink waved a dismissive hand and said, "Shuddap, Zurt! Ya didn't win. The filthy rat won. Bet's off."

"Psshhh. Whatever. Yer still buying the next round. Two more," Zurt insisted, motioning to the mugs. "What's to eat? Meat ready yet?"

"Too early for meat. Root veggie medley is warm and should tide you for a bit," Trinx answered.

"That's fine," Glink said. "We each'll take a dish of 'em. Make sure ya splits the tab down the middle. Not buying him nuthin'."

Trinx mentally gave herself a pat on the back for remembering the goblin's name. She had been trying to remember the more regular patrons' names and occupations. Glink's buddy, Zurt, was a carpenter, and they often ate together, swapping stories of jobs and the customers who hired them. She swung by the bar and picked up the four mugs of ale Gristle had waiting on a tray for her. Trinx dropped off one pair with the first two goblins and the second with Glink and Zurt, taking the empties into the back.

"You have a couple of admirers out there, Q. Don't worry. Told them that filthy critter in the cellar has a better chance with you," she announced on her way to the sink to drop off the mugs.

Quilka giggled. "Thanks! You're not wrong. Though I have my eyes set on someone better than the rat."

Trinx caught Brizla's attention. "Need two plates of the medley."

The cook humphed. "Sure. Sure. Here it is."

She ladled a heap of roasted vegetables in two shallow bowls and pushed them across the counter. Slipping the dishes onto a tray, Trinx headed back out. It took only a moment before she returned and stationed herself at the sink to make headway on the mound of dirty mugs, plates, and bowls. She scrubbed at the crockery with a wiry brush under a weak stream of water from the faucet. Quilka stood a couple of meters away, prepping more vegetables and cuts of meat, the sounds of her knife hitting the chopping board beating a steady rhythm.

Trinx's mind wandered as her hands automatically moved in familiar patterns. It drifted down dark passageways and stumbled on curious thoughts. A memory snuck up on her, then shrank away, back into a difficult-to-reach nook. Nervous fetters tried to bind her mind as she considered the coming meeting with the review board. They failed to catch hold, and she slipped free of the whirlpool, waiting to drag her down into a cavern of what-ifs and dread.

A soft voice in the background called, "Trinx."

"Trinx," it repeated. Louder this time. The sound wiggled into the maze of her thoughts.

"Trrrinxxx!!" Quilka yelled and reached over to shut off the water. The last cry yanked the daydreaming goblin from her mind's meanderings. Her eyes again focused. "Geez! How many times are you going to scrub that dish? I'm pretty sure it's clean by now. If there is anything left of it, that is."

"Oh!" Trinx said. "Sorry, I guess I was thinking about something."

She straightened up the dishes she had finished washing and dried them before placing them into stacks on the shelves.

"I never would have guessed," Quilka playfully admonished. "I thought we lost you there. What in the world were you so wrapped up in?"

"Um," Trinx started, then stopped, sheepishly shrugging. "I guess I don't know?"

Quilka laughed and patted her on the back. She gave an involuntary flinch and hoped with all her heart Q hadn't felt it. She didn't visibly react. Maybe she hadn't noticed.

"I'll finish these up and check on folks. Unless you already did recently?" Trinx asked.

"Yeah, that would be good," her friend said. "Haven't been out of the kitchen. Just been working food prep and doing a little thinking myself."

Trinx put the last of the clean dishes up, grabbed an empty tray, and ducked out of the kitchen to check on the guests. No one new had come in, which wasn't surprising. The dinner rush would soon descend on the inn. She enjoyed the idea of doing a quick cleanup and having a meal with Quilka.

Glink and Zurt sat nursing a couple of ales that Gristle must have served them. They chatted about bits of nonsense, cracking crude jokes, and taking turns punching each other to make the punchlines literally hit harder. They needed nothing else, for now, so she simply loaded their dishes on her tray.

The other two goblins had pulled out a deck of cards, and whatever game they played had them engrossed. They had moved all their empty plates and mugs to the floor. Grimacing, she squatted down and collected the forgotten dishes onto her tray. After fetching them a fresh set of ales, she returned to the kitchen to scrub some more.

Trinx was washing her latest dishes when Quilka said with a grin, "Don't get lost again on this batch. Brizla will have our pre-dinner meal ready by the time you finish them."

"For sure, Q. Keeping my head in the game." She meant it, too. Really, she always *meant* to keep focused. Sometimes, it was out of her control.

Brizla set out two plates of food on the small staff table. Tonight they would serve roast rockhorn with the root vegetable medley, now enhanced with some onions, peppers, and assorted spices. She ladled a thick gravy over the slice of meat and wedged a rye grain roll into the pile of veggies, then made another plate up and took it out for Gristle. Brizla rarely fixed an entire meal for herself. Instead, her style of cooking often involved a good deal of sampling. She constantly checked the spice level and flavor profile, snatching bits of meat and vegetables throughout the evening.

Trinx placed the last dried dish on the shelf and sat with Quilka.

"Thanks again for the tea earlier. I realize now I only had a few sips, but it was a nice way to start off the shift."

Quilka gave her a warm smile; then her mouth twisted up into a playful grin. "Figured you could use it. You've been out of sorts. Late more than usual, daydreaming with the dishes. I dunno, maybe not too much more, but seems a little off, is all. What's been going on?"

Trinx fidgeted with her fork, poking at a hunk of potato. "Just nervous, I guess. I have the review meeting coming up. Last time, they said no because I didn't have a steady job."

"But you fixed that now! You work here, and I'm sure even

grumpy, old Gristle would let them know you do great work," Quilka said.

"Yeah. I know. They can't complain about that this time," Trinx said, then put a small piece of rockhorn smeared with gravy in her mouth. She chewed thoughtfully before continuing. "I figure they'll have some other reason. I think they can't figure out why I want to adopt a youngling."

"Well, they aren't the only ones," Q said, laughing lightly. "I don't get it either. You're young. You don't need to get strapped down by a child. But I know that's what you want. I like that about you. Once you decide to focus on something, you go for it. I'm sure they'll see that, too, and grant you permission. But why focus on this?"

Quilka was great that way. She was always encouraging. As one of the few left in her life who knew her from before, she understood her in ways others couldn't. The entire staff here at the Tender was good like that. Unlike the rest of the warren, they accepted her.

"It's just—" Trinx started to say before cutting herself off to think. "I guess. I just think if I could get on the Council of Grandmas, then I could change things. Make it so the whole warren accepts me and people like Zigla and really anyone. I can't get on the council if I'm not a grandma, and I can't be a grandma without first having a child."

"I guess," Quilka said in a voice that sounded not at all convinced. "But do you even really want a child? It seems an odd reason to try to get one. And besides, you know how long it'll take to become a grandma? You'll be old!"

"I do," Trinx said, nodding her head. "I've always thought about having a child. Course, it would be really nice if I could actually birth a baby, but that's obviously not happening."

"Well," her friend said, "if they do say yes, we'll probably have a lot less time for fun. Maybe I can at least be the cool aunt."

"Totally!" Trinx agreed. "You can be their fun aunt, Quirky Quilka." She erupted into a fit of giggles at that, and her friend soon joined.

Composing herself, Quilka brought up an old topic, delicately dancing through it. "What about your family? You think your parents could help?"

Trinx dipped a piece of the roll in her dwindling pool of gravy. The earthiness of the rye paired well with it as she chewed.

"Pretty sure my parents spend most of their time mourning my dead brother. You know how they are. Probably hope to get lucky and produce a hob with better chances of surviving in the raids and battles. Better that than deal with me."

"I'm just saying. You could try, couldn't you?" Quilka pressed.

Trinx shook her head. "I am sure they wouldn't help me."

Her last statement hung in the air as they finished their meal. Then Quilka perked up. "I know! I'll help you pick out the perfect outfit. It will be hard for the board to say no if you look fabulous."

Chapter 4

Review Board

Trinx woke up early. Or rather, she stopped trying to sleep. If she had slept the night before, she likely would be impossible to drag out of bed at this hour. Working in the tavern fit her perfectly, as she naturally stayed up late. On the flip side, she often had trouble pulling herself from bed before noon.

She couldn't afford to be late this morning, and ruminating about it had kept her up all night. Setting five alarms had not helped to settle her brain enough. At best, she occasionally had dozed for a few minutes at a time before jolting awake again. During a longer glimpse of sleep, she'd had a dream, or, more accurately, a nightmare. For some reason, predatory hairy arachnids had comprised the review board, patiently waiting to ensnare her.

Excitement and dread clashed within her. She ran through all the questions she imagined they might ask, as well as the answers she had prepared. At least spiders wouldn't actually be on the panel. Probably. No. Don't be ridiculous. No spiders.

Awake and out of bed, she put on her best dress. It was

navy blue with flowers embroidered with a thread of the same color. Like all of her dresses, it had long sleeves that covered her arms. She looked at her hands and grimaced. Normally, she felt quite beautiful, but on days like these, her hands just seemed enormous. She knew they weren't nearly as big as she imagined, and they likely wouldn't notice at the orphanage, but she calmed her mind by taking a razor to some of the stubble on the back of her hands and knuckles.

Trinx wore dark stockings and a pair of blue flats. The simple leather shoes looked more mature. More motherly. She was admiring herself when she noticed the back of her left stocking had a run in it!

"Arg!" With some hurried disgust, she removed her shoes and hosiery. Rummaging around, she found a fresh pair and slid them over her legs.

She set two timers to help keep her on track and sat at her table in front of the mirror. Then she applied fresh makeup and pulled her hair back, securing it with a clip. She felt it had a more mature look than the braids she usually wore. A chime sounded, grabbing her attention. The alarms had been a smart idea as they each jolted her focus back to the task at hand. She may have set a record for how quickly she put herself together.

She picked up her handbag and the wooden beaded toy, which she debated for a moment. She really shouldn't fiddle with it during the meeting but, then again, she may not concentrate well enough without it. After a moment of hesitation, she thrust it into the bag and left her home.

Goblins and the occasional hobgoblin or orc filled the tunnels, swallowing her into their hustle and bustle. She found it best to flow with the crowd, only creating resistance when needing to take a fork in the walkway. Conversations melded into a symphony of overlapping voices, generating a constant hum. Despite the ebb-and-flow nature of traveling the tunnels, she made reasonable time walking briskly with determination toward the orphanage. In the end, the trek to Sulma's Home for Displaced Younglings took just over twenty minutes, which left Trinx plenty of time to sit and fidget impatiently, watching the hands on the standing clock creep ever so slowly.

Tick.

Tick.

Tick.

And yes, there were still 273 tiles in the mosaic covering the wall in the waiting room—no change from last time. She glanced around the reception area and once again read each of the posters on the wall.

"Small Hands, Big Hearts, Endless Possibilities"

And

"Hope and Happiness Begin Here"

And

"Only the Sky Can Limit Your Dreams"

They each had imagery complimenting the inspirational messages. Now, if only they would hold true. A positive ruling from the review board could be one of the endless possibilities.

The inner door opened, and the familiar face of Jigsai poked out with a warm smile. The older goblin had her graying hair styled in a bob. Grooves and wrinkles cut deep into her dark green skin. She had been the main point of contact in both letters and in-person discussions.

"Trinx. They are ready to see you now. Follow me back, please."

Jigsai led her to the audience room, where a long table seating five members of the review board stretched across the far end of the room. A much smaller desk that would make two people feel a little too cozy stood with two chairs closer to the nervous goblin.

Trinx entered the chamber and took a seat, trying her

hardest not to let her emotions reflect on her face. She glanced at the empty chair next to her. A frown broke through before she squashed it and painted a smile back on her face.

Three men and two women comprised the board. The man in the center of the desk spoke first.

"Thank you for joining us today, Trinx. According to our records, this is not your first time here with a petition. I believe I sat on a previous panel for you."

She hadn't pulled out her fidget beads. She didn't know what to do with her hands, so they hung at an odd angle, held up in front of her, occasionally kneading into each other.

Trinx attempted to make her voice soft and demure. She naturally spoke with a feminine tone, and adding this nuance felt right.

"Yes, sir. Yes. I've been here before. With your grace, I hope to not return." She gave her eyes a few seductive blinks, letting Vash's Extreme Lashes help plead her case.

"Unfortunately," the man began. An ocean wave crashed over her. Drowning her. Trinx's face fell. He continued, seemingly oblivious to the damage that one word inflicted. "The issue still remains. You are a single woman. You must get yourself a mate and prove you have tried to conceive children of your own before we will consider granting you guardianship of an orphaned youngling."

"But I proved I have a steady job—" Trinx started to explain before the judge cut her off.

"We appreciate that. We really do. However, the ability to care for the child is not the only issue at hand. If we grant you custody, what will happen if you find a mate and birth several children? The sire would surely want to put his offspring in line ahead of your adopted youngling. We've seen this kind of thing before. Too many times, the sire kicks out the adopted child, or worse, they meet some kind of *accident.*" He emphasized the last word with a meaningful stare.

The lead board member continued, "No. I'm sorry. We must decline again. You may reapply once your circumstances have changed. Take care, Miss." The rest of the committee looked at each other for confirmation and nodded in agreement.

Trinx sat still in her seat, working to keep her head above the water. They wouldn't listen. Last time, they said she lacked the resources to care for a child. It may have been true back then, but now, they had a new excuse. This one would be much harder to solve. She didn't want a mate. Never mind the complications of actually bonding with one.

At least they didn't rush her out. They were kind here. They had to be to care for the children. She stood. Smoothing her dress out to hide her trembling hands, she thanked them again and made her way back out to the reception area.

Jigsai looked up from a romance book with a beautiful pale-green woman wearing long flowing hair and a dress with barely enough bodice to keep her large bosom from spilling out. The woman on the cover stood between two men. On her left was a diminutive but wealthy-looking goblin. On her right, an enormous, powerfully built hob in simple clothes.

"You work at the Tender?" Jigsai asked while waving her book. "Seems there should be plenty of available gobs there. Maybe even find one as good as the men in my book here."

"Maybe," Trinx mumbled.

She left the building and stood next to the offices, staring up at the cavern ceiling far above. Trinx screamed empty nothings at the void. Passersby veered wide around her, giving her curious glances before focusing on their path. She stayed there for some time, surrounded and alone. Then she threw herself into the crowd and started walking, not entirely sure where her feet would take her.

"Trinx!" a voice called from across the tunnel.

She looked around for the source. Quilka sat waving at her in a fenced-off space that comprised the seating area for a cafe. A pastel-painted sign above the order window read "Mystic Leaf & Toadstool." Trinx wove through the crowd and took a chair across from her friend.

Quilka's smile flattened as she gathered the vibes emanating from Trinx.

"Oh, Trinx. I know you wanted it so much. Can you talk about it? It's okay if you don't want to."

Trinx pulled the comforting toy from her bag. Her fingers twirled and spun the beads, shifting them on the wooden spindle.

"I can talk about it. It's not like there's that much to say. It evidently doesn't take very long to say no."

Quilka reached a hand out and laid it palm up, close to her distraught friend.

"Working in a tavern isn't good enough for them? I'm sure you could raise a child from what you make there. It's a steady job. You proved that. Gristle can tell them."

Trinx snorted. "Gristle would need to take me as a mate to make them happy. That's what they want. No, I don't mean Gristle. I just mean a mate. That's what they want."

"Pssh," her friend said. "That seems like a ridiculous reason. Don't they want to send those kids off to good homes?"

Trinx sighed, exasperated, putting her free hand on the one previously offered. "That's the problem. They say if I got a man, he might kick the child back to them since they wouldn't be his."

"Well," Quilka consoled. "I can see their point, but of course, that complicates things, doesn't it? I don't want a mate. At least not now, I mean. But for you? Yeah, that's a tricky one." She squeezed Trinx's hand gently.

"See, this is a great example of why I want a child. I know you don't get it. You see me tied down and not able to have fun. But once I raise them, they'll be able to find their own mates, or not. Either way, they should be able to have children of their own. Then I'll be a grandma. I can petition for admittance to the council."

Excitement took hold. Trinx used her index finger to spin a bead in a pulsing rhythm and continued, "As a grandma on the council, I could change life here in the clan. Make it so others don't have the same troubles I've had with adopting a child. Or anything, really. Goblins should be allowed to live their lives how they want to."

"I agree with you," Quilka said with a gentle smile. "All goblins should be allowed to live their lives without harassment. I'm not sure it's as easy as some decree from the council, though. They care about the clan, right? If it was that easy, wouldn't they have done it already?"

"Well," Trinx said, her eyes searching the air for the answer. "Maybe they just haven't been close enough to the problems? Someone like me, with first-hand knowledge, I could make rules to make everyone feel safe."

"Maybe," Quilka said with a rueful shake of her head. "Maybe that would be the difference. I'm not so sure, though. And besides, I'm still not sure adopting a child is the best path to get there."

"*Please*," Trinx scoffed. "It's the only path. I mean, I guess I could produce a child with a woman. But that's not how I would want to have a child. If I could, I'd bear the child myself. But I can't, so I *will* find a way to adopt."

"If it makes you feel better," Quilka said, her cheeks taking on a faint purple blush. "I think you'd be a great mom. And an amazing grandma. Not just on the council, either."

"Thanks, Q," Trinx said, squeezing her hand. "I love how

you believe in me. We should have a failure party. After work, let's go out. I'd like to do something to take my mind off things. Something to put me in a better mood."

"Oh!" Quilka gasped. "That sounds great. And guess what? I meant to tell you. I bet you won't guess."

"What? Tell me. If you don't think I can guess, you have to tell me."

"Okay, are you ready?" Quilka asked with a mischievous grin, drawing out the suspense. "I got us guest passes to Club Unity! We can have our failure party there!"

"Seriously?" Trinx asked, her mouth slack in shock. "We've been dying to get in there. When is the next night they are open?"

"That's the best part," Quilka said, brimming with excitement. "*Tonight*! We can go tonight. I meant to tell you I got the passes, but there hasn't been a good time to go yet. But tonight is perfect. Do you need to go home and change before work? I'm sure you could wear that to the tavern and out dancing. But. It just. It just looks serious."

Trinx laughed. "Yeah, it's supposed to be serious. I had a serious meeting. But yeah, I'll go home and change before work. I'll pick out an outfit good for dancing. This'll be fun."

Chapter 5

Failure Party

Trinx breezed into work not only on time, but early. The entirety of the Tender's customers occupied a single two-top against a wall close to the hearth. Out of habit, she made a quick survey of their table and saw they appeared to have plenty of food and drink. She could check on them once she had settled in.

She turned from the table, catching Gristle's eye. His mouth slackened, and he took a moment before it engaged with his brain.

"Trinxy! Is everything okay, Luv? Don't get me wrong. Always appreciate seeing you early. Itches at my hackles, though. Tingly sense of worry, you know?"

She laughed away his concern. Of course, there was something wrong. Nothing Gristle needed to worry about, though. She had her mask fully in place. The review board business was tamped down in a cobwebby corner of her mind until she could further unpack it. For now, she had her failure party mask on, ready for fun with Quilka after they closed out their shift in the tavern this evening.

"Don't worry!" Trinx said. "Nothing's wrong. I'm just excited. Q and I are going out dancing after closing. She here yet?"

"No," he answered, waving her past him toward the kitchen. "Part of my shock, that is. You beat her in here. Go on back and see if Brizla needs help with the prep. Quiet still. Might as well make yourself tea and a snack if you'd like."

"Thanks, Gris!" she called over her shoulder as she pushed open the door to the kitchen.

Brizla stood by the stove, stirring a large vat of stew. The smell from the pot caused her stomach to reach out and try to grab it.

"That smells amazing! Need any help?"

"Doing fine at the moment," the cook said and looked up from her station. "Fix a quick bite and a cup before things pick up. What brings you in so early? Quilka isn't even here yet."

"Geez," she blew out. "I'm not always that late, am I? Can't a girl show up on time without a parade?"

Brizla just laughed at her absurd exasperation and checked on the dough rising for the loaves. It needed another punching. She got to work beating and kneading the large white ball of sourdough.

Trinx put scoops of dragonroot in a teapot. Using the Kwik-brew spout above the sink, she filled the pot with steaming hot water and set it on the counter to brew for a few minutes. She set out two cups and piled a plate with salty round crackers, thin slices of sharp, dark orange cheese, and thicker slabs of hard, cured sausage.

Trinx had just finished filling the second cup with tea and a healthy dollop of milk when she heard someone come through the door. Assuming it was her friend, she said, "Hey Q! I beat you here for once. Grab a cup. I put a plate together for us to snack on while we sip on dragonroot."

Turning around, she caught sight of Quilka. "Wow, that dress looks super cute."

Her friend blushed and swept away some nonexistent wrinkles in her gray-trimmed black dress. "Please. This is nothing compared to your outfit."

"What? This?" Trinx giggled and spun twice. The orange-and-green plaid skirt flared out, showing off her forest green tights. Her billowy matching orange blouse rippled in the breeze stirred up by her twirling. "I'm just ready for some dancing. Tonight's failure party is gonna be great."

"I'm glad you're focusing on tonight and not this morning," Quilka said and carried the snack plate and a cup to the staff table.

Trinx grabbed her tea, and they sat, eating, drinking, and talking about the latest Whispie Newsletter that lay on the table. Both danced from topic to topic, sidestepping any further discussion of the morning's events. Once they finished, they cleaned up, grabbed a tray each, and left for the main room.

The shift slid by smoothly. Tavern customers ebbed and flowed through the evening. Trinx served hot bowls of thick stew alongside hunks of bread slathered with butter. She passed out mugs of ale and, more often than not, refilled those glasses at least once or twice.

Gristle had to break up two brawls, making it one of the calmer evenings that week. Still, one of them ended with several bowls and a large pitcher upended. The resulting puddle of ale with bits of stew and shimmering rivulets of oily gravy turned her stomach while she cleaned it up.

She had put on an apron before starting the shift in earnest. Thankfully, it did a fine job of keeping her outfit pristine. It would have been a shame and put a major downer on the failure party if she had to run and pick out an entirely new ensemble.

Eventually, the last of the customers stumbled out to head home or some other convenient place to pass out. Trinx and Quilka cleaned up the tavern, following Gristle's regular checklist. Brizla served the last of the stew into four bowls. The group sat and enjoyed the late-night meal and sipped on a splash of wine that remained in the last bottle opened that evening. Once finished, they scrubbed the pot and the last dishes.

Trinx hung up her apron and double-checked herself in a mirror. Everything had held up, and she looked ready for dancing. She waved goodnight and left with Quilka, who led the way to the club.

The club was less a place than it was an event. It moved frequently, rotating between several locations, including warehouses, caves, or other sizeable areas where a mass of partygoers could gather. She and Quilka had heard about it, both rumors and first-hand accounts. You had to know the right goblins to get a guest pass. Rumor had it you could buy a permanent pass, but you needed to go at least once before you could get it. Tonight, an empty warehouse above ground near the river docks housed the club. Goblins, hobgoblins, orcs, and trolls mingled outside and queued up to enter. Couples and single women could bypass the line and an enormous troll bouncer waved Trinx and Quilka inside after checking their passes.

They entered the expansive warehouse, and the crowd quickly enveloped them. High above their heads, someone had converted the foreman's office into a DJ booth. Trinx could see a goblin wearing a bright outfit with a funny, oversized hat bouncing around in there, touching various controls. A mage had created spell glamours throughout the rafters that pulsed and cycled colors with the beat. From time to time, small orbs of prismatic light would launch out from the glamours and fly down, weaving through the sea of dancers before returning.

The music thumped as the DJ blended the softening beats of the last song into a rhythmic pulse of the next. *Dun-dun dun dun. Dun-dun dun dun.* Recognizing the intro, Trinx grabbed Quilka's hand and pulled her out onto the main dance floor.

I throw my spears up in the air sometimes
Singing, "Ayo, hunt'em down, yo"
I wanna dominate and take their life
Singing, "Ayo, raid the night, yo"

The two girls bounced and thrust their arms up in the air. Trinx's braids flew up and down. She watched Quilka's maroon ponytail whip around as her friend shook her head. The tension evaporated as the music coursed through her muscles.

I come to fight, fight, fight, fight
We stomp our feet
We got the might, might, might, might
I'm stirring up all that fright, fright, fright, fright
Gonna rend and gnash and now bite, bite, bite, bite

Along with most of the surrounding dancers, Trinx chomped her mouth open and closed, baring her teeth and grinning ferociously. She leaned in at Quilka, as her friend did likewise. Then they both pulled back, bending backward—all to the pulsing beat.

'Cause war goes on and on and on
And war goes on and on and on, yeah

I throw my spears up in the air sometimes
Singing, "Ayo, hunt'em down, yo"

I wanna dominate and take their life
Singing, "Ayo, raid the night, yo"

Two young hobs approached the girls. One looked incredibly hairy, with a coarse black beard. He kept the hair on his head cropped short, as was the popular style among men these days. His friend was slightly shorter, with a similar hairstyle in chestnut-brown, but a notable lack of hair on his face. They danced with the girls, the bearded one pairing up with Quilka, his buddy with Trinx.

'Cause we gon' rock this clan
We gon' fight all night
We gon' light it up
Goblin dynamite
'Cause I told you once
Now I told you twice
We gon' light it up
Goblin dynamite

All four of the dancers made exploding motions with their arms and jumped back from each other, expanding the cross formation into more of a square. The dance continued this way for the rest of the song, and Trinx wore a mad grin the entire time. Her heartbreak earlier in the day fell away with every chorus.

When the song ended, the two hobs pointed out a table and walked toward it. Trinx looked at Quilka with a shrug and a question in her eye. Her friend laughed and said something unintelligible over the music, then took her hand and dragged her through the crowd to the table.

Mages had spelled the tables in the club with noise-dampening fields. They didn't keep out all the racket but muted the music to conversational levels. Guests still had to speak up to be heard, but they didn't need to shout when seated. Trinx and Quilka slid into the two remaining chairs, and the change in acoustics temporarily deafened them.

The bearded hob spoke first. "I'm Draz, and my smooth-skin buddy is Vex. Oomph." Vex elbowed him hard, but he shook it off and continued. "Er. He don't like me pointing that out. So, best forget I said anything. What about you two?"

"I'm Trinx. And this is my best friend Quilka," she said. "We work at the Arsonist's Tender. Do you know it? You should come by sometime."

"You can bet we will. Right, Vex?" Draz quickly accepted the invitation for both of them.

"So, what do you do?" Quilka asked.

Draz thumped his chest and declared, "I'm with Jorgrim's raiding party. You've probably heard of him. He has had a lot of success lately."

Q nodded and turned to Vex. "And you?"

His cheeks took on a dusky purple tint, and he cleared his throat, but it still registered higher than most would expect.

"Um. I'm in between things. I haven't found a group I mesh well with." His words rushed out faster as he continued to speak. "But I've got some coin, thanks to my father. He'd rather I join a raiding team than take on a more peaceful profession in the warren. I'll land on a good team soon, I'm sure."

Before the conversation could proceed, the music changed again. Through the dampening field, they could hear deep bass chords, with several beats of silence between them, that gave way to a rising melody.

Trinx squealed. "It's Serenya! We gotta get back out there." She jumped up from her seat and waved the others to follow her. They obliged and danced as Serenya's voice filled the room.

Oh no, now we ate cursed food
Did we really need to indulge it
But who could blame our hunger
Oh no, now we ate cursed food

The four of them danced, jumped, swayed their hips, and pumped their arms. Trinx was in her element and soaked in the song. With a goofy grin, she chanted the lyrics along with Serenya's vocalizing.

Pain wracks our stomachs
And no magic can solve it
You cooked with a dark pact
And damn us, now we ate cursed food

Almost as if on cue, as she belted that last line out, her bounce caused one of her breast pouches to fly up out of her billowy blouse. She was sure Vex was the only one who saw it, but that was enough. He probably didn't even know what it was. It landed on the stone floor of the warehouse, and before he could stop himself, Vex stomped it. Gelatinous cube slime sprayed out in all directions, creating a slick area beneath their dancing feet. Draz and Quilka didn't seem to notice anything had happened. Vex looked confused.

Horrified, Trinx yelled in a rush of words. "Sorry! Have to go! Nice meeting you! See you tomorrow, Q!"

She raced toward the exit. She ran home faster than she ever thought her legs could move her. The blouse she wore really didn't show the issue because of all the loose fabric. Ironically, running made the situation worse. Rational thoughts had fled. She had lost a portion of herself. Not only had she lost it, but someone had *seen*.

She hoped with all her heart he wouldn't have a clue what he had actually witnessed.

Yes. He couldn't have known. It would be fine. Yes.

But she needed a replacement. How could she go out in public?

She had no problem sharing all of who she was with close friends and those she trusted. But some random guys she just met in a club? That could spell trouble. And she couldn't go to work like this. Her mind couldn't concentrate on tasks when she didn't feel herself.

It was the middle of the night. Dawn should still be a couple of hours away. At daybreak, Trinx would leave to call on Zigla. She could help. Trinx owed her a visit, anyway. It had been too long.

Chapter 6

Zigla's Idea

When Trinx had first laid down, sleep eluded her as her mind continued to race in circles. Every time she thought she had calmed one worry, more jumped to chase the last. Even if no one understood what had happened or why she had fled the club, she knew, and her mind projected that knowledge onto everyone in the warehouse, especially those she had been dancing with. The lack of sleep the night before, combined with the emotional crash of the day's events, caught up with her, and she fell into a deep slumber without realizing it. One moment, she was wide awake, fleeing her thoughts; the next, she was near comatose.

She woke hours later. It was still mid-morning and earlier than she usually pulled herself out of bed. She had hoped to leave for Zigla's cave at first light, but remembered there was no time set to meet, and she didn't even know Trinx was coming. The only time-related issue she had was the need to be back for work, ideally restored to whole.

After putting on a loose-fitting, full-length dress, she touched up her makeup. She would need to clean up and apply a fresh face before work, but this was fine for meeting Zigla. As she brushed on some of Vash's Extreme Lashes, she realized she should bring a gift. She fished around for an unopened bottle and slipped it into her bag.

In the mirror it was clear it was difficult to see anything out of the ordinary about her chest with this dress on. Her brain operated much more rationally this morning than it had last night. Still, she couldn't wear baggy dresses all the time, but she could walk calmly, out to visit her friend.

The cave was roughly an hour's trek from the outer entrance of the clan warren. Trinx let her mind wander as she made her way there and soon stood outside the door she had originally knocked on a couple of years ago. She rapped on the wood three times in quick succession and waited.

Zigla opened the door and looked down, her face breaking into a wide smile full of warmth.

"Trinx! It's been ages. Come in. Come in." Zigla pulled the door open further and waved her in.

"Oh, Zigla, it's so good to see you. I've missed you. I keep meaning to come out here more, but. But, well. You know how life goes," Trinx said as she stepped inside.

The cave looked much the same as it had. A pot simmered on the fire. Spicy aromas of cinnamon and nutmeg filled the room, and her stomach rumbled.

"Sounds like you could use a bite to eat," Zigla said with a laugh. "I'll toss some more oats in, and we can each have a bowl in a few minutes. The water for tea should be hot enough now, though. Dragonroot?"

"Tea sounds great," she answered, "but I think I need something more calming."

"Of course," the old hob said. "I'll fix us some lavender then. Should help take the edge off any anxiety." She put a couple of scoops from a small tin into a teapot and poured hot water from a kettle. She set out two cups and motioned for Trinx to sit at the table with her.

Once they both had sat, Zigla probed. "I do love seeing you and appreciate the company, but I can tell you've been holding something in out of politeness ever since you arrived. Let's hear it. What's wrong?"

Trinx took a deep breath, and words flew from her mouth in a tangled jumble. "It came out. And we were dancing. And it just came out. And he stepped on it! Do you think he saw it come out? Do you think he knew what he stepped on? It's gone now, and we were having a party to forget. The failure, that is. A failure party. Oh! And that. The whole reason we went out was because they said no. It was awful."

Zigla let the words spray freely. She had lived with the girl for close to a year and knew sometimes it was easiest to let it all come out first.

"We'll figure out a way to fix whatever is wrong. Let's start by going over what it was. What came out and got stepped on?"

Tears welled in Trinx's eyes, but she calmed herself before responding. She pulled out the remaining breast pouch from the bra she wore under the loose dress and held it up.

"One of my breasts. It must have been the bouncing. And he stepped on it. Slime squished out all over the floor. Everyone was stomping and dancing in it."

The old woman smiled reassuringly, trying to soothe her. She poured them both a cup of tea.

"Not to worry. I'll make you a new one. I have some fairly fresh cube. Try to harvest it regularly. There are other uses for it as well, so it's good to have around. In fact, I'll make you some additional sets. I should have done that the first time for you so you'd have backups, or at the very least, it would have let you swap them out for washing. I'll just use this one for size comparison."

Trinx was feeling ridiculous now. She had come unhinged over something easily fixed. Still, it had been mortifying how close she came to a stranger she just met learning her secrets. Likely, her tightly wound emotions after the rejection yesterday were to blame. She continued filling in the gaps.

"I'm sure I overreacted. Quilka probably covered for me with the guys. It was just so mortifying, having it out of my control. I had a meeting at the orphanage—my second one. The first time, they said I needed a steady job, but I had one—a fantastic one, even. So, I worked hard and waited, proving it was steady and that I could keep it. But that's not enough. Now they want me to have a mate. How am I even supposed to have a mate?"

"I don't have any answers for you there," Zigla said with a sigh. "From what I understand of your plans, that's why you are trying to raise a family in the first place. Being able to adopt a child as a single goblin is a small portion of it, but a strong first step. Eventually, goblins like you and I could be accepted no matter what we want to do. Though, I've warned you before. Getting on the council won't let you just wave a magic wand and fix society. It'll take time."

Zigla took a sip of tea and continued. "Still, it seems the path isn't going to be a smooth one. It's not unheard of for two people to form a union not out of love or desire to mate but out of convenience or obligation or societal demands. It ends up being a partnership for the public while keeping separate lives in private. I suggest you keep an eye out for someone who could use such a relationship as well."

Trinx had taken out her fidget toy and had been playing with it while sipping tea and listening to her mentor.

"That seems almost just as hard. But admittedly much more doable than finding a man who expects to mate with me. I'll keep my ears open at the Tender. People always talk in there as if no one can hear them. Most don't hear, but I do if I want to. I'm sure Quilka will help, too, if I ask her."

"That's a great idea," Zigla said. "Best to listen. It's safer than asking questions and poking around. While I said it's not unheard of, it isn't widespread, and folks are wary of deception. The oats should be ready. I'll grab us bowls."

She stood up and scooped two healthy ladles full into a couple of bowls and brought them back to the table. She set one down in front of the goblin, who inhaled deeply.

Trinx took a spoonful and blew on it lightly before putting it in her mouth. The oats were soft and buttery and molasses mixed with the spices she had been smelling. She enjoyed several bites before returning to the conversation.

"Thank you. I needed something hearty in my belly this morning. I didn't realize how hungry I was. Oh! I brought you a gift!" She rummaged in her bag and pulled out the bottle of Vash's Extreme Lashes. "I didn't wrap it, but it's still a gift. I love using it. Doesn't it make my eyes pop with such long and full eyelashes?"

Zigla took the proffered bottle and examined it. "It's for eyelashes? Yours look wonderful, by the way. It can make mine that nice? How's it work? Some kind of potion or elixir?"

"I don't know how it works," Trinx said with a shrug. "I'm not an alchemist, but yeah. It's some kind of potion you apply directly to the lashes. You don't drink it. It comes with a little brush. As you brush it on, the lashes just grow out and thicken. Really amazing stuff. Try it."

The hob stood and strode over to the mirror. She unscrewed the stopper and pulled it out, noting the tiny brush attached to the bottom of the cap. Gently, she brushed it onto her eyelashes. As she added strokes, her lashes filled in and grew longer. She kept at it until they were several centimeters.

Screwing the stopper back into place, she turned and asked, "How does it look?"

"They look great," Trinx said. "I can even see them from here. Isn't it wonderful stuff? I love Vash's."

"Yes, it's amazing," Zigla said as she returned to the table. "I had no idea the alchemists were making cosmetics now. It gives me a thought. I wonder what else we could use alchemy to enhance or change." She picked up the imitation breast pouch and looked it over while she spoke.

"Oh!" Trinx exclaimed. "You really think potions could change our bodies? I don't think I've heard of elixirs like that."

The hob absently hummed while thinking. "Hmmm. I don't know. Didn't even know they had lash-enhancing potions until today. I'm sure you could get a book or two and study. There are at least a couple alchemists in the Chubug clan. Start by asking one of them. Just be careful what you ask about. Don't make it too obvious what you're after unless you think you can trust them."

"That sounds right," said Trinx. "I can poke around the subject without being direct. I'll start by asking about a book. Maybe I can find answers on my own. I should head back soon, though, especially if I want to stop by an alchemist before work. I'll clean up the breakfast dishes if you don't mind making me a replacement." She patted her now flat chest before standing and gathering the dishes.

While she cleaned up, Zigla took the remaining intact pouch to a workbench. The pouches went together quickly, and both women finished their tasks about the same time. The hob had made her three of the fake breasts and handed them along with the original back to her.

Trinx stuffed two of them into her bra and adjusted her chest in the mirror. "Thank you. I can't tell you how much better that makes my mind feel."

Pulling her dress tight by cinching it in the back, she smiled at the body she saw in the reflection.

After a few more pleasantries and an extended goodbye with promises to visit again sooner rather than waiting for another emergency, she left the cave to return to the warren. Going mostly downhill for a good portion of the journey, and with her spirits much higher than they were on the trek out earlier that morning, she made it back home with plenty of time to stow away the extra set of pouches and get cleaned up.

Not all shops selling potions and elixirs had resident alchemists. Many of them were just businesses, and the owners ordered merchandise like any other storefront. General stores even stocked some of the more common concoctions. Trinx knew of one place called Zizzle's Fizzles, run by an older goblin named Zizzle, of course, who was an alchemist. She wasn't sure how much experience he had or if he just supplemented his ordered stock with some additional potions he crafted. It was worth checking out, though, as it wasn't too far out of the way from the path she normally took to work.

She arrived at the small wood and stone building in a row of shops in one of the larger expansive caverns in the warren. The sign had an open bottle with green vapors that twisted and turned, spelling out the name of the business in flowing script. She pushed the door open, and a bell tinkled as she entered.

An elderly goblin sat on a stool behind a counter. He looked up from some papers he had been reading and watched her warily.

It did not seem he planned to offer a greeting, so she walked to the counter and said, "Hi, I'm Trinx. Are you Zizzle the alchemist?"

"That's my name on the sign, isn't it?" he snapped.

Where had he learned his customer service? She fumbled; his response having caught her off guard.

"Er. Um. Sorry. Of course, you are. Well, see. I was wondering if you had advice for learning alchemy. Maybe a book you could recommend?"

Zizzle snorted. "And why would I want to encourage competitors to sprout up and push me out of business? Hard enough to run this place as it is. I have books, true. But they aren't for sale. If you would like to buy a potion, let me know. Just don't touch anything with those clumsy-looking hands of yours. Otherwise, go find someone else's business to steal."

He waved a hand, indicating the shelves lining the walls. Bottles, vials, and jugs filled the shelves with small placards showing names and prices. A layer of dust coated all of it.

Trinx was pretty sure she knew why he found it so hard to run the place and why the business didn't bring in plenty of profits. There were other shops and alchemists in the warren. This had just been the most convenient.

"Thank you anyway. I have no need for any potions today." She turned around and walked right back out the door. The little bell jingled, and the heavy door fell closed with a *thud*.

Trinx realized she had to get going to work, or she'd be late. As it was, she would likely be normal-late, but if she hurried, she could avoid being make-Gristle-angry-and-dock-her-pay-late. She breezed into the Arsonist's Tender a mere five minutes past the start of her shift, and Gristle simply grunted in acknowledgment of her presence.

"Sorry, Gris," she said. "I had to stop at Zizzle's Fizzles on the way in. He wasn't much help, though, so I need to find another alchemist. I'll look tomorrow. Don't worry, I'm here and ready to work today."

"Psssh," he said. "No worries here. Yer pretty much on time today, Luv. 'Bout as good as it gets. Days like yesterday are the stuff of legend. If you need an alchemist, though, ye could do me a favor? I know a goblin who runs a shop in the northeast quadrant. Ordered a couple bottles of Troll's Tooth Reserve. I have a solid connection for it, so my prices are better'n most. Still quiet, as ye can see. Ye should have time to run the bottles over for me and still get back before the crowd picks up. Name's Brinta. Calls the shop Distilled Magic."

He pulled out two bottles filled with dark amber whiskey and set them on the counter.

"Oh wow," she said. "Sure thing! I can do that. Let me just pop my head in the back to say hi to Q. I kinda left in a hurry last night."

He simply nodded and returned to cleaning some mugs and glasses with a rag.

Trinx walked into the kitchen and spotted Quilka by the prep board, cutting a large pile of onions.

"Sorry about last night, Q. Really, I am. Hope it wasn't too awkward."

Quilka turned to her. "Oh, don't worry about it. I was the one a little worried, but I also know yesterday was rough. It was odd that you ran out in the middle of a Serenya song. Don't worry. I covered for your sudden exit. Something about having an upset stomach earlier that must have gotten worse. Those guys were nice. They didn't seem to mind. That guy Vex looked a little disappointed, though."

"I'll tell you about it later," Trinx sighed. "Your place after work? I hope you had fun with them the rest of the evening."

"Oh. No," Quilka giggled. "After you left, I danced with Draz for a bit, and Vex wandered off. After the song ended, he left to find where his buddy went and I ended up dancing with some friends I spotted, then headed home to get some sleep. I never did find out how to get one of those permanent passes we've heard about."

"Thanks for the cover," Trinx said. "Gris asked me to run a

delivery for him. I'll be back in a few to help with the dinner rush."

She left the room almost as abruptly as she had entered, waving over her shoulder to Quilka.

Trinx grabbed the bottles from the counter, wrapped them in paper, and then slipped them into a cloth sack, slinging the strap over her shoulder. Waving to Gristle, she left the tavern to seek out Distilled Magic. Hopefully, Brinta would have a nicer demeanor than Zizzle.

Chapter 7

Distilled Magic

Trinx hadn't been to the northeast quadrant of the warren for quite some time. Her parents lived on the east side, and she avoided it to reduce the chance of running into them. She still had no idea how to explain where she had been or tell them about her true self. The warren was large, though, and seeing them was unlikely.

She found the shop with a sign depicting an apparatus with tubes and pipes that dripped luminescent purple-painted drops into a flask. The sign's industrial lettering read, "Distilled Magic." The building's stone walls with exposed iron girders continued the theme.

She pushed open the heavy iron door and entered the sparse shop with display tables littered with containers in a multitude of different forms and sizes. At the center of the room, a goblin stood in a U-shaped workspace. The middle of the curve looked like a service counter, while either side held lab equipment.

The goblin in the workspace immediately drew her eye. They had no hair on their head or exposed arms. They had five rings on the right ear and three on the left, barbell studs pierced both cheeks, and their nose had a gold circle through the septum. Full-sleeve tattoos covered their arms.

Trinx received a completely different welcome than Zizzle had provided; this goblin's voice was friendly and full of warmth. "Welcome to Distilled Magic! I'm Brinta. How can I help you today? If you give me an idea of the symptoms you'd like to remedy or the enhancement you'd like to make, I'm sure I can find just the right concoction."

"Hi, Brinta," Trinx opened, "nice to meet you. I'm Trinx. I have a delivery for you from Gristle at the Arsonist's Tender, but I also had some questions about alchemy, if you don't mind?"

"Oh!" they exclaimed. "I've been hoping that would come in soon. Thanks for bringing it over and saving me a trip. Gristle didn't need to send anyone, but I appreciate it. It's good meeting you as well, Trinx. I'd be happy to answer some questions. Are you looking for something in particular?"

Distracted with a stack of cards on the counter, Trinx picked one up and looked it over. It read, "Brinta of Distilled Magic, They/Them, Custom Alchemical Solutions," in a neat script. She realized Brinta had asked a question and set the card aside before rummaging in her sack.

Trinx pulled the wrapped bottles from the sack slung over her shoulder and set them out on the counter for Brinta. Unsure how to start, she took her usual approach and just let the words flow, hoping her brain or mouth would figure it out along the way.

"Well. No. No, I'm not looking for anything specific—or maybe it's too specific? I'm not sure what all is possible with alchemy. It can do wondrous things, I've heard, but what can't it do? I'd like to learn. Is that possible? How'd you learn? Do you sell books?" Okay, maybe her brain didn't fully connect with her mouth by the end, but she was pretty sure she used enough words to convey the idea.

Brinta politely listened to her rambling, smiling the entire time as if to encourage her. When it was clear the last question was the end, for now at least, they said, "I love that you are interested in experimenting and learning about distilling potions. I can let you borrow a book or two. You can read them. See what you think. After that, if you're still interested and have unanswered questions, we can work to figure out what it is you are after."

"Oh, wow!" Trinx said. "That's so generous. Are you sure I can just borrow them? I'll be sure not to let anything happen to them."

The alchemist pulled two books from under one of the work surfaces. They placed them side by side in front of Trinx on the counter. The first was titled *Alchemy Simplified*, and the second read *Interesting Uses of Common Ingredients*. Neither were large volumes, though the second was thicker than the first.

"Both of these are very approachable to most," they said. "You won't find anything very advanced in either of them, but there is enough there to be interesting. You are welcome to borrow these because Gristle sent you here with my whisky. If he trusted you to do that, I'm sure I can trust you to take care of these books. I expect that you not only return them but share with me what you learned."

Trinx ran a finger over the books, tracing the inlays in the covers. After reverently stacking them, she tucked the card she had picked up earlier between the cover and the first page of the top book as she slid the books into the cloth sack.

"Thank you so much. I'll bring them back as soon as I can. There is maybe one question I have now."

"Sure," Brinta said. "Lay it on me."

"Okay," she said. "So, one of my favorite products, that I'm pretty sure is alchemy, is Vash's Extreme Lashes. You know it?"

"Of course, I know it," the alchemist said. "It's very popular. Vash has done some amazing things. She's great, you know."

Trinx stared at them for a moment and asked, "You know Vash?"

Brinta laughed and spoke with a lilt in her voice. "Don't be so surprised. Just because her name is on some popular products doesn't mean she isn't approachable. Of course, approaching her is harder for some of us than for others. She lives in one of the largest cities, after all. I've only met her once, but we've traded letters for years. But did you have a question about her or the product?"

Trinx's gut told her she could probably trust the alchemist. Still, they had just met. Best to keep things vague for now. "Yes. Sorry. It's great how it makes the lashes grow, but I have an older friend with kind of the opposite problem. She has whiskers on her upper lip. Is there something that can get rid of them? Maybe even stop them from growing?"

"It's funny you should ask that," the alchemist replied with another chuckle. "It's actually something I've been personally working on. I, myself, have a few years behind me and noticed the same happening on my lip. I started with what I know best —a potion—but it didn't go as planned. Removed the hair from my lip. That part worked. But it also removed all of my hair. Everywhere. Head to toe." They patted their head and cackled, clearly having moved beyond the failure and seeing the humor in it.

Brinta calmed before continuing. "Turns out, I like it better this way. The potion lasts a while, so I only have to drink a dose every month, though, not everyone likely wants this extreme result. So, I still work on that project from time to time, even though my personal need for it is no longer there since I like this new look. I'll get my notes on the experiments back out and read over them before you come back to return the books."

"Thanks again," Trinx said with a wide grin. "I'll bring them back soon. Maybe I'll understand enough for you to explain the hair removal solution." She waved goodbye and left for the tavern.

As she walked, her imagination spun ideas of using the potion Brinta had mentioned. She was sure it would feel amazing, and she smiled, playing with a braid and daydreaming about the wider range of dresses she could wear. But then Trinx abruptly stopped, looking at the braid she held in her fingers—it wouldn't be worth it if she had to lose the braid and her full head of voluminous hair.

Eager to read the books right away, the idea of skipping out on work today danced through her mind.

No! Stay grounded, she scolded herself.

There would be time to read later. But probably not tonight. She had difficulty focusing on anything after a full shift and a complicated text would be too much. An early morning then. She could get out of bed early if properly motivated, and she found learning the secrets of alchemy very motivating.

So, back to the Tender, she walked. She wanted to have that talk with Quilka after work. Q would find it funny. Now that it was behind her, she could see it was pretty humorous herself.

The tavern had filled by the time she returned. The dinner rush would soon hit. She didn't bother disturbing Gristle on her way in and just flashed him a wave to show she had finished the delivery and was back at work. Quilka stood over a table on the far side of the room, taking an order. Trinx slipped into the kitchen, noted the special, and grabbed a serving tray before turning right back around and returning to the main room to tend to customers.

Her shift passed smoothly. The only interesting part of the night was when a traveling Gnoll bard stopped in. He had worked out a deal with Gristle to play through the evening for a good meal and a bottle of wine. The bartender had said he could keep any tips he pulled in as well. He wasn't half bad and did a fine job singing covers for popular songs. The bard hadn't played any original tunes, but the room enjoyed the songs they knew and loved.

The music made working the tables more pleasurable for both the barmaids. They each even dropped token tips into his hat in thanks. The evening slipped away, and before they knew it, they were washing and putting the last of the dishes back on the shelves.

"You ready to head over to my place?" Quilka asked. "I have an Elderberry Mist tea with ginger. It will help with your upset stomach." Her friend giggled at her joking reference to last night's cover story, putting air quotes around the words *upset stomach.*

"Sure, that sounds great," Trinx said as she joined in the laughter and patted her belly. "I think I've mostly recovered, but a nice cup of tea would round out the evening."

At her friend's place, Trinx sat on the couch, flicking the beads on her fidget toy. Quilka set out a teapot on the small table in front of her sofa. Steam rose from the spout, carrying the sharp spice of the ginger. She filled two cups and sat down, crisscrossed on the couch at an angle to face her friend. Picking up the closest of the cups, she blew across the surface to chase away some of the heat and took a sip.

"So, spill. What happened? You tore out of there faster than a rabbit fleeing a hawk."

Trinx picked up the second cup and took a sip. The sweet

tang of the elderberries collided with the spicy ginger. Q was right. If her stomach had been upset, this tea would be perfect.

With a sigh, she said, "Okay, so, don't laugh too hard. When we were dancing, I was hopping around a lot. I guess I landed too hard, and one of these flew out of my blouse." She touched her right breast pouch. "And then that guy, Vex? He actually stomped it! It blew open, spraying the gel inside all over the floor."

Quilka started giggling and even sloshed some of her tea onto the rug. "Sorry, I know you asked me not to laugh, but that was pretty funny." She contained her giggle fit and continued, "Seriously though. I really doubt they had any idea what happened. They had already had a few drinks, and the club was dark."

"You're probably right," Trinx said, shrugging. "But it shocked me. I felt embarrassed and needed to get out of there. Especially with those two hobs dancing with us. It was too much." She glanced down at the rug where the tea stained the carpet.

"Don't worry about the spill," Q said. "I'll clean it later. I've spilled worse on that rug."

"So, anyway," Trinx said, "I went to see Zigla out in her cave. She made me a new pouch and a couple of backups. She also had some great ideas. For the first idea, I need to ask a favor."

"Sure, of course. What can I help with?" her friend asked.

"I knew you would," Trinx said, flashing a grin. "Zigla said I should find someone who needs a marriage of convenience. You know, a man who needs it for other reasons, like me. So, he wouldn't necessarily want anything more from me. I've started listening in at work. Maybe I can find someone like that. That's the favor. Can you be on the lookout, too?"

"Hmmm, I don't think I like the idea of you married to

someone just for the agency's approval," Quilka said, wrinkling her nose. "That's a huge commitment and a pretty big lie to live. And long, too. All that to get a child? What about them? What would they think of that kind of family?"

"Well," Trinx said, "it doesn't have to be that big of a deal. We could always end the marriage after adopting the youngling. Then I'll just raise it like I was planning to anyway."

Quilka's frown deepened, and she paused before saying, "That seems like it might be complicated. Plus, this theoretical person would need the marriage, too. That's the whole point you were making: finding someone who needs the appearance as well. It wouldn't be fair to them to quit after you get what you wanted."

"Okay," Trinx admitted, "fair point. Maybe it would have to be longer than I thought. I got wrapped up in the part that solved my problem. I just wanted a way to get a child so I could raise it."

"And that's the other thing," Quilka said. "You keep calling the child you want to adopt, *it*. They are a person. You keep talking like it's a prop in this scheme you are making."

"Worg's breath," Trinx hissed exasperatedly. "That's not what I meant. You're twisting things. I would care for it—*them*. I know they would be a person. But fine, maybe Zigla's idea wasn't a good solution. She's not been in the warren for a long time and left when she was really young. Maybe that kind of thing happened more often back then. I'm not ruling it out, though. If I can find the right person. Well, it could work. I think."

"Maybe," Quilka said with some resignation lingering in her voice. "I'll keep my ears open around the tavern, I suppose. I still don't like the idea of a marriage like that. What if you found someone else you really loved? Or what if someone found you? Maybe someone already has."

"What's that supposed to mean?" Trinx asked, quirking an eyebrow. "Do you think someone has already fallen in love with me, and I don't even know it?"

"I don't know," Quilka said in a rush, blurring the words together. "I haven't heard. I just meant, what if you end up wanting to partner with someone else? But you are stuck in that fake union? But anyway, forget it. Didn't you say Zigla had another idea? Maybe it's a better one."

"Oh, right!" She clapped, oblivious to Quilka's redirection. "The other idea Zigla had. She thought I might find a way to change up my body with alchemy."

Trinx pulled one of the books from her bag. "Look at this. I got it today from an alchemist named Brinta. They said I could borrow these books to learn the basics of alchemy. I'm hoping I can find a way to make more structural changes to my body with potions. Like a more complicated version of growing stronger eyelashes with Vash's Extreme Lashes."

"Wow!" Quilka exclaimed. "That would be amazing if you figured something out. Let me know if I can help at all. Depending on what alchemy can do, who knows what kinds of solutions you could find? For now, though, I have to ask, did you sleep in your braids last night? I bet you did. They're all frizzed. Turn around; I'll grab a brush and brush out your hair."

"You don't have to do that," Trinx said, but her friend was already up and rummaging at her dressing table. Trinx turned herself around, switching to a crisscross position facing the opposite way she had been. She removed the two bits of stiff ribbon she used to tie off the end of her braids and tucked them away in her bag, sliding the book back in as well.

The couch sank in behind her, her braids loosened and unwound as nimble fingers untwisted the hair.

Quilka asked from behind her, "Do you think you'll learn to brew a potion that can remove your excess hair?"

Trinx started to nod but realized moving her head around would not be a good idea while Q worked on her tangles. Instead, she said, "Yes. That's actually what started the conversation with Brinta and led to me borrowing the books. I didn't tell them I wanted something for myself, though not having to shave was my goal. I told a fib about an older friend with lip hair. Brinta is fascinating. No hair at all—head to toe. Evidently, an experiment along those same lines went wrong. They liked the end result, though, and kept taking the potion. It gives me hope for a less drastic solution. I'd like to keep the hair on my head. I like my braids."

A light laugh chimed behind her ear, and Quilka said, "I like your braids too! You definitely shouldn't take that potion. Your hair is so thick and luxurious."

Fingers ran slowly through her hair, from her scalp down to the end. They repeated the motion several times, applying light pressure on the top of her head and shaking her hair on the way down, loosening it.

"Brinta sounds interesting," Quilka said. "From the name, I'd guess she is a woman, but I wonder. You keep saying they and them. Why is that?"

The brush tugged lightly as it began to work out tight kinks in her hair. Slowly, it made its way down, bringing the small tangles lower. Quick strokes with the brush stopped when hitting too much resistance, then started again with a wiggle.

"Oh, they had a card," Trinx said. "Plus, if you saw them, I'm pretty sure you'd think it fits. Brinta has crafted a very androgynous look."

Hands gathered a portion of her hair low down on her back. The brush began the quick strokes on the ends of her locks, sending the small tangles to the tips, where they vanished. The tension the hands kept on the hair prevented the pulling from being too painful.

"That makes sense, I suppose," Quilka said. "I'd love to meet them. Besides a solution for facial and body hair, what else do you think you can do with alchemy?"

Trinx sat thoughtfully as she felt her friend continue brushing out the last of her tangled ends. "I think, um, I think what I would really like—well, you know I lost a part of myself when we were dancing. I'd love it if that couldn't happen again. I'd love to have real breasts. A properly formed chest. One not so easily lost because I danced too hard. And—even if I couldn't actually bear a child, I'd like all the right parts."

The brush started long strokes down the tangle-free hair, smoothing out the waves the braids had taught her tresses. She described what she imagined as the perfect chest, the size and shape of the breasts. The brush stroked faster through her long hair. She spoke of losing the parts of her that bothered her the most and the desire to make herself whole. The brush continued to stroke faster through the loose hair. Hands danced with the brush as it smoothed and shined the blue-black tresses.

Quilka's voice whispered behind her as the brushing slowed, "I hope you can find all of those answers and more with the alchemist's help." Then, louder, she said, "I think I've got your hair in much better shape now. It should be easy enough for you to style it as you'd like tomorrow. Speaking of which, it's getting pretty late. I should probably get to bed soon."

Trinx turned around to look at her friend and said, "Thank you. It feels wonderful. You're right. It is late. I'll get going home. Thanks for the tea. I'll see you at the Tender tomorrow?"

"You bet," Quilka said, pushing her smile wider and giving her a pat. "Be careful on your way home."

They hugged briefly, and Trinx left for her apartment.

Chapter 8

A Solution

Trinx slept better than she had in ages. The poor sleep from the previous two nights most assuredly led to her deep slumber. But more than that, after the conversation with her best friend, the tension unwound from her body and mind like her braids had while Quilka brushed them away. She hopped out of bed, leaving her nightgown on.

Grabbing the ribbons from her bag, she parted her hair and tied two pigtails. Her tresses could use a rest during this morning's study session. She pulled out *Alchemy Simplified* and found a bag of granola. Absently, she munched on crunchy clusters of oats, peanuts, and tiny bits of dried fruit. She flipped through the pages slowly.

Trinx found the book surprisingly easy to understand. The basic ideas behind most potions and elixirs made sense. She simply had to learn how the bits of magic that infused the plants and animals of the world could combine to create the outcomes she desired. The more she read, the more she realized the concepts were straightforward, but there was a huge amount to discover about ingredients and how they might interact.

A larger issue appeared to be the danger lurking when combining some substances. The results could be disastrous and, in the worst cases, deadly. The book only contained a few very simple recipes. Most of it spoke about the basics of the craft and information on the common reagents that appeared regularly in formulas. More than once, she wondered if alchemists stuck with the ingredients they knew best rather than experimenting too broadly.

She found the number of different effects she could create to be much larger than she had dreamed. It really seemed like you could achieve just about anything with alchemy. The only trick was whether she could find the right combination and formula for the results she desired.

There were recipes for cures, wound closure, and health restoration. She knew of some of these from her time in the raiding groups. Of course, they never gave her potions like those, but the leaders often had an emergency vial or two.

Other formulas offered protective charms against elements, and some could toughen skin to make it act as natural armor, adding an extra defensive layer. She read of others that could enhance the mind and nervous system, making it easier to solve problems or dodge attacks.

The section that interested her the most spoke of recipes for elixirs that could alter the body. One page described a general solution for stimulating hair growth, similar to the product by Vash she used, but for a wider application. This was the opposite of what she wanted, but still noteworthy. The book listed several other body modifications; however, none were of the type she desired. This didn't surprise her. She needed to find more advanced references, learn a lot more from

Brinta, and maybe even break new ground in finding such solutions.

Most of the discussions did not have actual recipes or formulas. Instead, they spoke of the concoctions and their various uses. The book also focused on a variety of ingredients and the most popular effects rather than specific outlines for combining them into a potion. This was a beginner tome, after all.

When she reached the end of the book, she set it aside and checked the time.

"Oh, no!" she yelled to her empty room. Hours had sped by while she had her nose in the book. She still had to fix herself up for work, and today, she needed to shave as well. There wasn't actually enough time, but if she hurried, she wouldn't be too late.

She sat in front of the mirror at her changing table. No music. She must stay focused.

First, she scooped a small dollop of Glamour Dissolver and smeared it on her face. She massaged it into her skin until a bubbly foam covered her. Using a towel, she gently wiped away the residue, revealing her clean skin underneath. The stuff really was amazing, and she realized it, too, likely had been made with alchemy. It was magical, the way it worked, cutting through many layers of makeup and grease.

Yes. She definitely needed to shave. She lathered a thick cream over her cheeks, neck, and around her mouth. Carefully but deliberately, she used a razor to remove the layer of white and the black stubble underneath. She paused. Inspiration struck, and she made some notes in a notebook. She finished shaving and ran a hand over her baby-smooth skin.

It did not take long before she had applied a fresh layer of makeup, softening her features while adding emphasis to her lips and eyes. She opted to leave her hair in pigtails and swapped her nightgown for a purple dress. A thick black belt with a golden buckle cinched the dress around her waist. She wore pumps with short heels matching her belt, with little gold clasps on the straps.

That evening's shift at the tavern flew by until one major incident. Trinx approached a two-top with a couple of men who had recently sat down. The goblins likely came here straight after returning from a raid or a hunt. She caught the telltale scent of copper, confirming there was blood mixed in with the dirt covering them. It wasn't uncommon, and it was an unfortunate part of the job. In fact, there were quite a few goblins who felt coming in like this was to their benefit when looking to pick up women. In their minds, it showed off how successful a warrior or hunter they were.

"Welcome to the Tender," Trinx said. "Can I get you something to eat? Or just drinks this evening?"

A goblin with scraggly-looking, reddish-brown whiskers and a missing left earlobe said, "Food for me. Built up a rumble on the raid today." He patted his belly and flashed a grin.

"Same," said his buddy, who had a much nicer beard that was full and black. "And we'll both have the house ale."

"Of course."

Trinx turned to catch Gristle's eye. The table stood near the bar, and he had heard the conversation. He nodded to her to acknowledge it and set two full mugs out on the counter. She grabbed them and turned back around, setting them on the table.

"I'll be back with your food in a few moments."

In the kitchen, she had Brizla put together two plates. Tonight's dinner special was fried meadowlark served alongside a pile of fluffy mashed potatoes, with a crater crafted with the serving spoon. A gravy made with herbs and the greasy drippings from the birds filled the depression. Trinx took the dishes and returned them to the table in the main room, setting them down in front of the two goblins.

"There you go," she said. "Enjoy! Is there anything else I can get for you?"

"A date with you tomorrow?" asked the scraggly bearded one with a smirk.

"Sorry, tomorrow I've got another shift here," she apologized with a warm smile. She almost always had this excuse to pull out since she worked so much.

His black-bearded buddy spoke up and flicked him hard with an index finger that seemed spring-loaded. "Ya've only had one ale, and you're already hittin' this one up? Look at those gorilla hands. You know that's probably a *he*, right?"

Her cheeks flushed, and she opened her mouth at a loss for words. Before she could speak, in one fluid motion, Gristle had planted his single arm on the bar counter and swung himself up and over the bar. Standing behind Black Beard, the towering hobgoblin reached down and pulled the much smaller goblin up to his feet by the ear. "That's enough! Ye treat the women here with respect, or out ye go. Apologize. Or I haul ye both out right now."

"Sorry. I'm sorry!" he blurted, looking up at the scowling face of Gristle.

"Not to me! Ye dimwit! To her," he said, thumbing at Trinx.

The goblin looked like he might piss his pants right then and there. He looked at her and said, "Sorry. Didn't mean nothing."

"S'pose that'll do," he said, pushing the goblin back down into the chair. He turned to her. "Luv, swap this table for one of Q's. Ye don't need to serve these idiots."

Trinx retreated to the kitchen. Gristle really was an amazing boss. He took care of the staff here and didn't let anyone disrespect them. The old hob had accepted Trinx as she was when he hired her on at Quilka's request. He had known her before, yet he didn't seem to care. He treated her and Quilka the same, and she really appreciated him for that.

"Couple of obnoxious twits at the two-top near the bar," Trinx said to her friend. "Gristle told me to see if I could swap them for one of your tables. That work?"

"Oh, sure," Quilka said. "They better not be rude to me either, or we can have Gristle throw them out. But, yeah. Did you see Glink and Zurt at the table by the hearth? You can take that one instead."

"Thanks, Q," Trinx said and left to check on the table in question.

"Welcome back, Glink, Zurt," she said as she approached the table. "Gonna take over helping you for Quilka. Is there anything you need?"

Glink looked up from his meal and swallowed some ale to wash out his mouth before he said, "Don't tink so fer now. And don't worry about the swap. I saw Gristle with those losers. Never you mind them. Always happy to have you serving us."

"Thanks, guys," Trinx said, already putting the earlier rudeness from the other table behind her. "I'll be back in a while to check on you."

After her shift was over and the cleanup was done, she said goodbye to everyone and headed back home. She was eager to go through *Alchemy Simplified* some more before turning in for the night.

At home, she made a pot of dragonroot tea and snuggled up to read. She sat on the bed, her teacup perched on a side table, and the blanket tented over her head in a makeshift hood, fabric draping down around her. She held the book in her lap, re-reading interesting areas and familiarizing herself with the various ingredients, especially the callouts for dangerous combinations.

One section provided an overview of some information, and she wished it had more depth. Unfortunately, she likely needed an advanced text. It spoke to part of what she was looking for. In alchemy, you could craft concoctions in different forms, from liquids like potions and more concentrated elixirs to semi-solids such as creams and balms. Sometimes, an alchemist could even craft the solution in pill or tablet form.

Once she had finished the tea and gleaned as much as she could from the text for the night, she cleaned herself up and lay down, pulling the blankets over her completely. Sleep came to her easily, and she woke hours later feeling refreshed. There would be plenty of time to read through the second book before work, and she might even stop by Brinta's shop. Unfortunately, it wasn't on the way to the tavern, but she could likely make it there and back without being too late.

Trinx put the kettle on to boil and spread a soft cheese on several wheat crackers. While munching her cheesy snack, she flipped through *Interesting Uses of Common Ingredients*. This book had many more recipes, but they all produced only very minor effects. She quickly learned the benefit of this volume, however, and she smiled widely, wishing she had started with this one yesterday.

Every recipe in the book used common, easy-to-acquire ingredients. She even had everything needed for some of them right here in her home. The trick seemed to be that while the materials were easy to get, how you mixed them together was incredibly important. For instance, a Minor Elixir of Focus had an ingredient list almost identical to the tea she was about to make that morning.

Excitement rushed through her as she collected the necessary items.

Step one: grind dragonroot with a mortar and pestle.

Okay. So, she didn't have a mortar and pestle, but she had a bowl, and the end of her hairbrush could fill in for grinding. She scooped some dragonroot tea into the bowl and ground it with the brush. Next up: stir in a dollop of honey and mix thoroughly. She sometimes put honey in her tea but never mixed it with the tea first. She did as it instructed, though, stirring it vigorously.

The recipe said to add just enough hot water to loosen the honey mixture into a slightly viscous liquid. She wasn't sure exactly how much water that would be, so she used her gut and stirred while pouring hot water from the kettle. When it looked about right, she gave it a few more stirs and called it good.

Finally, the last step said to add a circular slice of lemon from the center of the fruit. She cut such a slice and added it to the bowl. The lemon floated in the center of the concoction. The instructions just said to leave it there until it finished. *How would she know when it finished?* She had no idea and just shook her head, thinking she would leave it in for a few minutes. Seconds later, the liquid in the bowl shimmered with a golden glow. That must be it! She removed the slice of lemon and looked at the elixir in the bowl. She had evidently made quite a bit—at least based on the elixirs she had purchased and consumed in the past. Most doses came in small vials, and she even had a few that she hadn't thrown out.

After washing the vials out and drying them as best she could, she filled them with the liquid in the bowl. She screwed a cap on each one and put them aside. She still had plenty left in the bowl and tried some by sipping directly from the container. It tasted like a very strong tea, and she immediately felt invigorated. She often drank dragonroot tea as a pick-me-up because it had a stimulating effect. This elixir blew away the tea and proved much stronger.

Did this mean she could call herself an alchemist? Probably not, but it was a good start. Trinx wanted to read through more of the book but also had a burning desire to show off her elixir to Brinta, and she could even tell them about the idea she had.

With that, she packed up the books in her bag in case Brinta needed them back and set off to Distilled Magic. She followed the tunnels in a northeasterly direction, traveling the twists and turns and floating through the ebbs and flows of the hallway traffic. Along the way, she thought about all the potions she might make once she had learned more. Hopefully, she could borrow some additional books.

When she pushed open the door to the shop, Brinta saw it was her and waved, saying, "Good morning, Trinx! Welcome back. Have you read through those books already? I would have thought it would take you longer. You must be an excellent study."

"What?" Trinx asked, looking confused for a moment, then shook her head. "No, I didn't finish. I'd like to keep them a while longer if that's okay with you. I came to show you what I learned. It's so awesome!"

"Oh," the alchemist said, and their smile widened. "I was hoping you would try one of the easier concoctions. Best way to learn is to do. Which one did you make?"

"Don't worry," Trinx said. "I paid close attention to the warnings in the books. And I kept away from the *Alchemy Simplified* recipes. Some ingredients sound difficult to get. I don't even know what some of them are. I made this, though, from the other book!"

She pulled out a vial, held it up, and said, "I followed the instructions carefully, and I had all the stuff I needed, and it wasn't even that hard. It just worked!"

Brinta took the vial and held it up to the light. They unscrewed the cap and took a sniff. Finally, they placed their finger over the end of the tube and inverted it, then righted it again. Brinta stuck their finger in their mouth, sucking the small amount of liquid off.

"Wow, that's a potent one. You made a Minor Elixir of Focus on your first try? The ingredients and procedure are pretty simple. But still. It often takes beginners more than one try, and they rarely turn out this nicely. You have a knack for this, it seems."

Trinx's face broke with a huge smile. She rarely received such compliments, and it was nice to hear.

"Thanks for saying that. It was really fun, too."

"Say," Brinta said, "I've actually been thinking of bringing on an apprentice for a while now. Do you think you'd be up for the challenge? I can't pay a lot, but if it works out, and I can pull in additional business with your help, then I can offer more."

"Seriously?!" Trinx blurted. "You'd really bring me on as an apprentice? Of course, I will, if that's not a joke. I have to go to work soon, but I could come back tomorrow first thing. I'll ask Gristle if I can start a bit later."

The alchemist smiled and held out a hand. "Deal. You start tomorrow. Come by in the morning."

Trinx took her hand and gave it a shake. "Oh, wait. I forgot. I wanted to tell you my idea for the hair removal potion. What if it was a cream? You know, like shaving cream? You could smear it on where you don't want hair, and instead of a razor, you scrape it off with a flat wooden stick. It would only remove the hair where the cream was, right?"

Brinta clapped their hands. "Ho! I think that might work. It will need some experimenting, though. You often can't just change the substance fundamentally like that. A potion differs greatly from a cream. I think it's possible, though. Great idea, Trinx. We can try an experiment tomorrow!"

Chapter 9

Juggling

At the tavern that evening, a huge brawl broke out between two raiding teams. It wasn't clear to those not involved what was driving the fight. What was clear was the enormous mess that the staff had to clean up at the end of the day, which pushed the end of the shift out late into the night. The clean-up couldn't even start in earnest until later than usual, as several of the customers were slow to wrap up and head home. Gristle held to his core tenets, though, and he insisted everything had to be in tip-top condition before leaving.

While scrubbing the floor with Quilka, Trinx said, "I actually made a potion, er, an elixir, I mean. Still figuring out the difference between the different concoctions. But I made one. It gives a boost of energy, like dragonroot tea, but I don't know, like ten times better?"

"You made a potion already?" Quilka asked, astonishment playing in her voice. "That's amazing. What else can you make?"

"It is amazing," Trinx agreed. "But I don't know what all I

can make. The books make it sound like anything could be possible with the right ingredients and procedures. There is so much to learn, though. But that's the thing. The other news."

"What other news?" Quilka asked.

"The other news from the day," Trinx said as if it was obvious. "I thought I told you I had news. Maybe I didn't. But I do. Brinta invited me to be their apprentice! They are going to teach me alchemy!"

"What?!" Quilka exclaimed. "That's incredible. When do you start?"

"Tomorrow!" Trinx proclaimed. "I can start learning right away. Plus, I gave them an idea on how we might tackle the hair removal potion. They said we could do some experimenting."

"Now, hold up," Gristle said from behind the bar. "What's that? Brinta is takin' ye on as an apprentice? How ye gonna do that, Luv?"

"Yeah, they said they wanted to take on an apprentice, and they offered it to me. Isn't it great?" she asked.

"Right, get that Trinxy," Gristle said with some exasperation. "I meant, how do ye plan on doing that and this?"

"Oh, right," Trinx said. "Well, I was going to talk to you about that."

"Were ye?" Gristle asked, raising an eyebrow. "And when were ye going to do that? Thought you jus' said ye start there tomorrow."

"Well, now," Trinx said, grinning. "So, what do you say, Gris? Think I can start my shift later? Brinta wants me to come in the morning and work most of the day. I'd finish there close to dinner and could come right here after."

"I see," Gristle said gruffly. "Hafta pull back on yer pay. But if ye can make it here before the dinner rush calms down, ye might still pull in plenty of tips. Brinta paying ye, Luv?"

Nodding, Trinx said, "Yes, Brinta said they could pay, but

not a lot. That might change if I help out enough and business increases, but probably enough to balance out what you take off for my shorter shifts."

"Well," Gristle said, "don't love it. But sounds like a good opportunity fer ye. So let's do it. Gonna need ye on time, though. Always needed that, truth be told. But it'll be more important now. And just like tonight, ye need to stay until closing and help with the cleanup."

"Of course," Trinx said with a grin she knew he couldn't resist. "I'll come here straight from there every day."

Maybe in response to Trinx's shift change or for some unrelated reason, both of the barmaids ended up staying late into the night before Gristle declared the tavern clean enough and released them from their shifts. Trinx gave Quilka a hug before leaving. By the time she got home, she was so tired she fell right into bed.

Excitement at the thought of starting her new alchemy apprenticeship drove Trinx out of bed early the next day. The lethargic speed at which she dressed herself proved *excitement* to be completely different than *energy*. Working late into the night had taken its toll on her. Being out late had cast a twinge of doubt on her new plan during her walk home.

That morning, the doubt plucked a little harder as she forced herself through the motions of getting ready. Before leaving her apartment, she remembered having crafted the perfect solution to this very problem yesterday. Rummaging in her bag, she pulled out a vial of the Minor Elixir of Focus and quaffed the entire shot. Her brain immediately engaged in high gear and ripped off the cozy blanket that had been trying to coax her mind to sleep.

With a fresh dose of energy, Trinx hurried to Distilled Magic and shoved the door open, rushing in after. Brinta looked up from the two customers they were speaking with and gave her a smile and a wave.

Trinx flashed a grin and a wave back, calling, "Don't stop on my account. I'll just get my stuff settled until you're done."

"Don't be silly," the alchemist said. "These aren't customers. Not usually, anyway. These are my partners. We had breakfast together at Mystic Leaf, and they walked me to the shop before heading out for their own activities. They'll be leaving in a few minutes. Come and say hello."

Trinx skipped to the counter to introduce herself. "I'm Trinx, but maybe Brinta already told you that. I didn't realize they had partners. But you don't work here? Are you just silent investment partners?"

All three of the goblins laughed, and one partner, a man with a stylish close-cropped mahogany beard, said, "Oh no, darling. We aren't business partners. We all live together. I'm Zerk. And this here is Lizznip, but we all just call her Lizzy." He gestured at an attractive, plump goblin. She wore her flame-red hair in a single long braid.

"Oh, I see," Trinx said while shaking hands with each of them. "I jumped to the wrong conclusion there. That must be an interesting living situation."

"Well," Brinta said and composed their laughter. "It adds just the right amount of spice to our lives. I'm glad to see it doesn't bother you."

"Bother me?" she questioned. "No, of course not. Your living situation is your own business. I'm very much in favor of people living how they want to."

"That's great," Zerk said. "We agree! But Lizzy and I should get going. From what we understand, you have a lot a learning in front of you. Good luck!"

"Well, now," Brinta said as the two left. "Should we experiment? Customers are rare first thing, but we will have to pause our crafting if someone comes in. I thought we would start by making the potion as it stands today, and then we can incorporate it into a cream. It's an advanced one, so I'll be crafting it. You can watch closely, though, and help by grabbing ingredients for me. The back cabinets have my primary stock of reagents."

Trinx nodded enthusiastically. "Sure thing! Just let me know what you need, and I'll bring them over."

"To start with," the alchemist said, "please find some witch's bane root and orb weaver extract. Those make up the base. The first causes hair to weaken, the second inhibits growth."

Trinx went to the cabinets and looked over the bottles, jars, and vials. After finding both, she brought them to the workbench, where the alchemist had set up various pieces of equipment.

"Great, now you'll need to find two essences," Brinta said. "Nettle leaf stimulates hair loss and works in combination with the witch's bane. Nightshade increases the potency of most concoctions."

Both items were near each other, and she found them easily.

Trinx turned to bring them back when the alchemist called while looking down at a scribbled notebook, "Oh, see if you can find some phantom orchid petals, too. Those should help bind the multiple effects together."

Trinx found the petals and brought all three ingredients over to the workbench. As she set them down, Brinta finished reviewing their notes and pulled out the last of the equipment needed.

As the alchemist worked, they spoke aloud, narrating what they were doing. "First, I cut the witch's bane into several small pieces and place them in a mortar. It's a dry, crumbly root. It powders easily. Then, I add the orb weaver extract. See how I mix it together well but with care? You want deliberate and slow folds with the spoon to combine them." The mixture developed into a thick black paste.

Once the compound had a uniform consistency with no undissolved root, they added the essences.

Brinta continued, "Now we add the nettle leaf, then stir in the nightshade. See how it loosens it up? Finally, we add three of the orchid petals."

They dropped in the petals, each dissolving as soon as it hit the potion. The dark brew glowed with a purple hue as the last of the ingredients disappeared.

"Do they always do that?" Trinx asked. "Glow, I mean. My elixir had a faint golden gleam when it finished. This one is casting a purple one."

"Not always," Brinta answered in a lecturing tone, "but it is very common. It's a nice way to know when you've finished something. However, sometimes, it will do that prior to completing the recipe. In those cases, you often made something but not the full elixir. So, you continue with the directions, and it may or may not glow again. For this one, we need to let it rest for at least an hour before we can experiment with it. You can help me clean up the equipment we used. We shouldn't run into trouble with any of this but keep this in mind, some ingredients will react in a nasty way with soap or water. I'll let you know ahead of time if that's the case, and we'll find an alternate way to clean."

The two set about washing and straightening up. An industrial-looking sink stood against the back wall. The alchemist dried while the apprentice built up a sudsy layer of bubbles, then rinsed it all away.

"Now, to find something to fold that into in order to develop a cream or foam," Brinta said, walking to the cabinet.

They pulled out a bottle full of a thick purple lotion. "This could work. Nado spittle. The nado are the tiny lizards found north of here. The spit can often successfully create a suspension."

After the viscous potion finished resting, the alchemist poured a portion into a small bowl. They added a dollop of the nado spittle and gently folded them together with a spatula. The spit darkened, creating a creamy, deep purple foam.

"Well," Brinta said, "we can definitely apply this directly to the areas with excess hair. The question is, will it still work like the original potion? See how this time there was no glow? Doesn't mean it didn't turn out right, but we'll have to experiment. I often try my creations on myself if I'm pretty sure they won't kill me. Not a suitable candidate for this one, though, with the potion in full effect. What about your friend with the lip? Are they adventurous?"

"Well...about that," Trinx said, grimacing and clearing her throat. "I don't actually have such a friend. It was for me. I have a problem with too much hair." She felt everything about her new teacher was trustworthy, and they had a pretty unique situation of their own going on at home. Rolling up the sleeve on her left arm, she said, "We can try it on a section of my arm."

"Now, that's quite the growth you have there," Brinta said, barking a laugh. "Sorry. Shouldn't laugh. You're fine. You know, some features tend to run stronger in families. You'd be surprised at some of what I've seen when people come looking for solutions to their problems. In any case, this will work well for a test. I'll try up here near your elbow."

Trinx blushed a faint purple but kept her arm out. The alchemist found a flat piece of wood that looked like a stirring stick. They used the mixing spatula to smear a layer of the foam on Trinx's forearm where it met the elbow.

On contact, the mixture bubbled, and a searing pain

flooded her arm. "OW! OW! OW! Get it off!" she screamed but tried to keep her arm still.

Brinta used the wood to scrape it off, and the hair in that patch came with it. The skin turned from her normal olive green to a bright purple.

The alchemist laughed again. They likely had to find humor in their job, especially if they often performed experiments like this on themselves.

"Wow. Okay. I think we can rule out nado spittle. Clearly, that burns too much. I wouldn't worry about the purple. It should fade over time. If it doesn't, you'll grow new skin, eventually. Either way, your arm will be green again. The good news is, we've proven the concept is possible. It removed the hair, which is what we want!" They clapped their hands excitedly.

Trinx rubbed at the discolored area on her arm that now itched as the burning faded. "I suppose that is good news. Really, if this purple fades away, I'd probably put up with the burning if it meant getting rid of the rest of this." She waved a hand over her hairy arm and then went back to scratching and rubbing the bare patch.

"No need for desperate measures," Brinta said. "This is just a minor setback. I have plenty of other similar suspensions we can try. We better let your arm rest a bit, though, before we try another one. For today, you can watch as I craft a few concoctions to restock the more popular items. I'm sure there will be time for you to see how I help a customer or two as well."

And that's how the rest of the day went. She watched the alchemist craft potions, some quite basic and others much more advanced. As customers came in, she saw how they identified their problems and needs and how Brinta made recommendations and sold solutions. By the end of the afternoon, Trinx was even handling the initial customer inquiry and then handing the information off to the alchemist.

She made sure she left with plenty of time to make it to her evening shift. As she arrived at the Arsonist's Tender, she drank a vial of her elixir. It proved to be a lifesaver and filled her with the energy she needed to make it through the rest of the night. She would have to brew another batch of it or maybe even get a better recipe from Brinta. Something told her she would need it more and more if she was to keep juggling these two jobs.

The evening flew by in a blur. The elixir fueled Trinx and enabled her typical cheerful disposition. Toward the end of the shift, the population in the tavern had waned, and she had time to talk with Quilka for a few minutes.

"Q!" she said. "I had the most amazing day at Distilled Magic. I'm learning a ton of useful information about ingredients and potions. But the best part! Check this out." Making sure no one was around to see, she pulled up her sleeve and showed off the bare patch of purple skin. It had stopped itching and now just looked like an odd purple bruise surrounded by the hair on the rest of her arm.

"The best part was bruising your arm?" Quilka asked, looking confused. "And what exactly did you do, anyway? Did you burn off your—" A light sparked in her eyes, and her friend's smile threatened to break her face in two. "Wait! You're kidding! You actually got it to work? But why is it purple?"

Trinx giggled, her joy overflowing, and she said, "Okay, so it's not supposed to be purple. And it hurt. Like a *lot*. Really bad. Then it itched worse than blisterbush. Brinta said it was a good first try, but we are going to find a better suspension for the potion."

"That's wonderful," Quilka said and gave her a hug. "Just

make sure you don't run yourself ragged. I can't believe you aren't tired."

More giggling erupted. Perhaps this was her tiredness finding a way through the elixir-fueled wave of energy.

"Well, I fixed that with alchemy, too. That elixir I made works great! I just drink a vial whenever I start to feel sluggish."

"Oh, Trinx," Quilka said while joining in the laughter. "That's great. Just be careful. I've known folks that get hooked on elixirs like that."

"Don't worry. I'll be safe. I swear," she said and held up two fingers as an oath.

The next several days repeated in nearly the same way as she barely slept and juggled the two jobs, supplementing with elixirs of different levels of potency. Brinta warned her about relying too much on the potions and took it on themselves to ensure the ones she used wouldn't cause lasting harm.

On the fifth day, they tried making a cream with dried marshmallow root ground and whipped into a thick foam with honey. Trinx rolled up the sleeve on her right arm. Two small patches on the arm were devoid of hair and discolored. One had nasty-looking red lines chaotically branching across her green skin. They found an area away from those that still had plenty of hair.

Brinta spread some of the mixture on with the spatula and held a wooden scraper at the ready. This time, Trinx didn't scream.

"It's tingly," she said. "I can feel something working, but it doesn't hurt. It's a light stinging sensation. Feels kinda like when someone slaps you really hard?"

"That's good news, then," Brinta said. "Now we just need to see if it actually still works the way it should."

They used the wooden scraper, gently removing the yellowish-foamy mixture. It stuck to the tool and tugged at the skin, but the hair came right up with it. The area underneath was smooth and hairless, with the same natural olive-green skin as the rest of her body.

Brinta and Trinx looked at her arm, then at each other, and let out a loud whoop of excitement.

"We did it!" Trinx cheered. "Thank you so much! Now we just have to make enough of this so I can use it properly."

The alchemist laughed and said, "You've learned a lot this week. I think you can even make it. Under my supervision, of course. We'll make up a batch for you to take home. And then I want you to stay there. Take a day off. You've been working too hard. Do your shift at the tavern if you have to, but don't come in here for a full day. You need to catch up on some sleep."

Chapter 10

Showing Some Skin

Trinx slept in for the first time in a week. She actually slept more than the four or five hours she had somehow been surviving on. She was grateful that Brinta had insisted she take a day off, but she still planned to go into the tavern that evening. The apprenticeship offered a modest amount of compensation, but she needed to make all she could from her job at the Tender.

There was time before she had to go in, though, and more importantly, she had a large tub of the hair removal cream they had made. She started a Serenya song on her music player.

I slept way too long
But I can't sleep all day
That's what my friends say-ay-ay
That's what my friends say-ay-ay

First, she removed her makeup using a generous amount of Glamour Dissolver to make sure she had cleaned off all of it. Her stubble was coming in, and she grimaced at the look of the dark shadow around her mouth and covering her cheeks. It even wrapped around most of her neck. She tied her hair up snugly on her head to ensure it would stay away from the solution.

Taking a spatula, she carefully spread the creamy yellow foam over her face and neck. She left it off her forehead, nose, and eyes but otherwise covered it all. Her skin tingled and began stinging. It wasn't comfortable, but it was easily bearable. Brinta had suggested leaving it on for at least a minute to ensure all hair would come loose and the effect would last longer. They mentioned that, like the original potion, this would have to be used every four to six weeks.

Using one of the flat wood sticks they had given her, she firmly scraped the sticky mixture from her face, wiping it on a cloth between strokes to clean it off. As she did so, she revealed the skin underneath, free of the dark shadow. She scrubbed her face with some soap and water, then toweled it dry. Her smile shone bright, and her smooth green skin looked vibrant as she admired her reflection in the mirror.

Trinx then drew a hot bath and removed her nightgown. Her face instinctively wrinkled when she saw her hairy, naked body. Thankfully, she and Brinta had made a large batch of the mixture. She used the applicator spatula to spread it all over her arms and under her armpits.

Scooping up a larger amount, she smeared it over her chest and stomach, then down in her crotch. As she did that, it occurred to her some areas were more sensitive. A mild burn flared up, but not that horrible. From there, she continued to apply the cream, covering her legs completely, front, sides, and back. She even smeared it on her feet as there were some tufts of hair on the tops of them, as well as her toes.

The next part was trickier. She found a longer cooking spatula and, reaching behind her, haphazardly moved it around, coating her back as well as she could. Turning this way and that, peering over her shoulder at her back in the mirror, she did her best to cover it completely. It would have to do. Surely, it would become easier with practice.

There was no good way to scrape it all off, which was why she had drawn the bath. After letting it sit a bit longer, she slid down into the tub. Trinx used the scraper to pull the goop off, swishing it in the water after every few strokes to rinse it. The bath became murky, with hair floating in it and a scummy slime building up on the surface.

She could not get completely clean with the water in that condition, and she stepped out of the tub. After draining it and wiping it out with a towel that already needed washing, she refilled it with fresh hot water. This time, she added a cap full of bubbling soap.

Easing herself back in, she used a cloth to scrub her body with the sudsy water. Once the bubbles had subsided, she stood up and poured clean water over herself to rinse off the soapy residue, then stepped out of the tub to dry her freshly smooth skin with a fluffy towel.

Trinx stood in front of the large mirror, her mouth agape at the amazing sight of her hairless body. She had shaved off her hair before, but never all of it. That was too daunting of a task. She rarely did because it would grow back so fast.

This, though. Her skin looked amazing. She ran her hands over her arms, her legs, and her torso. Granted, her chest was flat, but she wore a wide grin on her face. She had never felt more beautiful looking at herself naked in the mirror.

Trinx continued to stand there, swaying and twisting this way and that, looking herself over from head to toe. Mesmerized, happiness filled her, and she couldn't remember feeling this amazing before. Maybe when she had first put on a dress at

Zigla's long ago. But no, that had been wonderful. This was better.

Eventually, she pulled on some panties and strapped on her bra, filling it with two of her pouches. She traded them out regularly now to spread the wear and tear. Today she chose black undergarments with lace trim. Over this, she slipped on a dress she had never felt she could wear out in public. The dress was also black with thin dark purple accents. Sleeveless, it had two straps she positioned on her shoulder over the bra straps. The top of the garment fit snugly, then flared out, hanging loose down to her knees. So much exposed skin.

She painted her pointed toenails dark purple and, loving the look of them, so she painted her fingernails to match. After slipping on black sandals with a loose lattice, she turned to the mirror. She braided her hair in her usual style, evenly splitting the colors between the two. Then, standing back to look in the mirror once again, she flashed a smile and made a heart with her hands.

"Watch out, world! Here I come."

Still having time before her shift and desperately needing a shopping trip, she took off for the closest trading district. This was the only dress she had that didn't have sleeves. Prior to today, it wasn't feasible to wear it. Now, she would be showing some skin.

Trinx strutted the entire way to her favorite shop. With her head held high, she let the confidence surge through her. She waved at random strangers, flashing smiles and calling out greetings.

When she arrived at the shop, she waved hello to one of the employees she recognized. Trinx didn't remember her name, but she was friendly. With her help, Trinx found several new dresses and tried them all on, one after the other. Each had short sleeves or various patterns of straps across her shoulders and back. By the end of the spree, she found it necessary to show some restraint and put a few aside. Her eyes had been much larger than her wallet. Still, the trip ended with her holding a neatly wrapped package with three new dresses.

When she arrived at the tavern, she entered to find the room bustling. Gristle looked up to see who had come through the door.

"Good to see ye, Trinxy," he called. "Looking fabulous today. Get settled in the back and jump in. We have a crowded house this evening."

"Thanks, Gris," she said and walked into the kitchen, where she found both Quilka and Brizla.

Her friend had just loaded up a tray full of food to deliver but put it down when she entered. "Wow! Seriously? You figured it out! And it looks great."

Trinx beamed with pride at the compliments. It felt wonderful to look as good as she did, but it also was a great feeling knowing she had helped develop the alchemical cosmetic that made it possible.

"Thanks, Q. We finally figured it out yesterday, and Brinta insisted I take today off. They sent me home with a large tub of the stuff, and I spent all morning working on my makeover."

"That's so awesome! We can chat more about it later. Gotta get this food out. It's pretty busy. You should grab a tray and pick a table that needs help," Quilka said, filling her arms with trays before she left the kitchen.

Trinx slipped an apron on to keep her dress clean. She sampled a spiced meatball before grabbing her own tray and leaving to find a table waiting to order. The dinner rush passed with no major disruptions.

On her latest trip out to check on the customers, Trinx spotted a pair of faces she recognized at a two-top. Draz and

Vex were too busy speaking to each other to notice her approach.

"I can't believe I got passed up by another group," said Vex. "I thought for sure this one needed another hob badly enough they wouldn't care about my beard. Or, I guess, my lack of one."

"Can't your father pull any strings?" Draz asked. "He is the warlord, after all."

"He won't, though," Vex said. "It's complicated. He's annoyed I go out in public as it is. He even tried to use a hair growth potion on me, and it just turned out a complete mess. Worse than nothing at all, really."

"Frick," Draz spat the word out. "That's tough. If you aren't careful, one of your younger brothers is gonna end up warlord. Course, if you get a mate first, that should help." He looked up then and saw Trinx approaching. "Speaking of which, here comes that girl from the club. The one that ran out on you."

"What? Frick. Where?" Vex said, flinging his head around and straightening up. Draz laughed.

Pretending nothing was out of the ordinary, and that she hadn't just heard their conversation, Trinx asked, "Can I get you any food this evening? Or some drinks to start? Oh! It's you two. I remember. From the club? Sorry, I had to leave so quickly. I think I ate something that didn't agree with me that evening. Glad you came into the Tender."

"We came here hungry," Draz said. "I see people eating rice and meatballs. We'll take some of that and a couple of ales."

Vex just nodded and didn't bother trying to speak. He still looked flustered, and his cheeks were tinted lavender.

"Sure thing," Trinx said. "I'll grab your ale and be back with your food shortly."

Returning from the bar, she placed both mugs down for

them, then perhaps feeling inspired by how great she felt in her outfit, Trinx decided to tease the flustered hob.

"You know? I apprentice at Distilled Magic now," she said. "Brinta runs the place, and they are really terrific with potions. It's possible you just didn't try the best one. Come by sometime. I bet we can find something to grow out that beard of yours." Not waiting for a response, she giggled and turned, leaving for the kitchen. Draz burst into a laugh as she walked away.

A few minutes later, she returned with two plates heaped high with rice, a rich and fragrant sauce, and spicy meatballs. A roll glistening with butter and coarse bits of garlic rested on the side, slowly wicking up some of the sauce. She placed a dish in front of each of the two hobs.

"Will this be all? Or can I get you something else? Looks like you are still good on your ales. I can check on you again when those get lower."

By now, Vex had composed himself, and he said, "Actually, I've been talking with Draz. If you were serious, I think I'd like to see if your mentor can help. You said you work at Distilled Magic? I don't think I've been there. I think it's on the east side of the warren?"

"It is," Trinx said, nodding. "Northeast, actually. You should come in, really. I'm sure we can find a solution. Brinta is actually pretty talented with hair-related potions."

"Great," he said with a smile. "I'll come check it out. This food looks amazing, by the way." Vex grabbed a two-pronged fork and speared a meatball, not even waiting until she left.

"See you there," she said and looked to find the next table needing help.

Chapter 11

The Thing About Vex

Trinx wore a new orange dress with brown and green accents she had purchased the day before. This one had short sleeves that puffed out around her shoulders. The flared skirt came down to just over her knees. Although they would cover up a portion of her legs, she opted to wear some complementary socks. Her legs still presented plenty of skin.

Trinx was still amazed at how smooth her skin felt as she ran her fingers over her arms and legs. The hair was completely gone, unlike shaving, where signs of the hair still lingered, even after a close shave. Of course, it would grow back, but at the first sign of it, she would take a day off and perform another session with the cream.

Taking a few moments to brew another batch of her Minor Elixir of Focus, she filled ten empty vials and drank the rest to start the day strong. A few of the vials went into her bag and the rest she stocked on her pantry shelf.

Before she could leave, she still needed to take care of her face and hair. She didn't need as much makeup now that she didn't have to cover her beard, but she still wanted to accent her eyes and lips. She quickly brushed out her hair and wove two tight braids tied off with green ribbons to match the trim on her dress.

When she arrived at Distilled Magic, Brinta finished wrapping a parcel for a customer and sent them on their way. They smiled at the sight of her.

"Trinx! You look fabulous! I hoped there wouldn't be any issues with the larger trial at home. In fact, I had enough optimism. I pulled together a patent document for the hair removal cream. I just need a name and your signature."

"My signature?" she asked.

"Of course," they said. "I can't take all the credit for this. I have you listed as a co-inventor. Sure, it was my original hair removal formula, but except for odd folks like me, it would never sell as a potion. The cream idea and the solution we found together make this very valuable."

Trinx beamed with excitement. "How valuable? Where do I sign?"

Brinta laughed and pointed out the spot on the forms. They handed her a spelled quill that verified the signature was authentic, as it was written.

"I'd say this will sell incredibly well. Not just here in the warren but in all the big cities. The obvious uses are for things like the lip hair on older women like we first discussed, but there are a lot of women among the various races that have light hair covering their legs and often on their arms as well. Not like your extreme case, but the alternative is shaving, which many do. A cream like this will be very popular, but we do need a name. Something catchy."

"Have you any ideas to work with?" Trinx asked while

looking thoughtful and signing the documents with the proffered quill.

"For some reason, my creativity is eluding me today," Brinta sighed. "All I can think of are ridiculous names like Hair-B-Gone."

"No. Not that," Trinx said, wrinkling her nose. "What about Bare Essence? That's kinda catchy. After using it, my skin felt *so* soft and smooth. We could go with EverSmooth Cream?"

"Both sound great, but I love EverSmooth. Done!" Brinta filled in the name on the forms, tucking them into an envelope to take for filing. "Would you mind doing the honors of taking these to be filed? The sooner we do so, the sooner we can start producing it for the market. We'll also license it to other alchemists to further the reach. We don't have the resources to sell directly into other cities, but licensing can help with that."

"Sure thing," she said as she grabbed up the envelope. "Just, uh, where do I file them?"

"That's on me," Brinta said, chuckling. "Sometimes I forget you don't know the ins and outs of everything yet. The forms eventually need to go to one of the larger cities. Despite the fighting that goes on in rural areas like ours, agreements are in place to allow the trade of goods, services, and intellectual property. There's a clerk with an office here in the central district. He works as an agent for the Arcane and Alchemical Registry of Inventions. Most folks call it AARI. You'll also need the filing fee."

Grabbing the pouch that Brinta slid across the counter, Trinx waved the envelope.

"Got it!" she said. "I'll take it to the agent now. A friend I met at a club recently, Vex, might come by looking for me. If he does, see if you can help him and let him know I'll be back soon."

It took some asking around and reading small signs and placards in windows, but she eventually found the extension office for AARI and inside, a friendly older goblin clerk. The man had gray hair with streaks of dark brown, as well as a close-cropped beard. His appearance definitely made him seem like he'd be more at home in a larger city than here, but she guessed he might have family in the warren.

She handed the elder goblin the envelope. "This is a patent application from Brinta. Oh, and from me. I'm on there, too. I'm an apprentice, Trinx. Here's the fee."

She never was a smooth talker around new people. The nervousness of the situation made her stumble over her words. Trinx shoved the envelope and pouch of coins at the man as if to punctuate her statement.

The clerk chuckled and gathered the items as she pushed them his way. "Just have to see if everything is in order. Please wait a moment while I check."

He pulled out the forms and looked them over, then dumped out the coins and counted them.

"It all looks good. I'll have this filed right away. Let me draw up a temporary claim sheet for you. The full official documents should arrive in one to two months. Depends on how long the search and verification takes."

Trinx fidgeted while he wrote out a different form and stamped her papers. She looked around the small office. There wasn't much to it. Filing cabinets filled most of the space, and the clerk's desk occupied what little remained. He had a fancier glow lamp, clearly powered by a spell rather than oil or candles.

She took the completed document from him. Then clerk placed the forms Trinx had brought into a folder and tossed the packet on a stack in a tray labeled "OUT."

Looking up at her, he said, "That should do it. Say hello to

Brinta for me. It was nice meeting you, Trinx. I wish you the best in exploiting that patent."

Trinx still knew little about patents, why they needed one, or how exactly one might exploit one, but she was sure she would learn it all as she continued her apprenticeship. On the way back to the shop, she stopped and picked up two muffins and a jug of dragonroot tea. It still took some getting used to the idea that tea houses now sold tea in exchangeable, enchanted jugs to go. It was a rather new custom that had only caught on here in the warren a couple of years ago. Evidently, it had been popular in bigger cities longer. She had to pay a deposit and could either continue bringing the same one back for a refill or bring it back for a full refund of the deposit. The downside was that she now had several of these jugs in her apartment, as she was always forgetting to take them back.

When she arrived at Distilled Magic, she put her back against the heavy door and pushed the ground with her legs. The slab of metal gave way and opened into the shop, with her following behind, almost tripping over her feet. She spun around and away from the entrance, holding up the sack of muffins and the jug of tea.

"I brought us a mid-morning snack. Muffins and dragonroot tea."

The alchemist was at the counter talking with Vex when she finished turning.

"Oh! Hi Vex. You came by. Does Brinta have any ideas? I'm sure they do."

He turned to look at her, and she saw his chin, cheeks, and upper lip had several scraggly hairs growing from it. The rest of his face had soft fuzz filling in the gaps between the twisted whiskers.

The hob shrugged and said, "Knew I shouldn't get my hopes up. Pretty much the same thing happened last time I tried a potion. This one was different. Ended up the same anyway."

"That's so weird," she said. "Don't give up on one try, though. I'm sure we can figure something out. Brinta, do you have any initial ideas or thoughts about what might cause it not to work?"

The alchemist shook their head. "It's strange. Clearly, the potion is stimulating growth. That's what it's designed to do. Most folks use it to fill out a beard that is patchy or not very thick. But it should still work, even if there isn't much there to start with."

An idea struck Trinx based on her own history and experience.

"So, I brought the muffins and tea for us, but I'd like to talk privately with Vex. Do you mind if we rain check on my snack idea and I duck out with him for a chat?"

"No, no," Brinta said. "That's fine. I didn't really need anything right now, anyway. I had a large enough breakfast. Don't take too long if you can help it. I wanted to have you shadow some more today."

"Thanks!" Trinx said and went to the back room to grab a couple of cups. On her return, she waved for the hob to follow her. She stopped in front of the door and asked him. "Mind opening this? My hands are even more full than when I came in."

Vex shrugged and opened the door for her. She led them to a nearby bench that stood away from the main flow of foot traffic and offered a fair amount of privacy. Sitting down, she patted the seat and handed him a cup. She poured them both some tea and put the sack of muffins between them.

"What's this all about?" he asked and took a sip of the hot beverage.

Taking a small sip herself, she answered, "So, um. I'm going to tell you something about myself. It's not something I would normally tell someone I haven't known very long. So, I'm kind of putting myself out on a limb here, okay?"

"Uh, this sounds serious," he said, pulling his hand away from the muffin bag.

Trinx forced a smile onto her face. *Be brave*, she told herself.

"No. I mean, yes, it is. But have a muffin, I saw you going for one. I guess I think I can tell you because I'm pretty sure I'm right about something. If I am, then maybe it will help us both. If I'm not? Well, I guess I'll just find a hole to crawl into and die of embarrassment. Make sure you tell Quilka about my tragic death so she doesn't worry."

Vex snorted a laugh and stuck his hand back in the bag to grab a muffin. "Okay, now you've got me confused, but that's okay. Lay it on me."

"You know the night we met?" she asked, tensing her shoulders. "And I ran out? I wasn't sick. Just embarrassed, you see?" But it was clear Vex did not see, so she barreled on. "I dress like this," she said and flourished her hand over her body, "because I'm a woman. It makes me feel good. Like the world is right. But I only figured that out later. Only a couple years ago, actually, with the help of a friend. Before that, well, my father pushed me to join a raiding group. He wanted his son to be a powerful warrior, but that was never something I wanted." She paused, giving him a chance to say something. He did not, but his mouth stopped chewing the bite of muffin, and he sat there in silence.

UGH! What if she was wrong? Death by embarrassment it was. She had to continue forward.

"So, like I said. At the club, when we were dancing, a pouch flew out of my top. I don't have all the equipment I wish I had. So, I supplement, you know?"

By now, Vex had swallowed the bite of muffin and washed it down with a slurp of dragonroot. He sat quietly for a moment, and she let him. It seemed best to stop talking while she was already so far behind.

Finally, he spoke. "Okay."

Pause. "So, you weren't way off the mark."

Longer pause. "Fine. Yes. Your arrow hit the mark dead center. Female hobs are like myths, right? My parents certainly thought so until I started growing and growing. I don't know why we don't see female hobs. It was wrong. But not because I was a hob. That wasn't it. What was wrong was that my whole body felt off, not just because I was so big. But because I knew I was a guy. I just knew it. Does that make any sense?"

He paused again. Taking some tea and grabbing his leg with the other hand, kneading his thigh. "I think the only reason my parents didn't freak out is that my dad's the warlord. He wanted me to be a boy, anyway. So, they let me dress and act the part. But he's frustrated—my dad, I mean. I'm weaker than the other hobs, and I can't grow a beard. That *stupid* beard. Everything is about my damn beard. No true warrior is without one. Certainly no warlord."

Trinx patted his leg, not the one being mangled by his agitated hand.

"I get it. Really, I do. Until literally yesterday, my body had tons of hair all over it. But that's the thing: I worked with Brinta, and we figured out a solution. They are really cool. You have to believe me there. And I'm sure if we told them everything, they wouldn't tell anyone. They have some interesting stuff going on in their life, too. Not like us. But still. Different from what lots of folks expect."

"Well, you went out on a limb talking to me," he said, looking at her. "That's a lot of trust you just threw at me. If you think we can trust the alchemist, let's do it."

They finished their snack, and the conversation turned to much lighter and more frivolous topics. Once they drank the last of the tea, they gathered the remains of the snack and returned to the shop. The mornings really were quiet, no one had come in while they'd been away.

Brinta looked up and asked, "Did you have a good chat? Figure anything out?"

Trinx and Vex filled the alchemist in on everything. Trinx had never explicitly told them about herself, but figured they might have guessed something was up with all her hair. She was right; they had suspected. They even had suspicions about Vex as well, but professional courtesy prevented them from any personal questions that probed without an invitation.

After they finished, the alchemist said, "Well, now. Thank you for confiding in me. I know that isn't easy. Don't worry, I'm not one to babble on about a customer's issues to another like some old gossiping hag. It explains a good deal, though, and with that in mind, there may be some options."

"Really?" Vex asked excitedly. His husky voice raised half an octave.

"Yes, really," Brinta said. "The thing is. The potions you've tried. They all do basically the same thing. Like I said before. They stimulate what is already there to grow more fully, and it's working. You can see that. The issue is that what is there are a few random whiskers most women wish wouldn't show up and often get plucked out. The rest is all just fuzz. Now, you have thicker fuzz, thanks to that potion."

Brinta tapped their fingers on the counter in thought before continuing. "The trick, then—the thing about Vex, that is. We need to come up with something that doesn't enhance the growth that is there. Instead, we need something to stimulate and cause entirely new hair generation. It will take some experimenting, and you'll need to offer yourself as a test subject. What do you think? Are you in?"

Vex drew an enormous smile across his face and broke into a laugh. "You bet! I'm no alchemist, but you two get some options figured out, and I'll show up to try it."

Chapter 12

Experimenting

"With the hair removal cream, we started with a potion you had developed and turned it into a topical foam. Do you have a hair growth formula you own? One we can change?" Trinx asked.

"I haven't invented one from scratch, no," Brinta answered. "But we don't need to. The thing about alchemical patents is they protect the particular recipe. The recipe, though, is well known. It's in the filing. If you use it to make a batch and sell it, then the holder of the rights gets a share of the profit."

She nodded along as if she understood, hoping it wasn't clear she only partially followed.

Brinta continued, "If you don't want to run into issues, you have two choices. First, create a different recipe that produces similar results. This is like coming up with your own solution, but often takes inspiration from the existing one. The second way is to use the protected recipe as a base and add to it, creating a different effect. If the effect is completely different, then you can claim full rights. If it is similar but extended, then it becomes a derivative work and requires licensing the original.

You don't have to worry too much about that right now, but you should know we are going to start by taking the second path. It should be easier."

Trinx tugged on her braids. She found the pull soothing, especially when thinking. "I think I get that, but all this mess with patents is a lot to take in. I enjoy mixing up potions a lot better. So, if I get what you're saying, we can start with the potion you had Vex try and make modifications? Even though you didn't invent that one?"

"Exactly right," Brinta said. "I actually have the recipes for every item I sell in the shop here. I buy a lot of my inventory, but I find being able to make it myself can help in a pinch if stock runs low, or if I get a customer who needs modifications, I can do that as well. Let me go find this one." They flipped through folders in a large drawer until pulling one out with triumph.

Laying the papers out in a sequence on the counter, Trinx could see there was a lengthy list of ingredients, and several pages of step-by-step instructions. The recipe was much more complex than the simple ones in the books she had been reading. She held no illusions that she could make the potion herself, but felt she could be helpful, at least. Referencing the ingredient list over and over, Trinx found the reagents and laid them out on the counter.

Some items had definitive measurements for the amounts, while others were much more vague. Perhaps the vague ones didn't need precision, but she suspected it more likely required experience and intuition. Either way, if the measurements had exact requirements, she measured them out as listed.

Brinta read over the instructions carefully.

"Unlike with the cream we made, this is more complicated. With the other, all we needed to do was find the best medium to hold the potion without reducing the effectiveness and avoiding adding additional side effects. For this one, we must fundamentally change the formula. We want to keep the growth stimulation aspect, but in addition, we need to add something that causes spontaneous initial growth of the hair. Combined, it should produce the right type of hair that grows fast and fills out thick."

They made several notes on a sheet of paper as ideas came to them. Based on the alchemist's ideas, Trinx found additional ingredients to set out. After writing out several sets of modifications, Brinta tried the first one out.

"The trickiest part to this," Brinta said while working, "is not just finding the extra ingredients, but adding them in the right order and fashion."

While talking, they added different reagents, following the original recipe and altering it with their modifications at the spots they determined the best. The whole time, narrating what they did so Trinx could learn.

"And now we'll dissolve several strands of dreamweaver silk. The spiders live at the intersection of two dimensions. They spin silk capable of stimulating the growth of anything, even when nothing has existed before."

They carefully added the strands of silk into a cauldron holding the work-in-progress potion. The instant they began to dissolve, the entire contents furiously bubbled and shot the entire batch into the air with such force it splashed across the ceiling.

"Get back!" Brinta yelled, and both Trinx and the alchemist jumped out from under the mess on the ceiling. Once out of danger, Brinta said, "We must be extra careful with touching a work in progress potion, especially one we are modifying. Don't let it get on you."

Potion dripped from the ceiling, splashing into puddles on the floor and covering the workbench where they had been mixing everything together. It gradually stopped actively raining the toxic liquid, and Brinta took the opportunity to teach Trinx how to clean up a dangerous mess.

"Go in the back and fetch the bucket of triple-A. That's Doc Puddlefoot's Antireactionary Absorbant Alabaster Powder. We'll also need a broom and some rags."

She ran off to fetch the bucket and cleaning equipment. The alchemist took a large scoop of powder and filled a bellows. They squeezed it up at the ceiling, and the white powder fused with the remaining liquid. Repeating this with the floor and counter, the surfaces covered in the potentially dangerous substance now had thick layers of white dust.

Using the broom to knock it down, Trinx swept at the ceiling, dislodging the inert crust and powder. She similarly brushed and pushed the dry residue from the floor and counter. The alchemist assured her everything was safe, and she continued to sweep the dust into a large pile. From there, it was simple enough to fill a waste can.

And so the experimentation went. The alchemist eventually found a stable part in the recipe to add the silk, but they still didn't know if having the silk in the solution would be part of the answer. As customers entered, Trinx helped them, allowing Brinta to continue experimenting. The wary shoppers kept their distance, especially when they saw volatile reactions, bright colors, and billowing smoke.

She spent more time cleaning up after their failures than actually watching the attempts. It was worth it, though, as she felt she learned much more than any book might teach her. The alchemist was great at narrating the procedure but somehow was always aware of the world around them while working. That was something she felt she may never do because once she had her head set on a project, very little could ever pull her attention up and away from it.

Case in point, she watched in fascination as Brinta stopped right in the middle of an attempt and said, "Trinx, don't forget to mind the time." They said it off-handedly and seemingly without even looking at a timepiece themselves.

And yet, when she looked at the clock, Trinx exclaimed, "Oh! Oh! Now I've done it. Thanks, Brinta. How'd you even know what time it was? I gotta go. Gristle is not going to be happy this evening."

She ran from the alchemy shop the entire way to the tavern. Trinx threw open the door with such force it banged against the wall. Everyone in the room looked up at her as she came rushing in. She caught sight of Glink and Zurt, but after finding the source of the commotion, they and the other patrons returned to their meals. Gristle, on the other hand, shot daggers of ice through her heart with his eyes.

She shrugged off the freezing glare and rushed to the kitchen. In her hurry, she didn't take the care she normally would when opening the door, and she crashed right into Quilka, causing a tray with two full plates of food to fly into the air before crashing to the ground. The goblins nearest the kitchen hooted, hollered, and laughed uproariously. From the looks of the food sprayed across the floor, she guessed tonight's dinner included cured pork and spiced baked apples. The soft fruit squished, creating a chunky apple sauce.

"I'm sorry! So sorry!" she said while pulling thick slabs of ham off the stones. It made a squelching sound as it came loose, revealing a thick, syrupy puddle.

Quilka waved her hands frantically to dispel the sentiments, but it felt ineffective as she was laughing uncontrollably. Between fits of giggling, she assured her, "Glad you could make it to work."

Once composed, Quilka helped clean up the mess.

Trinx huffed and grumbled at the snarky comment. "We

were experimenting today, and I completely lost track of the time. We made such a mess. Worse than this, even."

She swept her arm out to show off the mess and grabbed a mop to scrub at the floor. Gristle had a thing about keeping everything clean. That's why the crew had such a thorough end-of-shift routine. Most messes could wait until then, but if something impeded a major walkway like the kitchen doorway, it needed attention right away. He would not put up with a mess like this tracked all over the tavern as they passed through the sticky film all evening.

Her friend grabbed another tray of plates from Brizla and carefully walked around Trinx's mopping effort. Returning with an empty tray, she asked, "What kind of experiments? You just solved the hair removal cream. You dove into something else already?"

"More hair related experiments if you can believe it! This time for growing it," Trinx said while taking a towel and drying the clean but now-soaked floor.

"So, this isn't for you, then?" Quilka asked after flashing a sign to the cook for three plates.

"Nope," she said. "This one is for Vex. When he and that Draz guy were here, I overheard them a bit. I suggested he stop by Brinta's for help with his beard. Turns out he has a complicated condition and needs a custom formula."

"That'd be great if you could help him," Q said. "I had to let his friend down. That night, he was angling for a date. The dancing at the club was fun, but you *know* he's not my type."

"Yeah, but speaking of that," Trinx said with a giggle. "I'm hoping I can help Vex because I overheard a few other things. Did you know he's one of the warlord's sons? Eldest even. And he needs a mate, but it's complicated. I'm going to dig in a little deeper there."

"Woah," her friend said. "That would be something. Son of

the warlord. We should talk more later. For now, it looks like you cleaned most of that up. You should help the four-top by the hearth. I haven't checked on them since they got here."

The rest of the shift had much less excitement than her spectacular entrance. By the end, Gristle had softened to his usual kind but prickly self, seeming to have forgiven her again. She missed going out after work, but her new schedule still took a lot out of her. Hopefully, she would find a routine that would allow for more fun. For that evening, though, she headed home to sleep.

Despite trying to be responsible, she slept in through her alarms. Trinx spun into gear quickly in the morning once she woke up and threw herself together. Thankfully, Brinta didn't seem to mind her mild tardiness.

The alchemist looked up from the workbench where they worked.

"Morning. I've been brewing some basics for restocking. I also made and portioned out tubs of some of the cream. Now that the patent's filed, I want to put it out on the shelves. We'll be the only shop to buy it for a while."

"Good morning," Trinx said. "Sorry about the lateness. I don't know how I slept through my alarms. It took the fifth one to get me out of bed. I can jump in and help now, though. Are we going to continue experimenting today?"

"Yes!" Brinta said. "I'm eager to jump back into that. Once I get to working on a new project, I have trouble focusing on anything else. That's why I've been restocking this morning. I wanted to free up the day for more work with you."

Trinx put on a lab apron and helped clean up the bench from the morning's efforts. The two of them spent until mid-afternoon trying combinations and inevitably cleaning up large messes from the results of some of them. They had yet to even make a stable solution so they could move on to a first trial.

Brinta assured her they eventually would, but it can often take a lot of experimenting.

"But that's the fun, don't you think? Plus, you've seen I captured all these notes. Sometimes, a wrong turn for one project might be the key to unlocking another later. When I see an interesting effect I didn't expect, I make a note of it."

A moment later, Vex came into the shop and walked straight up to the counter with a big smile on his face. "What's the good news? I'm ready to be a test subject. Have something to test out on me?"

"Oh. Oh," Brinta said, somewhat flustered. "That's on me. Sorry, I wasn't more clear. I definitely will need your help to test, but this is likely going to take some time. Quite a bit of experimenting, actually, from the results so far. I hate to think I got your hopes too high or gave the wrong impression. I'm sure I can find the solution, but it won't likely be right away. We'll send word when we need you for testing."

"Figures," he mumbled as his face fell. "Thanks for working on it, though. Guess I'll get out of your way. Good seeing you, Trinx." He turned to leave and walked toward the door.

"Wait!" she called after him. "I'm pretty much done here for the day. I have to be at the Tender soon, but I think I have time for a cup of tea and a chat. Want to hit up that Mystic Leaf on the next street over?"

"Oh sure," he said. The disappointment left his face. "Let's go get a cup."

She pulled off her apron. "That's okay with you, Brinta? I think this looked like a good stopping place. Do you mind if I take one of the new tubs of EverSmooth you made? I want to give a gift to an old friend. I think she'll love it."

"That's fine," Brinta said, looking up briefly. "Catch up with your friend. And sure, grab a tub. If she does like it, she'll likely want some more. Always good to get people using a new product, even if you give some away at the beginning."

Trinx put a tub in her bag and left with Vex for the nearby Mystic Leaf and Toadstool outlet. The chain didn't have the greatest tea and snacks, but they had spots everywhere. The big cities had tons of them. She thought she remembered five here in the warren.

As it turned out, Vex enjoyed dragonroot, too. They both bought a cup with milk and a spice-filled pastry coated in a sugary glaze before finding a table on the patio. Mystic Leaf outlets almost always had a fenced-in seating area. Inside, if they had one, it was usually cramped with only a few tables.

Trinx took a nibble of the pastry. The flaky pastry melted on her tongue, coating it with sugary spices. Reluctantly, she washed it down with a sip of tea. Her fingers found a frayed edge on the placemat and picked at the loose threads.

"So, I wanted to ask a few questions. If you don't mind, I mean. The other evening at the Tender. I heard you talking about your beard, but also some other things."

Before Vex could answer, a passing couple stopped and turned around. A woman's voice she knew all too well asked, "Traz?"

Chapter 13

Parents

"**O**h, I'm sorry," the woman said, looking over at the couple sitting at the table, eating pastries and drinking tea. "We were walking by, and I swear I heard the voice of my son, Traz."

The goblin with her had a thick black beard and creased brows from what appeared to be a permanent scowl on his face.

"It's clearly not him," he sneered. "I wish you'd give up on your dreams of finding him. That raid was a total wipe. Not a single gob returned."

"I know. You're right. It's silly of me. I just could have sworn," she said apologetically, trying to placate him.

Trinx took a sip of tea, centering herself, and forced a calm response. "Don't worry, ma'am. It's okay. Have a nice day."

That was too much. She winced as the woman looked closer at her curiously.

"No. No. Vilk, don't call me crazy. You had to hear that. And look at the eyes and the face. I'm not wrong. If Traz had a twin sister, this would be her."

"My name is Trinx and—" she started.

"Worg's breath!" her father blurted as he looked closer. "You're right. It is him. The nine hells you wearing all that paint on your face? And a dress? What's wrong with you, boy? And where have you been these years?"

Trinx shrank into her chair, feeling smaller than a mouse. She could feel every eye in the area staring right at her.

"Don't yell at him. Her? This is a public street," her mom pleaded with the irate goblin.

"I'll yell at him if I want, after all the worry he put us through," he spat.

"That's enough, sir," Vex said, surprising Trinx as he spoke up in her defense. "This is my friend, Trinx. And *she* deserves some respect. Do you know who I am? I'm Zogar's eldest."

Her father took a step back, and his chest deflated, but he spoke with vitriol. "I don't care what web of lies he's caught you up in, but you'd best be careful. I always knew he had issues. We're going, Gwix. I say he's still dead." He grabbed his wife's arm and tugged.

Her mom looked at her with betrayal, tears welling in her eyes. "I wish you had come home Tra—er, Trinx, was it?" she said, but Vilk was already yanking her down the street.

Breath rushed out as Trinx released everything held tight in her lungs. She looked at Vex and the agitation on his face.

"I'm sorry." She paused, taking several shallow breaths. "Thank you."

"Obviously, I get it. And I couldn't let him rant at you like that. But you let them think you were dead?" he asked, pressing his lips together in a tight grimace.

She put her face in her hands and answered in a muffled voice, "I knew my father. I knew he'd react like that—or worse. I'm pretty sure the only reason he didn't slug me is you and all these people were here. Once I figured out who I truly was, I couldn't go home."

"I guess I can see that," Vex said, chewing on his pastry thoughtfully. "Every situation is different. You know what your home was like better than I do. Your father didn't really seem the accepting type. That's for sure. I even worry about your mother."

"My mother?" she asked, raising her eyebrows.

"Yeah," he said, nodding. "I don't know. That was a brief encounter. But your father, he seems like a cruel goblin and the way he yanked her away—I just met her, but I worry he may take some of the frustration of that encounter out on her."

"Oh," she breathed, shrinking again, folding up on herself. "That. Yes," she said, forcing a nod. "He did. Likely still does. That's part of why I couldn't go home. I got the lash for much less. To show up like I was when I came back to the warren after finding myself?" She fell silent, picking at the placemat.

"Well," Vex said, forcing an odd laugh that he cut short. "That got dark quickly. Sorry. I use humor to defuse." Taking a sip of tea, Vex continued, "It's not your fault, though. It's pretty common with goblins, much less so with the hobgoblins. You'd think it might be the other way around, with the hobs being so large and prone to aggression, but that's the thing: hobs don't have nearly as much to prove. Quite a few gobs around the city are always taking out their frustration on anyone around them. I've heard my father talk about the problem with the grandmas on the council."

She perked up slightly at the mention of the council.

"That's one of my greatest wishes," Trinx said. "To be on the council. To be a grandma."

"Really?" Vex asked, raising his right brow. "And how do you figure that would work? And why?"

"Obviously, I can't birth a goblin child," she said with a shrug. "I've been looking into adoption, but they are tough. They need me to have a mate before they'll consider it. I didn't come out to them. Maybe I should. That's the why. If I was on the council. If I was a grandma. Well, then, I could help change life here. Make finding and sharing our true selves with the world easier."

Vex snorted another burst of laughter. "So when you ask a guy for a cup of tea, you don't like to keep the topics light, do you?"

"I guess not," Trinx said, giggling. "But in a way, it's part of what I wanted to talk to you about. Obviously, you can't have children either, or at least not in the way people would expect it. And if you are going to be a warlord? That's something expected: to keep the line going. So, I thought, what if we formed a union? One for the warren to see and accept. And we adopted a youngling or two. Made a family. Help each other reach our goals."

He swallowed some more tea, choking on the last of it, and cleared his throat. "You move pretty fast, don't you? I think we need to get to know each other more. And I know I need more time to think about all that. I'm not sure how well my father would take that idea."

A frown flashed across Trinx's face before fading away. It seemed her shortcut ideas never worked out the way they did in her head. Of course not. She was being silly and moving too fast. She always became too focused on her plans and ideas without thinking them all the way through. Taking a deep breath, she realized he hadn't said no, though, just that he needed more time to think.

"That makes sense," she said, trying to cover her racing thoughts. "It is a big decision, I suppose, and I'd love to get to know you better. I still have some time before work at the Tender. I need something to take my mind off my parents. What music do you like? I'm the biggest Serenya Dawnwhisper fan in the warren. Quilka thinks she is, but I'm pretty sure it's me. Are you a Whispie?"

Vex laughed heartily and calmed himself before saying, "Oh. You were serious?" He chuckled. "No. No, I'm not a Whispie. I'm more into heavier stuff. I love Thraxx Bloodhammer. Besides, I'd much rather listen to a hob than an elf. Serenya's stuff isn't bad, though. I'll listen to it."

"You would listen to that," Trinx said with a pout. "I bet I'm a bigger Whispie than you are a fan of Bloodhammer."

"And how does one prove how big a fan they are?" he asked. "I bet I've been to more of his concerts. Have you ever even been to a Dawnwhisper concert? She only plays in the big cities."

"It's not about how many concerts," she said defiantly. "I'd love to go to a concert. It's about how much you know about them and their music. How many Bloodhammer songs do you know?"

"A lot!" he proclaimed. "In fact, I know them all." He triumphantly ate a large bite of his pastry after his boast.

"I bet you don't," she shot back. "But I do know all of Serenya's songs."

"Done. It's on, then. Are you ready?" he asked and took a sip of tea to clear his throat.

"Ready for what? What's on?" she asked, looking at him, confused.

"Our knowledge showdown!" he said excitedly. "We each take turns saying the name of a song. Whoever gets stuck first and can't think of one loses."

"That's the silliest game I've ever heard of," Trinx said, giggling. "But I'm in. I can win this one. Easy."

"Ironclad Fury," he said immediately.

"Whispers in the Wind," she responded.

"Thunder of the Ancients," he said, making a drumbeat on the table.

"Moonlit Promises," she answered and whistled part of it.

They traded names back and forth for several minutes, taking only minor breaks to nibble on their snack or sip the tea.

Vex hesitated only a moment before adding, "Warrior's Wrath."

"Echoes of the Heart," she shot back without faltering.

"Blood and Steel," he said and mimed swinging a sword through the air.

"Starlit Serenade," she added.

A small crowd had gathered around their table, watching in fascination. Ignoring them, the two continued to lob names between them. At one point, Vex paused a little longer, and Trinx looked ready to pounce and claim victory. He pulled a song out, though, and the crowd applauded. She responded instantly with her pick, and the onlookers cheered even louder. He caught a second wind and must have remembered an extensive set and spit out titles as fast as the beginning.

"Forge of the Titans," he said.

She countered with, "Enchanted Love."

"Battle Cry of the Damned," he thundered.

"Gossamer Dreams," she sang to the melody of the song.

The crowd continued to grow as more goblins caught the excitement of the impromptu contest. Newer arrivals murmured whispers to those who had been there longer, asking about the spectacle. The names kept flowing, and some in the group wondered if they were all real. Others assured the doubters that they, in fact, recognized the songs. It was clear. Two super-fans took part in the showdown.

He looked up, trying to pull a name from the sky before he said, "Wild Dominion!"

She giggled at his effort and said, "Twilight Ballad."

A pained look fell across Vex's face. He looked up and to the left and right as if he could somehow find another name hiding somewhere. He held a finger up, trying to stall, but failed to recall a song.

"Veil of the Forest!" Trinx yelled as she jumped out of her seat.

The entire crowd erupted with hoots and hollers. Clapping thundered. Trinx made several curtsies. She turned this way and that to face different sections of those who watched.

Vex slapped his head and mumbled, "Echoes of Destruction." But it was too late. The crowd laughed and wished him better luck next time.

Trinx fell back down into her chair and reached for her cup of tea, only to find it empty. She sighed.

"Good game. I'm sure you are *almost* as good a fan as I am. My tea is gone, and I need to leave for the Tender if I want to come in close to on time."

"It was fun," Vex said with a smile and then slumped into his chair. "I was sure I could beat you. I'll think on what you asked. For now, please keep working with Brinta on that potion. Having a beard would make me feel much better about myself and would also get my father off my back."

"You know it," Trinx said as she stood up. "I'm sure we'll have one ready for testing soon. I'll send word as soon as we do."

With that, she left him there and made it to the tavern just after her shift started, which really might as well be considered right on time. She missed the days when her shift started earlier, with a quiet room and a slower pace. It always gave her time to chat with her friend more. If she wanted to stick with alchemy, she would have to make trade-offs like this. She jumped into helping the crowd of guests in need of food and drink.

At the end of the night, one of the side dishes still had a fair amount left. Brizla didn't think it would keep, as it was a salad made of boiled root vegetables, a creamy dressing, and small bits of pickles and onions. The cook filled bowls for everyone.

Trinx sat with Quilka to eat their late-night snack. She filled her in about the run-in with her parents.

"That sounds stressful and pretty rough," her friend said, squeezing her hand. "Do you think you're going to talk to them?"

"I don't know," she answered. "I've been avoiding them because I suspected this kind of reaction. My mom, though. It seemed like I might be able to talk to her. I don't know. Maybe not. Definitely not if my father is around."

"Then that's what you should do," Quilka said, looking into her eyes. "It might take some maneuvering but find a time he isn't around. It's been forever since I saw your mom, but I know most mothers care. Yours probably isn't that different."

"I'm sure you're right," Trinx said. "I'll try to find a time I can talk to her. Of course, finding time for anything these days is hard. I need the money from the job here, plus I'd miss seeing you, Gris, and Brizla. I want to get out to see Zigla. Maybe I'll go tonight. I don't need that much sleep."

"You do, too, need sleep," Quilka admonished with a light laugh. "But if you can get by on the money front, don't worry about work here. You can always come and visit. You'll be my favorite customer."

"I'll keep that in mind," Trinx said as she stood up and reached out her arms. "I will skip a bit of sleep tonight, though. I'm going to run and give Zigla some of my cream."

Quilka pushed her chair back and stood. She walked into Trinx's awaiting arms and wrapped her own around her sleep-deprived friend. Squeezing, she said, "Fine. I can't stop you. Now go before it gets even later."

Trinx let go and nodded. "You're the best, Q," she said as she ran out the door.

She still had the tub of EverSmooth in her bag and left the warren straight for Zigla's cave. The stars and the two moons bathed the night with light. Goblins had strong low-light vision because of their tendency to live in networks of caves and caverns. Before long, she stood outside the familiar door set in the stone entrance and knocked. The hour was late, so she waited several minutes before rapping on the wood again.

Eventually, Zigla answered in a long nightgown and asked with a yawn, "Is something wrong? I thought it might be you. Who else would come calling at this time of night?"

"No," Trinx said with a shake of her head. "Nothing wrong. My schedule is just so horrible. I've been meaning to bring you something. Brinta and I developed it." She pulled out the tub and held it up for her elder to see.

"Come in. The stars are bright tonight, but not so much I can see with you in the shadows of the doorway," Zigla said and stepped out of the way to let Trinx come in.

Zigla lit several more lamps and candles, filling the cave with warm light. She looked over at Trinx and what she held in her hand.

"Is that what I think it is? Your arms! I can't believe it. And this, is it?"

"Yes! Isn't it amazing?" she asked, beaming. "You had a wonderful idea. I'm an apprentice now. To Brinta. They run Distilled Magic, an alchemy shop. We made this. And it totally works. You have to try it." She shoved the tub into her older friend's hands.

Trinx told Zigla everything that had happened since her last visit. She told of the experimenting, the marshmallow root, and the patent filing. Throughout, she showed her friend how to apply the cream and scrape it back off.

She talked about Vex and their new project but also about running into her parents.

"Q thinks I should find time to talk to my mom. I'm not sure I agree."

"Yes," Zigla said. "I think so, too. My own mother understood. Supported me even. There was only so much she could do. That's why she sent me out of the warren, but she sent runners with supplies regularly. She took care of me. I never could look as good as you. No one would be okay with me in the warren."

"I don't think that's necessarily true," Trinx said with a sigh. "It sounds like your mother loved you. She sounds like a good goblin."

"Oh, she is," Zigla said. "I don't think I ever told you, but she's on the council, you know? She's wise. My siblings gave her grandchildren. It was her position that let her pull the strings to get me out here safely."

"Wow," Trinx said. "I didn't realize you had someone close on the council. Speaking of that, I suggested a marriage of convenience to Vex. You know, so I can try to adopt? He doesn't seem sure, though. He said he'd think on it. It might be my best bet for the council."

Zigla gave her a reassuring pat. "I know you have your dreams. I don't want to stop them. But I just don't know if it will solve everything you think it will. You should talk to my mother. Maybe she can help you see your path may not lead to where you think it will. I could write a note of introduction."

"I'd love to meet her," she said. "Please *do* write that note. Maybe she can give me some tips for earning a seat on the council with her."

Trinx helped scrape the foam off Zigla's back. They had used it on her face, chest, arms, and now her broad back. Her elder said she could handle her legs and other areas now that she knew how it worked.

Zigla stood at the mirror and admired herself. Tears welled in her eyes and ran down her now smooth face. She sniffed deeply.

"Thank you. This is amazing. This cream will change lives."

Trinx let her admire the reflection in silence for some time before she said, "I'm so glad you like it. I should go, though. Brinta will expect me at the shop first thing, and that's only a few hours away."

"Nonsense," Zigla said, composing herself and turning from the mirror. "Stay the night. I'll put together some pillows and blankets. I can see you are exhausted. You can head straight to the shop from here."

Weariness filled Trinx's eyes, and walking back to the warren tonight did not appeal to her.

"That sounds wonderful. If you are sure you don't mind. I know where things are. I'll put my bed together."

The next morning, she woke to find Zigla assembling a simple breakfast and tea. They chatted about lighter topics than the night before. As she stood to leave, Zigla pulled out a sealed envelope.

"I wrote this when I woke this morning," Zigla said. "Drop it in the post at the warren, and once she reads it, she should reach out to you for a meeting."

"Thank you," Trinx said. "I can't wait to meet your mother. I should go, though, if I'm going to make it to the shop on time. I'll visit again soon."

Chapter 14

The Grass is Always Greener

There was just enough time to swing by her home and change before Brinta would expect her at Distilled Magic. As she prepared to leave her place, Trinx looked at the sealed envelope. The front read, "Vorti, Care of the Council."

Zigla believed her mother might be able to lend assistance. Trinx wondered if Vorti could swing the review board at Sulma's Home for Displaced Younglings in her favor. That would certainly help. Once she explained to her about her dreams of joining the council herself, Vorti was bound to offer what assistance she could.

On the way to the shop, Trinx stopped by a post drop and sent the letter on its way. The clerk who took the letter glanced at the recipient, and said, "Oh, a Grandma? We'll get this to her right away."

He then opened a tube on the wall behind him, and air hissed in, then rose to a roar as the vacuum pulled at anything near. He held the envelope up, and it flew up the tube as he shut the hatch.

Trinx always wondered how the postal system worked. All she knew was that goblins stole the designs during a war several hundred years prior. The gnomes had originally invented it, but the plans had enormous amounts of details. Goblin engineers recreated the system, or a version, anyway. The engineers in goblin society were just as good as their gnomish counterparts. However, they focused more on explosives and combustion. Most of the gadgets with more day-to-day uses originated from the gnomes. Supposedly, this mail system even connected with other settlements, as well as the larger cities.

Trinx waved to the clerk. "Thank you! Have a great day."

He waved back and tipped his hat. Soon, she rejoined the crowd, moving through the tunnels in the general direction of the alchemy shop.

When she arrived at the shop, Brinta was mixing a set of ingredients she recognized. Evidently, they had already tried several variations, as this set should be further down the list of options than when she left yesterday.

"Excellent! Good morning, Trinx," Brinta said, looking up from their work. "Come on over and observe. I think we are getting close."

She dutifully skipped to the workbench to watch as they added a furry moss to the solution. They had ground it into a fine powder and then gently sifted it into the flask. Chartreuse fumes built into a cloud and billowed out, filling the air around the workbench. Trinx's eyes stung.

"Out of the shop!" Brinta yelled.

Trinx ran for the door, and the alchemist followed right on her heels. They pulled the door closed, trapping the gas inside.

Panting, Trinx asked, "What are we going to do now? The shop is full of poison!"

The alchemist flashed a somewhat mischievous grin and laughed.

"This certainly isn't the first time. It's a good part of the reason for the materials used in the shop's construction. Surely you noticed all the stone and the heavy metal door?"

"Of course, I noticed," Trinx said with a nod. "That door isn't light. But that just explains that it is good at trapping the toxins. How does that help?"

"Well," Brinta said. "It doesn't help with dispersing the fumes, but it helps keep the neighborhood safe. I'd have been run out long before now without a building this sturdy. However, I also built a robust ventilation system."

They pointed up at the roof, where a metal cylinder rose until it disappeared from view in the upper reaches of the enormous cavern.

"I just have to come around here." Leading the way around the shop, Brinta said, "And turn this dial here. I always have it running, usually on low. At times like these, we just turn it up. A powerful fan will suck all the fumes up."

The tube on the roof shuddered as the machinery spun to life, and a whooshing sound filled the air. Clearly, the fan they spoke of attached directly to the pipe, causing the vibration.

"Hard to say how long that will take," Brinta commented, dusting off their hands. "Seems like a good time for a sweet treat and a cup of tea. Don't you think?"

"That sounds wonderful," Trinx agreed with a grin.

They walked to the same Mystic Leaf she and Vex had visited when her parents stumbled on them. Brinta ordered, and they found a spot to sit in the enclosed patio, well away from the street. A server soon brought a wooden tray laden with a pot of tea, two cups, and two plates, each holding a piece of cake.

The sweet cake tasted heavenly, with a dense vanilla biscuit, rich, thick sweet cream, and sliced sugared berries. The alchemist chose a white tea that paired perfectly with the acidic fruit. They nibbled their cakes and sipped tea, enjoying the moment.

"Have you finished reading through both books?" Brinta asked between sips. "I wonder if it is time to have you pick out a few more. Maybe some with advanced topics?"

Excitement sent Trinx's smile stretching to her ears. "Yes! I would love to read through more books. From what I've seen, a lot of alchemy seems to be just trying stuff out, but I need a better idea of what I can even try."

"Excellent," Brinta said with a clap of their hands. "I'll get you set up with a few more books once we get back to the lab."

They passed the time, happy to enjoy the cake and tea.

Eventually, Trinx asked, "We've been so busy experimenting, and I've been learning all I can, but we've never really talked much about each other. You learned a lot more about me when Vex and I came out as transgender to you. I'm curious about you, though, if you don't mind. What's up with that interesting living situation you have?"

"What's up with it?" Brinta questioned back. "Well, I suppose I have to admit it's not normal goblin behavior to most, but it seems normal enough to us, so I don't think about it. My two partners and I love each other. We live together, and, well, yes, we do all the things you might imagine might happen in a situation like that."

"So," Trinx said before thinking about what she actually wanted to ask. "You are all bisexual, then? If you all love each other?"

"Hmm," Brinta hummed while sipping their tea. "We aren't much for labels. That label is close, but still not even right. It's hard to say we're bisexual when there are more than two sexes involved. I like to think of myself as flexible or fluid. I'm more of a toy that is fun for a girl or a boy." The alchemist let out a melodic burst of laughter and smirked mischievously.

Trinx clapped and joined in the laughter. "That's a fun way of putting it. It sounds like you have quite the home. At least you all know what you're attracted to. I'm still trying to figure that out. I'm really not sure if I've ever found anyone attractive, though I love some of my friends dearly."

Brinta shrugged. "I'm glad you have such good friends, and I'd like to hope I'm making my way into the group of people you consider friends. As for sexual attraction, it's not for everyone. You wouldn't be the first asexual goblin I've met."

"Oh, yes!" she quickly clarified. "I do consider you a friend. I can't believe how much you've helped me. Hopefully, I can help you as much."

"Well, there we go then. Friends, it is," Brinta declared, standing and extending their hand. "Let's shake on it and go see if the fumes are gone."

Trinx giggled and gave the extended hand a shake.

Back at the shop, the fumes had completely cleared, and Brinta turned the fan back down to the lowest speed. The annoying noise Trinx had always heard and tried hard to ignore now had a source and an explanation. Knowing didn't make it less annoying, but it was understandable.

The alchemist showed her to a set of books in the back. They invited her to take any that sounded interesting, except for two.

"Most of these are fine for you to take and study in a comfortable spot. These two; please leave them here. You can look at them while you are here, but don't leave the shop with them."

"That sounds more than fair. Thank you again," Trinx said as she scanned the titles on the shelf.

Brinta went out to clean up the mess from the past experiment and get everything ready for another try.

All the books on the shelf sounded like they could contain

wondrous recipes and theories. Her eye landed on *Phylo's Morphology*. That sounded like it had potential. She plucked it from the shelf and added it to her bag to read at home later. The alchemist called her, so she returned to the workbench to see what the next experiment would be.

The next experiment turned out to be—another failure. Not nearly as catastrophic, but a failure nonetheless. That seemed to be how things went in alchemy. Many failures with the very rare success. At least when figuring new recipes out. Creating concoctions that an alchemist had already solved was almost always straightforward. Of course, they could still be dangerous without the experience and skill to perform the steps correctly and handle the ingredients with care.

After experimenting through the afternoon with Brinta, Trinx left for her shift at the tavern. It seemed to blend with all her other shifts recently. Before she knew it, she was finishing up the cleaning and saying goodnight to Quilka, promising they would do something together soon.

At home, she drank a vial of her focus elixir and settled onto the bed to read the latest book she had borrowed. The time had arrived to find out what morphology was and what Phylo had to say about it. She settled the book on her lap. However, before she could open it, a painting on the wall across from her caught her eye. The still-life captured a vase full of tulips, her mother's favorite flowers.

Without warning, tears filled her eyes as the full force of the emotions she had been ignoring since the altercation with her parents crashed into her. A mixture of sadness, anger, and fear swirled into her own unique concoction. It threatened her more than any failed experiment in the lab so far. She could only let it wash over her, swirling in a tempest.

The focus elixir took hold of her emotions. It had been meant to focus her on the book, but instead, she fell into herself. A well had opened within her, and somehow, she tumbled into it, plummeting down into the darkness.

She eventually climbed out and found her tears had fallen all over the book in her lap. Horrified, she grabbed at her blankets and wiped the cover frantically. She removed the dampness, but a spiderweb of black from her eyeliner stained the brown leather. At least she hadn't had the book open. She couldn't even imagine explaining the damages to the pages if it had been.

Setting the book aside, she went to her dressing table and removed her makeup. She scrubbed at her face and washed away the tears. Slumping back in the seat, Trinx toweled off her face. What in the world had come over her?

She centered herself with several deep breaths. Some tea would be good. She nodded to herself and put on a kettle of water to heat. Just before it began boiling, she poured it over a generous scoop of chamomile. She pulled out her favorite mug. It held a lot of tea and had a starlit sky with twin full moons painted on it.

Settling down on her bed again, she put her mug on the side table and set the book in her lap. She once again returned the emotions to their cage, and she cautiously opened the book and read.

Phylo had many interesting ideas on transformation. They focused primarily on transforming all or part of a person into an animal or the other way around. All of them were temporary, though. The longest one would last only a handful of hours.

She needed something similar to this, but for transforming a person's features. Ideally, she could make it last longer as well. Having the transformation come undone at any time would not work. But first, she needed to get the changes she wanted before worrying about how to make them last. She continued reading and sipping tea, absorbing knowledge late into the night.

Several days passed in much the same routine: experimenting and helping Brinta in the shop, serving customers and cleaning in the tavern, reading late into the night, and sleeping very little. She relied heavily on the focus elixirs and more than once thought about trying something stronger.

One day, in the late morning, they had a success—or at least, it appeared to be a *potential* success. The potion did not explode or fume or attempt to take their lives in some other fashion. They added all the ingredients and changes without issue and created a stable, light green, translucent potion. The basis for the changes in this version involved the furry moss that had created all the fumes the other day. However, they added it at a different point. The recipe also leveraged several other natural ingredients known to encourage growth.

Trinx flagged down a runner. She gave the speedy goblin three copper coins and sent him to deliver a quick note to Vex. Keeping it simple, the letter merely asked him to come by the shop for a test as soon as he was able. The runner tucked the paper and the coins in a pouch and ran away into the crowded streets and tunnels.

Brinta took a guess at how much a dose should be based on the original formula they had built this work on. They measured it out into a vial and screwed a cap on. Setting it aside, the alchemist took time to capture all the latest steps and ingredients in detail in a journal.

Trinx looked over the bookshelf for additional volumes to read. She still had a lot left in Phylo's tome, but spending time on the same topic and book became difficult for her. A trait like that may end up making her studies as an alchemist harder, but there was nothing for it. Best to work within her limitations and juggle reading a few different topics at once.

She had just picked out a book to add to her bag when Vex pushed his way through the door. His hobgoblin strength sent the heavy iron slamming into the stone wall. Everyone winced at the noise, and Vex sheepishly shrugged.

"Sorry about that. I don't think I broke anything. I was just so eager to get here and try the potion."

Brinta replaced their wincing, scrunched face with a smile and waved him over.

"Oh please, it was just startling, is all. This place is sturdy. Come on over and see how this potion tastes. I ran a few standard tests, and it shouldn't kill you or cause gastronomical distress. Probably."

He walked to the station, shaking his head while muttering to himself more than anyone else, "Probably, they say."

"Please drink the entire contents at once," Brinta said, handing him the vial. "Don't sip on it. I can't speak to the taste, but I don't imagine it will be a delight for your tongue. If this works, we can always make tweaks to adjust the flavor."

Vex took the vial, unscrewed the cap, and set it on the counter. Then, in a quick motion, he tossed the entire contents of the tube into his mouth, swallowing quickly.

"Did it go down smoothly?" Brinta asked. "What about the taste? I hope it wasn't too horrible."

"It barely registered on my tongue," Vex said. "I swallowed pretty fast. The liquid burned a bit. It had an oily finish and left an earthy aftertaste of decomposing forest."

"That good, huh?" Brinta said with a chuckle. "Definitely could have been worse. If this works, we'll need to adjust that. Decomposing forest is unlikely to attract a lot of customers."

As they spoke, Vex began patting his face. Something changed, and dark, thin hairs sprouted on his cheeks, chin, and lip. He scrunched his face. The process clearly pained him. The beard kept growing, but not in the way everyone expected.

Those were not hairs sprouting. A dark green grass grew out of the entire area of his face where they would have expected to see chestnut-brown hairs.

He looked absolutely ridiculous. Trinx and Brinta couldn't help but laugh despite their attempts to stifle it. Worry cast a shadow over him as he tried to determine what they laughed at.

"What is it? What's wrong?" he asked, feeling his new beard with his fingers. "This doesn't feel like the hair on my head. It's wider and flat."

Trinx grinned and said, "I'm pretty sure that's because you just grew a field of grass on your face." Giggles slipped out and intensified, until turning into a burst of laughter.

Brinta held it together and stifled their amusement. With a straight face, they said, "Don't worry. We can trim it close to your face. No one will know it's grass. It should fall out completely by tomorrow. Might even be tonight. We make sure our trial runs won't last long."

Vex wanted to see firsthand what they had been on about. He walked to a mirror on the wall and examined his new beard.

"At least it gives me an idea of what it could look like. If we can just make something that grows hair and not wild grass."

With the help of the alchemist, he trimmed it quite close. It didn't look that different from a normal beard. The short, dark green hair looked more black than green. He could keep it this way until it fell out.

Chapter 15

Sleepover

The Arsonist's Tender was quiet when Trinx arrived, something she hadn't seen since before her life became hectic with juggling two jobs. Gristle looked up as she entered.

"Hey there, Luv. Wasn't expecting to see ye so early. Quilka's in the kitchen same as Brizla. Have yerself a snack before things pick up if yer feeling peckish."

"Hi, Gris!" she said on her way to the kitchen. "We had a partial success this afternoon. Brinta suggested I leave early. Didn't have anywhere else to go. So here I am, a bit early."

"Trinx!" Quilka exclaimed when Trinx walked into the kitchen. "You're here so early. Something must be going on. Spill it."

Brizla stood at the stove cooking. Not much food appeared to be done cooking yet, but several enormous bowls of salad sat out on the counter, resting in an ice trough. Trinx grabbed two plates and handed one to her friend.

"Let's have some of that salad, and I'll tell you while we eat."

They both loaded up their plates with a medley of lettuce and vegetables. It all looked fresh, with a mix of greens, plump cherry tomatoes, crisp slices of cucumber, deep purple onion, a rainbow of sweet peppers, blue button mushrooms, sunflower seeds, and sprigs of herbs heavily dressed with oil, vinegar, salt, and black pepper. Grabbing a couple of forks, they sat down at the staff table with their heaping dishes.

Before sharing the story of her afternoon, Trinx stabbed a tomato with her two-pronged utensil and popped it into her mouth. The juices squirted across her tongue when she bit down in a satisfying spray.

Swallowing, she said, "You're going to love this. We came so close but failed. The failure was pretty funny, though."

"What happened?" Quilka asked with a mischievous grin.

"So, get this," she said. "Brinta found a stable way to add in the furry moss. The potion ended up kind of greenish. Vex said it tasted like a decomposing forest."

"That sounds pretty gross, actually. Not funny," Quilka said and then stabbed a forkful before poking it in her mouth.

"That's not the funny part," she said. "Vex knocked the whole vial back like a shot of liquor. Then he looked pained, and his beard started to grow out!"

"What? Notthicknuf?" Quilka asked around a mouth full of leaves. "I thought you said it didn't work?"

"Oh, it worked for growing a beard," Trinx said, stabbing a slice of cucumber glistening with oil and coarse ground pepper and then slipping it into her mouth.

"Now you are just being confusing again," Quilka said. "Are you just teasing me at this point? Did the beard fall out right away?"

"Nope," Trinx said with a wide smile. "He'll want it to, though." At this, she couldn't hold it in any longer and let out a burst of laughter. "His beard came in vibrant and lush—just like those manicured lawns some humans take pride in. It was made of grass!"

"Oh, no!" Quilka said before joining in Trinx's laughter. "Poor Vex."

"He'll be alright," Trinx assured her after her laughter died down. "Brinta says it should fall out tomorrow, maybe even tonight if he's lucky."

"That's good, at least," her friend said and nodded while composing a large bite of assorted veggies on her fork. "So, does Brinta know what went wrong?"

"We're not entirely sure, but it seems the plant related ingredients aren't going to work out," she said and crunched on a piece of orange sweet pepper.

"Hopefully, you can find inspiration in one of the alchemy books," Quilka said. "Sounds like it's back to the drawing board."

"Speaking of that," Trinx said. "I know we never have much time for fun anymore. Probably would think it's boring, but want to just hang out tonight and read? We could get some junk food and get lost in some books? I've been making my way through a big stack of alchemy books. Some company while I read would be nice."

"It's not dancing," Quilka said, wrinkling her nose, then she smiled. "But I'll take it. I enjoy spending time with you. You're my favorite person, you know?"

Trinx blushed, her green cheeks turning a light purple. "You're my favorite, too. Best friends forever."

"Yeah," Quilka said. "That's exactly what I meant. Best friends forever." She shook her head slightly with a smile and added, "I'll come to your place after work, then. I just need to go home to get a book or two. I'll bring some snacks for us."

Their shift came and went. However, by the end of the evening, they found that Brizla could have made a better choice than salad. While both girls found the salad delightful to eat prior to working, they found it entirely unappetizing to clean slimy bits of lettuce and vegetables from the tables, chairs, and floor—at least none of it made it onto the ceiling.

Trinx brewed a pot of dragonroot and straightened up her place after returning home from the tavern. She made the bed —something she didn't do nearly often enough. Really. What was the point of making it if no one saw it but her? The single-sized bed was pressed lengthwise against one wall with a side table at each end. She didn't have a good sofa, not that one would fit in her small apartment. Instead, she put several throw pillows on the bed, propping them against the wall. In this way, she turned the bed into something akin to a deep couch.

Hearing a knock at the door, she wondered why her friend hadn't just come in.

"It's open!" she called.

Some shuffling outside suggested Quilka may be rearranging her load to open the door. She came in soon after with two bags clutched in one hand only long enough to make it inside, where she dropped the heavier of the two on the floor. From the other, she pulled out a box of cookies coated in powdered sugar and a gigantic bag of popped corn.

"I brought treats!" Quilka proclaimed as she laid the treats out on the counter. "Smells like you've got some dragonroot brewing. I'll take mine with some milk. No sugar, though. These treats should be sweet enough."

Trinx poured two mugs of tea, adding a healthy pour of milk to both. She placed a cup on each of the two tables at the ends of her bed. Getting out two plates, she said, "Those cookies look delicious. What flavor? Vanilla?"

Quilka set the bag of popped corn on the bed and shook her head while opening the box. "Nope. Better! Lemon!" she said with a squeal. "Tart and sweet. The popped corn is sweet and salty. Hopefully, our teeth don't ache after all of this."

They tossed their books on the bed and put a few cookies on each plate. Then, both girls hopped up on the bed and shimmied backwards until they rested against the pillows that leaned against the wall. Initially, they ignored the books and focused on their tea and sweet treats.

"So, the trick now," Trinx said, "is figuring out a fresh set of ingredients for stimulating growth."

Quilka licked some powdered sugar from her lips and, with a mouth full of cookies, asked, "Innyideeth?"

"No," Trinx said. "No ideas yet. That's why I wanted the study session. Hopefully, I can find something in these books."

"Well, you can dive in once your hands are clean from the snacks," Quilka said and licked a couple of her fingers.

Once they had eaten their fill, they continued to sip on tea while reading their books. Quilka used her hands against the bed to lift herself and twist a quarter turn. Leaning back, she rested partially on the pillows and partially against Trinx's arm.

While Trinx read over recipes interwoven with notes and theory, she paused from time to time to think out loud about ingredients she could suggest to Brinta they try.

"Ooh. This might work. Ground hydra scales. I don't think we've tried that yet. This says it can stimulate growth because of their ability to regenerate."

"Maybe?" Quilka said with a question in her voice. Then, trying to sound more supportive, continued, "I mean. I don't know much about alchemy, but that sounds logical enough."

"I hope so," Trinx said. "I'll tell Brinta and see if she has any we can experiment with. Oh! Tell you what, if it does work and leads to a potion—you know, that actually works—we should all go out dancing! You, me, Vex, and Brinta. I know you've been wanting to. Celebrating gives us a great excuse."

"Now that," Quilka said, "is something I can for sure say is a good idea. Let's hope hydras hold the key!"

With the deal sealed, they went back to reading, occasionally munching on the popped corn. The salty-sweetness made it easy to keep reaching for one more handful. Trinx ate with her left hand and turned the pages with her right.

They read until late in the night, until the candles burned low. Each girl shifted from time to time to get a bit more comfortable and lean into the other more. Eventually, they woke to find it was morning, and their books lay open, falling out of their laps. What they had meant to be a late-night reading session had turned into a sleepover.

Trinx looked at the time and realized how late she was. "Stay here and sleep longer. I gotta go. I don't want to show up late! Plus, we have to experiment with those scales."

Her friend waved a hand in acknowledgment as she fell back to sleep, her head resting on a pillow. The would-be alchemist gathered up her books into her bag and picked out a fresh outfit. She touched up her makeup and bolted out the door, shoving two of the sugary tart lemon cookies in her mouth on the way.

Brinta simply shook their head upon seeing her when she pushed open the door. "Don't worry. Calm down. No customers have even come by yet. Though that will probably change soon." Looking closer at Trinx, they pointed a finger at their own mouth.

Trinx realized she must have sugar stuck to her lips. She brushed it off and grabbed an apron.

Rummaging on the supply shelves, she called, "Do you have any hydra scale powder? Or maybe the whole scale and we can make powder?"

"There should be some in there. Powder, that is," Brinta answered. "Are you thinking of that for the beard growth potion?" They scratched their chin and kept talking before she could answer. "Yes. Yes. That may actually work. Or at least part of it, anyway. Bring it over when you find it."

Trinx brought the powder to the workbench, and the alchemist sketched out a new recipe incorporating the scales. They mixed several steps of the base potion they had been using, then added a measure of the hydra powder. The liquid bubbled and frothed. Every time it appeared to calm down, it gained new vigor and produced even larger bubbles.

The alchemist continued to stir the mixture, trying to calm it down. Eventually, the glass stir rod clinked against the empty flask. The entire potion had bubbled away, leaving only a dusty residue.

"Well," Brinta said. "That clearly was not the right way to do that. I think it still holds potential. It may take a fair amount of trial and error. Hydra scale powder can be quite volatile depending on what ingredients it is mixed with. We likely need to find some inert ingredients to reduce the volatility."

They spent three days attempting various versions of the recipe using the hydra scales. On that third day, around three past midday, a potion stabilized. About ten percent of the potion bubbled away during the mixing procedure, but that was an acceptable amount of loss. They clearly had something successful because the potion pulsed a dark blue before fading into a paler hue.

Trinx sent a runner to summon Vex again. She hoped he would come and not stay away in fear of something worse than the grass on his face. The thought of the green beard made her chuckle to herself as she gave instructions to the runner.

"If this works, would you be interested in going out dancing to celebrate?" Trinx asked. "Quilka and I were talking the other day about how fun it would be to go out after we finally succeed. You, me, her, and Vex?"

"I'm always up for celebrating an outstanding success," Brinta said. "Just don't get your hopes up. This could just as easily give him a scaly face as it would a hairy one."

"I know. I know," Trinx said. "I can be realistic. It would be amazing, though, if it worked. I can't help but be hopeful."

While they waited for Vex, they straightened up the shop and cleared the excess ingredients and equipment off the workbench. The alchemist measured out a single dose into a vial and then poured the rest into a large, stoppered flask.

"It's best we seal this since those scales are so volatile. I can imagine it may eventually evaporate away into nothing if left open."

Vex cautiously entered the shop. He demonstrated more restraint and less exuberance than the first time he came for a trial. He still managed a large smile, though, and had a hopeful look on his face.

Brinta waved him over and handed him the vial. "Just like last time, unscrew the cap and then drink the entire contents at once. Don't sip it. Until we know what it might do, it's best to get the full dose in quickly. If it works, we can always do follow-up tests to see how much is needed and if timing on the delivery matters."

The hobgoblin nodded his head and took the vial. He removed the lid and dumped the liquid in his mouth, swallowing it all immediately. His tongue involuntarily stuck out as he made a gagging noise.

"Do your best to hold it in," Brinta said, grimacing, and grabbed for a nearby bucket.

He waved the bucket off. "Nah. I'm fine. That one tastes like fermented rat shit. It's fine now that it's out of my mouth. At least it didn't have an oily finish that stuck to my—"

He braced himself mid-thought against the counter and lowered his head. The skin under his cheeks, around his mouth, and on his neck rippled like insects crawling underneath. Chestnut-brown hair erupted from his face, growing from stubble to roughly 10 centimeters long. He let go of the counter, brought his fingers to his face, and began furiously scratching.

Trinx looked at him, then over at Brinta. "Did that? Did that just work? It looks like it worked! That's hair, definitely not grass or scales. What's wrong? Does it hurt?"

"No," he answered. "Not pain. Itch! It itches so bad. You wouldn't believe it."

"That should subside once the growing settles down," Brinta said. "It looks to be slowing already. And it looks like it worked. You have a vibrant-looking new beard, Vex."

Chapter 16

Mid-Afternoon Tea

T rinx had just finished twisting a fresh set of braids into her hair when she heard a knock at the door. That was certainly strange and definitely out of the ordinary. Hardly anyone ever came knocking. It was unlikely to be Quilka, and she didn't have many other visitors. Her place was small and not built for entertaining.

A second knock struck the door, this time a three-beat knock with two, a pause, then one. Whoever stood at the door didn't seem likely to give up and go away. She had been on her way out anyway, so she went to the door and pulled it open.

She saw, standing before her, a goblin runner. He was tall and lanky, with a mid-length beard and a shock of orange on the top of his head. He simply smiled and held out an envelope.

She took it and fished a copper out, pressing it in his hand. He ran off, and only then did she look down at the delivery. A red blob of wax embossed with vines climbing up a stylized V sealed the cream-colored envelope. Turning it over, she saw the front simply read, "Trinx."

After breaking the seal, she found it to be less of a letter and more of a formal invitation. The paper had a neat, flowing script.

Trinx,

It seems Zigla has many good things to say about you. I would be delighted to speak with you about the prob-lems you have experienced. Please join me for tea service this afternoon.

You are cordially invited to mid-afternoon tea.

Location: Vorti's Home
Time: Afternoon tea hour
Date: Today

Sincerely,

Vorti, High Council of Goblin Grandmas

Tea? With a grandma? Today?

What to wear? She couldn't wear the dress she had randomly picked out that day. She needed something with intention. What does one wear to afternoon tea with a grandma? And not just any grandma. Vorti was Zigla's mother.

Her mind continued to race as she flipped through the dresses hanging in her wardrobe. A conservative dress. That's what she needed. Did she have one? She finally landed on an older dress, black with blue trim and stitching. The dress had long sleeves, and buttons ran up to a high neckline. It fell to beneath her knees, midway down her shins. It would do.

She removed the dress she had been about to wear and hung it back in the wardrobe. Picking out some high stockings that reached her lower thighs, she pulled them on before slipping into the black dress. She chose black pumps with mid-sized heels. As she looked herself over in the mirror, she felt something was missing.

Some jewelry would complete the outfit—something silver. She sifted through a jewelry box and found a thin silver chain with a flower-shaped pendant. This would work. She fastened the chain around her neck and centered the charm while on her way out the door.

Trinx hurried off to Distilled Magic, hoping the entire way that Brinta wouldn't mind her taking the afternoon off. Despite her mind focused on the thought, she couldn't help but feel a sense of importance as she raced through the crowd. She would meet with a member of the council today.

When Trinx arrived at the shop, she explained everything to Brinta, even showing her the invitation.

"Of course you can go," Brinta said. "Don't let me and our experiments keep you from a meeting like that. Besides, with our success yesterday, a small break would be good. You look fabulous today, by the way. Not that you don't usually, but I think Vorti will appreciate it."

"Thank you," she effused. "I'm so excited. Don't worry, though. I'm here to help for now. I won't have to leave until early afternoon."

"I don't want a mishap with an experiment ruining that outfit," Brinta said. "Today, let's focus on some chores in the shop. I've been neglecting them recently with all the experimenting."

"Sure," Trinx said. "We can do chores. I'll work on organizing the supply shelves. Lately, it's been harder to find the ingredients you want to use. That's probably my fault. I didn't think when putting things back on the shelves. I may have been too random."

"Wonderful!" Brinta exclaimed. "I like that idea, as

handling the ingredients to organize them will get your mind thinking more about them and how they interact. Use that to get a feel for where to put them and which should be shelved next to each other."

Trinx braced her hands on the counter and leaned in.

"Remember how I told you Quilka and I thought it would be fun to go out dancing to celebrate if we solved Vex's beard potion? Are you still up for it? Have you had any ideas?"

"I do remember," Brinta said with a sly smile. "I've got an idea for tonight. I just need to check on some details. I'll send word on where to meet this evening."

The two spent the time organizing and cleaning everything in the stockroom, lab area, and the shop itself. By the time they finished and the hour had almost arrived for her appointment, the place looked better than it had in a long time. With a wave and a last call of thanks, Trinx left for tea.

She knew the general area where Vorti lived, and as she got closer, helpful passersby pointed her in the right direction. Eventually, someone motioned at a house. The dwelling did not appear overly fancy, and she realized she didn't know what she should expect. Despite being on the council, the grandma was just another goblin after all.

With deliberation, she approached the door and noticed a pull chain for a bell. Rather than knock, she gave the chain a small tug and heard a muffled chime from within. Shuffling noises soon followed. The door opened, and she saw a woman about her age wearing a cleaning staff uniform.

The goblin had a plain look but a friendly smile and demeanor.

"Welcome. Trinx, I presume? I'm Wobblet. I help Vorti out around the house. Please, come in."

Trinx entered a foyer that held a simple coat rack and a small table with two chairs on either side. A chandelier filled with candles hung from the ceiling. Above the table, a painting of a forest with a clearing holding a single flower hung on the wall. On the opposite wall, a large mirror with ornate metal fillagree hung.

The housemaid beckoned her to follow and led the way down a hall, deeper into the home. The hallway had pictures of what she presumed were the extended family lining the walls. She spotted one of a hob that had a striking resemblance to a young Zigla, and she thought it might actually be the last picture captured of her before she left home to find herself.

Wobblet opened a door on the right-hand side of the hall and held it open, gesturing for her to enter. She did as requested and entered a sitting room with a couch and several armchairs. The couch was filled with more pillows than she felt she had seen in her entire life and was upholstered in a flowery fabric. The seating formed a cozy circle around a large cocktail table that stood low to the ground. She sat in an armchair with alternating stripes of blue and green.

"Vorti will be with you shortly, and I will return soon with the tea service," the maid said before leaving the room and closing the door behind her.

Trinx looked around the chamber. Several oil lamps illuminated the room with a soft glow. A writing desk with a chair stood against one wall under a large mirror. A fireplace adorned another. It held no fire but a grate holding a large log. Several tools rested on a stand on the hearth. Despite the lack of a fire, she felt cozy and peaceful sitting in the room.

After only a few moments of waiting, she subconsciously pulled out the toy Zigla had made for her so long ago. Her fingers danced over the beads, spinning them, stopping them, and then spinning again. It really had been a very thoughtful gift, and she relied on it in any situation that needed her attention.

She couldn't help that her mind wandered. It always had. She knew it must be part centipede, and its legs constantly tried to carry it away. The beads helped calm those itchy feet. They grounded her focus. Maybe they wouldn't be enough for this conversation. Her host had not yet entered the room, and she unscrewed the cap on a minor elixir of focus.

Quickly, she downed the entire vial and had it stashed back in her bag. She almost felt guilty for some reason. Her mind played tricks on her like that at times. Surely there was nothing wrong with a little help to focus on the conversation ahead and give her a small boost of energy. She still regularly ran herself ragged, with much less sleep than her body needed.

She continued to look around the room and saw a hutch in one corner with glass doors. Small figurines lined the shelves of the hutch. Birds, animals, and even goblins in various poses. Her mind counted the miniature statues, starting with the top shelf and working her way down to the bottom. *Forty-seven.* The lower half of the hutch had solid wood doors with brass knobs. *Did that cabinet hold more of the figurines?*

The door opened, and an elderly goblin with long white hair tied up in a bun stepped into the room. She wore a navy blue dress with matching stockings. A pair of brown flats with blue trim poked out from the bottom of the long garment. Her eyes looked enormous behind a pair of octagon-shaped glasses, and Trinx could see they were the same color as Zigla's eyes.

The woman, presumably Vorti, wore a warm and inviting smile on her face, causing deep wrinkles around her eyes. Dark green and brown age spots dotted her cheeks and forehead. She crossed the room and took a seat near the fidgeting goblin.

"I am so glad you could come today, Trinx," she said. "Wobblet will be in shortly with the tea and, I'm sure, a few sweet treats as well." The right side of her smile drew up higher, causing additional crinkling, giving her a mischievous look as if she hid a much younger girl inside her ancient body.

"N-nice to meet you. Er, yes. I'm Trinx. Zigla is such a good friend of mine. It's good to meet her mother," she said in a rush, tripping over the words to get them out.

The elder goblin clucked. "Please, dear. Calm down. I'm here to help. Don't be nervous. My child wrote to me about you but only gave some basic information. From what I understand, you and my child have a lot in common. I would love to hear more about yourself from you."

She swallowed, and her fingers spun the beads of her toy. Taking a deep breath, she said, "Of course. I can start at the beginning, I think. Zigla took me in when I needed help. She helped me learn who I truly was, and I lived with her in the cave for around a year."

Trinx filled in the details of her time with her mentor and described how helpful she had been. As she finished, Wobblet entered the room carrying a large tray. She set it down on the table and filled two cups. Trinx could smell the blend. She caught notes of dragonroot, black tea, and strong spices.

"Milk? Sugar? Honey?" the maid asked, looking up at her.

"Just some milk, please. A healthy dollop," she answered.

Wobblet added a generous pour of thick, creamy milk to her cup, then added both milk and sugar to the other. She then set out a plate and a set of silverware in front of each of them. She motioned at a serving tower that rose from the back half of the tray. Cakes, tarts, cookies, and pastries filled the shelves.

"Please, help yourself to a sweet treat." She then curtsied and left the room, pulling the door closed quietly.

Trinx let it all sit for a moment, waiting to see if Vorti would act first. Seeing her hesitation, the grandma reached out and placed a custard-filled tart on her plate. She brought it to her lap and cut a small bite with her fork.

"Please, help yourself, or stick to the tea if you aren't hungry. I always need a little something something to get by in the afternoon, or my tummy gets too rumbly by supper."

That was enough of an invitation, and Trinx reached out and took a round shortbread with a thick layer of chocolate spread on top. Normally, she would just pick it up with her fingers and bite it, but feeling self-conscious, she used her fork to carve a piece of the crumbly cookie off. She awkwardly scooped it onto the fork after failing to impale it with the tines and placed the bite in her mouth before it could fall into her lap.

"Such proper manners," Vorti said with a chuckle. "Feel free to use your fingers if you'd like."

As if to prove it would not break any rules, she broke off a small piece of her tart and popped the cream-covered crust into her mouth.

Vorti put the plate with the tart down and picked up her cup of sweetened tea. "From what I gathered in my child's letter, you could use some help. There are many ways I might help, but rather than presume, why don't you start by telling me what you most need help with?"

Trinx put down her plate and took a deep breath. She had been waiting for this question and knew what she wanted, but as usual, the connection between her brain and her mouth didn't follow a straight path. The words fell from her in a tumble, rushing as if to make sure they could not be left behind.

"I am a transgender woman. Just like Zigla. She showed me I could be, and I am. And it's not fair she's in a cave, and I'm in the warren, but I'm always sort of hiding, you know? Not from everyone. My friends know all about me. Well, mostly. And most of them—except the ones that don't—we don't usually talk about it. Because what's to talk about, really? Right?

"Except, sometimes, the looks and comments I get, they

make me feel small. You know? Like a mouse? And I bet other people feel that way, too. Another friend hasn't told me that, but he's not small. But that doesn't mean he doesn't feel that way, right? And there have to be others. Others hiding. And I should be able to help them.

"Of course, grandmas on the council can do anything. They run the clan, right? I mean, *really* run it. Not like the warlord, but the important parts, and if I was a grandma, then I could help run it. I could make goblins treat everyone right, and people wouldn't feel small."

This was too much, too fast, Trinx thought. *Did any of it even make sense? What else could she do, though, but barrel on?* She had questions and needed help.

"But how can I be a grandma? Well, I know how. I just need to adopt a child. Quilka says I'm too young. I should have more fun, she says. But a grandma needs a child who has a child. So, I need a child first. Then they can have a child, and the council would let me join.

"But I can't birth a child. That would be wonderful, though, wouldn't it? To birth a child of my own? But you know that, you're a grandma. Of course, you know that. But I can't. Even if I figure out some potions. That doesn't seem like it would work. The insides just aren't the same.

"And Sulma's, the review board, said no. Twice even. They want me to have a mate. Vex said he didn't know. I get that. Makes sense, right? But maybe he'll say yes. Maybe he doesn't have to, if you help, though, right? You could just tell them to let me have a youngling. Maybe two? Do you think I need two? But you could help, right? You said you could help."

The words ended, and she found the beads on her wooden toy spinning faster than they ever had before. Trinx breathed in and out in quick puffs, trying to refill her lungs and calm herself. Her eyes met the elder goblin's, and she stared. Hopeful. Pleading.

Vorti had sat silently, watching her fight to release all of her words. She took a long sip of tea and swallowed. A kind smile filled her face.

"Well, now. Those were a lot of words. I can tell you've been holding on to them for quite a while."

Taking another small sip, Vorti said, "I believe I understand what you are asking of me. I also believe that *you* don't understand what you are asking of me. You are asking me to help you onto the path toward joining the Council of Grandmas, and you are specifically asking me to pressure the orphanage to allow you to adopt a child. Those are two separate requests, and I'm not sure either is actually what you need."

Trinx's face grew tense. She could see the old woman had more to say. It took all of her willpower, but she held her tongue.

"If you'll indulge me, let me tell you a story," Vorti said. "When I was a much younger goblin and pregnant with my first child, my husband and I were excited. We could tell by the size of my belly that we would likely have a hob. Bliz was a hob himself and led his own raiding squad. As our child grew, he gained mass and muscle, proving us right. We also had several other children, some hobs, some not, and we had two female goblins as well."

Vorti paused for another sip of tea before she said, "Our oldest child grew up and trained as a warrior but was often very sad. He kept to himself most of the time. One day, I entered my room and found him looking in a dressing mirror. He had fashioned a dress out of a huge potato sack. He had covered his lips with a red gloss I had and poorly applied dark eyeshadow around his eyes. I saw all this from the doorway. What struck me more than anything, though, was the look on his face I saw reflected in the mirror. He had the largest smile I had ever seen on him."

Another sip of tea and Trinx had relaxed some, listening intently to the story.

Vorti continued, "I, of course, did not know what to think other than, despite the scene before me, he wore that smile. That smile told me I had to help my child find a new way through life. We got him cleaned up before Bliz returned. I hatched a plan to find my child a home. With some effort we found the cave I know you've visited. My child chose a new name, one better fitting, and moved into the cave. I sent regular supplies and still do to this day. Occasionally, my child sends letters."

The grandma took a small nibble of her tart and washed it down with another swallow of the tea. "You may wonder why I told you that story. I know you have talked and even lived with my child for a spell. You surely know that story, or at least a version. What you don't know is what came later."

Finding her cup empty, Vorti fixed another, stirring in the milk and sugar. "Life went on for me, and I missed my child, but I had a family full of other children to raise. I raised them well, and some had children of their own. Eventually, those on the council asked me to join them. And I did. I joined them."

She blew across the fresh cup; a wisp of steam swirled up, and she took a sip. "I thought, just like I see you thinking now, that I could use my position to further help my child. But what I found was what I am trying to tell you now. The council is a group of wise women. Goblins look to us for advice. But we do not weave spells that somehow transform how those in the community think and act. I could no more change the clan's opinion of my child than I could tame a wild vornash."

Trinx could take it no longer and jumped back into the conversation. "But there has to be a way. I'm sure I could do it if

I was just on the council. Do you even want to change anything? I couldn't help but notice in your story that you always called Zigla 'my child' but never by her name or even by saying her or she."

Vorti shook her head gently and continued smiling. "I want change. Believe me. If I could somehow wave a wand and have the clan accept my child, I would. As to my references, please understand, it's difficult for me. I have accepted I no longer have the son I thought I once did, but I fully accept Zigla as my child."

"I suppose that's better than nothing," Trinx said, grimacing. "And I believe you would like her back home and nearby. But I don't believe you when you say that nothing can be done. I'm sure I could do something. I just need to become a grandma myself. Will you please help with the adoption?"

The kind grandma shook her head again. "Perhaps I could. Perhaps not. But I won't. I agree with your friend that you are too young. I also am not sure that would be the best life for a youngling you might adopt. There may even be other paths to the council you could pursue."

"But I thought you were going to help me," Trinx whimpered. "You have to know I need help."

This time, Vorti nodded, and she said, "Yes, you need help. And help, I will give you, but it is the same help I give most every goblin that comes to me seeking aid. I believe there are many paths that can take you where you want and allow you to achieve what you desire. First, though, you need to understand that you have all the power you need. You must become the change you desire."

"What?" Trinx asked, staring blankly at the older goblin. "What is that supposed to mean?"

"Just think about what I have said," Vorti said. "Take your time. A change does not happen today. It does not happen tomorrow. It does not even happen next year. A change happens always. Continue on the path you have set out on. Become the change. I think that has been enough for today. I enjoyed meeting you, Trinx. Wobblet will show you out."

Trinx looked up to see that the housemaid had returned and stood waiting in the doorway. *How did she know the conversation was over?*

She stood and said, "Thank you," but she really didn't mean it. She walked to the door and followed Wobblet out of the house.

Trinx wandered toward the Tender. Her shift wouldn't start yet, but that was good. There would be more time to talk with Quilka. *Become the change? What did that mean?*

Chapter 17

Unity

For the second time in as many days, Trinx graced the Arsonist's Tender with her presence early. It was quiet again when she arrived, and Gristle pulled his shocked jaw closed before saying, "Trinxy! You'll have me questioning my sanity if ye keep popping in so early. Is everything good with ye, Luv?"

"Oh, Gris!" she said with a wave of her hand. "I had an errand this afternoon and got here a bit early. You talk like it's never happened before."

"Well, truth be told," Gristle said, "pretty sure it hasn't. Even so, good to see ye and hear nuffin is wrong. Q's in the kitchen. Feel free to chat for a bit before things pick up in here."

"Trinx!" Quilka exclaimed when she entered the kitchen. "Early again? And look at you. Fabulous! What is it this time? The way you are dressed, it must be something good."

Over at the enormous cauldron near the stove, Brizla stood stirring what appeared to be a stew. Heavenly aromas of spices filled the kitchen. Trinx picked out coriander, cumin, cardamom, and cinnamon.

She called over to the two girls, "This is coming along well enough. Grab a bowl so you can eat before things get busy."

Trinx grabbed two bowls and handed one to her friend. "Let's have some of that stew, and I'll tell you while we eat."

Brizla ladled a heaping portion into each bowl, and they sat at the staff table to eat. Quilka handed Trinx a spoon, and she used it to scoop up some of the thick broth. Blowing on it lightly, she then sipped and found it also had garlic and a powerful kick from some spicy peppers.

"Try some, Q," Trinx said before swallowing the rest of what had been on her spoon. "It's amazing. Brizla, great work today!"

Quilka dug in and began eating, making noises that seemed to indicate she agreed. "So, what's the story? Fill me in."

Trinx handed Quilka the invitation and ate another spoonful of the spicy stew before she said, "This came this morning. I was ready to leave for the shop and had to throw those plans out the window so I could find something nicer to wear. You think this was appropriate?"

"Oh yes," Quilka said, nodding. "You look marvelous. Fancy even. I'm sure you made a strong impression. So, is she going to help you?"

"Well," Trinx started. "She said she would help me. No. She said she was helping me, but she said she wouldn't talk to Sulma's. So, I don't see how she is helping. She said I had everything I needed."

"What's that supposed to mean?" Quilka asked and put a spoonful of saucy potato in her mouth.

"That's just it. I don't know," Trinx said. Then, in a poor imitation of Vorti's aged voice, said, "You must become the change." She let out an exasperated sigh. "Become the change? How do I do that?"

"Hmm," Quilka mused. "You sure that's all she said?"

"Obviously, that's not all," Trinx said with a shrug. "But the rest of it didn't make any more sense. Stuff about change happening all the time and to keep doing what I'm doing." She chewed a piece of meat with determination. Or maybe it was frustration.

"At least it's easy enough to follow her advice, even if you don't understand it," Quilka said in a chipper tone. "I mean. If what you need to do is what you are doing? You're doing it, right?"

"I guess," Trinx said while absently swirling her spoon in the stew. "I was hoping for more, though. Thought she would have more answers or, you know, pull some strings? She thought I was too young, maybe?"

"Well, you are!" Quilka said, letting a giggle escape. "I've told you that. I barely get to have fun with you as it is with your two jobs. Can you imagine if you were raising a child? It would be years before we did anything fun again."

"You're both probably right," Trinx admitted. "I honestly don't even know what I would do with a youngling. What time would I have for them? I guess I've just been seeing a child as a step in the process. Not really fair to the kid, though."

"Right," her friend said and nodded while scooping another spoonful from her bowl.

"Someday, it might be nice to actually birth a child," Trinx said wistfully. "I doubt anything could make that happen, though."

"Careful what you wish for there. I could, but I don't think I should. Don't think I'd want to, either. Maybe someday?" Quilka said and shook her head as if to clear away the thought.

"Wait!" Trinx said, dropping her spoon into her bowl.

"That's it. That's what Vorti meant. She said I had to become the change. She must think I can make a potion to fully transform my body. Like all the way. Internal changes and everything. If I did that? Well, yeah. That would do it. I *could* birth a child of my own. I wouldn't need to adopt. I just have to work even harder to find the right potion."

"Wow," Quilka said. "That would be something. A change like that could be amazing. You really think that's what she meant? And you think you can do it?"

"Not alone," Trinx admitted. "But Brinta has been such a great help. If I tell them what I really want, I'm sure they will help me. Oh! And speaking of Brinta. They said they had an idea for celebrating Vex's beard tonight. We should get word on where to meet up at some point this evening. Maybe Gris can let us leave a bit early so we can get dressed for a night out."

"You should ask him," Quilka said. "I'm pretty sure he's still amazed you came in early two days in a row. He's sure to let us leave a little early or at least not make us stay late."

Brinta had a membership at Unity, and it turned out Vex did as well. That's why he'd been there when they met during the failure party. Brinta liked it because they labeled it as a safe place for people of any race, gender, or sexual persuasion. Enforcers dealt with anyone who had a problem with the club's primary clientele. That was news to Trinx and Quilka, but that made them like it even more. It was the perfect place for them.

That night, the club organizers set it up in an expansive cavern at the end of a closed-off mine shaft. At one point, this mine had produced iron ore and the occasional gemstone vein. It had long since been exhausted and eventually closed down.

Trinx, Quilka, and Vex met Brinta and their two partners, Zerk and Lizzy, outside the entrance to the mine shaft. The club organizers had removed the boards, closed them off, and replaced them with a thick rope net. Two orc enforcers stood guard.

The alchemist led the way up to the guards, showing them a flat piece of metal with a multifaceted prism embedded in the center, and pointed at Zerk and Lizzy. Vex showed off a similar card, gesturing at Trinx and Quilka. The guards gave affirmative nods to each member of the group and pulled up the heavy netting, allowing them all to pass.

Bioluminescent plants in a rainbow of colors lined the mine shaft, creating a well-lit walkway down the center.

Brinta stowed the metal card away before saying to the girls, "If I see the organizers, I'll introduce you all, and if you want membership, you'll have the opportunity to join. There are dues, but they keep them reasonable. They use the funds to put on these events. You just need a current member to vouch for you and both Vex and I can."

As they continued down the tunnel, the music grew louder. A deep bass beat thumped, sending vibrations through the ground and causing the plants to shake. The haunting sound of a woman's chanting voice beckoned them forward.

> *I would give that gob a munch*
> *Days like this I know I've won*
> *As I smack her little bun*
> *Yeah, she's my favorite snack*
> *You know she be coming back*
> *Something I need, not a want*

The gently sloping mine shaft eventually opened into a cavern full of lights, sound, and people having an enormous party. A natural stone platform rose in the center, swarming with dancers. Smaller groups of partiers bounced in open areas on the lower floor. Tables of different heights stood in a haphazard layout. Shorter ones had chairs around them, while the taller ones seemed a convenient place to stand around with a spot to set a drink down.

The group was large for a sit-down table and opted to stand around an open high-top. Brinta flagged down a server and asked for two bottles of sparkling wine.

"It's the best way to start off a celebration," they told the gang.

Trinx and Quilka stepped back from the table and danced while waiting for the server to return. She had crafted fresh braids and wore one of her newer dresses. The crimson dress had crisscrossed shoulder straps and left her arms bare. The red complemented her smooth, olive-green arms, and it hugged her torso tightly.—there would be no flying pouches tonight. A wide matching red belt with a large buckle on it came with the dress and cinched at her waist before the skirt flared out, hanging mid-way down her thighs. Instead of tights, she wore knee-high white socks and a pair of red boots.

Her friend opted to wear a green dress with thick vertical navy-blue stripes. The green closely matched the shade of her skin. It fit snug and looked like it would need to be peeled off later. The net result made it appear that she was only wearing some dark vertical strips of cloth strategically applied to her body.

At the table, Vex watched them dance with a smile on his face. Brinta's partners flanked them, Lizzy holding onto their arm. Zerk looked distracted and read from a Mysti Message Scroll. The alchemist noticed and patted his hand, prompting him to put it away.

The server returned with the bottles of wine and six glasses. She popped the cork from both bottles in a controlled fashion.

"Sorry, can't let people open their own bottles anymore, too many minor injuries from flying corks. I'll pour you all a drink to start with." She then filled each flute half full, set the bottle down, and disappeared to help the other guests.

Vex waved the dancing girls over, and they stopped their bouncing and returned to the table. He gestured for everyone to take a glass and grabbed one himself. As if it was a completely natural thing he did all the time, he stroked his beard thoughtfully. Clearly, he wanted all eyes focused on his new facial hair, which he had already groomed with a comb and wax.

"Thank you all so much for everything," he said. "I can't believe I not only have a beard, but it's so thick and full. To the best alchemists in the Chubug clan. No, wait—the best alchemists in the world."

Holding his glass out, everyone clinked them together, and they all drank the fruity wine that danced effervescently across their tongues.

Brinta clapped and said, "It's always great to crack a tough problem, and much of the thanks go to Trinx. She had the determination to keep learning and experimenting. Her idea of using hydra scale powder turned out to be just what we needed. Great work!"

The praise caused Trinx's cheeks to flush purple, and she pushed away the words with a quip. "Thanks, but now you better watch out, Vex. If you aren't careful, you'll get fleas in that new beard of yours."

He laughed and swore an oath with his hand on his heart. "I swear I will care for this fine beard like it's my most prized possession. No fleas invited."

The alchemist brought things back down to earth with a reminder. "Besides grooming that beard, you'll also need to stay on top of taking that potion. Otherwise, it will fall out. I'll work on improving the flavor and add in some longevity agents. The improved formula should last a month, but if I were you, I'd take it every two weeks to keep it nice and full."

"Ha!" Vex snorted. "I don't care about the cost. I'll take it weekly, to be sure."

Brinta chuckled and shook their head. "You likely don't need it that often, but it won't hurt. You do you. Now, Trinx, what's next up on our experimental journey?"

"Maybe we should talk tomorrow at the shop?" Trinx asked, looking pensive. "It's pretty loud in here."

"Fair enough," Brinta said with a nod. "That's a good point. I'm shouting as it is."

"Trinx, you up for a dance?" Vex asked.

"Sure!" she exclaimed, pulling away from the table with him to an empty spot on the floor.

They danced, bounced, and jumped to the heavy bass beat. This song didn't have many lyrics. On the downbeats, a deep voice rumbled suggestive phrases. It actually made it possible to talk while dancing, albeit at a high volume.

"Wanted to let you know," Vex shouted.

Thump. Thump. "Been thinking what you asked."

Dum. Bum. Dum. "I owe you so much." He tugged at his beard.

Thump. Thump. Thump. "But I just can't."

She nodded even more than her head already bopped to the beat of the song and shouted back, "Was too much to ask!"

Thump. Thump. "Wouldn't work, anyway."

Thud. Thump. Thud. "Just have fun. Okay?"

She flashed him a smile, and he returned it. They continued dancing until the song ended. Returning to the table, they found Quilka holding down the fort, and the Distilled Magic trio danced several meters away. Her friend poured more wine into the glasses at their approach, and they each grabbed one to join her in another drink.

Before long, Brinta and their partners returned to the table as well and joined in, finishing the last of the wine. The alchemist spotted someone they recognized and waved him over. The goblin had impeccably styled black hair and a full goatee trimmed very short. He wore a brilliant, bioluminescent-yellow, crop-top shirt that would challenge the sun with its brightness. A pair of chocolate-brown pants fit extremely snugly, looking painted onto his legs. Chunky black leather boots rose all the way up to his knees.

As he approached the table, he squealed, "Brinta! So good to see you! And, of course, Zerk and Lizzy." He paused as his eyes fell on Vex. "And you're with Vex as well? But who are these fine-looking young goblins?"

"Mungo!" Brinta exclaimed. "Meet my apprentice, Trinx, and her friend Quilka."

The snazzy-dressed goblin gave a shallow bow toward them and said, "My most sincere pleasure to meet you. Welcome to my club!"

"Your club?" Trinx asked. "You're an organizer?"

"Yes, I'm an organizer," he said with a nod. "But I also started the entire club. It's my baby. If you are a friend of my favorite alchemist, then you must join. The membership is quite reasonable. Five silver a month. I try to keep it low to encourage more to join and come regularly."

"This club's great," she said with a wide grin across her face. "I love it. Quilka and I came on a guest pass when it was in a warehouse. That's where we met Vex. I'd like a membership. I don't have a coin purse on me tonight, though. Interferes with the dancing."

"Me too!" Quilka said in agreement. "But same deal. Where would I even fit it?" She ran a hand over her skin-tight dress.

"Not a problem," Vex said, coming to their rescue. "I owe

them anyway. I've got it covered." He stroked his beard with a knowing glance at Trinx and pulled out the fee for both of them to hand to Mungo.

"Wonderful," Mungo said. "Glad to take the fee and get you your membership cards. I will bill each of you for the ongoing dues."

Without another word, he disappeared into the crowd, only to return a few moments later with two cards just like the one Brinta and Vex had flashed at the guards on the way in. He gave one to each of the new members.

"There you go. You are now official members of Unity. I'll just record your names, and you will receive messages about upcoming locations." He scribbled down their names and a few notes in a notebook and left once again.

Trinx looked at her new card and caught beams of light in the prism. Realizing that just with her lack of a coin purse, she had nowhere to put the card, either. She took the matching card from Q and handed them both to Vex.

"Need your pockets again. Can you hold on to these? At least until the end of the night. Better yet, maybe bring them by the Tender when you have a chance?"

He nodded and took the cards and tucked them in his pockets. "No problem. That's what I'm here for: a walking set of pockets."

The group continued dancing late into the night until it couldn't be rightly called night anymore and had threatened to become morning. Brinta danced exclusively with their partners. Trinx and Quilka danced a lot together, so much so that Vex asked many other clubgoers to dance. Occasionally, all three of them would dance together, much like the alchemist's trio.

As the latest song ended, Trinx stifled a yawn and said, "Need to visit the restroom. Coming Q?"

Her friend nodded and followed her to the back of the club, where they found an offshoot of the cavern leading to a cave with lanterns hanging from the ceiling. Somebody had brought in wooden outhouses and set them up over a long grate embedded in the stone floor. The drainage system must have been there originally from the normal mine operations. It was a smart idea to bring in the stalls, even if a little disgusting.

"Maybe we can hold out until we get back home," Trinx said, wrinkling her nose. "It's not an emergency. At least not for me."

Quilka shook her head. "Nope. I should have sought this out earlier. I need relief now. That one looks empty. Wish me luck." She made a beeline for a shack with a door slightly ajar.

Trinx wondered how she would manage in there with the cramped space and that form-fitting dress. She leaned against a wall far from the line of stalls and the grate underneath them. She yawned several times. Her energy was fleeting at this late hour.

After several minutes, Quilka emerged from the stall and headed to a wash station. They then walked back out to the club proper, and Trinx suggested they find the others.

"I think it's late enough. We should head out."

They made their way back to the table they had been using as a base of operations throughout the night and found the other four sipping an orange cocktail of some sort.

"I think we're about done for the night. I need some sleep, and I'm pretty sure you are going to want to see me in the shop first thing in the morning," Trinx said.

"That is a fair point," Brinta said with a nod. "I should get some sleep, too. We will take it easy tomorrow. Straighten up the lab, maybe tweak the taste on Vex's potion, and other simple tasks. Neither one of us will be in exemplary condition."

Chapter 18

Traveler's Tonic

The morning came much too early for Trinx. To be fair, it had been nearly dawn by the time her head hit the pillow. With only three hours of sleep, she seriously wondered how she would make it through the day, but she had to try.

Still, her eyelids weighed a literal ton. It took all her concentration to keep them open and force herself to sit up. Gradually, as her mind awakened, the memory of her new plan helped clear some of the fatigue. Thanks to Vorti's insights, who, in retrospect, was quite helpful after all, Trinx knew what had to be done. She simply needed to invent a potion, elixir, or pill that could transform her body completely, giving her female anatomy inside and out.

Simple.

Okay, so maybe it wouldn't be simple. But that was the point, right?

The focus elixir she had made should help, and she fumbled around to find a vial. Luckily, she found two. After downing one, she tucked the other into her bag for a pick-me-up later.

Trinx cleaned herself up and applied fresh makeup. Flipping through her wardrobe, she picked something simple to wear and put her hair up in a single ponytail. Her stomach rumbled, demanding food. She looked around her kitchenette for something quick. Finding half a bag of granola, she tossed some nuts in, along with some dried fruits. It would have to do.

Her stomach reached for the snack bag, and she tossed back a handful. Saliva filled her mouth as she chewed, her body clearly craving more. As she swallowed, the food occupied her stomach, allowing her to focus on the rest of the world. Deciding that trying to eat while walking to the shop might not be the best plan, she sat down and read through Phylo's book while eating the rest of the bag.

Once her stomach was satiated, she headed to the shop.

When she pushed open the door to Distilled Magic, Brinta looked up, and she could see the bags under the alchemist's eyes from across the room.

"Hey Trinx. Looks like you're handling the lack of sleep about as well as me. Which is to say, not at all."

"Definitely agree. I feel like I should be walking like this," Trinx said. Her feet shuffled across the floor, and she hung her head, tilted to one side, her eyes half closed. She kept this up only halfway to the center counters, then shook it off and walked the rest of the way with a giggle, despite her exhaustion.

"Well," Brinta yawned. "I'm glad we decided to take it easy today. If you haven't already, it would probably be a good idea to have some of that focus elixir you brewed."

"Way ahead of you there," Trinx said with a nod.

"Despite the lack of sleep, I'm just still super excited about our success yesterday," Trinx added. "I'm ready to work on the next project. I have some ideas. Phylo's Morphology has been an excellent read. He mainly works with animal transformations. But why couldn't it work on goblins and other people?"

Brinta nodded and stifled another yawn. "Yes, that's a good one. Lots of good ideas for body transformations and enhancements in there. So, that's what's next? You want to do more augmentations? What are you thinking?"

The topic infused Trinx with an extra boost of energy, and she bounced lightly on her toes.

"I want to do it all. Go all the way. I want to be me inside and out. I want to give birth to a child. You can help me, right? It's possible? We can find a potion that can transform everything?"

Brinta put a hand on the countertop to brace and sat in a chair. They leaned back and looked the woman over.

Nodding, they said, "I thought that's where all this might lead. I think it's a good idea. I'm sure you aren't the only one wishing for such things. It likely will be tough. Harder than the last two experiments. And we'll want to make sure we brew them to be as short-lived as possible. It's likely we'll grow some things we don't mean to and remove some others we'd rather keep. So best if it wears off quickly."

"But you think we can do it, right?" she said, her eyes wide and bright.

"Yes," the alchemist nodded. "I believe we can. I have a lot of confidence in myself, and you have proven to have some very intuitive ideas as an apprentice. Today, however, is not the day we start. I'm wiped. We need to take it easy, like I said last night."

"But—" Trinx said, then stopped when she saw the weary expression on Brinta's face. Keeping her emotions in check, she said, "That's fine. We should at least tinker with the beard formula some, don't you think? What Vex drank may have already worn off since it was just a trial. We need to increase the duration and improve that nasty taste."

"Fair enough," Brinta said. "We can work on improving the elixir for Vex. He'll probably be by today looking for more, anyway. You have a point there. Besides, if we can fix it up, then we can get an application filed."

Over the next few hours, the two made several small trial batches of the beard formula, focusing on adjusting the taste. Changing the flavor of an elixir or potion was fascinating. Brinta knew several well-known ingredients that were nearly magically inert, making them safe to add without fear of disrupting the effects of the elixir. The *nearly* part was the key. They had a magical effect capable of masking the most foul flavors with several pleasant choices. As long as the elixir was not also involved in changing the taste receptors, they wouldn't react negatively.

Similarly, there were ingredients for increasing potency. These were simply amplifiers that impacted the duration of the potion's effects. Unfortunately, the most powerful of these could only increase the duration to roughly a month. It was never exact, so if one wanted to sustain an effect, then another dose needed to be consumed before the first ran its full course.

Brinta was in the middle of brewing a large batch containing a year's worth of doses when Vex entered the shop. He still had his beard, but it did not look nearly as full and regal as it had the previous day. It was starting to look thin and patchy.

"Hello! I hope you're working on more of that beard growth potion. My beard is just about at the end of its temporary life," he said, scratching at the whiskers.

"I am," Brinta said as they added the ingredients that Trinx handed them. "Should taste a lot better, and you can expect it to last roughly a month. Like I mentioned at the club, you'll want to take it regularly to keep it looking full. We never talked price, but you also seemed to indicate price was no issue. I'm not going to gouge you. As the first customer, and in thanks for helping to test it, I'll just charge my costs for the first year's worth."

"Not a problem," Vex said. "I'm still very grateful and happy to pay that and even toss in some more. I'm sure you invested quite a bit during the testing. How much for this first year?"

"I'm setting you up with twenty-six doses, enough for you to take one every two weeks. Each dose has about two silver worth of ingredients."

"But don't forget all the time you put in," Vex said. "That and the failures. Here, have a gold piece. That seems more fair."

Trinx stared at the gold as he handed it over. Being the son of the warlord definitely had its perks. Without thinking, she blurted out, "Do you always walk around with that much coin?"

Brinta cast her a disapproving look, but Vex just laughed.

"No, not usually. But I knew I had to pay something for this elixir. Truth be told, I'm just glad the cost wasn't higher. I only brought the one gold piece and then I have some silver and copper, like I usually do for walking around money."

"That's very generous, Vex," Brinta said and swapped his coin for a box of small vials. "Here you go. Since your beard is looking pretty rough, take a dose now. You can let us know if we hit the taste right. Also, if you have any ideas for a name, I'm all ears."

Vex pulled a vial from the box, removed the lid, and emptied it into his mouth.

"Mmmm, smoked meat. Much better than the rat sh—" He cut off his words with a grunt as he gripped the counter. His patchy beard filled in, and soon, he had a luxurious chestnut beard again.

"I thought the meat flavor might work out for such a manly elixir," Trinx said proudly. "Any ideas on a name?"

Vex scratched at his fresh beard and said, "Not sure I'll ever get used to that itch. But a name. Hmmm. Something about hair or beards, obviously. The potions that never worked well for me took most of the good names. They are all I can think of right now."

"What's the name of the elixir we based this one on?" Trinx asked Brinta.

"Oh, it has a cheesy name. Hair Today, Beard Tomorrow," Brinta answered.

"That makes it sound like you have to wait for the beard," Trinx said, frowning. "What about InstaBeard? Or maybe since it even works in extreme cases like Vex, Beard From Scratch."

"That could work," Vex agreed. "Especially since I have to scratch my face after taking it because it itches so much."

"Love the wordplay," Brinta said. "We'll go with that, then: Beard From Scratch."

"Thanks again for all the work on this," Vex said, picking up the box. "I should get going. I have a number of things that need my attention today."

"See ya later, Vex," Trinx said with a wave.

"Let me know if anything odd happens," Brinta said. "It shouldn't, but sometimes side effects don't show up until later on."

Vex paused on his way out the door but said nothing. He just shook his head and continued on his way.

"I put this together this morning before you came in," Brinta said, pulling out a folder full of papers. "It's a derivative patent application. I just left out a few things I didn't know yet. I'll fill those in now."

"Does that make a big difference?" Trinx asked. "The derivative part?"

"It's much like the first one, but this one is based on that other formula, which has protections of its own," Brinta explained. "It means when we sell this potion, or others brew it for sale, a portion of the profit will go to the original IP holder. AARI magically enforces all of it."

They slid an application over to Trinx to read over and sign. Trinx read the parchment and then signed with the special pen Brinta used for these types of documents.

"Should I take these to the clerk like last time?"

The alchemist shook their head and said, "No. I'll take it. I have a couple of other errands to run near the clerk's office. You can stay here and work in the shop."

They packaged the documents, stuffed them in a large messenger-style bag, and slung the bag over their shoulders.

"I'll be back later. Just do what you can to get things in order."

"Sure thing," Trinx called after them as they left the shop.

She turned and looked around the room. Things weren't in horrible shape. She gathered up several ingredient containers and put them back on the storage shelves. Scanning the reagents, she saw they weren't really out of place that much. It took only a few swaps to put things in order.

The books needed straightening, so she ordered them, but there wasn't much else to do, at least not without more instruction. So, she grabbed a book the alchemist had said she couldn't take out of the lab. It seemed as good a time as any to learn what she could.

The title on the cover read *Advanced Alembic Alchemy*. Inside, she found recipes for several dangerous-sounding potions. Her skills had been improving, and she felt she could likely brew one of these if she focused.

As she was flipping through the pages, a recipe caught her eye. At the top of the page, she found the title *Traveler's Tonic*. Under it was a tagline that read, "Nodding off on long journeys? Let Traveler's Tonic keep sleep at bay."

The description was perfect, and she read it aloud to herself. "*Traveler's Tonic* may be used to ward off sleep indefinitely. Taking a small sip every few hours or when sleepiness manifests will remove the need for sleep. This tonic is the perfect solution for long journeys or other activities that may span multiple days. Once the mission is complete and the traveler stops sipping the tonic, the traveler must rest for a full day once sleepiness sets in. See Appendix D for a full list of potential side effects."

I'll be able to get so much more done with this, she thought.

She read over the ingredients and instructions. They were not overly complicated, and having recently organized the storage, she knew she had everything needed here in the shop. Trinx skipped looking up Appendix D and figured she could always look it over later. If it contained anything truly important, she was sure it would be listed here with the recipe.

But should she brew this tonic? Technically, Brinta had never told her she couldn't make things. They said Trinx couldn't take the book from the shop, not that she couldn't make the recipes they held. They'd probably just laugh and say, "You're welcome to try." She heard the words in her head as if the alchemist had actually spoken them. And, of course, she would clean up afterward.

Placing the book on a work counter, she gathered the ingredients, setting them out like she often did for the alchemist. She measured everything carefully and precisely, double-checking each step. The recipe came together even easier than she thought it would. It likely helped she used little tricks like reading several steps ahead to understand the purpose of the current step.

Before stirring in the last ingredient, she set out enough vials to hold it all. She added the last ingredient and stirred twice clockwise, four times counterclockwise, and twice clockwise again. The mixture glowed brightly and turned a brilliant shade of purple. She quickly filled all the vials and capped each one tightly.

After loading nineteen of the doses into a box with a five-by-four grid of holes, she tucked the box away in her bag and looked around the workspace. Brinta would likely be back soon, and the place needed to be tidy. Trinx had been tasked with straightening up the shop after all.

The lack of sleep from the night before was catching up with her, and she felt sluggish. So, she took a sip from the vial of tonic she had left out of the box. Its pleasant taste reminded her of thimbleberries. Immediately, the tension melted from her shoulders, and she felt the sleepiness recede. After tucking the rest of the vial into her bag, she looked around the room.

Trinx made quick work of putting the ingredients away and then put the book back on the shelf where it had been. Why did it feel like she was hiding something? She was learning, after all. That's why the alchemist had made her an apprentice—to learn. She was just being paranoid. She assured herself she would rationally observe and take notes if her paranoia continued.

The heavy stone door scraped lightly on the floor, and Brinta called, "Trinx, you still here?"

Exiting the back room, Trinx welcomed the alchemist with a smile. "Right here. I just finished straightening the bookshelves. How's it look in here?"

"Fabulous. Wonderful job," Brinta said while looking around appraisingly. "Now we can get to experimenting tomorrow. I was thinking on the walk and have a few ideas I remember from Phylo. Perhaps we should sketch some of them out to prepare for tomorrow?"

"That sounds great," Trinx said. "However, I can't stay much longer. I still need to get to the tavern."

"Of course," Brinta said. "Leave whenever you need. We can work until then. So, I recalled he had a serum for dosing milk-producing farm animals like cows and goats. It enlarges the udder and grows additional teats."

Wrinkling her face, Trinx said firmly, "I do not want an udder, and my nipples better not turn out that large." She broke into laughter, unable to hold a straight face.

"I warned you that there may be some undesired growths during the experiments," Brinta said with a playful smirk.

"Just make sure we keep it very temporary," Trinx said, rolling her eyes. "But still, let's avoid an udder if we can?"

The two of them spent the next hour reading through Phylo's book and jotting down ideas and recipe variations in a notebook. Trinx definitely had a knack for brewing potions and elixirs correctly. However, the creative ideas for modifying them spilling out of Brinta were fascinating.

Noting the time, Trinx grabbed her bag and said, "I better get going. I might actually be there right on time if I leave now."

The alchemist looked up briefly from their notes to wave but was too much in the zone to engage any more.

"Trinxy? Right on time?" Gristle asked. "Q barely made it here today. Said she slept in very late after a party ye all had last night. Figured ye wouldn't be poking yer nose round here until later, if at all."

While she didn't have the energy to skip across the room, she felt as awake as ever and walked with determination toward the kitchen.

Pausing briefly at the end of the bar, she said, "Guess I got all the sleep I needed, or maybe work at the alchemy shop invigorated me?"

"Looks pretty busy this evening," she said, scanning the room. "I'll get ready and start picking up orders."

She pushed open the door to the kitchen and found Quilka pouring out some dragonroot tea for the both of them. Her friend looked up. "Well, I thought you'd be needing a fresh cup of tea to make it through the shift. From the looks of it, you already had some? I can't believe you look so awake."

"Always good to have more tea," Trinx said, grabbing a cup Quilka had just poured milk into. "Thanks for thinking of making me some. You're so good to me."

Her friend moved roughly half as fast but took up her own cup and sipped. "I'm just glad you are here, and I'm not dealing with that crowd all alone tonight."

Trinx laughed and broke into a wide smile. "Never going to leave you hanging, Q. I'll head right out there." She took a big swallow of the hot tea, singeing her mouth slightly, but not enough to slow her down.

The shift flew by, and she only had to stop for a small sip of the tonic once when she had begun to feel run down. Quilka headed straight home after finishing her portion of the chores, while she continued to not only finish hers, but she helped Brizla and Gristle with theirs.

At home, Trinx curled up in bed with a book. With Phylo's book at the shop, she tried reading *The Wondrous Uses of Monster Parts* instead. She found a page on a mimic's mana locator gland particularly interesting. Whenever she felt her eyelids begin to droop, she took a small sip of the tonic and perked right back up. She read through the entire book that night and found she didn't feel tired at all. Though, at times, it was difficult to keep her focus or keep her mind from wandering.

Chapter 19

A Slow Process

Once the morning officially arrived, Trinx cleaned herself up and dressed in fresh clothes. Transitioning right into the new day without spending time unconscious in bed felt strange. Considering how often she needed multiple alarms to pull herself into consciousness, this was a welcome change. The best part was not having to worry about being late.

On her walk to the shop, her stomach, once again rattled from within. It demanded food, and she had not yet eaten, so she stopped at a Mystic Leaf and picked up a basket of muffins. The scent of warm spices escaped the cloth covering them, and the smell of fresh baked goods teased her nose.

When she entered Distilled Magic, Brinta eagerly eyed the basket. "Oh! Are those muffins from Mystic? Please tell me you brought enough to share."

Trinx nodded and placed the basket on the counter. Her stomach had been gearing up from the aroma during the walk, so she took one for herself after handing one to the alchemist. They both enjoyed the dense, chewy bran muffins filled with nuts and berries. It took two of them to settle her belly.

"Did you get enough sleep last night?" Brinta asked after swallowing her bite of muffin. "You have some dark circles under your eyes."

"I think I probably got enough," Trinx said as she thought how best to fully answer. For some reason, she wasn't sure it made sense to tell Brinta about the tonic she had made. It almost seemed like not telling her when she had returned to the shop yesterday made it seem too late to do so today.

"It's always hard to tell, but if my body is getting me around, it should have been enough."

"Hmmm," they hummed. "Could just be left over from the night before when you had so little sleep. Besides the eyes, you look chipper enough. Ready for some experimenting?"

"You bet!" she exclaimed.

The experiments proved tougher without a base to work from. After a full day of failures, they had only one solid lead toward a workable formula. However, that was primarily because only one hadn't evaporated, exploded, or caused some other minor catastrophe.

She stayed busy all day as they tried various combinations to make a stable base but never exerted herself too much. As needed, she would sip a bit of the tonic to ward off the sleepiness.

Maybe Quilka would have some tea made. That would perk her up. She was great that way, always doing small things for her. Waving goodbye to Brinta, Trinx left for the tavern.

After the walk to the Tender, she didn't feel tired as much as just blah. The tonic didn't give her energy or help her focus —it just kept the sleep away. Some dragonroot would definitely help.

Inside, customers filled half of the tables. Gristle poured

drinks for a group gathered at the bar and simply nodded to her in acknowledgment.

"Hey, Gris. I'll grab a tray and help once I've had some tea."

When she entered the kitchen, Brizla was making meat pies. The cook had just pulled a fresh one out of the oven and carved slices for the plates waiting on Quilka's tray.

"Is there any tea? I could really use a cup today," Trinx asked.

Quilka shifted the loaded plates on her tray to distribute the weight. "Sorry, Trinx, we've been busy."

"Don't even worry about it," Trinx said. "I just thought there might be, but I get to make it for us for a change. I'll get it steeping and check on some customers. It should be ready once you make it back to the kitchen."

She went to the stove and filled a teapot with dragonroot and hot water from the Kwikbrew. Quilka left with the tray of food, and Trinx followed soon after with an empty tray to find a table of customers to help. Out in the main area of the tavern, she spied two hobgoblins chatting at an empty two-top.

"Good evening! Can I get you two something to eat or drink?"

The hobs paused their conversation, and one said, "Ah, great. We were hoping someone would be by soon. We'll each take an ale and some of that meat pie we've been smelling. Is that thyme in the gravy?"

"Could be. I'll check with Brizla when I grab your pies," she said and turned to leave.

Trinx caught Gristle's eye, pointed to the table, and flashed two fingers. By the time she reached the bar, he had two mugs of ale waiting for her. After loading them on the tray, she dropped them off with the hobs and then returned to the kitchen.

Quilka was standing, taking a hurried sip of tea. She had poured a cup for Trinx, who said, "Thank you so much. This should help put a bit more bounce in my step."

"Thank you for making it," her friend said with a warm smile. "I didn't realize how much I needed it until I started drinking. But now I have to get back out there."

Trinx nodded. "I get it. Just having a quick sip myself and need to deliver some meat pies to that two-top with the hobs."

"Thanks for checking on them," Quilka said and left the kitchen with a tray full of food.

Trinx soon followed to deliver the meat pies, which did, in fact, have thyme in the gravy. The rest of the shift went smoothly, and she only needed to sip her tonic once when she could have sworn iron plates began to weigh down her eyelids.

By the end of her shift, her stomach had begun rumbling and shifting regularly, so she sat down to eat some of the left-over meat pie with Quilka.

"Did you ever catch what type of meat is in the pie tonight? It has a slightly gamey flavor, but it's sweet. I think that blends nicely with the spices Brizla used."

"I wish I didn't like it as much as I do," Quilka said with a sigh. "It's bunnycorn. They are just *so* cute. I always feel bad eating them. Not so bad that I'm willing to miss out on this flavor, mind you."

"They may be cute, but there's a reason no one ever has a pet bunnycorn," Trinx said as she swallowed another bite and licked the rich sauce from her spoon. "They can be vicious. I've heard rumors we've even lost an entire raiding squad to them before."

"You're right," Quilka admitted. "I've heard those same rumors. I wonder what they do with the horns."

"I know that one," Trinx said, her face beaming. "We've got a jar of powered bunnycorn horn in the backroom at Distilled

Magic. I can't remember what it's best for, but it is definitely an alchemy component."

"If you're done eating, I suggest you clean up so we can close down for the night," Gristle said when he poked his head into the kitchen. He had a point, and Brizla had already left for the evening.

The two women cleaned up the small remaining mess in the kitchen and walked out together.

"Bye, Gris, see you tomorrow," Trinx called.

Gristle shook his head. His mouth pulled up at the corners, causing his lower fangs to look longer than usual. He watched them leave the tavern and went back to wrapping up the closing routine.

Back in her apartment, Trinx put on a kettle to boil and pulled out the latest book she had borrowed from the shop. The book bore the title *Alchemical Solutions of the Bunadh Clan*. She hadn't been very sure it would help in any of her current endeavors to create a full-body transformation, but it had looked interesting, and she thought it would help expand her expertise with alchemy.

She spent the night reading the dwarven alchemical recipes, taking several breaks to sip her tonic, make a fresh cup of tea, or eat a small snack. It seemed she needed to eat more when she went without sleep—or she at least *wanted* to. It was hard to tell the difference.

Eventually, an alarm sounded and yanked her attention away from the book. She had decided to set an alarm, much like she had when she slept. There was no reason to be late anymore if she was already awake. She just needed to make sure she had enough time to get ready for the day.

Looking in the mirror, she sat down to apply some makeup. She definitely needed it. The circles under her eyes Brinta had commented on were more prominent. The tonic clearly didn't push off all the side effects of foregoing sleep. However, a little concealer would cover the circles. Her mind was awake enough, even if her body was beginning to show weariness. After pulling her hair into a ponytail, she picked out a dress and headed to the shop.

Unfortunately, the day yielded many failures at the lab bench, and she felt completely drained by the end of the experiments.

"This is never going to work, is it?" she bemoaned.

Brinta chuckled. "It's only been a couple of days. You know this can be a slow process. Look how long the other trials took, and we had something to start with for those."

She frowned, creasing her brow. "Still, you'd think we'd have something more than a bunch of wasted ingredients. Maybe I don't have the patience for alchemy. I think that's probably enough for today. I gotta get to the tavern, anyway."

"I don't believe that," Brinta said. "You have plenty of talent, but maybe patience isn't your best quality. Still, you have fun trying these experiments, don't you?"

"I do," Trinx said, the thought bringing a smile to her face. "There's that moment when you're about to put in the last ingredient, and something tickles your brain like it's teasing you. Will it work, or won't it? That bite-sized mystery that needs an answer."

"See. I knew the curiosity was in there," Brinta said and slapped the counter for emphasis. "Please put these reagents we used in the last trial away before you head out."

"Of course. No problem," Trinx agreed, gathering the jars and bottles into a box to take to the back room. "I just wish more of those little mystery presents had something good in them. That's when the payoff really hits, and my brain gets a super dose of excitement."

Trinx took the box into the back and found homes for

each of the items on the stock shelves. She put the book from the Bunadh clan back on the shelf and took another that looked interesting: *Knob's Effervescent Elixirs*. She tucked the gnomish volume in her bag and left the shop for the Tender.

Trinx opened the door to the tavern and found the room nearly full. Only two small tables were open, and Quilka was zipping around, checking on the customers. Her friend noticed her and waved with a smile. Gristle nodded and pointed to the kitchen. So, she walked into the back area to grab an apron and a tray and see what Brizla was cooking.

Butter melted on top of loaves of cornbread resting on a side counter. Brizla stood stirring a pot of thick stew that smelled of tomato, spicy peppers, and rockhorn meat. Trinx's stomach leapt forward, but she had no time for a bowl of stew. Instead, she popped a small piece of the cornbread into her mouth and left the kitchen to help balance the tables and relieve Quilka. She was sure there would be time to eat later.

One of the two-tops she had seen open on the way in now had a pair of goblins she recognized sitting at it.

"Glink, Zurt, what can I start you with? Brizla has cooked up a spicy rockhorn stew this evening."

"Hey, Trinx," Glink said. "Couple ales to start, but we can both use some food, too."

"Sure thing," Trinx said and walked to the bar to get the mugs of ale.

On her way back to their table, Trinx tripped on nothing and her tray with the full mugs went flying from her hands. She really hadn't tripped on anything. It was more that her feet had lost focus and tangled up and forgot how to work right. Shattered glass and foamy puddles of alcohol filled the floor ahead of her and continued under the table that had been her destination.

"I'll get a mop," Quilka called while running to the back room.

Trinx looked embarrassed and shuffled to the bar, mumbling, "Sorry, Gris. Can I get a couple more?"

He shook his head more to himself than her and put two more mugs full of amber ale onto the counter for her.

"Try to be more careful this time, Trinxy."

She nodded and loaded the drinks onto her tray. Trinx took the long way around the mess and managed to deliver the fresh mugs without spilling any more of the alcohol.

"Don't worry about nuthin," Glink said.

"Yeah, t'was more funny than anything else," Zurt agreed.

"Glad you find it funny," Trinx said in a whimsical tone. "For an encore, you can watch me clean it up."

Quilka returned, juggling a mop, a broom, a dustpan, and a bucket. "Little help?"

"Thanks, Q," Trinx said as she grabbed the broom and dustpan.

She swept the broken glass and emptied the dustpan into the bucket of water. Trinx mopped the floor to clean up the ale and any remaining bits of glass. Once she and Quilka were done, they took everything out behind the tavern. There was a faucet on the backside of the building they used to rinse everything before putting the broken glass in a large garbage can.

"I have to run an errand this evening," Quilka told her. "Gristle already gave me the go-ahead, but I wanted to make sure you could handle everything while I'm gone. Especially after that accident. What happened anyway?"

"I don't know," Trinx said, shrugging. "I guess my feet forgot what way they were supposed to walk. But don't worry. I have things covered."

"Thanks, Trinx," Quilka said and gave her a quick hug.

The next few hours were less exciting, and she sipped on a

cup of tea she left on the kitchen counter whenever she passed. At one point, she had taken a brief break to take a sip of the tonic. It hadn't perked her up, but it had stifled the yawns she'd felt coming on. Thankfully, the tea kept her feeling good, and she made it to the end of the shift without any more significant messes to clean.

Since Quilka left early, Trinx didn't feel like eating a late-night meal in the tavern without her friend. Instead, she packed up a hefty portion of the stew and a large hunk of the cornbread. Her study sessions throughout the night needed fuel.

Over the course of the night, she made it through a cursory reading of the entire gnomish text she'd brought home, taking care to keep her food away from the book. The last thing she needed was to explain to Brinta why the book smelled of spicy peppers and rockhorn, so she snacked on the food from the tavern while standing in the kitchen at the sink. It wasn't nearly as relaxing as sitting down, but the bed was her only furniture, and she hadn't wanted cornbread crumbs in her sheets.

The gnomish recipes were interesting, but many of them focused on industrial solutions useful in factories. She found many oils and lubricants but nothing that would directly help her quest, not that she had expected to. At least she picked up some techniques for making reductions that might be applicable over a wide variety of use cases.

When morning approached, she flipped off her alarm before it could sound and drew a hot bath. Her tonic was keeping away the sleep, but her body protested at the constant exertion. It didn't seem to matter that she had just sat on the bed reading all night. The bath was most welcome.

She added a small amount of bubbling soap while the water filled the tub before she slid down into the fluffy pile of white, sudsy bubbles. Setting her music player to random, she enjoyed a nice long bath, scrubbing lightly at her body to clean any grime from the past few days. Her muscles relaxed, and she almost let herself fall asleep.

Instead, she realized what was happening and shook herself awake. That had been close. She knew from the instructions on the tonic that in order to stop taking it, she just had to allow sleep to come naturally. However, she was not ready to fall asleep for a full day while in the tub. A fit of giggles helped wake her up as she thought of what she might look like as a shriveled green prune.

That was it for the bath. One close call was enough. She climbed out and toweled off before making up her face and slipping on a purple dress. The thought of prunes had put the ideas of plums in her head, and she felt the dress was just the thing for it.

Trinx put a fresh vial of tonic in her bag after taking a small sip, shut off the music player, and left for Distilled Magic, imagining at least one of today's experiments actually working instead of ending in a minor explosion.

Chapter 20

Do You Smell a Rat?

"I've been making my way through the books I've been borrowing," Trinx said as she put her bag down under a workstation at Distilled Magic. "Unfortunately, I haven't found any direct ideas for body transformation, but Phylo's book might be best on that topic. It's all helped with my understanding of alchemy, so no time wasted. Is that the transformation potion you have cooking this morning?"

"It is," Brinta said. "Come and join in. After going through Phylo's work some more, I realized we maybe don't have to start fully from scratch. I first joked about his potion to increase milk production in a cow or goat. But after reading his notes more carefully, I think it might help to start there. If we can take a bull and craft a potion capable of giving the bull some udders, it may yield a base we could work from."

"Does it have to be a cow? Or a bull?" Trinx asked. "I don't know about you, but I don't have a barn full of cows attached to my small apartment. Could we use a smaller animal?"

"That's a very solid point," Brinta agreed. "In fact, I don't actually have any cows. But I could get some rats. It's already going smoother now that you're here to help. Let's brew the potion as-is for now, and then we can see if it works the same on a rat as it does on a cow."

"You know, um," Trinx started before realizing she didn't know what she was going to say. She had been reading over the potion formula during the conversation and knew she wanted to add something, but what it was escaped her. She continued reading until her brain clicked with the answer. *Oh, that's right, rats.*

"You don't think the experiments will hurt the rats, do you?" Trinx asked. "I'd hate to be torturing them, even if they are rats."

"That's quite commendable of you," Brinta said. "I don't believe they should be in much danger. I have a contact who is an exterminator. Since he usually just kills them anyway, it works out well for both of us. Just because they are rats doesn't mean I inflict undue harm, and like with goblins, I make sure everything is very temporary."

"Oh!" Trinx said. "That doesn't sound so bad. Should I go and pick up a cage of rats from your friend, then?"

"If you don't mind," Brinta replied. "That would be quite helpful. I can continue putting together the potion so that we can test it when you return. Just make sure he gives us both male and female rats. His name is Pox, and he can usually be found out on a job or in his home office in the southwestern portion of the warren."

Brinta fished around under the counter and pulled out a lockbox. After opening it with a small key, they pulled out an empty pouch and added some coins to it.

Handing it to Trinx, they said, "This should compensate him well enough for the rats. He lives in a tunnel named Gritstone, which is a loop off of Hinox. You know Hinox, right?"

"Oh, yeah, sure. I walk Hinox practically every day," Trinx

said as she picked up the coin pouch. "I'm sure I'll be able to find Pox. Before I head out, I'll make sure you have all the ingredients you'll need."

"Thanks," Brinta called after her as she disappeared into the backroom.

Trinx pulled all the ingredients she remembered from the formula she had read over in the other room. She put the bottles in a crate and hauled it back to the workbenches.

"Here you go. Now you don't have to go rummaging around for them. I'll be back in a bit."

"Excellent. Be sure to say hi to Pox for me," Brinta said while waving after Trinx, who was already on the way out the door.

Once she reached Hinox, she began to pay attention to the signs on the haphazard smaller tunnels branching off the principal thoroughfare. Before long, she spotted the small sign marking Gritstone. There was a large cavern with several buildings off the tunnel loop. A two-story building with a sign containing a spring-loaded trap caught her eye. Sure enough, when she got closer, the sign read, "Extermination Services by Pox."

Trinx walked up to the yellow-painted wooden door and gave it a solid knock. She thought she heard something from inside, but the door remained closed. Taking a moment to look around, she noted that there were twelve small bushes growing in planter boxes. She counted them again, just to be sure she hadn't missed any. Then, she reached up and gave the door two more quick knocks.

Now, she was sure she heard something inside and the noises were getting louder. The door opened with a whimpering whine from the hinges. A goblin who looked to be in his late twenties or early thirties peered out at her. He had a wart on his left nostril that drew her attention in an uncomfortable way. She didn't want to look at it and usually made a habit of ignoring physical oddities, but for some reason, this particular feature kept drawing her eye. His dirty-blonde beard also appeared slightly singed. *What might have caused that?*

"Can I help yeh?" he asked.

"I hope so," Trinx said. "Are you Pox? Brinta sent me. We need some rats. They said Pox should be able to get us a cage full of them. They're for an experiment. But I guess that only matters if you are Pox. Are you?"

"Aye, that's me," Pox affirmed in a scratchy voice. "I can get yeh a cage of them. Matter of fact, just did a job this morning. Was gonna put 'em down, but now I can offload them on yeh. Brinta happen to send along some coin? Most folks figure rats aren't much value, and they be right about that. Even so, some coins always help. Come on in."

"Don't the folks who hire you pay you for your services?" Trinx asked while entering the exterminator's shop.

"Seems like getting paid to collect them up and then paid again to rid yourself of them is..." she trailed off as the odor of the room assaulted her nose. The smell was musky, mixed with acidic urine and an undertone of stale rat droppings.

Not sure of where she was going with that thought as it jumped right out of her head, she said, "Sorry. Don't even know why I asked. But yes, Brinta sent some coins." She handed him the pouch, and he gave it a shake before slipping it into a pocket.

"Oh, don't worry about the questions," Pox rasped. "Good instincts. That's exactly what I'm doing. That's the beauty of this job. Doesn't always work out that way, but when it does, well. Well, it certainly helps. Let me go get that cage from this morning."

A muffled cacophony of squeaking escaped the door the goblin had left through. Trinx took a moment to look around the cluttered room. Stacks of cages of different sizes were piled haphazardly against the walls. Several large bins held an assortment of traps, from common spring-loaded snapping bars to large snapping jaws with wicked teeth. One wall had shelves crammed full of bottles and sprayers holding noxious liquids and vapors. From the looks of things, it seemed Pox could handle a wide variety of pests and likely even some large beasts.

Her eye caught movement as Pox pushed the door open with his back. Once he was sufficiently in the room, he turned and stepped forward with a large wire cage in his hands, letting the door swing shut behind him.

"This should do for Brinta. Tends to like a variety. Got some big ones and smaller ones, too. Got some bucks and does."

He lifted the cage out from himself toward Trinx, who took it and said, "Thank you. I'm sure this should provide Brinta with plenty of options for test subjects." Looking at the writhing, squeaking swarm of rats in the cage, she wasn't exactly sure how much she meant the thanks. Her nose involuntarily wrinkled at the sight.

"Excellent," he said while dusting his hands. "If yeh needs more, just come on by again. Never a shortage of rats in the warren. I'll get the door for yeh. That cage is a bit much but wanted to get Brinta's money's worth."

He was right. The cage *was* too much. It was difficult to hold in her arms. The constant movements of the rats inside kept shifting the weight, forcing her to concentrate in order to keep it steady and avoid dropping it. Trinx didn't love holding it against her body but holding it in outstretched arms would be very difficult. The thought of the rats being so close to her made her skin crawl. With effort, she managed, and left the shop through the door Pox held open for her.

On the way back to the shop, Trinx noticed she was receiving a lot of unwanted attention from the goblins crowding the tunnels. She likely would have stared, too, if she saw someone hugging a large cage full of squirming rats while walking the streets of the warren. She hurried, partly to outrun the eyes watching her and partly just to get to the shop so she could put this smelly cage down somewhere. The musky odor from the rats made her nose wiggle, and she hoped it wouldn't permeate her clothes. Smelling like a swarm of rats for the rest of the day would not do.

When Trinx reached Distilled Magic, she copied the move Pox had used and pushed open the iron door with her back. Brinta looked up and smirked upon seeing her.

"Go ahead and put the cage down against the back wall. By now, you likely figured out why I didn't insist on going myself when you offered to fetch them."

"Hilarious," Trinx moaned. "You know, these things are disgusting. I don't even know how Pox operates in that shop. The smell was not pleasant."

"Not just operating," Brinta said. "He also lives there. The upper floor is his home. I'm sure most of the smell and noise are contained below, but some must travel up to his living quarters." The alchemist shuddered.

Trinx set the cage on the floor in the back corner and went to the sink to scrub her skin. "Probably. The smell was pretty strong. Did you get very far with the potion?"

"I did, in fact," Brinta said. "I brewed the original potion, just as Phylo described. The first thing we want to test is whether it works regardless of the type of animal. I have a few smaller cages in the back. Can you grab one? We'll want to isolate the test subjects to make observing easier."

There were two small cages in the back room, and Trinx grabbed one before walking back into the main room. Brinta had pulled out a doe from the large cage. The rat wriggled and squirmed in their hands. The alchemist dropped it into the cage after Trinx set it on the worktable and closed the hatch.

"I'm going to add a bit of sugar to the potion," Brinta explained. "It should not react and change the effects, but it should entice the rat to drink it. They like sugary drinks and snacks."

Trinx watched as the alchemist measured out some of the potion into a small bowl and stirred in some sugar. They then placed the bowl in the small cage and yanked their hand away to avoid a nip from the eager rat. It seemed they would not need to coax the rat into consuming it.

That rat flicked its tongue into the bowl, pulling up mouthfuls of the liquid. After a few moments, she stopped drinking and backed away. The rat rubbed her body against the mesh of the cage. If Trinx had to guess, it looked like it itched a lot. Before long, the rat calmed down and stopped pressing itself into the wall of the cage, but the underside of the rat looked swollen. All six pairs of nipples were now clearly visible and had grown in size. While not a full udder like a cow, the skin holding the two rows was fuller and bulged from the body.

Brinta clapped their hands. "Wonderful! I'm so glad that worked. I had a good feeling it would, but one must always experiment and test to be sure. Phylo suggests the potion can be used on a variety of milk-producing animals—not just cows. The notes specifically call out cows and goats, but I think we can officially add rats to the list as well. Not that I want to actually milk this rat."

"So, this increases the chances our final potion will work on a wide variety of species, even goblins?" Trinx asked.

"Yes," Brinta said with a nod. "I'd like to think so anyway. Cows and rats are quite different, but this worked as expected on the rat. I don't see any reason it wouldn't work on even more species, even sapient ones. But this is not the only test."

"Right," Trinx said enthusiastically. "We need to see what happens on a buck!"

Brinta returned the test subject to the larger cage and pulled out another rat. The alchemist brought it over and placed the buck in the small cage. It immediately started lapping at the potion. Much like the doe had, the buck began scratching himself against the wall of the cage. He eventually settled down, and Trinx could see the underside looked swollen, just like the previous rat.

"Look!" Trinx exclaimed. "I think it worked. See the swollen underside?"

"I see it," Brinta said. "It's a good sign, but let's take a closer look."

The alchemist pulled the rat from the cage, and he squirmed in their hands. Unfortunately, while the torso of the rat had enlarged, it had no nipples.

"I'm afraid it's close but not there yet," Brinta said. "Don't worry. It can't be that far off based on the resulting swelling."

Working together, the two brewed an alternate version based on an idea Brinta had. However, it did not achieve the results they were looking for. It was never as much fun to end a day on a failure, but the evening was already well underway.

"I think this is a good place to wrap up for today," Brinta said. "You're welcome to borrow Phylo's book this evening. I won't be needing it. Of course, I'm not sure how you have time to fit in reading. But that shouldn't stop you from taking it, just in case."

"Thanks, Brinta," Trinx said as she scooped up Phylo's book and a couple of others into her bag. She then slung it over his shoulder and, with a wave, walked out of the alchemy shop and toward the tavern. The heaviness in her eyelids faded as she took another sip of the tonic while she walked.

For some reason, the Tender was quiet that evening. There

were enough customers, but never too many, and certainly not all at once. Toward the end of the slow shift, she and Quilka sat down for a meal.

"So, it seems one of the exterminators in the warren is named Pox," Trinx said as she cut her sandwich in half. Thin slices of pink vornash formed a mound that was likely a little too high between two halves of a fluffy white roll. She pulled out a couple of slices to shrink the sandwich. "Brinta had me collect a huge cage of rats from him for our experiments."

She popped the slices of meat into her mouth. The thin slices practically melted in her mouth as she chewed gently.

Quilka giggled and almost choked on the bite she had been chewing. "That's an ironic name."

"Yeah, I thought so too. He seemed nice enough and gave me plenty of rats. Too many, if you ask me. It was hard to carry them back to the shop," Trinx said and dipped her sandwich into a bowl filled with a salty brown broth.

"So, you are testing the potion on rats?" Quilka asked. "I like that idea better than you trying random potions yourself."

"Brinta is pretty careful when we experiment on ourselves," Trinx explained. "We never add any extension ingredients until we know it works as intended. So, unless it kills you, it's more annoying than anything else."

"Hmmm, okay," Quilka said, taking a bite of the sandwich she had just dipped in her bowl of broth. A rivulet of the liquid escaped and ran down her chin. She wiped it away with a finger. "Just make sure you don't go trying one that actually kills you, then."

"I'll be careful," Trinx promised. "But I'll have to try some, eventually. Once we get past the stages where we can run on animals like the rats, that is."

Chapter 21

Snixil and Nibbles

Trinx put her bag down and slipped into a pair of comfortable linen pants and an old baggy shirt. Curling up on the bed with her feet under her, she pulled a blanket up onto her shoulders and opened *The Wondrous Uses of Monster Parts*. She read through the night until the words began to swim in front of her eyes. Blinking, she cleared the bleariness away.

"I should take a break from the tonic and get some actual sleep," she said to the empty room as if saying it out loud might somehow convince her to actually do so.

As it turned out, that wasn't enough to convince her, and instead, she took a sip of her tonic. *Who needs sleep anyway?*

She pulled herself out of the cozy nest she had been reading in and found a tin containing a few gingersnap cookies.

Happy to have a small snack, Trinx climbed back onto the bed, this time sitting crisscross with Phylo's book in her lap. She nibbled on a gingersnap as she engrossed herself in the book. The most curious thing to her about this book, as well as several of the others she had read, was that each time she picked it up to read, she gained more information and insights into alchemy. This held true even when she read the exact same text she had previously read through. The text clearly wasn't changing, but her ability to pull new information out kept improving each time she read the books.

Once more, weights began to pull her eyelids down, which made it very hard to continue reading. She thought another sip of the tonic should take her the rest of the way through until morning. She ate a couple more cookies to feed it and looked at the small pile of books on the bed.

"You know," she spoke to no one in particular. "I haven't cleaned the kitchen or bathroom in quite some time."

With a nod to herself, she grabbed several rags, a bucket, and some soap. She spent the rest of the night meticulously cleaning her sinks, toilet, and bathtub. Trinx turned on her music player and queued up a playlist of cleaning songs. She scrubbed every counter and then swept the floor for good measure. Surprisingly, she had enough energy for all of those tasks. The time slipped by more quickly than when she had been reading.

As morning approached, Trinx's kitchen and bathroom were cleaner than they had been in quite some time. She had really been ignoring the less important tasks when juggling her two jobs. As she made a final trip around the room with the broom, she swept around several piles of various items.

Trinx thought briefly of doing something about the piles, but even with her energy, she just couldn't muster enough to deal with them. Besides, piles were often the best way to organize things. Trying to find a specific home for them could be tedious and a pile could be a perfectly fine home.

However, when she swept around some empty tea jugs, she noticed the containers had "Mystic Leaf & Toadstool" stenciled on them, along with their logo.

"I don't suppose I can complain about not having any money if I just leave it piled up in a corner," she admitted to the empty room. "First task tomorrow, or I guess it's today, isn't it? Is to take these to Mystic and return them for the deposits."

Mystic wouldn't be open yet, so Trinx put together a small plate and ate some crackers and cheese. She was getting used to not sleeping and wondered why more people didn't put off sleep. It seemed like such a waste of time now that she wasn't doing it. However, she still remembered how nice it could be to bury her head in a pillow and see what her dreams brought. But not today. Today, she had things to do.

Trinx slung her bag over her shoulder and headed out the door. A moment later, she popped the door right back open, muttering, "Worg's breath," and grabbed two of the Mystic jugs. After three trips to the tea shop, while she was walking back to her apartment for what should be the last time, some movement down an alley caught her attention.

A young goblin, younger than Trinx by several years, likely in her early to mid-teens, played with a raccoon outside a tent. The movement from their game had caught her eye, but the tent made her curious.

Walking down the alley, she saw the goblin had long, dark-brown hair and wore a simple blue dress stained in several areas. Dirt covered her face and limbs. Getting closer still, the goblin and the raccoon froze. They both looked up at Trinx, which she found quite funny, especially the animal's curious gaze.

"Hi," she opened. "I'm Trinx. I saw you playing down this alley, but then I saw the tent. Are you camping out here? In an alley? Or are you living here?"

The goblin looked wary. "I'm not hurting no one. Please don't call the guards."

"I'm not calling anyone," Trinx said with a smile. "I just

thought you looked young to be on your own, and an alley isn't a good home."

The young one petted the raccoon, and the animal settled at her feet. "Sorry, others have done that. Can't be too careful. I'm Sk—I mean Snixil." She tripped over her name, catching it partway and changing direction.

"And what's your friend's name?" Trinx asked.

"Oh, him?" Snixil said, looking down at her pet. "This is Nibbles. You hafta watch him. He nibbles just about anything that he gets his paws on."

"Hi, Nibbles," Trinx said to the raccoon. "It's nice to meet you and Snixil." Turning to the goblin, she asked, "Can I pet him?"

Snixil shoulders relaxed when she saw Trinx talking to her pet rather than her. She nodded, and Trinx came closer, reaching down to pet the masked animal. She noticed as she did so that not all the darkness on the goblin's skin was dirt. Snixil had a lot of hair on her arms and legs, and she didn't have a full beard, but there was thick growth on her face.

The young goblin noticed the glances at her arms and face and then spoke with some defiance in her voice, "It doesn't matter, really. Not everyone can have perfectly smooth skin like you. Besides, it helps out here on the streets. It can get cold sometimes."

"Oh, I'm sure it does," Trinx said while petting the raccoon. "I wasn't going to say anything. I think goblins should be able to live however they want."

"Good," Snixil said curtly. "Cause that's what I'm doing. Living life my way. Never mind what he thinks."

"He who?" Trinx asked.

"What?" Snixil asked in reply. "I didn't say anything. Never mind. Anyway, I live my life my way. Just me and Nibbles."

"Still, you must have some trouble out here," Trinx said. "Are you hungry? Do you mind if I come back by sometime and give you some food and supplies? It doesn't look like you have much here in this alley."

The young goblin shrugged noncommittally. "I guess. Wouldn't say no to food, that is. Nibbles might want some too."

"Deal," Trinx said as she stood up. "I'll come back later with some things for you. Take care of yourself out here, okay?"

"Thanks, ma'am," Snixil said and waved goodbye.

The title struck her. This was the first time anyone had called her ma'am. Compared to this young goblin, she was older. But really, was it that much? Maybe she was just acting older these days.

"See you later," Trinx said.

At home, she realized she didn't really have that much to give Snixil. She needed to do some shopping, and even then, what she bought wouldn't be impressive. Still, the young goblin deserved something nice.

"I know!" Trinx announced to her apartment and grabbed up the last two empty jugs, leaving a lot more space in her room.

Trinx returned the final two jugs to the Mystic teahouse she had already been to several times that morning. She now had a small pouch of spending money from the returns and used a portion of it to purchase three muffins. Returning to the alley, she found Nibbles standing guard outside the tent.

Approaching the shelter, Trinx said, "Hi, Nibbles. Is Snixil inside?"

Upon hearing her name, Snixil stuck her head out. "Oh! You're back. I didn't think you meant so soon."

"I've been running errands this morning," Trinx explained. "I had to return several tea jugs to Mystic. Since I was there anyway, I thought maybe I could bring you and Nibbles something.”

“Really?” Snixil’s eyes lit up, and she crawled the rest of the way out of the tent.

“Yup,” Trinx said and held out the paper bag. “I bought us all some muffins. Even one for Nibbles.”

“Wow, that’s very nice of you. They smell fresh and delicious.” She took the bag, peaking inside with a smile on her face. “Did you want to sit down?”

“I’d love to,” Trinx said and folded herself into a crisscross sitting position, leaning against the wall of a building.

The young goblin took a muffin from the bag and put it on the ground near the tent. She made a curt whistle, and Nibbles pounced on the baked treat. After giving the raccoon a scritch on the head, she took another muffin before handing the bag to Trinx.

“Thanks,” Trinx said and pulled the remaining muffin out. She took a bite and found the tender cake-like bread full of dried thimbleberries, talisnuts, and cloves. “Wow, these are amazing.”

Nibbles clearly agreed as the raccoon had almost finished his muffin. Snixil took a large bite and then asked through puffy cheeks, “Did you make’em? Very good.”

“Oh, no. These are from Mystic,” Trinx said, pushing away the credit. “Maybe I’ll try baking you something sometime, but don’t expect it to be this good. I’m not known for my baking skills. I wonder how related baking and alchemy are? They both have recipes.”

“Alchemy? Why would you wonder that? I don’t think you can make baked treats with alchemy,” Snixil said, making a face like she was trying to figure out what she was missing.

“Because I’m an Alchemist!” Trinx exclaimed. “Or an

apprentice, at least. I've been studying. It's a very important job. Brinta and I are working on important potions."

"Who's Brinta? She's an alchemist, too?" Snixil asked, seemingly becoming more engaged in the conversation.

"Yes, they are an alchemist. A really good one," Trinx said. "I'm learning so much. We made this one cream, and it's ridiculous how cool it is. It removes excess hair and leaves smooth skin behind and even lasts for like a whole month."

"That sounds really useful," Snixil said, glancing at her arm and then immediately flicking her attention back to Trinx.

"Not to be too presumptuous, but I'm pretty sure you and I are a lot alike," Trinx said. "I used to have that much hair on my arms, legs, and face, too. But, thanks to EverSmooth, it's gone. I could bring you some if you want, but it might be hard to use in the alley."

Trinx looked around at the tight walkway between the buildings. There was room for the tent, but not a lot more.

"That EverSmooth stuff sounds nice, but I wasn't kidding earlier," Snixil said. "I don't love the look of it. And I definitely get stares from goblins if I leave the alley, but it helps keep me warm. Maybe someday. I can't believe you really looked like me."

"I did. Really. But the EverSmooth is amazing," Trinx said. "But it's not really about that. I love how my skin looks and feels, but you and I are beautiful, with or without some extra hair. Plus, I'm sure you're right about it being warmer."

Snixil picked at her muffin and said nothing.

"I'm glad you have a tent, at least," Trinx said, giving it an appraising look. "If you had somewhere to live—like a building, I mean, I know you have a place to live. It's right here. But if you had options, would you still choose here?"

"Depends," Snixil said and took a bite of her muffin, chewing thoughtfully. "Not if it was anything like where I grew up. I know that. But I can't afford nothing, and no one would give a kid a job."

"If it was anything like my home growing up, I can understand that." Trinx took another bite herself. "I don't really have any good suggestions. I was just curious how much of living here in the alley was a choice or not."

"Definitely a choice not to live with him," Snixil said, now gazing at a piece of thimbleberry. "But this tent in the alley? More like it's my only real option. Cause I'm not going back."

"I wish I could offer something, but my place is super small," Trinx said. "I'll keep an ear out. Never know when something might come up. Besides the alchemy shop, I work at the Arsonist's Tender, too. I hear about all kinds of things there."

"Thanks. I guess," Snixil said and popped the last bite of muffin into her mouth. "And thanks for the muffin. I liked it a lot, and Nibbles ate it faster than either of us."

"I'll try to come again soon," Trinx said, standing up. "For now, I have to get to work."

"Having two jobs is impressive," Snixil said. "No wonder you can afford fancy muffins and jugs of tea from Mystic. You don't have to bring anything next time. I mean, if there is a next time. It would be nice to talk again. Thanks again, Ma'am."

There it was again, that title. It was so strange. With a small shake of her head, Trinx smiled and waved as she left for the shop. She thought to herself, *two jobs definitely didn't pay that well, but it probably seemed like a lot. Especially to someone without a job at all.*

When Trinx arrived at Distilled Magic, she found the door secured with a padlock. She realized this was likely the earliest she had ever arrived at the shop. With nothing better to do, she sat on a nearby bench. After a sip of her tonic, she opened up Phylo's book to read while waiting.

Before long, Brinta approached and waved to Trinx.

"Spells and fancy tricks, this is a surprise! Ya beat me here this morning. You must be catching on to balancing the two jobs. You never struck me as a morning person."

"I've been feeling great," Trinx said, not bothering to acknowledge there was a lot more to it. "I'm ready for a day of experimenting. Do you think we can give that buck some nipples?"

"I'm not so sure about that," Brinta said with a shake of their head. "Last night, I realized we need to trigger more of a transformation. I've been working on an idea around insects that transform via metamorphosis. Don't worry. I'm not going to turn you into a butterfly. But I think we might coax a trans-formation using insects from the different stages."

"That's worth a try," Trinx agreed and followed Brinta into the shop.

They spent the day trying all forms of insects, from grubs to caterpillars to moths and butterflies. By the end of the day, they weren't any better off than when they started. However, they had eliminated numerous possibilities.

At one point, they had thought they were on to something. The rat test subject had lapped up a potion and then huddled in a corner of the cage. The rat then developed a soft shell around him, growing out of his fur. When it had later emerged, instead of a set of nipples, the extra growth had been on his back. Two leathery bat-like wings. It was interesting but some-what disturbing. The effect didn't last long, and the rat simply shed the wings half an hour later.

"Well," the alchemist said. "I guess that line of thinking didn't pan out. It's worth trying a few more, though. There are some monsters that also go through forms of metamorphosis. I may have to order some parts, but magic infuses the essence of many monsters, and using their parts may yield better results than these insects."

Trinx had been wandering around the room and hadn't really heard what Brinta had said. While looking in the rat cage, she asked, "What was that? You want to switch from using rats to monsters? Seems dangerous. Does Pox have monsters he catches?"

"What are you talking about?" Brinta asked, confusion written across their face. "I said I might have to order some monster parts. From monsters that go through metamorphosis. I know it was a long day today, but keep your head in the game, girl. Actually, strike that. Not sure if you noticed the clock, but your shift at the tavern is starting soon. We'll dive in again tomorrow."

"Yeah," Trinx said. "Good idea. Glad we aren't experimenting on monsters. I'll see you tomorrow."

After gathering up her things, Trinx left the shop and pushed away the sleep beckoning her with another sip of the tonic. On the way to the tavern, she stopped and bought a few things at the market since her cupboards at home were getting bare. She kept to the basics and even got a few raw ingredients. Thinking more about it, she realized cooking and baking weren't that different from alchemy. She thought she could try cooking a few meals or even some treats.

Other than telling Quilka all about meeting Snixil and Nibbles, her shift at the tavern was boring. When Brizla heard Trinx was planning on trying some cooking and baking, she gave her some small spice pouches.

At home, she put away all of her supplies from the market and the spices Brizla had donated. Trinx then spent the night studying Phylo's book and skimming through some others.

The next several days went by in much the same fashion. During the day, she would experiment with Brinta. In the evening, she would put in her time at the bar. Sometimes, it yielded humor and excitement; sometimes, it was just another shift to get through. Trinx would stay up all night reading, but also had begun to practice cooking and baking. She even found that she wasn't too bad of a cook. Most of the time, that was.

One evening, she attempted to make muffins. When she pulled the pan from her small oven, she found they had not risen and were missing the classic domed muffin tops. Trinx dumped the small pucks out onto the counter. Picking one up, she gave it an experimental nibble. She found she had to work at it with her teeth to get a piece separated into her mouth. Chewing the small bite, she found it extremely chewy. Surprisingly, it didn't taste half-bad. The texture was what was wrong, and it made the would-be muffin difficult to eat.

Still, Trinx had made plenty to share and took some with her in the morning. She stopped in Snixil's alley and found her tossing a ball for Nibbles.

"Hi, Snixil," she called as she entered the small walkway. "I brought you and Nibbles something to nibble on." She giggled and snorted more than the wordplay deserved.

"Good morning, Ms. Trinx," Snixil said and came forward to see.

Handing her a small bag with a handful of the muffin-pucks, Trinx said, "Here you go. I made them myself. I've been experimenting with cooking and baking lately."

"Thank you, ma'am," Snixil said as she took the bag and looked inside. "You shouldn't have. But thank you. But, um, what are they?"

"Well, the recipe said they were muffins," Trinx explained. "But I suspect the person who wrote the recipe hasn't had a proper muffin before. They didn't turn out as I would expect."

Snixil took an experimental bite. "Mmph. Chewy. Tasty,

too. But chewy." She noticed Nibbles looking up at her expectantly, so she dropped one of the pucks down for him.

The raccoon snatched the snack up in his little paws and gnawed on it. He didn't seem to make much progress, so he opted to bat it around the ground. Sometimes, he sent it flying too far, so he bounded after it with a pounce and then began to bat it around again.

"Well, I think they are tasty enough," Snixil said. "He can play with that one. More for me then, anyway. Did you want to sit and talk?"

"Sorry they aren't better," Trinx said. "I'll bring something a bit less chewy next time. Unfortunately, I have to get to the shop, but I promise to find a time to come and chat again soon."

With a wave goodbye, she left for Distilled Magic. Along the way, Trinx decided she would keep the rest of the muffin-pucks to herself for snacks. She didn't want Brinta to make fun of her baking.

Chapter 22

Unexpected Growth

When Trinx arrived at Distilled Magic, she found Brinta already there and busy restocking the shelves. They looked up and said, "Morning, Trinx. I'll be ready for more experimenting soon. The shop needs some attention this morning."

"Hi, Brinta," she said as she bounced over to the workstations. "I had an idea last night. I just have to go over it with you."

"Well, that sounds promising," Brinta said. "What is this idea of yours?"

"I got it while thinking about Phylo's work. I know we've used a lot of his ideas as the basis for our experiments."

"Right," Brinta said, nodding in agreement. "Like our first experiments based on his udder enhancer. We only had marginal success with the male rats."

"Yup. That's what I mean," she said. "But I've been reading through his notes and recipes a lot. He has some advanced notes that go beyond enhancement and actually cause full transformations. Kind of like what we were trying the other day with the insect metamorphosis."

"Yes," they said. "I remember that from his writings, though it's been a while since you've basically permanently borrowed my copy. I should just get a new one and gift that book to you. You've had it long enough you might as well keep it."

"Oh, I have it with me. You can look at it today," Trinx said as her cheeks flushed purple. "I shouldn't have kept it so long. His most elaborate recipe is for a potion that he made into a spray. He sprayed wasps, which are just nasty, changing them into honeybees, which everyone loves because they make delicious honey."

"I remember that," the alchemist said. "I don't sell any here because most goblins don't keep bees. But I know it's used a lot by the gnolls. They have farms of bee hives and extensive fields of flowers for cultivating honey. If there are more wasps than bees in an area, they use that potion to spray all the nasty insects."

"So Phylo," Trinx began. "He uses ground-up bees as a major component of the potion. It has a bunch of other stuff in there, too, including some honey. The solution then uses the essence of the bees to provide a blueprint for turning the wasps into their much nicer cousins, the bees."

"Wait a minute!" Brinta said. "I think I see where you are going. We need to stop trying to augment the body. Stop trying to force it to grow breasts. You're suggesting we actually try to transform the male body into a female body. But—"

"That's it!" Trinx interrupted, her excitement bubbling over. "Yes! I mean, I don't think we should grind up any goblins or anything like that. But I think if we used some hair, maybe some claws. Something that grows back easily enough. We'd have to figure out a different base, I think. I'm not sure if one of our insect bases might work. But maybe it wouldn't be too far off?"

The alchemist wore a rueful smile and shook their head. "I was trying to say, I'm not sure how easy this will be. Turning an insect into another insect is one thing. Turning a goblin into another goblin? That's a tall order. Plus, we don't actually want that. We wouldn't want to transform their mind. And for that matter, we don't even want to transform the body exactly. We don't want a clone, after all."

"But we've done that before, right?" Trinx questioned. "Like with the beard growth formula we made for Vex. The potion just grows out a beard. It doesn't grow hair all over his body. It seems targeted at the face only. And not just the face, but the part that is supposed to have hair. Imagine if it made his nose hairy?" She snorted a burst of laughter at the silliness of the idea.

"Hmmm." The alchemist paused, looking deep in thought. "I suppose. Yes, I suppose that's true. If we could pick the right reagents to target specific parts of the body for the transformation, then yes, yes, it might just work. We'd want to make two distinct lines. One based on samples from female goblins to transform males into females. Then another to do the opposite."

"So, you think it could work?" Trinx asked hopefully.

"Well, what I think is that it has the potential to work. But it's going to take a lot of testing. And, now that I think of it, even in those two distinct lines of potions, we probably need variations. We'll want to collect samples from a variety of goblin donors. This would let you pick a potion that would give you the right size and shape of the parts you want. I'm getting ahead of myself, though. For now, we need to get one version to work on one person, namely you."

"You know what?" Trinx asked. "I bet, if we can make this

work, we could make it work for anybody. Not just goblins. Anyone. I'm sure goblins aren't the only ones that have people who feel this way about their bodies."

"No, of course not," Brinta said. "We could definitely make this a wider solution once we had an initial success. Okay. I'm really getting on board with this idea now. It could be the winner we've been looking for. Let's get to work."

"First, we need the ingredients, though, right?" she said. "I mean, you could provide some claws, but you take that potion, so you don't have any hair. Oh! Quilka! Worg's breath. I only get to see her at the tavern these days. We haven't just hung out in forever. What's wrong with me? And now I'm just going to go and ask for some hair and claws?"

"I'm surprised you haven't been spending more time with her," Brinta said. "But I know it's hard finding time to fit everything in. You manage to fit in a lot of reading somehow. Still, she's a good friend. I'm sure she would love to see you, even if you come with strange requests."

"She is the best. That's true," Trinx agreed. "I'll go see her now. She should be home. It's too early for her shift at the Tender."

"That sounds like a plan," the alchemist agreed. "I'll finish getting the shop in order and then work on plans for a base for the elixir."

"Sure thing!" she called, already on her way out of the shop. The door slammed shut behind her.

When Trinx got to Quilka's apartment, she knocked as she opened the door.

"Good morning, Quilka!"

She walked in smiling. Talking at the Tender was nice, but she hadn't been spending enough actual time with her friend lately.

"Trinx!" Quilka shouted with delight. She hopped up from

the couch where she had been sipping on some tea. Trinx noticed she still had on her sleeping clothes and hadn't fully gotten ready for the day.

"Sorry, it's been forever," Trinx said. "I kept thinking I should come and see you, but it never seemed a good time. Do you have time now?"

"I do. But shouldn't you be at Distilled Magic?" Quilka asked, then continued on without waiting for an answer. "But I'm so happy to see you. We need to spend more time together. I miss hanging out with you. We need to go dancing again."

"Well, I'm here now," Trinx said with a fancy pose. "But it's probably not the best time for dancing. I can stay for a little while, but I need to ask you a favor. Is that too boorish of me? Just popping in out of nowhere asking for things?"

"Please," Quilka said. "It hasn't been that long. We just got busy, is all. Sit down. I'll get you a cup."

Trinx walked over and plopped herself down on the couch. "I really did mean to try to come sooner. We've just been wrapped up in figuring out the potion. I had an idea and Brinta thinks it might be possible. We need to test it, though. Brinta says it could take quite a bit of testing, but that's why I need your samples."

"My samples?" Quilka asked as she returned to the couch and handed Trinx a cup of milky-white tea. "What are you talking about?"

"Well, that's the reason I came. I told you that when I came in," Trinx said, giving her an admonishing look.

"You said you needed to ask a favor," Quilka corrected playfully. "You didn't say what the favor was."

"Oh, I guess that's true," Trinx admitted. "Well, anyway. That's the favor. I need samples. Some extra hair, like from your hairbrush? Oh, and some claws. Not the whole nail, obviously. Just some shavings or clippings."

"That's certainly strange," Quilka said. "And it sounds kind of gross until you think about it and it's not really. It's just weird. So, yeah, sure. I'll get some hair from my brush, and I'll file down the claws on my hands a bit while we talk."

Quilka set her tea down and went to her vanity. She brought back a brush full of maroon hair and a file. "Have you seen that girl with the raccoon again? What was her name?"

"Snixil?" Trinx said. "I brought her some muffins I baked. I didn't have time to sit and talk. It seemed like she wanted that more than muffins, so I'll need to go back sometime."

"You baked?" Quilka asked, and her right eyebrow quirked up. "I bet they turned out fabulous."

"I'm not sure you'd win that bet," Trinx said, taking a sip of tea. "They were edible. Nibbles played with it instead of eating it. That alone gives a good idea of how good they were."

"I'm sure it just takes practice," Quilka assured her. "You will improve if you want to. It might just take some time."

Trinx popped up off the couch and walked over to the kitchen to rifle through the cupboards. "We'll see. Do you have an empty jar? I need something to hold your samples."

"Should be an old jam jar or two in there," Quilka answered. "I try to clean them out when I empty them. They make nice storage for bits and bobbles."

Trinx found an empty jar and returned to the couch. She pulled some hair from the brush and stuffed it in. Then she swept the fresh claw shavings in as well. "These should work. Thanks, Q."

"Oh, are you leaving already?" Quilka asked softly.

"I'd actually love to stay and talk more if that's alright with you," Trinx said. "I can at least finish my tea. Sorry, these days, I tend to get focused on something, and I can't let go until it's done. But let's talk. Have you heard if Serenya has any new songs coming out soon?"

And so, the two friends sat on the couch, drinking tea, swapping stories, and laughing for the rest of the morning until Quilka needed to get ready for work. At this point, Trinx gave her a hug and left with the samples tucked safely in her bag.

"I'll see you later at the Tender. Before then, I'm going to see what Brinta and I can do with your donations."

Back at Distilled Magic, Trinx found Brinta brewing a base for their experiment.

"There were a few customers while you were gone, and with the interruptions, I didn't get the base going until just now. It will be a little bit still. Did you get what we need from Quilka?" they asked.

Trinx fished the jar full of hair and claw shavings out. She waved it around like a prize and then set it on the worktable.

"It was nice catching up with Quilka. She didn't mind giving these to me, but she thought it was odd. I suppose it was a weird request." She gave a shrug of her shoulders and pulled Phylo's book over in front of her to flip through while Brinta worked.

"What about this one?" Trinx asked idly.

"What?" the alchemist asked. "What one?"

"This one here," she said. "He calls it the Seed Remover. It's a bath. You stick fruits and vegetables in it. Like apples, melons, cucumbers. You know, anything with seeds."

"Oh, yes," Brinta replied. "I've seen that. We don't stock that here. Goblins import most of their produce. But that's why the fancier fruits you buy in the market don't have any seeds in them. What about it? You don't have any seeds we want to remove."

"Psssh," she dismissed the silly idea. "No. Not the seed part. Or the seeds are part of it, I guess. It's the phase spider gland."

"What's he using that for?" Brinta asked.

"That's the thing," Trinx answered. "The gland helps the spider phase between planes of existence. He uses it to target the seeds, so the bit of the potion that removes the seeds removes them and not any other stuff."

"Oh!" Brinta said, crinkling their face with a smile. "That makes sense. Yes. We could try that. We could combine that with what I was trying to extrapolate from the beard growth potion. It might work. This could be the missing part. Could you grab some from the back?"

Trinx ran to the back room and soon returned with a jar containing several small shimmering orbs. She set it on the counter near Brinta and wandered around the room, eventually stopping to watch the rats squirm in their cage.

"Don't go too far," Brinta said. "It would be good practice for you to try pressing one of those to collect the oil."

"Oh, right, sure," Trinx said and tore herself away from the rats to rejoin the alchemist at the workbench.

"You'll want to use one of these trays," Brinta instructed. "Put the gland on the tray, then using that small tool there—the one with the head that looks like a mallet? Use that to press gently on the gland to release the oils. Don't press too hard, or you'll rupture the gland and need to start again."

Trinx did as she had been instructed and gently pressed the gland. Small beads of oil began to form on the surface. As they increased in size, they eventually fell off into the tray.

"I only need a small amount," Brinta said. "Once you've pressed several drops, you can stop and put the gland back in the jar if it seems it still has some left."

Brinta took the tray with the oil and sucked it up with an eyedropper. They squeezed several drops into the base, and, after checking the notes, added the rest of the ingredients. The solution flashed yellow. Then, they gently stirred in a strand of the hair and a small pinch of nail powder. On the fifth stir, the potion pulsed three times before turning bright pink.

"Well," they said. "This is promising. It appears to be a stable solution. I believe we've gone beyond the usefulness of rats at this point. Are you ready for another trial?"

"Yes!" Trinx enthusiastically said and reached out for a sample.

Brinta measured out a small dose into a vial and handed it to the eager goblin. "This should physically change you in some way. Hopefully how we want, but regardless, it might be uncomfortable."

Trinx drank the vial of pink liquid and immediately felt her stomach do a flip. She grabbed onto the counter to steady herself and hung her head down, breathing steadily. She felt insects, worms, and other creepy crawlies under her skin, moving up and down her entire body. Then the itching began, and it was all she could do to fight the urge to scratch. She gripped the counter tighter and let out a strained groan—desperate to find relief.

Eventually, the itch subsided, and she no longer felt anything crawling around inside her. However, Trinx felt something strange on her neck, and her eye caught movement to her left. Brinta froze and simply stood staring at her. Trinx turned her head to the left and gasped at the same time Brinta inhaled just as suddenly.

"What? What is that? What did it do?" she frantically asked.

Brinta managed to compose themselves and finally sighed, "It appears to be a second head. It looks quite similar to your friend Quilka. It should wear off soon. Don't panic. The bigger issue is why that happened. I've got another book in the back that might have some ideas. I seem to remember something in it about unwanted extra limbs and even an extra head."

"At least it doesn't hurt, and I don't seem to have an extra brain," Trinx said while reaching out to probe gently at the head. "It better go away. I don't like it at all. And besides, what would Q say if she ever saw it?"

"True. That might disturb her quite a lot," Brinta called from the other room. "Just sit down and let it wear off. I'll be back out shortly."

Trinx sat down, leaning back against a wall. She realized her chest felt tight. Pulling out the pouches from her bra, the pressure subsided, and she realized her bra was still full. Calling out, she said, "There were more changes. I think I grew breasts. If it wasn't for this weird head, we'd be pretty close."

She pulled out her wooden toy and began to spin the beads while trying to ignore the weird growth on her shoulder. As the minutes drifted by, the head began to shrink. Eventually, it was just a raised lump with a tuft of maroon hair on her shoulder.

Brinta came back into the room, wearing a pensive look on her face. "I believe I know what the issue is. Based on what happened, I have good news and what is likely to be bad news."

"Maybe the bad news isn't that horrible," Trinx said hopefully. "But just in case, start with the good news."

"Very well," Brinta said. "The good news is, I'm fairly certain we are close, and with a slight change, we should have a stable potion that does what we are looking for."

"That's amazing," Trinx said. "I thought we must be close. I didn't strip out of my underwear to check, but in addition to the breasts, that feels different, too. The bad news can't be that bad. Give it to me."

"Like I said, I think it's likely to be bad news, but it's possible it isn't. I'm not an expert on your personal life," Brinta said. The alchemist looked down at Trinx, sitting against the wall. "The problem is, the samples deviate too much from you. Obviously, we need them to deviate. We're switching out parts of your anatomy. But with such a major change, according to what I found, we need samples that are much closer to how you are now."

"I don't understand," Trinx said. "I'm super close with Quilka. She's been my best friend forever. How can I get samples that are closer?"

"I'm not talking about the closeness of your relationship," Brinta explained. "It's the similarity to your biology that matters. We need a sample from a close female relative. Ideally, your mother."

Trinx crumpled and rested her face in her hands. *Why? Why did she need to be involved?*

Chapter 23

A Long Night

Brinta dropped to a squat beside Trinx. "You can control this," they said. "Yes, you must ask your mother for something, but you don't have to let her or your father set the terms. From what you told me of the altercation at the cafe, I'd suggest not involving your father at all. Invite your mother here. I'll be here, and you should be comfortable."

"I'll admit I'm probably over dramatic here," Trinx said, pulling her hands from her face. "I'm definitely not involving my father. I like the idea of having her meet me here."

"You know, she may even be anxious to talk to you," Brinta offered. "She only recently found out you were still alive, and you are her child, even if you've changed from the person she used to know."

Then, the alchemist stood up and went to the back room while saying over their shoulder, "I'll grab some paper and a pen. You can write your mother a note, and we'll grab a messenger. There are always plenty running by the shop."

Trinx pulled herself off the floor, using the wall for support.

She walked over to a workstation and found a clear spot. She idly toyed with a glass beaker and a small metal bead. As she swirled the beaker with her hand, the bead spun along the container's wall.

Brinta emerged a moment later with a pen, inkpot, and a few sheets of parchment. They laid them down on the counter next to Trinx and said, "Here you are. Keep it short and to the point."

Picking up the pen, Trinx held it thoughtfully for a moment, then said, "What do I even say? 'Hey, Mom, it's been a while. I know you thought I was dead, but can I have some claw shavings?'"

Brinta stifled a chuckle. "No. No, I don't think that would work. Like I said. Keep it short. Tell her you want to talk to her and invite her here."

"That's it?" Trinx asked. "You don't think I need anything else?"

"She's your mother," Brinta explained. "I'm certain she will come if you ask."

Sighing, Trinx set the pen to the parchment.

Mother,

I would like to speak with you. Please come to Distilled Magic tomorrow or reply with a time you can come.

Do not bring Father.

Trinx

P.S. I mean it. Do NOT bring Father.

"Will this work? I thought formal might be best." Trinx asked, pushing the parchment toward the alchemist.

Brinta read it over, nodded, and then said, "You kept it short. You said what you wanted. You also added what you didn't want. Twice even. And the formal titles add some distance. Yes, I'd say this should work. I'll give it to a messenger."

Folding the note, Brinta left the shop and returned shortly without it. "Well, it's off. No turning back now. We'll see if and when she comes. I think she'll come tomorrow if she is able."

Trinx let out a long breath of air. "Now what? There isn't really anything to do with the potion until I can meet with her."

"She won't be here until tomorrow at the earliest," Brinta said. "It's almost time for your shift at the tavern. Why don't you head over there and try not to dwell on what may or may not happen tomorrow?"

"I'm pretty sure that's all I'm going to be thinking about," Trinx said while packing up her bag. "But that's probably best. Thanks for all of your help, Brinta"

"Of course, Trinx," Brinta said with a reassuring smile. "And remember, I'll be here. I promise. You don't have to do this alone. If it helps, I really do think this will work."

"I hope so. I'll see you tomorrow," Trinx said and shuffled out of the shop.

When Trinx opened the door to the tavern, a cacophony welcomed her. Nearly every table was full, and an elven bard played a lute and sang in the corner. The elf was an interesting twist. She must have been on quite a journey, as they rarely showed up in a goblin warren. For a moment, Trinx thought it might be Serenya herself because she was singing a song she knew well, but she had seen pictures of Serenya Dawnwhisper, and this was not her. However, the bard sounded nice, and it lifted her spirits to hear a song she loved.

Trinx spied Quilka helping a table across the room, but Gristle caught her eye and called, "Trinxy! So glad yer here.

The bard has brought quite a crowd. Grab what ye need and jump in to help."

"Sure thing, Gris."

Thoughts of tomorrow slipped out of her mind as her focus turned toward the work in front of her. She hurried to the kitchen, slipped on an apron, took a sip of her tonic, and grabbed a tray.

Both Trinx and Quilka worked the room and split the tables between them. Neither had time to stop and say much other than small pleasantries. One of Trinx's tables held an elf, two humans, and a dwarf. They turned out to be an adventuring party, and the bard was with them.

"What brings you to Chubug?" Trinx asked as she set down a fresh round of drinks at the adventurers' table.

"We're out seeking our fortunes," said a human she later learned was named Travis. "We often sleep under the stars, but when we find ourselves near a settlement, we jump at the option to rent some beds."

"Which inn are you staying at here in the warren?" Trinx asked, mostly for conversation but also because she was curious to find out more about the travelers.

"One not too far from the entrance to the warren. Name is the Slumbering Boar," Travis answered. "The rooms are nice enough, but the tavern space is small. After some asking around, we eventually found this fine establishment where Kamina could entertain and make some extra coin."

"She sounds wonderful," Trinx said, glancing over to where the elf was singing. "I hope she knows a lot of Serenya's songs. I'm a huge Whispie."

"Dontcha worry," the dwarf said with a snort. "Kamina be the biggest Whispie I've ever met. Likely knows more'n Serenya herself."

"Drumhill exaggerates, of course," Travis said. "But we do

have to stop at any city we hear Dawnwhisper is playing so that Kamina can go to the concert."

"I wish I could go to one of her concerts," Trinx said wistfully. "She always plays so far away. I don't travel much."

"Maybe someday, lass," Drumhill said.

"I hope so," Trinx said. "Enjoy your drinks. I'll be back to check on you in a while. As you can see, it's busy in here. Seems folks really like Kamina's performance."

The crowd kept both Trinx and Quilka busy the entire evening and well into the night. By the time the last of the crowd filtered out, both women were starving. Thankfully, Brizla still had some of the soup they had been serving all evening and a small pile of flatbread left over. The cook dished up two large bowls and set them down on the staff table next to a plate piled with remaining bread.

"Thanks, Brizla," Trinx said as she sat down.

"Yeah. This is perfect," Quilka added and sat down across from her.

Trinx's mouth watered at the sight of the food. She had been smelling the fragrant soup all evening while serving bowls to the customers. Now, she could finally have some. The broth looked creamy with bubbles of red chili oil with pieces of broccoli, bell peppers, and mushrooms drowning alongside some type of red meat.

After tearing off a piece of flatbread, she dredged it through the soup and took a bite. The bread released the spicy flavor of the soup as she chewed. Trinx let out a soft moan of pleasure. She had been so hungry, and this soup was divine.

"Oh! Did my samples help?" Quilka asked, yanking Trinx from her infatuation with the soup.

"They were helpful," Trinx said. "But...they didn't do what we needed. In fact. Well. It's a little disturbing. I grew a second head that looked like a warped version of you."

"What?!" Quilka exclaimed. "That's creepy. But it went away? I don't see anything."

"Oh yeah," Trinx said. "It didn't last long and didn't leave anything weird behind. But it was helpful. Brinta realized the issue was we weren't related. They figured out I needed samples from a female relative."

"Oh," Quilka said softly. It was clear to Trinx that she already saw where the story was going.

"Exactly," Trinx said, and her mouth turned down, instinctually exposing her fangs. "Brinta assures me it will be okay. I'm not convinced. I sent her a short note asking her to come to the shop tomorrow."

"You can handle it," Quilka assured her. "I know you can. Do you think she'll bring him?"

"If she does, she's not coming in," Trinx said firmly. "I asked her not to in the letter. But if he comes, I'll just figure something else out. I don't know what, but I'm not dealing with him."

"If you asked her not to, I'm sure she won't," Quilka said. "And I doubt she'll have a problem giving you the samples you need."

"Rationally, that all makes sense," Trinx agreed. "I'm still nervous. The crowd tonight was a lot of work, but it kept me busy and my mind off of tomorrow."

"Speaking of the crowd," Quilka said after swallowing a spoonful of soup. "That Kamina sure could sing. Sometimes, I could have sworn we had Serenya right here, in the bar."

"Wouldn't that be amazing?" Trinx asked. Her face lit up at the change of another topic. "But you're right. Kamina was very good. It's not often we see folks traveling so far."

"I know, right?" Quilka said and wiped some soup broth from her bowl with a piece of bread.

"It sounded like they were just here for the night," Trinx

said. "They are on a grand adventure and never seem to stay any one place long."

"We should go on an adventure," Quilka suggested. "Travel to one of the large cities."

"Oh!" Trinx exclaimed. "That would be amazing. Then maybe we could see Serenya perform instead of a bard singing covers."

"I don't know when we'll have the time or money," Quilka said. "But I'm in."

"Great," Trinx said. "It's a date."

Quilka blushed lavender, then stood up. "We should get this cleaned up so we can head out. You should make sure you get a good night's sleep before tomorrow."

"I will," Trinx lied and got up from the table to help finish the cleanup.

When Trinx got back to her apartment, she put down her bag and looked at the bed. As usual, the sheets and blankets were in a pile. She never bothered making the bed. Still, it looked very inviting. It had been far too long since she had last slept. There never seemed to be a good night to catch up.

However, that night was not the night for sleep. She was tired, and the bed looked *so* good. But if Trinx slept now, she risked losing the entire next day, and she had to be at the shop. Shaking her head, she took a sip of the tonic and pulled out a book.

The time crawled by. More than once, Trinx found herself re-reading a page, having no memory of what she had read the first time. Her thoughts kept drifting to her mother, the shop, the potion, and all the things she could do nothing about that night. It was a long night.

At one point, she had to put the book aside because she realized she had been crying, and the tears threatened to fall from her chin onto the pages. Instead of stopping the flow of tears, she let them all out. Eventually, they ran dry, and she decided a bath was in order.

After another sip of the tonic to ensure she didn't fall asleep in the tub, she climbed into the warm, sudsy water and tried to relax. It helped. Eventually. The tension in her shoulders eased, and she even felt several small pops in her neck when she twisted to reach for a washrag.

Still feeling worried but now more refreshed, Trinx stepped out of the tub onto a mat and toweled herself off. She slipped on some clothes and sat at the vanity to do her hair and makeup. When she turned on her music device, a song she had just heard the evening before played, and she smiled, thinking of the chaos of the bar.

It was too early yet to go anywhere, so she put the kettle on and fixed a slice of toast with jam while the water heated. Trinx sipped dragonroot tea with not only cream but a dollop of honey as well. She realized she shouldn't have wasted the jam on her toast when she popped the last bite into her mouth with no memory of having eaten the rest of it.

Finally, enough of the early morning had passed, and it was time to head to the shop. She briefly considered visiting Snixil but then thought better of it when she realized how distracted she would be. There would be time to check on the young goblin later.

Trinx waved to Brinta when she opened the heavy door to Distilled Magic.

"Good morning. She hasn't come yet, has she?"

"Your mother?" Brinta asked. "No. No, she has not. I wouldn't expect her this early in the morning. But I'm sure she'll come today. I know it gets lost sometimes with all the experimenting we've done since you came on board, but there's plenty to keep you busy in the shop until she does."

"Oh, right," Trinx agreed. "I'll work on cleaning and straightening things. Maybe we'll even get some customers in."

She dove into the chores, putting away items that had been left out, wiping and dusting the shelves, and sweeping the floor. Every time the door opened, she caught her breath, and she would freeze, looking to see who had entered. When she inevitably saw it was just another customer, she assisted Brinta in helping them, then went back to her chores.

While trying to focus on her work, she rehearsed potential conversations. She imagined all the ways the day might play out and found herself looping back and repeating the same scenarios in a way that quickly stopped being helpful. Unfortunately, she found she couldn't get her brain to stop and instead kept replaying different variations of the same conversation.

"What was that?" Brinta asked from across the room.

Trinx shook her head and looked up. "What was what?"

"I thought I heard you saying something," Brinta said. "Did you need something?"

"Oh, that. No. Sorry. I was just mumbling. Thinking about what to say," Trinx explained.

"Quite alright. Try not to think too hard on it. You might twist your stomach up," Brinta said with a light chuckle.

Trinx went back to work and did her best to focus on her tasks and not on what conversations may or may not happen. She might not even get a chance to talk to her mother today. Maybe she wouldn't even answer at all.

Chapter 24

Mother

When the door opened for the fifth time that afternoon, Trinx looked over to see her mother walk inside. She glanced around the room, taking it in until her eyes landed on Trinx, who was drying some glassware.

Brinta saw the recognition between the two and stepped in to diffuse the tension.

"Welcome to Distilled Magic. I'm Brinta and judging by the recognition you both have on your faces, you must be Trinx's mother. Thank you for not bringing your husband as she requested. But please, come in. I can pop over to Mystic and get you both some tea and something to nibble on if you'd like. Feel free to talk in the back room."

"Thanks, Brinta. As you suspected, this is my mother, Gwix," Trinx said, setting down the rag and the beaker she had been drying. "Would you like any refreshments, Mother?"

"What? Oh, dear," her mother said, sounding flustered. "I guess. I guess I didn't know what to expect when I came here.

Refreshments? No? No. I don't need anything like that. I suppose I just want to find out why you asked me here."

Trinx took a deep breath in, then let it out. *I can do this.* "Then let's go in the back room like Brinta suggested. Follow me."

She led the way into the back room, followed by Gwix. They each took a seat in a chair. The furniture was not elaborate, typical of the backroom of a shop. The two chairs they used were simple, utilitarian wooden chairs.

"Thank you for coming," Trinx opened. "I know it was quite a shock to see me the other day. You seemed surprised but not angry like *he* was. I hope he didn't take all that anger out on you."

Gwix self-consciously rubbed at her arm. "Not more than usual. Don't worry about that. But yes, he was angry. And after I got over the shock, I was angry, too."

"Well, you shouldn't be angry. I'm not going to apologize for who I am," Trinx said firmly, just like she had rehearsed in her head all afternoon. "I knew I couldn't come home. If he even let me in, it would just be to beat me and not let me leave the house again."

"Ah," her mother started. "Er. That may well be true. I just don't understand. How could you do this to us?"

"Do this to you?" Trinx practically yelled. "I didn't do anything to you or him. You know I was never happy. I didn't want the life Dad pushed on me. I just didn't know why. But I figured it out."

"What do you mean, you figured it out?" Gwix asked. "What's to figure out? Did that Brinta person put you up to this? She certainly looks strange. How is dressing like this and wearing braids and makeup something you figure out? It's not normal."

No need to bring Zigla into this, Trinx thought to herself. "I mean, the child you raised and thought you knew was not the real me. This is the real me. I feel so much more at peace with myself like this. I feel like I should be. And Brinta had nothing to do with it. I figured it out before I even met them."

"I've heard of this kind of thing," her mother admitted. "But I never understood it, and I still don't. All of this? This is all just pretend. Just because you wear a dress doesn't make you a girl."

"You're right," Trinx acknowledged. "The dress doesn't make me a girl. It just helps me express that aspect of myself. I'm a girl because that's what I *am*, whether I'm wearing a dress, or pants, or a flour sack."

"I can't say I'm okay with any of this," Gwix said, dismissing her explanation. "But I'm glad you reached out. I'm sure you had a reason. Why ask me here?"

"I need something from you," Trinx said. "Brinta and I have been working on a potion. If it works, it will align my body with who I am. And no, that won't make me more of a girl. Like I said, I already am. But, like the dresses, it will make me feel more at peace."

"What could you need from me?" her mother asked. "And I'm not at all sure I want to give you anything to encourage this."

"Nothing you say, do, or don't do, will stop me from being me," Trinx said. "But if you care for me at all, consider giving me what I want. I'm not asking for much. I need some of your hair, like from a brush. I also need some shavings from your claws when you file them. I need some of both now, but I'll also need some in the future as well to keep brewing the potion."

"I don't understand how that will help," Gwix said. "If that's all you need, though. Fine. You can have it. Maybe I'll eventually understand you better. Right now, though, I'll give you what you want and ask that you let me think and process this."

"I know you used to carry just about everything in that bag," Trinx said, motioning at the blue fabric purse embroidered with white flower designs. "Do you have a brush and a file for your claws?"

Her mother nodded and pulled the bag into her lap. She dug through it and pulled out a brush full of loose hairs and a file. Trinx stood up, grabbed a beaker from a shelf, and brought it over. Taking the brush, she peeled away a handful of hair and placed it in the jar. Then, handing the jar to her mother, said, "You can file your claws directly into here. I don't need a lot, but please take off as much as you are comfortable with."

Gwix did as requested and filed her claws, catching the shavings in the beaker. "Despite what I said earlier, I am glad you asked me here. I'm still confused, but perhaps we can talk again in a few weeks?"

"We can do that," Trinx agreed. "Thank you for this. And please, don't tell *him* you saw me or that we talked."

With a forced chuckle and a shake of her head, Gwix replied, "I won't. I'd suffer the consequences more than you if I did."

Trinx took the beaker from her mother and placed it on a counter. She helped her mother stand and asked, "Can I—do you think I can have a hug?"

Her mother looked at her, eyes roving from head to toe and back. Then she opened her arms and allowed Trinx in. The embrace was not long, and Gwix broke it first.

"I should be going before I need to come up with excuses."

Trinx led her mother back out into the shop and then to the door.

"I'll write soon," she promised as her mother walked away.

When the door was closed, Trinx slumped against it, letting out an enormous sigh.

"I heard some raised voices," Brinta said, "but not a lot of yelling."

"There was less yelling than I thought there would be," Trinx agreed. "She's more confused than anything else. I can kind of understand that. I was confused for a long time, too, until I wasn't. She gave me the samples, though. I hope you are right."

"Well, let's find out," Brinta grinned. "Bring them to the workstation. I already have a base prepped and ready. It's at the yellow stage."

Trinx shuffled to the back, her mind still lingering on the interaction with her mother. She returned shortly with the beaker.

"I collected it in here."

Brinta took the beaker and extracted a hair and a pinch of the claw shavings. They added them to the mixture and stirred it five times. The solution pulsed a bright pink. They measured out a vial and handed it to Trinx.

"Drink up."

Trinx took the vial and swallowed the contents. She felt the creepy crawlies return, writhing under her skin. Her entire body itched from head to toe. Gripping the counter for support, she forced herself to breathe normally. The entire time, she mentally begged for the sensations to pass.

The itch finally subsided, and she again felt her chest was extremely tight. Trinx looked up at Brinta.

"I don't feel any weird growths on my neck. How do I look?"

"You look good!" Brinta exclaimed. "Go to the back room and see for yourself. Shut the door. Lock it if you'd like. You should see what's changed and what hasn't."

Trinx walked deliberately to the storeroom and shut the door. There was a mirror on the wall, and she stood in front of it. Her face looked the same but softer and less angular. She removed her dress and then her undergarments. When she removed her bra, her chest felt relief; it was no longer tight. She put the breast pouches aside with her clothes and looked herself over.

Everything appeared as she had dreamed it would. She smoothed her hands over her body, experimentally probing and feeling the differences. A wide smile broke on her face. Overwhelmed by the emotional pendulum of the day and this success, tears streamed from her eyes.

Trinx stood there for quite some time, admiring herself in the mirror and exploring her body. She imagined her belly growing and holding a child. Eventually, the cold of the shop's storeroom overcame her amazement and joy. She redressed and returned to the main shop area.

"It's everything I imagined," Trinx said, her throat still clogged with emotion. "And more even. This is wonderful, Brinta. Thank you for all of your help."

"Of course," Brinta said, their smile reflecting Trinx's happiness. "Let me just adjust this to extend the duration. With the samples your mother left, we should be able to brew plenty of this for you, but I'll stretch the duration out as long as possible. It should last nearly a month."

With that, the alchemist added several ingredients they must have had at the ready in case the potion had been a success. They stirred them in, and the brightness of the pink intensified. Brinta filled vials with the potion and arranged them in a box before sliding them over to Trinx. "Here you go. Take one now, and then you'll want to take one every three weeks or so to keep the changes in place."

"I'll definitely stay on top of taking it," Trinx swore. "I don't want to revert back. Besides, once I find someone, I'd like to have a child. That's been the whole point of this work. Well, not the whole point. I mean, I wanted this body. But what's been driving me so hard is the idea of a child. I can't have the potion wearing off halfway through a pregnancy." She snorted at the thought.

"So, if having a child is a major part of your goal, we need to run some tests," Brinta explained.

"Tests? What tests?" Trinx asked.

"Obviously, you have changed your body," Brinta said. "Biologically, you look female now, which is what we were trying to achieve. However, there are changes that need to happen internally as well. I think they should have, based on our research. Don't worry, they are simple and harmless."

"What do they involve then?" Trinx asked.

"I'll need samples of your humours. You'll need to collect some spit and urine in separate containers," Brinta said. "In addition, I'll collect a small amount of your blood. With these samples, I have a series of tests I can run that will determine your capability of birth. That is to say, do you have the right internal makeup? They will also reveal how fertile you are. Or rather, how likely you are to become pregnant."

Trinx grabbed two fresh beakers and walked toward the back room. She called over her shoulder, "I'll be right back with my spit and urine. Er, that sounds really weird and gross." Shaking her head, she left the room.

A few moments later, Trinx returned, holding out the two jars. "That was interesting. I basically had to teach myself how to relieve myself. This equipment is different. I made a small mess, but I cleaned it up. I wasn't sure how much of each you needed. Despite my fumbling, I got quite a lot of pee. I made my mouth dry with all my spitting, though. I got what I could, but it's not a lot."

"That's more than enough," Brinta chuckled. "I'm glad you figured things out. Now, let's just draw some blood. I don't need a lot. Hold out your hand."

Brinta grabbed the wrist of her outstretched hand and maneuvered it over a beaker. Using a needle, they pricked Trinx's finger and squeezed several drops of blood into the container. They then put a small cloth over the wound.

"There we go. Just hold that there for a few minutes, and that should close up."

The alchemist prepared two vials with different reagents in each. Then, they took a small measure from the urine and spittle and added it to the blood. Brinta added a small amount of water and mixed the fluids thoroughly. Finally, they measured several drops into each of the prepared vials.

"You should be able to see the reaction take place as the magic from the reagents mingles with your samples," Brinta said. "The one on the left is dark and murky. It should clear up and turn a vibrant yellow if our potion worked as we hoped and transformed your insides as well as your external features."

Trinx nodded along at the explanation and said, "Looking for yellow, got it."

"On the right, you'll see it is already clear," Brinta explained. "We are looking for it to turn red. The deeper the red, the more fertile you are. Don't worry if it only becomes pink. That's still workable. But some goblins will turn that test blood red."

Trinx nodded again. Her eyes studied the two vials, waiting for the reactions to play out.

"So, while we wait. There's something I wanted to tell you," Brinta said. "I'm glad we found a solution for you, but it turned out to have a complication. We can file a patent and even produce it for others who also want to change. The good news is, it should work for any race, I would think. The bad news is this will be what is known as a designer potion. Since it needs samples from a relative, each batch must be custom-made for the client. And, as you saw with your own case, it may not be easy for everyone to get the needed samples."

"Oh yeah," Trinx frowned. "That will make it harder. My closest friends should be able to get what they need. But others might not be able to."

"Who knows?" Brinta shrugged. "It's possible we may find a more generic solution someday. But yeah, for now, this limits things."

"Oh! Look!" Trinx exclaimed. "It's yellow!"

Sure enough, the vial on the left had cleared up. The darkness was gone, and in its place was a bright yellow hue. The vial on the right remained clear.

"Excellent," Brinta said with a clap. "Seems the potion did work on the insides as well as the outsides. I love it when a plan comes together and fits the research."

"But why is the other one still clear?" Trinx asked. "How long does it take to turn red?"

Brinta frowned and peered into the vial on the right. "Honestly, I would think it should at least be pink by now. We can try running a second test. Maybe I measured the base reagents wrong."

The alchemist prepared a second vial and added drops from the collected humours. They stirred it and it again became a clear solution.

"Give this one a minute or two. It should turn pink or red."

After five painful minutes, Trinx looked over at Brinta and said, "So..." and just left it hanging there, hope in her eyes.

Brinta sighed and said, "I'm sorry, Trinx. I don't know what's wrong. Your body changed. I don't see why you would be infertile. There must be something else at play here. If I had to guess, you likely weren't fertile before taking the potion.

Have you ever had a major accident? Or perhaps a horrible sickness?"

"No, never," Trinx said, shaking her head. "Sure, I've gotten small wounds, but nothing big. And I've never been horribly sick..." She trailed off as a thought occurred to her.

But it couldn't be. Could it?

"What is it?" Brinta asked. "Did you think of something?"

"You know how I was exhausted for a while? From working so hard? But I've had more energy and been on time recently?" Trinx asked.

"Yes. I still don't know how you juggle everything between here and the tavern. Not to mention all the reading and studying you do," Brinta said. "But I love seeing how much you enjoy the work here."

"Well, I've had some help," Trinx said slowly. "I've actually been so productive because I can work all day and still read and study all night. I don't even remember the last time I slept. I stopped needing to sleep quite a while ago."

"What do you mean you don't sleep?" Brinta asked with apprehension. "Everyone needs to sleep."

"Well, it all started after the party at Club Unity," Trinx said. "I was so tired the next day. I found a recipe for Traveler's —"

"Tonic?!" Brinta cut her off. "You've been taking that? And not sleeping? At all?"

"So, yeah," Trinx said. "I keep some on hand and sip it whenever I start to feel sleepy. I've been meaning to find a good time to take a break and catch up on my sleep, but it never seems like the right time."

"Yes. I see," Brinta said exasperatedly. "That is a powerful tonic, and it can stave off sleep for as long as you take it. But that doesn't mean you should. Especially for such an extended period. That solves that mystery."

"How does that solve the mystery?" Trinx asked. "Does the tonic interfere with the test?"

Shaking their head, Brinta said, "No. It doesn't interfere with the test. The test was working just fine. I think it's safe to assume you didn't look up the side effects and complications in the appendix of that book containing the recipe?"

"Oh," Trinx said and swallowed hard. "No. I didn't. I read all of the instructions and how to properly take it. I always meant to go back and look at the appendix later."

"That's what I thought," Brinta said with a grim look on her face. "If you had read through the appendix, you would have seen that infertility is a potential side effect. The longer you take it, the more it can build up and cause the issue. There are other side effects as well; most have to do with going without sleep for too long. The mind needs sleep and dreams to reset. Go too long without sleep, and you can lose your mind."

"So, if I get some sleep and stop taking the tonic—" Trinx said before Brinta cut her off.

"You'll help your mind, and I can't stress how important it is you let your mind rest. But if you were going to ask about the infertility, I'm afraid there's no unringing that bell. At least none that I know of. I'm sorry, Trinx, but you won't be able to bear a child."

"What?!" Trinx screamed. "How could you not tell me?"

"Tell you?" Brinta balked. "I didn't even know you were using that tonic. How would I have known to tell you? You should have told me what you were doing. Then perhaps we could have stopped it earlier before it was too late."

"I need to go," Trinx stated, doing her best to hold back tears. Today's pendulum of emotions had evidently not finished swinging.

"I'm sorry to put such a wet blanket on your success today," Brinta said. "You should go home and get some sleep. I'll send word to Gristle that you aren't feeling well. Don't worry about coming in here until you feel rested. Based on how long you've been taking it, you can expect to be out for quite a while."

Trinx felt numb and simply nodded. She left the shop and walked home, cursing the tonic, fate, the gods, and eventually herself. Another door closed. She would never have a child. She would never become a grandma.

Chapter 25

Project Snixil

By the time Trinx made it to her apartment, she was an emotional wreck. Her overwhelming sadness had turned into anger, which she had directed at anything and everything. Eventually, it had found its true and rightful target when she faced the reality that her own choices had led her here.

Why didn't I at least look at that appendix?

What kind of alchemist am I if I don't read all there is about a potion?

I should have told Brinta about the Traveler's Tonic before I even took it.

Why didn't I ask them about it?

I can't just keep things from them.

All they ever do is help me.

Trinx found herself at a loss with no anchor or plan. She threw her bag down on the floor. It had been so many days since she had last closed her eyes. She removed her shoes and socks, pulled off her dress, and then removed her undergarments. Turning to drop everything in her to-be-cleaned pile, she caught a glimpse of herself in the mirror.

Walking over to stand in front of the mirror, she once again saw her new body. All of her work hadn't been a total loss. It was hard to be as happy as she should be, but the sight of herself still brought a crooked smile to her face. This was something she had dreamed of for a long time, and she knew her life would be different now, even if she couldn't achieve her other goals. *Wait until Quilka hears about this.*

Tearing herself away from the image in the mirror, she slipped on a nightgown. Then she crawled under the covers in her bed and pulled them up and over her head, creating a cocoon. She had been getting sleepier since her last sip of tonic. That sip was quite a few hours ago, and she could feel the dreamworld pulling at her, causing her eyes to sag. Trinx let them close and allowed the sleep to envelop her, pulling her into a deep slumber.

The lack of any set alarms allowed the sleep-deprived goblin to sleep through the entire night, the next day, and most of the following night as well. When she did wake, she found it was early, before dawn, not that she could see the sky in the caverns. Her clocks told her it would still be an hour before the sun rose. That, combined with the gurgling and rumbling in her stomach, indicated she must have slept for at least a day.

Trinx pulled herself out of bed. She felt well rested. The feeling was much better than what the tonic had provided. The tonic put off the need for sleep but didn't fully refresh everything that actual sleep provides. After putting a kettle on for tea, she scrounged around the kitchenette for some food. Finding a hard roll, she cut it in half and smeared a thick layer of creamy butter on each side. She put a pan on the stove and grilled the roll, butter-side down. Once it looked sufficiently toasted, she removed it, placed the two pieces on a plate, and spooned on a healthy dollop of berry preserves.

The kettle began to whine as the water threatened to boil. She pulled it from the heat and poured it over some dragonroot in her teapot. Between taking bites of her crusty jam delivery device, Trinx drew a hot bath. She finished her toasted roll and poured a cup of tea into her favorite mug, finishing it with a large dollop of milk.

Mug in hand, Trinx carefully lowered herself into the bath. She spent the early morning in the tub, sipping her tea and contemplating everything that had happened the day before. *No*, she thought, *the day before that*. It amazed her to think about everything that had happened that day. Tears began to well up, but she wiped them away.

"No, there will be none of that today. I need to move on," she said aloud to the empty apartment.

But what would she move on to? She had achieved almost everything she wanted from alchemy, and it was her own fault she hadn't gotten more. Trinx liked alchemy, though, and there were always new mysteries to solve. *Not everything has to be about you*, she told herself.

Eventually, the bath water cooled enough that she found it too uncomfortable to stay in the tub. She toweled off and dressed, choosing her sleeveless black dress with purple accents. Sitting at the dressing table, she applied some makeup and crafted fresh braids. At the ends of the braids, she tied dark purple ribbons that matched the highlights of her dress.

When she grabbed her bag from the floor, a few items fell out, having been jostled close to the opening when she had dropped her bag before sleeping. One of her muffin-pucks rolled out. It likely was no longer chewy and was now just a dense rock-muffin.

"Snixil," she whispered to herself.

Trinx decided to visit Snixil and bring her and Nibbles some breakfast. No, not the rock-muffin. She would splurge for some pastries from Mystic and get a jug of tea as well. It was definitely time she spent some time visiting with her. Trinx stuck a couple of mugs in her bag so they would have something for the tea.

"Oh!" Trinx exclaimed. "I should bring Snixil a dress. She might only have the one. Even if she has more, who wouldn't want another one?"

She flipped through the dresses in her wardrobe and picked out a brown dress she thought would look nice on the young goblin. After carefully folding it, she slipped it into her bag and left her apartment.

Trinx set off for the nearest Mystic and picked out three flakey pastries filled with apples and cinnamon. She was sure Snixil would love them, and there would be enough for her to share with Nibbles.

When she entered the alley, everything was still. It was early in the morning, so this wasn't too surprising. Trinx approached the tent, and when she still didn't see any movement, she stood outside, cleared her voice, and said, "Knock, knock!"

A ball of fur flew out of the tent and landed a short distance away. Nibbles had flipped in the air and somehow landed facing Trinx. The raccoon settled some when he recognized it was her. His little nose twitched, sniffing toward the bag of pastries. Shortly thereafter, a sleepy Snixil poked her head out of the tent.

"Hello? Why are you knocking? I don't have a door."

"Of course, you don't have a door," Trinx said with a giggle. "That's why I said it rather than knocking your tent over. Breakfast delivery! Hungry?"

Snixil's sleepy eyes popped open wide. "Really? You

brought more food? Why are you so nice? No one ever is this nice to us. You must be hoping for something."

"Nope. I just want to help. It's my new thing," Trinx said. "Mystic had apple turnovers that looked amazing and smelled of cinnamon sugar. In fact, I think Nibbles can smell them. I brought one for him, too. Are you up for a chat this morning?"

"Thanks," Snixil said. "I'm sure they will be great. And I'd love it if you stayed for a while, Ma'am."

Trinx mentally sighed at the *ma'am* title. She would have to cure Snixil of that.

"You are very welcome."

She sat down and leaned against the wall of a building and began pulling things from her bag.

Handing a turnover to Snixil, she said, "You can have Nibbles start on his. I can tell he's hungry."

Trinx pulled the two mugs from her bag, set them down on the ground, and then poured hot dragonroot tea from the jug. "Oh! And I brought you something else. The blue dress you have on looks really cute on you. But I thought you might like another one. This one is brown."

She pulled the dress out, handing it to the young goblin.

"Really? This is too much. Thank you. It looks beautiful."

"You don't have to keep thanking me," Trinx said as her cheeks continued to darken with purple. "I just know how hard it can be sometimes. A friend of mine gave me my first dresses, and I adored her for it. Think of it as me paying it forward. I've been focused too much on myself lately. I want to do more for others."

Trinx passed a mug over to the girl and handed her a turnover on a napkin.

After taking a small bite of the pastry, Snixil set it down. She then took a sip of tea and said, "Mmmm. I love dragonroot, but I don't get to have it very often. I used to have it at home sometimes."

"Do you miss home? Is it really better out here? You're just so young. It must be hard," Trinx said as she took a sip of her own tea.

"Sometimes I miss my mom," Snixil said as she pulled off a layer of the flakey crust while picking at the pastry. "But she died, and that's when I left. I couldn't stay there with him after that. He got worse than he ever had been before."

"I thought I had it rough," Trinx said, wincing. "Sounds like your father and mine would get along well on a keffleball team. They don't sound very different. I worry about my mom sometimes. She even helped me recently, even though she doesn't understand me."

"It's not so bad," Snixil said and popped a full bite with a gooey cinnamon-glazed piece of apple into her mouth. "The shops on either side of the alley don't care much that I'm here. And most people walking by don't even notice."

"I'd still like to help you find someplace better," Trinx said. "I'm sure there are other folks without a lot of options. I would help them all if I could."

"You've already helped me a lot, Ma'am—"

"Please, just call me Trinx," Trinx interrupted, softening it with a smile. "Sorry. I'm just having trouble thinking of myself as 'ma'am.'"

"Sorry, Trinx," Snixil said. "You've just been so nice, and my mom always insisted I call her 'ma'am.'"

"No need to apologize. Really," Trinx said and took another sip of tea.

"I like to act like I don't need nothing," Snixil said, picking at her napkin. "But I appreciate all your help. If you find a better place for me to live, I'd love it. I just won't count on it."

"I tend to make things happen when I try," Trinx said.

"That's how I reinvented myself and how I learned alchemy. So, I'll make it an official project. How's that sound? Project Snixil."

Snixil wrinkled her face. "I'm not sure I want to be a project."

"Fair enough," Trinx agreed. "I didn't mean it like that. The project is finding you a home. I just named it after you. But I'll keep that in my head. It doesn't need a name. Don't worry. You aren't a project. Of course, you could be your own project. You can change yourself and the world if you try."

"Are you sure about that?" Snixil asked, doubt creeping across her dirty face.

"Oh! Worg's breath! I'm an idiot," Trinx suddenly said.

"I don't think you're an idiot," Snixil said, her doubt turning into confusion.

"No. Really, I am," Trinx said. "Someone tried to help me and told me that I needed the be the change I wanted to see in the world. I totally misunderstood what they meant. But here I am telling you the same thing. I get it now, and this goes beyond you and me."

"I don't know if I get it," Snixil said with a shrug and took a bite of her turnover.

"That's okay," Trinx said. "You don't have to get it. Not now, anyway, but just know you can change stuff if you want. But you were right. This isn't Project Snixil. Like I said. I bet there are lots of folks who could use a better place to live and some help. I have a friend who lives in a cave. She seems happy there, but I wonder if she wouldn't like someplace better."

"That sounds like quite a project," Snixil said and finished the last of her tea.

"It might be," Trinx said. "But I'm going to see what I can do. I should get to the alchemy shop. I just finished sleeping for two nights and a day. It's time to get back to work."

"What?" Snixil asked, confusion apparent in her eyes.

"I'll tell you about it another time. I'll see you later," Trinx said as she gathered everything up and left for Distilled Magic.

Snixil waved after her while shaking her head and giving Nibbles a scritch.

Trinx entered Distilled Magic and waved to Brinta, who was behind the counter.

"Thank you for encouraging me to sleep. Based on how long I was out, I really needed it. But I've rejoined the world of the living. I'm sorry I didn't tell you about what was going on and that I blamed you for it."

"I understand it was an emotional day for you," Brinta said warmly. "I also understand if you need a bit more time before diving back into work. Unless you have more project ideas, we should focus on the shop for a while. Maybe go through more of the basics with you, like reading all of the warnings on advanced recipes."

"That's a good idea," Trinx said sheepishly. "I really should have read more thoroughly. And I should have told you I wanted to make the tonic instead of just making it while you were out. I really didn't think you would mind, but I realize if I had told you, you would have had me read everything."

"You're right," Brinta said. "You should have told me. But you're also right that I didn't mind. In fact, I'm proud you could. That was an advanced concoction. But while Traveler's Tonic is very handy, it can be dangerous with prolonged use. Most folks who use it only do so occasionally and usually just to put off sleep for a few hours or a night at the most. Get your-self settled, and we can figure out what to focus on."

"I want to help you today," Trinx said. "But...I was wondering if I could take another day. I wanted to tell Quilka about everything that happened."

"That sounds like a good idea," Brinta replied. "I'll be fine here without you. Say hi to Quilka for me."

"Thanks," Trinx said. "And I will."

It was early enough that Quilka might not even be awake yet. She had already had breakfast. However, she thought she could still splurge on a treat that they could eat while chatting. Trinx stopped at a Mystic outlet near Quilka's apartment and found they had a special on a new item she hadn't seen before. The discount price made her decision for the treat even easier, and she purchased two and got a refill for the jug of tea she still had from earlier. Quilka would appreciate not having to brew tea this morning.

Trinx knocked on Quilka's door as she swung it open and entered the apartment. She found her friend in bed reading a mystery book. "Morning. I brought us a treat!" she said, holding the bag up to show it off.

Before waiting for a reply, Trinx put the bag on the counter and pulled the mugs out of her bag. She washed them in the sink and dried them off.

"Hi, Trinx," Quilka said with a yawn as she put her book down. "I wasn't expecting you, but I'm glad you're here. I was a little worried when you didn't come to the tavern the past couple of nights. Gristle said you weren't feeling well. What kind of treat? I smell cinnamon and nutmeg!"

Trinx pulled a plate from a cupboard and two fried cakes from the bag. One had a thick layer of chocolate icing smeared across the top, and the other had a similar treatment with whipped maple frosting. She cut each one in half so they could try the different versions. Then, she filled the two mugs with tea from the jug and pulled a container of milk from the coldbox to add a dollop to each.

"Mystic had a special on a new treat," Trinx said. "Fried

cakes with frosting. They smelled amazing, and the discounted price helped a lot."

"Those sound delicious," Quilka said, wiping her mouth. "I think I just started drooling a little bit. And you brought tea too? We could have just made some."

Quilka slipped out from under the covers, pulled on a robe, and cinched it loosely. She then took a mug to the couch, offering her friend a smile of thanks.

Trinx took the plate of cakes to the table in front of the couch and set it down before sitting herself.

"So," Quilka began, "what brings you by this morning? You look like you are feeling a lot better."

"So, yeah," Trinx said. "I wasn't exactly sick. But I wasn't exactly well either. I'm sure Gristle won't mind the difference. I've been taking a tonic to stay awake and not getting all the sleep I needed."

"Oh no," Quilka said. "You shouldn't do things like that. Everyone needs sleep."

"I thought maybe I didn't," Trinx beamed. "I found this amazing tonic that puts off the need for sleep. I had to make up for it, though. If you can believe it, I slept for two nights and the whole day in between!"

"That's a lot of sleep!" Quilka said, raising her eyebrows. "I don't think I could sleep that long even if I tried."

"I definitely needed it," Trinx said. "Especially after the day I had before I went to bed. *She* came to the shop. Thankfully, *he* didn't come with her."

"Did she agree to help?"

"She came," Trinx said with a slow nod. "And she did help. She provided both hair and claw shavings. It wasn't as bad as I thought it would be, but she still didn't know what to think about me."

Quilka took a sip of her tea. "I'm glad it wasn't too bad and that she helped. But I'm not surprised she isn't fully on board yet. I can't wait any longer to try these cakes. The smell is killing me."

Trinx laughed and liked how Quilka lightened the mood of the story. "It's a good spot to pause and try these treats."

They each took half of the chocolate variety. Trinx found the cake was decadent. A thin, crispy, fried crust broke easily when she bit into it. Inside, the dense crumb was soft and spicy. The warm chocolate icing stuck to her teeth and the top of her mouth. The cocoa flavor complemented the cake nicely. After swallowing the sticky bite of cake, she washed it all down with a sip of her creamy tea.

"Mmmph," Quilka grunted as she swallowed her bite. "By the fae, these are amazing."

"So, the best news of the day got overshadowed by the worst," Trinx said. "But I think I'm coming to terms with it and trying to celebrate the good. I'll start there. You are looking at a changed woman. The potion worked when we used the samples from my mom."

"That's wonderful!" Quilka exclaimed. "I thought maybe your face looked a little softer, but it could have just been my eyes still blurry from sleep. How does it feel?"

"I feel at home," Trinx said. "So much so that I almost don't even think about it. It's weird that way. I don't have to waste extra time when getting ready. I just feel like I can breathe."

"I can't even imagine," Quilka said. "That is definitely good news. It's what you've been wanting. What could be so bad that it overshadowed that?"

"Well, I mean, it is what I wanted," Trinx said. "And I wanted it so that I wouldn't need the extra pouches and could look the same way I felt. But I also wanted the change so I could have a child. You know that. I've wanted one so much.

And then to have the opportunity some day to join the council. But that's the problem."

"Problem?" Quilka asked, sipping her tea.

"Yeah," Trinx said. "So, that tonic I mentioned? The one that put off sleep? It turns out if you take it too long, it can have side effects. Infertility is one of them."

Quilka let out a gasp. "Oh, Trinx. I'm glad you didn't hurt yourself more."

"I know. I know," Trinx said, shaking her head. "It was short-sighted and stupid. And now I'll never have a child. But I'm not going to shortcut things anymore. And I'm giving up on my quest for a child. I've decided to help people."

"Help people?" Quilka asked. "How?"

"Any way I can," Trinx said with a shrug. "I don't need to be on the council. Zigla tried to tell me that and I wouldn't listen. Her mom did the same and even told me to be the change."

"Right. Be the change," Quilka said. "I thought you said that was the potion to change your body."

"That is what I said," Trinx admitted. "But now I don't think that's what she meant. I was talking with Snixil when it hit me. I was encouraging her to think about how she could change and improve her life. I realized right then. I decided to change my life, and then I did. I decided to learn alchemy, and then I did. I decided to help the community of people like me, and instead of doing that, I had it in my head that I could only do it if I was on the council."

"I see," Quilka said with a clap. "That does make sense. You don't need to be on the council to help people. You can just help them."

"Exactly," Trinx said. "So that's what I'm going to do. I'm going to help people. I'm starting with Snixil, but I'm going to find others to help as well. I don't know exactly how I'm going to do it yet, but I'll figure it out."

"Snixil wants your help, right?" Quilka paused to ask as her cheeks started blushing. "You aren't just forcing your help on her? I know how you can be sometimes."

"She seems happy to have it," Trinx said. "She even calls me 'ma'am.' I need to stop that."

Quilka let out a giggle. "Ma'am? That's too much."

"I figure, maybe I can just make things better for people like me, one at a time. Bit by bit," Trinx explained.

"That still sounds like an ambitious plan," Quilka said. "But it is at least more doable. More realistic than raising a child, in my opinion."

"Probably," Trinx said and reached down to try a bite of the maple-covered cake. She didn't believe it could have been possible, but it was even more divine than the chocolate. The maple frosting was fluffy and airy, and it blended perfectly with the cinnamon and nutmeg in the cake.

As she was chewing, there was a knock on the door.

"Who could that be?" Quilka asked rhetorically and stood up to open the door.

"Letter delivery," the goblin at the door said. "Are you Quilka?"

"Yes," she said, nodding and holding out her hand.

"Here you go, then," the goblin said, handing the envelope to her.

Quilka thanked him and wished him well before shutting the door. She turned and opened the letter. Walking back to the couch, she sat down and pulled out the parchment.

Scanning the letter, Quilka said, "Oh! It's from Mungo at Unity. You probably got one, too. It has the latest location of the club. Woah."

"What?" Trinx asked, bending over to read.

"You know that ancient old house in the outskirts of the northwest part of the warren? It's not that far from the Tender. You know. The one everyone says is haunted?"

"Yeah, everyone knows that place," Trinx said. "Or at least they know to stay away from it. Weird noises come from there sometimes."

"Evidently, those noises might be Unity," Quilka said. "The club is sometimes *under* that old house."

"That's sneaky," Trinx said with a grin. "We should go check it out."

"I'm sure it will be there for a while," Quilka said. "We can find a time to go soon."

"No, I mean like now," Trinx said. "We have memberships. We should go check it out. I want to see what a club under that old house is like."

"What?" Quilka asked, raising her eyebrows. "I don't even know if the club operates during the day. We've always gone at night and left before closing. But I assumed they did actually close at some point during the night."

"I don't know if it does either," Trinx said. "But don't you want to see? If it's not open, we can at least see how the entrance works and come back sometime when it is open. We don't have to stay long. Just a bit of dancing, and then we can go to the Tender to work."

"Okay," Quilka said, grinning conspiratorially. "I'm in. Let's see if it's open for dancing and have some fun before work. We can see that spooky old house close up."

Chapter 26

TQ House

Trinx and Quilka approached the large house that sat on the edge of town. It wasn't horribly far from the Arsonist's Tender, but farther to the west. Trinx looked up at the imposing structure that loomed three stories in front of her. A portion of the roof was missing, and she could see through a large hole in the wall of the third floor that it had collapsed in. She couldn't tell what color the house had originally been painted due to all the grime and dirt, but whatever hue it was didn't matter as the paint peeled from the house in curls.

Shutters hung limply from several windows, while others were missing coverings altogether. Trinx could only spy a single window that wasn't at least cracked, if not outright broken. Several planters lined the walkway in a haphazard pattern leading up to the house, with more on either side of the front door. The planters contained dry dirt and small twigs that likely had once been bushes or flowering plants.

Quilka pulled out the letter and skimmed it again.

"It says here that the club entrance is separate from the

house, around back. We should look for something that looks like the entrance to a cellar near an old outhouse."

"So, let's head around back then," Trinx said and led the way behind the house.

As they passed by, her nose wrinkled when the pungent odor of a backed-up sewer and death washed over her.

"That smell probably helps people get into the perfect mood for dancing," Trinx said with a laugh.

"No kidding," Quilka agreed. "They can definitely keep the club secret in this location. Oh! Look, I think that's the entrance."

Trinx looked where Quilka was pointing and veered in that direction. She found the doors open and a stairway leading down. Although the stairway was dark, she could see some light from the depths. The girls looked at each other, then shrugged and walked down the stairs.

It was much quieter than when they usually came to the club. As they approached the bottom of the stairway, Trinx called out, "Hello? Mungo? It's Trinx and Quilka. Is the club open? We got the letter."

Shuffling and movement from ahead beckoned them on, and the hallway opened into a large room. It was fully lit up, very different from how it would likely look when the next event started. Goblins hurried around the room, cleaning and preparing it.

"The club is definitely not open," Quilka said. "We should go. We can come back in the evening sometime. Maybe Gris will let us leave early one night when it's slow."

"You're probably right," Trinx said, nodding. "It's pretty neat seeing how it all comes together."

As she turned to leave, a nearby goblin spotted them and ran over. "Hello, hello. Did you need something?"

"Oh? Us?" Trinx asked, feeling silly they had come down.

She thought she better say something so it wouldn't be even weirder. "Do you know where we can find Mungo? Is he here?"

The goblin looked at her, then around the room, and finally pointed to an area across the way.

"Looks like he's over there. See him talking with that group?"

Sure enough, Trinx recognized him and said, "You're right, that's him. Thanks!"

Quilka hissed a whisper, "What are you doing? Why are we bothering Mungo?"

"I don't know," Trinx said, shrugging her shoulders. "I felt like I had to say some kind of reason we were here, and that's the first thing that came to mind."

Trinx marched across the room with Quilka in tow. Along the way, she caught Mungo's eye, and he wrapped up his conversation by the time the girls reached him.

As they finished their approach, he smiled widely and said, "I remember you two! Friends of Brinta, right? I never forget faces, but names sometimes slip right out of my mind. Forgive me! Remind me again of your names?"

"I'm Trinx," she said and gestured at her friend, "and this is Quilka. And yes, we're friends of Brinta, you remembered."

"Wonderful!" Mungo exclaimed. "I'm thrilled to see you again, but there is much to do. As you can see, the club isn't open. Is there something I can do for you?"

"We weren't sure when the club was going to be open," Trinx explained. "It didn't say in the letter, and I wanted to see what the new location looked like. You know, I never knew this creepy old house hid this club. A lot of people even say it's haunted, and they hear strange noises sometimes."

"I know!" Mungo squealed. "Isn't it grand? The house was condemned quite a few years ago. It sat empty for quite some time, and I got an excellent deal on it. It seemed the perfect cover for one of my clubs, so I bought the place and built the club underneath. The noises people hear are just the club, but everyone jumps to the scariest conclusion."

"You bought this house, and no one lives there?" Quilka asked. "So, it's just like a giant prop?"

"It *is*," Mungo said, nodding enthusiastically. "A prop is exactly what it is. No one would want to live there. It's falling apart. The plumbing is wrecked, the roof is falling in, and hells, there's a sizeable portion of the third floor just missing. Inside is even worse than out. Vermin moved in and left droppings all over. They gnawed on the inside walls and fixtures, too. I bought it for the land and what I could build underneath. The house helps deter people."

"Seems a waste," Trinx said, thinking of Snixil and her hunt to find her a home. "Especially when some goblins don't even have a home."

"Maybe," Mungo said with a nod, "but I don't see anyone wanting to live in a wreck like that, so it's not like I could rent it out. I don't have the time, energy, or money to invest in fixing it up. It serves its purpose well."

"Wait!" Trinx burst. "I just had an idea. What if someone else could fix it up? Then people could live there."

Mungo just laughed. "Who would want to fix it up if they don't own it? And I don't plan on selling. I like the location of the club. I've put in a lot of work down here."

Trinx screwed up her face and thought out loud, "Well, I know some people who don't have a lot of options. And while I have an apartment, it's expensive despite how small it is. I'd rather put my money toward living in a house like that. I bet I could fix the house up myself. Well, maybe with some help from friends. We could make it a safe place for any goblins that need a home."

"Honey," Mungo said. "If you can put in all the work it

would need to make that a safe home, I'd gladly let you have the house for that. As long as I can continue running the club down here when it comes around in the rotation. Do you actually think you could do that?"

"I would help her," Quilka said. "And I bet we can find some others to help, too."

"I'm sure we could," Trinx agreed. "I can make this the best home for displaced goblins. Zigla might help, and if she wanted to, she could live there, too. Oh! Maybe Zigla could even help run the house? You think she'd want to?"

"You should ask," Quilka said, grinning. "From what you've told me of her, she seems like the sort that would handle that well."

"Okay, Mungo," Trinx said. "We have to get started. Thank you so much for the chance."

"Good luck," he said. "If you manage to get it renovated, we can spread the word in the club. Folks in the club won't need it, but they likely know of goblins who might."

Trinx led the way back to the surface and walked to the front door. She found it wasn't locked, and it swung open easily on loose hinges. Inside, it was truly a disaster. Upon entering the house, Trinx heard small claws scampering across the wooden floors. She thought she spotted an enormous rat scurrying beyond a doorway deeper within the house.

"Uh, Trinx," Quilka said. "You were so excited down below. I just got wrapped up in the idea. But do you think we can actually do this? This place is a wreck, and it stinks."

"It will be fine," Trinx announced, seemingly unphased by the state of the house. It was dark, making it hard to see exactly how much work needed to be done. "First thing, we need to get some lights in here. But right after that, we need to get rid of the current residents. I know just the guy. The only question will be how much."

"How are we even going to have time?" Quilka asked. "I don't think you should go back to using that tonic, and you work all day and evening. It'll take forever. Even if I help."

"I'll just have to talk to Brinta and Gristle," Trinx said, nodding. "If I explain what I'm doing, I bet they'll let me have some time off. You can help during the day if you are up for it."

"If they give you time off, I'll definitely help during the day," Quilka agreed.

"I'm going to make this my home," Trinx announced. "I'll cancel my apartment. You can live here too if you want, but I understand if you don't want to. Your place is so nice. But if I live here, I can easily use my free time to work on it. Just need to get the vermin out and clean up at least one room."

"Oh," Quilka said quietly, her cheeks a soft purple. "I could live here, too? It would be fun living so close. We get so busy at the Tender, and with your job at the shop, I feel like we never see each other."

"Totally," Trinx said. "We'll clean up enough space for both of us!"

"So, maybe let's wait on that," Quilka said. "If I kept my place for a while, we could have a place to bathe and clean up. I don't really want to camp out for that long."

"Good point," Trinx said. "I hadn't thought about that. I can't think of everything. That's why you and I fit together so well."

Quilka's cheeks turned purple, and she coughed, making a point of looking around the room.

Trinx joined her in the appraisal and sighed happily. "We can do this. Do you think you could round up some basic supplies? Candles, maybe a shovel? I'm going to see about a solution for the vermin and tell Zigla and Snixil."

"I can do that," Quilka said, nodding. "I'll have to get to the Tender for my shift, but I'll leave some supplies here before I do. I'll come back and check on things after work. I'll tell Gristle you are feeling better but need a bit more time. You'll need to go talk to him soon if you want more time off."

"Thank you so much for helping," Trinx said. "You really are the best. When I said I wanted to help Snixil, I had no idea it could turn into something so much bigger so fast."

"You never have thought small," Quilka said and flashed her a grin. "At least with this idea, you are in control. You can make this happen if you try hard enough."

"Right!" Trinx said excitedly. "I am the change. Just like Vorti said.

"Oh!" Trinx exclaimed again. The ideas seemed to have been exploding in her head during the entire conversation. "That's what we could call it! TQ House. Trinx and Quilka." She giggled, and it turned into a laugh.

"I love the name," Quilka agreed. "And you really are the change. You are practically change incarnate."

"I'm even more sure than before that this is what Vorti meant," Trinx said, beaming. "I'll see you soon. So much to do."

She turned and set out as Quilka yelled, "Goodbye," from behind her as she raced off to track people down.

Trinx ran all the way to Hinox in the southwest portion of the warren. Before long, she stood in front of the extermination office. She caught her breath before she opened the door and found Pox standing behind the counter, filling out some paperwork.

He looked up as she entered.

"Hello again. Does Brinta need more rats for your experiments?"

"What?" she asked reflexively. "Oh, no. They still have some. No, I need to get rid of some rats and maybe other stuff, too. Honestly, I'm not sure what all is in there. How much does it cost to rid a house of vermin?"

"Depends," Pox answered. "How big is the house? What's infesting it? Yeh said rats? But maybe something more?"

"Yeah," Trinx said. "It's the new TQ House. It's a mess. I'm pretty sure I saw a giant rat. Just a glimpse. Might have been dire, maybe not. I don't know what all is living in there. We just got the TQ House."

"The TQ House?" Pox asked. "I've never heard of that. If yeh don't know what all is in there, I'll have to come take a look to give you a proper estimate."

"Oh, right," Trinx said, nodding to herself more than the exterminator. "You wouldn't know about the TQ House. I just named it. The old haunted house in the northwest. Do you know it?"

Pox snorted. "Yeah, I know it. In fact, I'd bet that house is the source of many of my clients up in the northwest. Yeh actually trying to fix that place up? Did yeh buy it? Hope yeh didn't pay much."

"No, I didn't buy it," Trinx explained. "But I'm fixing it up. It's complicated. Anyway, it's called TQ House now. It's going to be a safe home for displaced goblins."

"Yeh don't say?" Pox said, raising an eyebrow. "Like some kind of shelter?"

"That's the plan," Trinx said, excitement overflowing. "It's going to be amazing. I'll live there, and Quilka said she'd move in once it's fixed up, and I'm inviting Snixil and Zigla."

"Don't know any of those folks," Pox said, shaking his head. "Should I? Doesn't matter. Got a question for yeh, then."

"What's that?" Trinx asked.

"I have a nephew," Pox began. "I suppose that's what I'd call him. It gets confusing, yeh know? And my brother. Well, let's just say he's an ass. Kicked the child out well before he was ready for the world. Yeh think there would be room in that house for him?"

"Oh, yes!" Trinx squealed. "TQ House is big. I don't know how many it will hold yet, but once it's done, he can move in. We have a lot to fix up first. Like the vermin. That's why I'm here."

"Well, in that case," Pox said with a grin. "I can clear the vermin out of that place for yeh. Donation to the cause. Besides, depending on what kind of critters are holed up in there, might be able to make some money on the back end," he added with a purposeful wink.

"Oh, that would be wonderful," Trinx said. "Thank you so much. Tell your nephew about the house. And that is what you should call him, nephew, that is. But what should I call him? He's got a name?"

"Right, right," Pox said. "He asks people to call him Flek these days. Name's just as good as the one his ass of a dad gave originally, so fine by me if he wants people to use Flek."

"It's a great name," Trinx said. "Come by when you can to clear out the vermin. We're going to be busy cleaning the place up. But if no one is around, just do your thing. Once we get it fixed up, I'll let you know, and Flek can come move in."

"Sounds good, take care," Pox said, waving as she left.

Trinx went to find Snixil and Nibbles next. This time, she was bringing something better than food—a new home—well, almost. It did need a lot of work.

"You're back already?" Snixil asked when Trinx found her and the raccoon in the alley. "The pastries you brought this morning were wonderful. Thanks again. But what brings you back, ma'am?"

"You won't believe it," Trinx said, ignoring the ma'am title Snixil kept using. "I've found you a new home!"

"A new home?" Snixil asked with a quizzical expression. "What do you mean?"

"You can live in TQ House!" Trinx announced. "It needs

some work. Okay. It needs a lot of work. But when Quilka and I finish fixing it up, you can live there."

"So, almost a new home," Snixil said. "But what's TQ House?"

"TQ House is a new safe place. I'm going to live there, too. So is Quilka. That's the name. TQ House. Get it? But also, it's a home for anyone like us that needs some help."

"What about Nibbles?" Snixil asked, petting her raccoon friend. "I can't leave him. He's basically my only friend."

"Of course, he can come," Trinx said. "I bet he'd liven up the place. It would be fun."

"Where is it? Is it far?" Snixil peppered in more questions.

"You know that old house in the northwest? The one everyone always says is haunted?" Trinx asked.

"Wait!" Snixil cried. "You want us to live in a haunted house? No, thank you, Ma'am."

"It's not haunted," Trinx said with exasperation. "People just think that because of the weird noises. But I know the secret. The noises are because sometimes Club Unity uses a place *under* the house."

"Really?" Snixil asked, her curiosity peeked. "Could I visit the club sometimes?"

"Maybe in a few years!" Trinx said with a laugh. "You're a bit too young to be going to clubs. But sure, once you are older, you could visit the club. Quilka and I go dancing sometimes."

"Fair enough," Snixil said. "Do you think I could help fix the house up? It might go faster with more hands."

"It would be amazing if you helped," Trinx assured her. "But you don't have to. I'm trying to make a safe place for people like you to live. You don't have to work to have a place."

"No. But I want to," Snixil insisted. "I'm sure you could use the help. I've seen that place. Not up close. But close enough to see it's a dump. Sooner *we* get it fixed up, the sooner I can move out of this tent."

"If you really want to, I won't stop you," Trinx said. "And I would appreciate the help. You're right—it'll go faster with more people. It might get a bit crowded, but if you want to, you can sleep at my apartment until the house is ready."

"Sounds good," Snixil said. "I don't like just leaving my stuff here. I'll pack it up and head over there later. I really don't mind helping clean it up. Thanks, ma—I mean, Trinx."

"See you later," Trinx said, running out of the warren, this time to track down Zigla in her cave.

Chapter 27

House Manager

Trinx knocked on the wooden door of Zigla's cave. As she waited for a response, she realized she had a lot to share. It hadn't been long since her last visit, but so much had happened. Eventually, shuffling noises gave way to the creak of the door as it opened into the cave. Zigla stood in the doorway, looking better than ever. The EverSmooth worked wonders for her. She had her hair drawn up in a bun and wore heavy but neatly applied eyeshadow and liner. It was clear she had also been using the Vash's Extreme Lashes, as her long lashes looked incredible.

"Good afternoon, Trinx," Zigla said, her bright smile revealing how pleased she was to have Trinx visit. "Come in, come in. What brings you out here? Have a chance to talk with my mother?"

"Thanks, Zigla," Trinx said. "It's wonderful to see you, too. I did talk with your mother, and so much has happened since I was last here. I need to tell you everything."

"Well, then, don't just stand there," Zigla said, encouraging her with her arms to enter the cave. "Have a seat, and I'll put a kettle on. If you have that much to share, we should have some tea with the chat."

Trinx entered and plopped herself down in a chair at the table. It was the same one she always used, falling back into the habit as if she still lived there. She looked around the cave and noticed it didn't seem very different. Perhaps a little tidier, but other than that, nothing had changed. Zigla's life didn't seem to have much outside of her solitary routine. Trinx wondered if she would even want to come back to the warren.

"If what you have to share doesn't need me sitting there, you can start talking while I make the tea," Zigla said. "You always seem to have more words than there is time to get them out, so might as well start now."

"I have so much. Where to start?" Trinx mused aloud, then jumped right in. "I guess I'll start with Vex. Oh! Vex! I need to tell him, too. Maybe he can help."

"What was that?" Zigla asked. "You need to tell Vex what?"

"Sorry, I just remembered," Trinx said. "But I'll get there. I need to tell you first, don't I? That's why I'm here. So anyway, like I was saying. Vex. We solved the beard potion. Now, he has an amazing beard. Oh, but maybe he won't even need that potion anymore. We'll have to see if he wants to try the new potion."

Zigla continued making tea. She looked almost ready to ask more questions, but shook her head and continued to listen.

"And then your mother invited me to tea," Trinx said. "That was so kind of her. She's really nice, you know? Oh, right, of course, you know. At first, I was sad and upset, though. She wouldn't talk to the agency. I thought she would help me adopt a child. She didn't make sense, just talking about how I needed to become the change."

Zigla let out a snort. "Sounds about right. You should trust in what she had to say, even if it didn't make sense at the time."

"I know, right?" Trinx said. "It turns out she was right. I can be the change! I'm pretty sure, anyway. I'm almost positive that's exactly what she meant. But I'm doing stuff anyway, and I think it will help Snixil and Flek and loads more people."

"Snixil? Flek? You've never mentioned them before," Zigla said as she brought over the teapot and two cups. The tea still needed time to steep, but she set it down and joined Trinx at the table. "You might be jumping ahead again."

"I haven't technically met Flek yet," Trinx said. "I met his uncle, Pox. But Flek needs a safe place to stay. His father kicked him out. Pox didn't say if he had a room in his place, but if you saw, or smelled, the place, you can imagine Flek wouldn't want to live there."

Zigla nodded along, taking in the information with a smile.

"I met Snixil in town," Trinx explained. "She has a pet raccoon named Nibbles, who is just the cutest! Snixil also needs a place to live. She has a home, but it's not the greatest. I just told her about TQ House. She is excited; she even wants to help out so she can move in sooner. I told her she doesn't have to, but she really wants to."

"TQ House? What's that?" Zigla asked as she poured some tea for them. The steam rose from the cups, exposing the chill in the cave.

"That's the whole point," Trinx said, giggling. "We have to fix it up, but we have a house. TQ House. Isn't that an awesome name? It's a house for displaced goblins that need a safe home. Quilka is moving into the house with me, too. So, it's a house for Trinx and Quilka."

"That's quite the undertaking," Zigla said. "How do you have the time or resources? And how did you even get a house in the first place?"

"Oh, that's easy," Trinx said with a wave of her hand. "Mungo said we could use it. He didn't need it. He just had it for the club—it's underneath. Well, sometimes it is, anyway. But it is going to be a lot of work. That's part of why I came."

"So, you are getting to a point with this story. That's good," Zigla smirked.

Ignoring the jab, Trinx continued, "I want you to come live there, too. I think it would be loads better than this cave. And if you are up for it, you could help run the house. It would benefit from someone more mature as the house manager. You were so kind to me when I first stumbled in here. Just like a mom, only better, really. But my mom isn't so bad, it turns out. She still has issues, though. But she helped with the potion. So, that was amazing."

"What potion?" Zigla asked.

"The potion!" Trinx said, exasperated. "Oh, wait. That's right. You made me jump ahead. I hadn't gotten to the potion part. I did it! Brinta and I did. We made a potion that can transform the body. I don't need pouches anymore. I grew these myself!" She cupped her breasts and bounced her hands twice. "I should have been able to even have a child, but I messed that up. That part isn't important now, though. I'll tell you more about that later. I still don't like to think about how I wrecked that plan. But now I have a better plan that isn't even about me anymore. This house is a way I can help others."

Zigla choked on her tea as Trinx explained all of that. "Trinx. That's amazing. Will it work on anyone?"

"It should," Trinx said. "But not the one I made. That one's for me because of my mom. Brinta said it's a designer elixir. It has to be custom for each person. We could make one for you. But we need some samples from your mother. Just some hair and claw filings. She's so nice. She would do that for you, wouldn't she?"

"I'm sure she would," Zigla answered, her eyes looking a

little misty as Trinx's avalanche of information washed over her.

"Great!" Trinx exclaimed. "We can ask her for the samples and get you a designer elixir just for you. So, what do you think? Will you move into TQ House when it's ready? I'm sure the house would run smoothly if you were in charge. And it has to be better than this cave. Not that there is anything wrong with your cave. It's very nice. I loved living here. But don't you get lonely out here?"

"I don't know," Zigla said. "It sounds nice, but I haven't been in the warren in ages. My mother and I agreed it would be for the best. But I can see how, with so many changes, it would be a different experience. I loved having you stay with me and being able to teach you how to find yourself. I was so happy to have that chance. Being around people who need me sounds really interesting."

"That settles it," Trinx said. "We'll move you into the house. Once it's ready, that is. Unless you want to come now? You could help us fix it up. It's not in great shape."

"Oh, I can help," Zigla said. "In fact, you could probably use someone of my size and muscles. I'm still not so sure about the warren. I've lived out here alone for so long."

"You wouldn't have to leave the house until you are ready," Trinx offered. "It wouldn't be that different from staying in the cave, except it would be loads nicer, and there would be other people in the house."

"Well, I suppose that works," Zigla conceded. "I'll move in. I'll start gathering my things. Might take a few trips. I have an old cart that should help. Where is this house?"

Trinx went on to explain where the house was and how to get there. "Come as soon as you can. Pox should have the vermin gone soon. Then we just have to deal with the mess. And the plumbing..." she said, trailing off.

Zigla laughed. "It does sound like a project. I'll be there when I can. And I'll reach out to my mother for the samples. Maybe you can introduce me to this Brinta you've told me about. I'd like to thank them for taking you under their wing."

"Definitely!" Trinx said with a nod. She took one last sip of the tea and stood. "I've still got so much to do. I should tell Vex, but maybe I'll do that tomorrow. I want to get to the house and start clearing it out."

When Trinx arrived back at the house, she found Snixil and Nibbles outside. The girl had her tent and a small bag next to her. She heard a lot of rustling and banging about inside.

"Hi, Snixil. You found the place. Why not go inside? Is it because of the noise? Are the vermin riled up?"

"Oh, they're riled up, I think," Snixil said with a couple of snorts. "It's pretty messy in there. I was poking around, checking the place out. Then, this guy shows up with a kid. Said he was there to get rid of our pests. I figured you knew what was up and let him have the house to himself. Surprised me when the kid went in to help him, but he said his uncle often has him help and pays him for the work."

"That must be Pox and Flek," Trinx explained. "Yeah, he's here to clear out our vermin. I didn't realize he would come so soon. Flek is going to live here with us. He needs a new home, too."

"He seemed nice enough," Snixil said. "That should be fun having more people around."

"Speaking of people," Trinx said, scanning the area. "Is Quilka here?"

"Quilka? Who's that?" Snixil asked, scrunching her face.

"Only my best friend in the world," Trinx said. "She's moving in, too. Eventually. She said she wanted the plumbing fixed first. I don't blame her." She punctuated the thought with a giggle.

"I think Pox probably doesn't want us in there," Snixil said. "Is there anything else to do?"

"Loads, I'm sure," Trinx said. "Look at that place. It's a dump. But we need supplies. Where can we get some supplies?"

"I don't know," Snixil said, looking like she was trying to figure out a solution.

"Of course you don't," Trinx said. "I was talking to myself, not you. Sorry. I have some things in my apartment, and I can pick up what I don't have at a store. Oh, there are two shovels. Quilka said she would track one down. Looks like she found two. We can empty these planters. But you don't have to. I can take care of it myself."

"No way," Snixil said. "I'm helping."

The two of them used the shovels to remove the dry dirt from the old planters. Some of the soil was packed in with time, but with some effort, they were able to remove it. Eventually, the long stone containers were empty except for some traces of dirt and dust. With Snixil's help, Trinx aligned the planters to the walkway and straightened the ones up against the house. They would look wonderful once they had fresh soil and Trinx had a chance to plant some flowers.

Right as they were taking a step back to admire how much neater the planters looked, Pox and a young goblin came out of the house. Pox was pushing a large cart loaded with traps and cages. Many of which contained vermin of one type or another, though most were rats.

"Oh, there yeh are," Pox said. "Only one I found here when I showed was, um, her? And she didn't know why I was here. Figured I'd just start in. Pretty sure I got everything living out of there. If yeh don't get it cleaned up, more are likely to just move on in."

"Thanks, Pox," Trinx said. "I didn't think you'd come so quickly. Is this Flek?" She waved at the boy. "The plan is to dig right into clean up. Well, maybe right after dinner. I'm getting hungry. But we'll have it cleaned up in no time."

"Not so sure about that," Pox said, wringing his hands. "It's pretty filthy in there. Yeh have your work cut out for you. Found some candles in the entry. Hope yeh don't mind, but I set them up throughout the house. Made it easier to see for clearing the critters out."

"Mind?" Trinx said. "Course I don't mind. Saves me the trouble. We'll need to see all the dirt and grime we're removing."

"I should be getting on. Need to get all these critters stowed," Pox said. "This here is Flek, as yeh guessed. Come on, Flek. Trinx said she'd let us know once the house is ready."

"Uncle Pox? Do you think you could just pay me for the job now?" Flek asked the exterminator. "I don't have a reason to go back to the office and would rather stay around here."

"What?" Pox said as it seemed to take a moment for him to register what he had been asked. "Oh. Right. Sure. I got the coin on me. I guess you can check in with me or Trinx from time to time to see when the place is ready."

Pox fished several coins out of his pocket and gave them to Flek. "Thanks for your help today."

He turned to Trinx and said, "Right, well. Like I said, I'm heading out. Sounds like Flek is going to stick around."

"Thanks, Pox!" Trinx said and waved as he dragged the cart off. "Hi, Flek, I'm Trinx. Your uncle probably told you that. Welcome to TQ House. It's not really open yet. You were inside, so you know what a mess it is. At least the vermin are gone! Thanks for that."

"No problem," Flek said. "Uncle Pox has me help him every once in a while. Usually when he has a bigger-than-normal job. It's a good way to get some extra money. You're right about the house. It definitely needs a lot of work."

"I'm going to be staying here, too," Snixil said. "I'm Snixil and this here is Nibbles. Trinx insists I don't have to, but I'm going to help get the place fixed up."

"Why you doing that?" Flek asked her. "Sounds like a sucker move."

"Because Trinx is super nice, and I want to," Snixil said, crossing her arms. "It's not a sucker move if you want to. I bet you can't even help that much. That's why you don't want to try."

"Says who?" Flek said, crossing his own arms. "I could help. I'm not that strong and pretty small, but I could help if I wanted to."

"Uh huh," Snixil said with an eye-roll. "I'm sure that's true. You have me convinced."

"Hey now, Snixil," Trinx intervened. "Just like you, he doesn't have to help. Don't go making him feel bad that he isn't. He can just move in once it's done."

Taking the lifeline Trinx extended, Flek said, "Yeah. See? I'll just move in when it's done. Thanks for helping that happen faster, sucker."

"Watch it, Flek," Trinx warned. "Just because I said she shouldn't pressure you doesn't mean you can be rude to her."

The two fell into glaring at each other. Trinx thought, *What have I gotten into?*

"Oh! I wasn't kidding when I told Pox I was hungry," Trinx said, interrupting the stalemate. "How about you two? Hungry? We could go to the Tender. I work there in the evenings. I'll buy us some dinner, and you can meet Quilka. She's working there this evening. I bet Gristle will even give me a discount."

"That sounds great, ma—Trinx," Snixil said, catching herself again when she caught the look from Trinx.

"I could eat," Flek agreed.

That was good enough for Trinx, and she led them to the Tender. On the short walk, the two younger goblins got to know each other and exchanged stories. It seemed they had put aside their temporary feud.

Trinx pushed open the door to the Tender and walked inside with the younglings in tow. "Hi, Gris, Look who's here! It's your favorite barmaid."

"What?" Gristle whipped his head around in mock confusion. "I thought Quilka was in the kitchen."

"Gristle!" Trinx admonished. "You know I meant me. Even if I haven't been in for a couple of nights."

"Oh, I know, Luv," Gristle said with a chuckle. "Just giving a good yank on yer leg. Glad to see ye feeling better. Hope that means you'll be back ter work tomorrow. And who are these two?"

"Meet Snixil and Flek," Trinx said. "They are moving into TQ House. Did Quilka tell you about it?"

"Briefly," he said with a nod. "Don't know if I caught the full of the how or why, but I got the gist. Sounds like a noble goal on your part."

"It's going to be amazing," Trinx said as she finally took a moment to look around the room. About three-quarters of the tables were full. "Think we could get a table? Maybe that four-top over there? We're all a bit hungry. Any chance for a friendly discount?"

Gristle laughed while nodding and waving them over to the table she had identified. "Sure, Luv. I'll make sure the price is right for ye."

Trinx escorted her entourage to the table, and they all sat down.

"So, about tomorrow evening," Gristle said. "You'll be back to work now that you are up and about?"

"Um, about that," Trinx said and saw his face scrunch. "If I could just have a bit more time off. I want to make some progress on the house. I'm going to take time off from the alchemy shop, too. I think if I work at it, I can have it fixed up quickly."

"From what I heard, that isn't likely," Gristle said, shaking his head in bemusement. "But I'll let you have a couple more evenings. I already brought in a temp to cover since I didn't know how long you'd be out. Speaking of which, there she is. Hey Jixnet, let Q know Trinx is here for dinner. She can take their table."

"Sure thing, Gristle," Jixnet said and ran to the kitchen.

"Gristle," called a familiar face from a nearby table. "What about a discount for long-time loyal customers? Heard you giving Trinxy a special price tonight."

"Just be lucky I don't charge ya extra, Glink," the bartender shot back. "You and Zurt spend at least twice as long at a table and order about half as much."

Glink waved it off. "Can't blame a goblin for trying."

Quilka came out of the kitchen holding a tray with three loaded plates. She approached the trio at the table.

"Hey Trinx, glad you decided to take a break for some food. Is this Snixil? And who is this other one?"

"Yup, this is Snixil, and that's Flek," Trinx said. "His uncle is Pox, that exterminator. Turns out Flek needs a place like TQ House, and Pox took care of the vermin for us. They're all gone. We just need to clean the place out before everyone can move in."

"That's amazing news," Quilka said and laid the plates down, one in front of each of them.

The plates were laden with thick slabs of rockhorn covered

in a mushroom gravy. On the side was a pile of fluffy white potatoes and some roasted carrots. The potatoes had a crater formed in the center, filled with the same gravy.

"This looks great. Make sure to tell Brizla," Trinx said as she stuck a saucy bite of potato in her mouth. The younger goblins didn't need any more encouragement than that and began devouring everything on their plates.

"You know," Quilka said with a grin. "With the vermin gone, that's a big step forward. I thought that would be a lot more work. If we just had working plumbing, I'd move in right away."

"Something wrong with the pipes in that house I heard you two talking about," Glink butted in from two tables away. "What's with that house, QT, or whatever you said? How'd you get a house?"

"Long story," Trinx said. "The important part is, I'm opening a safe place. For goblins that need a home like these two here. It just needs a lot of work. Not sure how I'll get it all done, but I'm sure I'll figure it out."

"Admirable cause," Glink acknowledged. "Pretty sure you know I work with pipes. I could see what needs fixing for you."

"Really?" Trinx asked, somewhat in shock. "I don't think I can afford it. I was just going to borrow some tools and try to figure it out."

"Worg's breath," Glink blurted. "Guarantee, if you don't know enough about what you're doing, you'll make things worse. Maybe even flood that whole house. You've always been good to Zurt and me. Don't worry none about the cost. Anyone asks, and you can tell them I did a great job. Maybe stir me up some business."

"Don't go trying to show me up," blurted Zurt. "I can help out, too. I'm a woodworker and carpenter. You know that. Got some wood scraps and paint. Might not all fit together the best, and maybe the colors won't all match, but I can help."

"I can't believe both of you are willing to help," Trinx effused. "Thank you so much."

"Glad to do it," Glink said. "We'll be around tomorrow, won't we, Zurt? Maybe you can give a good word to Gristle. Let him know how generous we are? How we earned that discount?"

Gristle belted out a hearty laugh from the bar. "I heard that. Fine. Fine. Ye beat me down. If yer pitching in to help Trinxy, I'll make sure yer price is right tonight. Just tonight, though, ye hear me?"

Both tables erupted in a cheer.

"Okay then," Quilka said. "We get enough cleaned up tomorrow, and I'll move in, no more excuses. Think you can get another day off from Brinta? Maybe with Gristle's newfound generosity, I can have tomorrow evening off, and we can work on the house the whole day."

"It's a date!" Trinx declared and dove back into her meal.

Chapter 28

House Renovations

That evening, Trinx reflected on how much easier everything would be with the Traveler's Tonic. But no, she had decided there would be no more of that, at least not for a while. She surveyed the large room just off the house's entryway. Piles of dirt, dust, and debris climbed up the walls. The corners were the worst. Random papers, scraps of wood, and assorted trash covered the floor, leaving small pockets where the filthy floor peeked out beneath it all.

With her hands on her hips, Trinx announced, "This looks like a pretty big job, and it's late."

She turned to Pox's nephew, "Flek, thanks for joining us for dinner. You're welcome to stick around in the area or go do whatever it is you do. Feel free to check back in a day or two in order to see how things are going."

Turning to the young girl whose pet was slinking in and out between her legs, she said, "Snixil. I know you've offered to help, but it's pretty late. I can take you back to my apartment and get you settled. Then I'll come back and work for a while. I need to go to my place for some cleaning supplies anyway. You can help out some tomorrow."

"Thanks for dinner, Trinx," Flek said, shrugging his shoulders and kicking at some dirt on the ground. "I wasn't expecting that, and I guess I don't have a lot else I actually need to be doing. I could help, after all, if you thought there was stuff I could do."

"I knew you'd come around once you got to know Trinx," Snixil said with a wicked grin. "And I know it's getting late, but I have plenty of energy. It would be good to start tonight."

"Thank you, Flek, for offering," Trinx said, beaming a smile at him. "And, of course, you too, Snixil. But really, you don't have to."

"Right. I don't have to," Flek said. "I decided I wanted to. That's different. Doesn't make me a sucker if I want to."

"You may not be a sucker, but let's see who's the loser," Snixil said. "There are two shovels. Let's each make a pile outside. We can see who removes the most. Smaller pile is the loser."

"Oh! You're on!" Flek said, then ran out to grab a shovel.

"Hey! I didn't say it started yet," Snixil screamed after him, but his laughter was his only answer, so she followed after to get the other one.

Trinx smiled, knowing that this house was going to be amazing with goblins like these living there. She double-checked the coin she had in her purse, then set off to the store. There were a few things she knew she didn't have at home, like another shovel. After that, she could head to her apartment for supplies she already had.

The closest general store had everything she thought she might need. Trinx bought two more shovels, a broom, a pile of cheap cleaning rags, and a small cart. After loading everything in the cart, she set off for home—*home? It wouldn't be for long.*

At her apartment, she first remembered she needed to cancel her lease. She found an envelope, a piece of parchment, and a pen. Keeping it simple, she wrote that she would be out by the end of the month. It would actually be much sooner, but as far as notice went, the end of the month was good. She put the note aside and then began collecting supplies.

Before long, she had two buckets filled with brushes, soap, and some rags. A broom and a mop stood tall out of one bucket. Trinx stuffed the envelope for her landlord in her bag and slung it over her shoulder. The cart she had purchased proved useful as she loaded everything in. It was a small cart, and the load was precarious, with the long poles from the shovels, mop, and brooms hanging well over the edge. If she was careful, it should all make it to the house safely, if not speedily.

Along the way, she stopped and set her load down outside the post office. Although they were closed for the evening, there was a slot next to the door that accepted letters and small parcels. She stuffed the note through the slot and gathered up her supplies again.

When she approached TQ house, she found two decent-sized piles of refuse growing near the side of it. Snixil and Flek took turns running through the door, wielding shovels of filth. They dumped their latest loads and stopped when she approached. Trinx dumped her supplies on the walkway leading to the front door.

"Looking great! I can't believe how much you've cleared out."

"Thanks," Flek said. "As you can see, my pile is a bit bigger."

"No, it's not," Snixil rebuked. "Mine just spread out more."

"Whatever," Flek said and sucked his teeth. "There's a lot more in there, but that large room is mostly clear. I've been working in the kitchen, and Snixil has been in that other large room.”

“Great! So, I’ve brought some supplies from my house, and I bought a couple more shovels at the store,” Trinx said. “I’ll join in on the shoveling. We can’t do much actual cleaning until tomorrow. The pipes are busted. Deeper cleaning will have to wait until Glink can fix our sink.” She laughed at her rhyme, then grabbed a shovel.

“Make your own pile,” Snixil warned. “I don’t want you giving Flek an advantage.”

“Yeah. Keep your junk in your own pile,” Flek said. “Don’t want Snixil to cheat with your help.”

Trinx just chuckled and found a room with plenty of debris. She shoveled it all out, making sure not to get her shovelfuls anywhere near the piles the kids were building.

Once they had cleared out the entire first floor, Trinx took up her broom and began sweeping. There were still spots that would need scrubbing once they had water, but the broom caught plenty of lighter dirt and dust. Snixil or Flek stopped by from time to time with empty shovels, and she would sweep a pile onto the shovel for them to take outside.

As the evening turned into night, a deep thumping reverberated throughout the house. Trinx stepped outside and noticed goblins, hobgoblins, and even a few orcs, gnolls, and trolls passing by the house toward the back. Trinx realized the club must be in full swing, and behind the house, she spotted bouncers flanking the stairway down. The noise really wasn’t that bad. It was the vibrations, more than anything, that caught her attention. However, all the goblins passing by could end up being an issue. Maybe they could build a fence and a pathway.

Trinx was mulling over what they could do to better corral the clubgoers when two caught her eye, and she waved them over. “Hey, Vex! Draz! Over here.”

The two hobs jogged over to her, and Vex said, "Hey, Trinx. You're going to Unity tonight, too? It's been a while since we've had a chance to see each other."

"I wish," Trinx said with a laugh. "I'm fixing up TQ house. It's going to be amazing."

"TQ House?" Draz asked. "I thought this place was condemned. Figured that's why Unity set up underneath."

"I know!" Trinx said. "That's what makes this place great. Mungo said I could use it. I'm creating a safe place for goblins who need a place to call home. My dad would have flipped if I went home to my parents after I figured out who I really was. I was lucky I had a good friend who let me stay with her. Then Quilka got me that job at the bar. But some folks aren't as fortunate, and when they can't go home, where can they go?"

"All of those house renovations have got to be a lot of work, but I think it's a great idea," Vex said, looking over the house appraisingly. "Oh, hey, Draz. Your father runs the lumber mill, doesn't he? Looks like some of the house needs repairs. Think he could donate some wood?"

"He does, yup," Draz acknowledged. "I could ask him. He's probably got some he could spare. I'll bring what I can if he agrees."

"And I've got nothing pressing going on," Vex said. "I can come over tomorrow and help clean and do some of the rebuild."

"That would be amazing," Trinx said. "You know Glink and Zurt that hang out at the Tender? They both said they'd help. Glink's going to work on the pipes. Zurt said he works with wood a lot. You could help either of them. Oh! And I need to talk privately tomorrow. I have some news you'll want to hear."

"You got it," Vex said. "But that's definitely a tomorrow

activity. We're going to head to the club. Don't work yourself too hard."

"Too late," Trinx said with a giggle. "I want to get this place ready to open soon. That's going to take a lot of work." She waved as they headed to the club and then got back to cleaning.

Before long, the first floor was free of dirt and debris that they could sweep away. The three goblins gathered in the large front room of the house off the entryway.

Trinx looked around and said, "It's cleaner. Passable even, at least until we can scrub and mop. We don't have any furniture yet. Quilka and I will have to see what we can find at some second-hand stores. Do you have somewhere to stay, Flek? I'm going to take Snixil back to my place. It's not big, but you can come too. I'm sure we'll figure out how to fit."

"Can't I just stay here?" Snixil asked. "Pox took care of the pests, and we got downstairs cleaned up. I can set up my tent."

"If you spread it out, we can both lay on it," Flek said. "I'm sure I can find a place to crash, but staying here works, too. But, um, Trinx? Is there any way you could stay here with us tonight? I know we've been out on the streets alone, but somehow this feels different here. I think Snixil might feel better if you stayed."

"Hey!" Snixil cut in. "I don't need her to stay. Besides, I got Nibbles. I need to find him, though. He ran off while we were cleaning. I think he's allergic to cleaning. But even though I don't need her to stay, I wouldn't mind."

"If you two really want to stay here, then of course I'll stay with you," she said, glimpsing hopefulness in Snixil's eyes. "But really. I know I said my place is small. And it is. But we can all go there. You two could have my bed, and I'll sleep on the floor."

"We're already here. Plus, we can get an early start in the morning that way. Flek was right," Snixil said and threw him a glance. "We can use my tent, so we don't have to sleep directly on the wood floor."

Snixil began laying the tarp she used for her tent out flat before Trinx could say anything else.

Trinx shrugged and sighed. *If that's what they want...*

They all found a spot on the tarp to curl up, and Nibbles managed to find his way back in. The raccoon snuggled next to Snixil, who fell asleep almost immediately. Trinx found sleep more elusive, but soon the thumping rhythm from the club deep below lulled her, and she drifted off.

Without her alarms to wake her, Trinx slept until she heard a knock at the door. She was confused for a moment as to where she was. Looking at the two goblins sleeping on the tarp and the empty room around her, it all snapped back into focus.

She stood up and brushed her dress to smooth it out. Another knock at the door reminded her of why she had woken up. Trinx walked to the door and opened it to find Zigla standing there, looking around nervously. She had never seen Zigla anxious, and it was disconcerting.

"I decided to come early," Zigla said. "I thought if I came before too much of the warren was up and about, it would be both easier to get my cart through the tunnels and easier to avoid interacting with many goblins."

Looking behind the large hob, Trinx saw a wagon piled high with what looked like just about everything that had been in the cave. "That was smart. I'm sure it was less busy. Come in. Snixil and Flek are here, but they are still asleep."

Zigla stepped into the house and looked around the room. Trinx took her on a tour of the downstairs.

"We've only managed to clear out the trash and debris from the first floor so far. But I found a room you might like. It still needs a good scrubbing, but I think the house manager deserves a nice room on the first floor."

"Oh, this is nice," Zigla said as she entered the room Trinx had mentioned. "It's close to the kitchen and the downstairs bathroom. The other bedrooms are on the upper floors?"

"Yes," Trinx said, nodding her head. "There are common room areas downstairs. I suppose some of them might make bedrooms? But probably better to have some areas for folks to gather and relax. The second floor has a few rooms. The third does, too, but as you probably saw, the third floor needs some work before anyone can live up there."

"I noticed the kitchen needs a deep clean, but the oven and stove looked usable with some work," Zigla said.

"The sink needs work," Trinx said. "Or, rather, all the sinks need work. And the tubs. And the toilets. The pipes have issues. Not sure what's wrong. There's no water. But a friend is going to fix them up."

"As soon as we have some water, I don't mind scrubbing," Zigla said. "Until then, I can help with clearing the upper floors."

"That would be great!" Trinx said. "I've got to visit Distilled Magic. I'm supposed to be working today, but I'm going to ask Brinta for some time off. I hope they don't mind. Then I'll be back. Snixil and Flek seem to be sleeping pretty hard. Even though it still needs a lot of work, they must feel safe here already. Introduce yourself to them when they get up."

Trinx made her way across the Warren to Distilled Magic. Taking Zigla on a tour of the house had eaten away the early morning, and now the warren tunnels teamed with goblins. When she reached the shop, she pushed open the heavy door and found Brinta measuring a potion into a set of bottles.

"Good morning, Brinta."

"Hey, Trinx," the alchemist replied. "Good to see you this

morning. Hope you had an enjoyable time catching up with Quilka."

"I did!" Trinx exclaimed. "But so much more happened, too. You won't believe it."

"I might," Brinta grinned. "Let me have it."

Trinx then proceeded to unleash a torrent of words, explaining how she received permission to fix up and use TQ House as a safe haven and all the work she had already sunk into it, all in the course of a day.

"You did so much," Brinta said in a cautious tone. "And that was with you getting a good night's sleep? No dipping right back into the Traveler's Tonic?"

"What?" Trinx balked. "Oh, no. I got plenty of sleep. Maybe if an emergency comes up, I'll try the tonic again. But now that I know more about it, I'm giving it a rest for now. I'm just so motivated. It's my new thing. Helping people out. TQ House is going to be amazing."

"I'm sure it will," Brinta said. "It really sounds like a wonderful idea. I'd ask if helping people included helping me in the shop today, but based on your story, I suspect you are about to ask me something to the contrary."

"So," Trinx said, drawing the word out. "I could help you today. It's just that so many people are counting on me to get the house in working order."

Brinta laughed a loud and hearty laugh. "I can't say no when it's such a good cause. Especially after Mungo helped out by providing the house itself. I've been to the club under that house a few times, and I know what a sorry state it has been in."

"Thank you," Trinx said, letting out a sigh of relief.

"Tell you what," Brinta said, with a finger on their chin, "take the time it needs to get it ready, even if it's a few days. Then, I want your mind on alchemy. It's time we broadened your skills. With a few months of dedication, we may even have you ready to get a certification."

"That would be amazing," Trinx said with a bounce. "Once we finish, I plan on having an open house party to celebrate. You'll have to come."

"I wouldn't miss it," said Brinta. "Before you go, I realize I've got something that might help with the house. You can take a bucket of triple-A. It's good for more than just cleaning up alchemy messes. It should cut through whatever layers of grime have built up in that house. Then you'll just have to sweep up the powder."

"Oh, wow," Trinx said. "I had no idea it could do that, too. Thank you. That should help. There is definitely a layer of greasy grime. I thought we'd be scrubbing it for days. I'll get a bucket from the back room."

"Don't forget to grab a bellows," Brinta called after her when she ran to the supply area. "It works a lot better that way."

Chapter 29

It Took You Long Enough

When Trinx returned to the house, she found a flurry of activity. Snixil and Flek were flinging shovelfuls of debris out of the upstairs windows, most of it landing in the refuse piles they had been building. Zigla was scraping the peeling paint off the house siding. Even Nibbles seemed to be helping. He would grab stray bits of garbage that had missed the piles and add them to a heap.

Several new arrivals stood waiting to get her attention. Vex and Draz were next to a large wagon piled high with boards of all shapes and sizes. Zurt stood with them, engrossed in a conversation, occasionally pointing at various parts of the house.

As she came up the walkway, Glink came out of the front door.

"Good! You're here. That older woman, the large hob? She said you'd likely return soon. I need to talk to you about the pipes."

"Thank you for coming!" Trinx said with a wide smile. "What did you find out? Can you fix the plumbing?"

"I figured the problem, or should I say problems," Glink said, scratching his head. "Ya have two issues, one I can easily deal with. No problem there. Started in on it already. The other...well, I can likely get some water flowin', but it could take a while."

"Oh, that doesn't sound good," Trinx said, unable to keep a frown from her face.

"It's not good, but not all bad," Glink explained. "Seems there is something nasty blockin' the main pipes outta da house. Got some tools. Usually can break it up, but it's gunked up pretty bad."

"Do you think this would help?" Trinx asked, holding up the bucket of triple-A. "Brinta let me have a bucket to get rid of the greasy gunk built up on the walls and floor."

"Dunno, what's that?" the plumber asked, peering at the branding on the bucket. "Never heard of Doc Puddlefoot's Antireactionary Absorbant Alabaster Powder. What's it do?"

"I don't know exactly how it works," Trinx admitted. "We use it at the alchemy lab if we have a dangerous spill. Cleans it right up."

"Guess we can try it," Glink said, stroking his chin. "Don't think ya can make it much worsen it is. I'll show ya where the main blockage is."

Glink led her around to the back of the house, where two large pipes led into the building. He had removed two elbow joints exposing the pipes that led down into the packed dirt of the cavern floor.

"See here? This one brings the water in. That one takes the water out. Ya can see the pipes are mostly clear that go into the house. Cleaned them out easy enough. Had to replace a few pieces that had broken. But look down into these two leading into the ground."

Trinx peered into the dark pipes. She couldn't see much. It

was quite dark, but Glink reached an arm past her and probed a metal bar down. The rod didn't go far before it hit something. The blockage was further down in the one he said brought the water in, but both pipes were blocked.

"I'll see what happens on the outbound one," Trinx said, setting the bucket down and removing the lid. She picked it back up and slowly poured the white powder into the pipe.

A foam developed, piling up out of the pipe. It then broke apart into clumps of fine gray powder. She cleared it out and poured some more of the fresh white powder; this time, it went further in, and the pipe held more. Again, it foamed up in a bubbly, sickly gray. She was about to brush it away again when it fell back into the pipe.

"Lookit that!" Glink shouted. "Ya said ya got that from an alchemist? Gonna have to get me some of that miracle stuff."

"I should put a bit more in just to be sure we got it all," Trinx said and then poured another measure in. She didn't notice any foam this time, but it could have been farther down the pipe. "Okay, I'll try the incoming pipe now."

Trinx dumped a healthy portion of the powder into the pipe. A moment later, the same foam came up. It began slowly overflowing from the pipe as it grew in volume. A fine gray powder similar to ash piled around the base of the pipe. Then, she heard a gurgling from deep in the pipe. The next moment, a geyser shot up, spraying muck, powder, and water everywhere.

Glink sprang forward and clapped a cap on the pipe. "That sure cleared it good," he said, wiping water from his brow. "Ya just saved yourself lots of time and me lots of effort. I should have this all back together soon, and you'll have water throughout the house. In the pipes, of course, not gonna flood the house." He cackled at what must have been a plumber's joke she didn't understand.

"Thank you," Trinx said, beaming. "That's amazing. I'm going to see about clearing up the rest of the grime in the house. But first, I should check on the guys over by the wagon of wood."

As Trinx approached the wagon, the men stopped talking with each other, and looked over at her.

"Morning, Trinx!" Vex said. "Check out the load of wood Draz got from his father. It's mostly odds and ends, but Zurt assures us there are plenty of usable pieces. We should be able to get the major damage fixed up."

"That's wonderful!" Trinx said, bouncing on her toes. "Be sure to thank your dad, Draz. This is amazing. Let me know if you need anything; otherwise, I've got work inside. But first. Vex? Can we chat for a moment?"

"Of course," Vex said, his smile beaming. "It's been a while. Happy to hear what's new." He walked from the other two men and the house, and she followed him.

When they reached an area that seemed far enough away from everyone for some privacy, he asked, "So what's new? Nothing wrong, I hope."

"No, nothing wrong. The opposite," she said. "Brinta and I had a major breakthrough. We did it. We made a potion that actually changes the entire body. No more accidents like when we first met."

"That's amazing," he said, his smile threatening to break his face. "So, that potion works on hobs, too?"

"It should," Trinx replied. "Well, not the same potion I took. It's a designer potion. So Brinta will need to brew you a specific batch if you want some for you. You'll need some hair and claw filings from your father. He'd give you those, right?"

"Hell yes," Vex shot back. "I'm sure of that. He'll give me those samples in a heartbeat."

"Great! Just take the samples to Brinta and they can brew you a batch," Trinx instructed.

"My father is going to owe you for this," Vex said. "I'll encourage him to consider making a donation to your house project."

"That would be a huge help," Trinx said, smiling widely. "We're still getting everything set up and trying to do so as cheaply as we can. But I know stuff is going to add up quickly. Anything he can give would be wonderful. Thanks again for all your help with the house. I'm going to focus on cleaning the inside."

Trinx entered the house and filled the bellows with triple-A. She sprayed clouds of powder up onto the ceiling, on the walls, and all over the floor. Sizzles and pops filled the room with noise, and then everything settled. Taking a broom, she banged on the ceiling. A shower of powder rained down. Trinx then beat the walls, knocking the crust loose.

As she swept up the mess, Quilka came in carrying more cleaning supplies and said, "I can't believe how much you've accomplished already!"

"I know!" Trinx said, grinning. "It's all coming together. Glink will even have the water on shortly."

"Really?" Quilka questioned. "Well, I guess I can give my notice. No reason I can't move in soon."

"This is going to be so fun," Trinx said. "If you help me remove the grime with this triple-A, then maybe we can go out furniture hunting. We need to find some furniture and supplies for the house. Hopefully free or cheap."

"I'm in," Quilka said. "I even know a few good spots where we might find some stuff."

The two spent the next couple of hours removing the greasy grime from every surface in the house. They were eventually joined by Zigla, Snixil, and Flek, who had finished removing the easy piles of dirt and debris. By the time they swept the last of the powdery residue from the house, the entire place looked practically brand new.

Trinx announced to the crew, "Quilka and I are going out to scout for furniture and supplies for the house. You should all take a break. You've been at it all day. Quilka brought some food over. Have a bite to eat, too. After you rest, if you want, check if you can help with any of the repairs. But only if you feel up to it. You've done too much already. If there is any wood left, we might want a fence to help keep the folks visiting the club from wandering in and around the house."

"I'm sure we'll find ways to keep busy, but we'll get some rest," Zigla assured her. "I also still need to get unpacked."

Outside, the men had unloaded all the wood and had begun repairing the third-floor walls and roof.

Trinx approached Draz. "Do you think Quilka and I could borrow your wagon? We need to collect furniture for the house, and move our own stuff."

"Oh, yeah. Sure," Draz agreed. "I doubt my dad'll mind. The dire goat should be rested plenty from earlier."

"Thanks!" Trinx called as she and Quilka took off for the wagon.

The girls approached the enormous goat with wickedly curved horns on its head. Trinx reached out and gave it a pat.

"We're going to find some furniture, and you're going to help pull it all. Does that work for you?" she asked. The dire goat snorted, and the girls hopped up onto the wagon.

They drove the cart through the warren's tunnels. Everyone stepped aside, keeping plenty of distance from the goat. Quilka guided Trinx to the places she thought they might find free or inexpensive used furniture. Stop after stop, they piled random pieces of furniture and housewares into the wagon. They found beds, small tables, and couches. They even found an elderly woman willing to part with an entire dining set, including a table and chairs. That set was too large for the cart, with everything they had gathered so far, but the older goblin said she would have her sons deliver it to the house.

In addition to furniture, they collected lanterns, bedding, towels, and a random assortment of dishes with cutlery. Trinx realized they would likely need a lot more supplies, but if she could at least get the basics, everyone should be comfortable in the house until they could get more. For now, they had filled the wagon and directed the goat back to TQ House.

At the house, Trinx and Quilka unloaded the furniture. They didn't bother taking it inside yet, and instead left it beside the house. They could haul it in later, or the others could if they needed something to do. The men were still working on the third floor, though they had made amazing progress. The walls looked complete, and they seemed focused on the roof. Zigla, Snixil, and Flek were all painting the outside of the house. The house manager had finished scraping the old paint off earlier, and now the trio was painting it in a motley set of colors, using whatever paint Zurt had brought.

It seemed like the perfect time to move their belongings over, so Trinx and Quilka once more set off in the wagon. Along the way, they stopped to collect some boxes and crates from the alleys behind several shops. Stores always had extra boxes, much like the ones Trinx had emptied at Distilled Magic earlier that day. After gathering quite a few, they decided to head to Trinx's place first.

"This should be pretty easy," Trinx said. "I don't have that much stuff. I'll want all my furniture: the bed, the end tables, the dressing table, and the wardrobe. We don't even have to empty the wardrobe—it's already a box!"

"I suppose so," Quilka said, a little unsure. "I guess there's no point in packing the clothes separately. But what about all these piles of stuff around the room? Some have clothes, and some have odds and ends. Why is it all piled up like this?"

"Oh, those are just my piles," Trinx said as if that was all the explanation needed.

Seeing Quilka's puzzled look, she decided to continue further. "Sometimes it's easier to just deal with stuff like that. It makes it easier to find. If it's hidden away in a chest or box, how am I going to remember where it is? Or if I even have it?"

Quilka shook her head with a rueful grin. "Maybe we can help you organize when we unpack it all."

"Maybe," Trinx said with a shrug of her shoulders. "At least it's easy to pack." With that, she started putting each pile, just as it was, into a box or crate. Quilka just watched with fascination, seemingly at a loss for words.

They loaded everything onto the wagon and closed the door to Trinx's old apartment. During the packing, Trinx had found an old whistle. As she drove the wagon to Quilka's place, she held the whistle between her lips, blowing shrill noises. She gave the reins a snap to urge the goat to go faster. The combination of the noise and the snapping soon had the goat racing through the tunnels. Goblins and hobgoblins darted aside to avoid the thundering beast. Even a large troll stepped out of the way, not eager to find out how it would fare against the enormous goat.

As they approached Quilka's apartment, Trinx pulled on the reins, and the goat calmed and slowed, eventually stopping just past her door. The girls hopped off the wagon and went inside. Quilka's place looked as neat as it always did when Trinx visited. She wondered how she ever found anything when she needed it. Packing took longer since Quilka insisted on placing each item into the box that she said it belonged in.

They chatted while they worked until Quilka paused and asked, "There are quite a few rooms in that house. Have you thought about which one you'll take?"

"I haven't thought too much about it," Trinx admitted. "I figured I'd see where everyone wanted to settle. I suppose it might be nice to be up on the third floor. Being up high in the house might be fun."

"That does sound fun," Quilka agreed. "There is a large room up there and two smaller ones. You could take the large one."

"Oh, no," Trinx said, shaking her head. "I don't need nearly that much space. Besides, even if my room is small, there is still the rest of the house. Considering I've been living in a single room, that already feels huge."

"That's so true," Quilka said. "But what if we shared that large room? What would you think of that?"

"Oh!" Trinx exclaimed. "That could be fun, like having a sleepover all the time. But, even though it is large, it might be crammed with both our beds. Maybe we should each take the two smaller ones and be next door to each other."

Quilka sighed in exasperation. "My bed is pretty big, probably even big enough for two. We could just share the one bed, and then we would have one more bed for another resident's room."

"Oh," Trinx said. "Share your bed? I mean, I guess we've fallen asleep in the same bed before when we stayed up too late. That could work. Should we sleep going in opposite directions? No. That won't work. Then you'd have to smell my feet." She giggled at the thought.

Quilka looked her in the eyes to get her full attention, placing her hand on hers. "Trinx, I have a feeling you still don't understand me, even when I lay it out there plain as day. You never have, and I think we need to clear this up. It's okay if you don't feel the same, but I need you to actually understand me."

"Understand what?" she asked. "I thought it was clear. You want me to share a room, right?"

Quilka couldn't help but laugh at this point. "Trinx, I've told you how much I like you, and maybe I didn't use strong enough words. I don't just like you; I *love* you. I want you to be mine, and I hope that, even after all this time, you understand that and feel the same."

"Oh. Oh. OH!" she said while processing what she heard. Her cheeks blushed a deep purple. "I just. I thought we were best friends."

The mirth left Quilka's face, and her eyes softened. "Yes, we have been best friends. I just thought we could be more. Thought we were more. I'm silly. Forget I said that. We can just use the two rooms next to each other."

"What?" Trinx waved her hands. "No. Don't take it back. You aren't silly. I'm just not very bright. I love you, too. I love spending time with you, and I love everything about you. I guess. I guess I just never thought of you the way you've been thinking of me. But that doesn't mean I don't want to. I've just never thought of anyone like that. I don't know why. It just hasn't happened. But it could be fun, and I love you."

An enormous smile filled Quilka's face, and she squeezed her hand. "Whew. You had me worried. I'm so glad to hear that. I was really out on a limb."

"Sorry," Trinx said, her blush deepening. "I really don't pick up on subtle sometimes."

"It took you long enough," Quilka said. "But it's more than okay. I'll be less subtle from now on."

Quilka leaned in closer.

"Oh," Trinx said. "Are we supposed to kiss now?"

Quilka's intensity faltered and shattered. She let out a peel of laughter and said, "There's no 'supposed to' about it. But yes, I wanted to."

"Okay, then," Trinx said. "I was just checking."

Quilka stepped forward and kissed her.

Chapter 30

Elizabeth Vash

The dire goat pulled the wagon laden with Trinx's and Quilka's possessions up next to TQ House. The pile of furniture and housewares they had unloaded earlier had vanished. Diligent helpers had taken it into the house and found suitable places for all of it. Snixil, Flek, and Zigla had painted the house in a kaleidoscope of colors. The paint still appeared wet but looked fantastic. Looking up at the third floor, Trinx wouldn't even be able to guess that a large section of the wall and ceiling had once been missing.

Trinx stood staring at the house in wonderment. She snapped out of it when Quilka voiced what she had been thinking.

"Wow, that's amazing what they managed to accomplish today. Should we get this stuff unloaded from the wagon? I imagine Draz will need to take it soon."

"Oh, right. Yeah," Trinx agreed, nodding her head and shaking loose the spell the house had cast on her. "Let's get it all unloaded out here, then we can take it in."

As the women unloaded the boxes and furniture, an entire

crew of goblins came out of the house. It seemed everyone was still there, and they all were jockeying for her attention to tell her about what had been accomplished.

The two youngest pushed forward first. Flek proudly boasted while pointing at the house, "We finished the painting! Doesn't it look great?"

Snixil thrust forward a wooden sign that had letters carved into its face reading, "TQ HOUSE."

"Look at this!" she gushed. "Zigla carved it. Me and Flek painted it. We used cerulean and magenta, just like your hair."

"It all looks fabulous!" Trinx told them, her voice singing with joy. "You did a wonderful job. What do you think? You like living here?"

"Without a doubt," Snixil said, nodding her head vigorously. "I even have my *own* room now. It's across the hall from Flek's room on the second floor. Zigla helped us get the furniture up there. She's so strong."

Zigla took that moment to step forward, offering a tray with two mugs to Trinx and Quilka.

"I just do what I can. Might be a bit stronger than some." Her eyes twinkled, and she gave Trinx a wink. "We've all been having some tea to relax after what's been a busy day. Thought you two might like a mug as well."

"Thank you," Trinx and Quilka said in unison, each taking a mug.

"It's still hot!" Trinx said with some shock as she took a sip. "I didn't expect that if you all have been enjoying a tea break."

"You can thank Glink for that," Zigla chuckled. "Isn't that right? Come on over and tell her what you did."

Glink shuffled over, looking bashful, and absently scratched his head, then scratched the inside of his left ear.

"Wasn't much, really. After I got all the plumbing sorted out, I inspected everything. That's when I found someone, prolly a long time ago, mind ya, built some cabinets around some pipework. Cabinets had collapsed in, so we hacked 'em out."

"Yeah, I thought we'd have some work cut out in the kitchen," Trinx said, nodding. "Seemed a lot of damage in there, but we were happy to see it still had a sink and the oven looked good, even if it was old."

"Right," Glink continued. "Sink works now. No worries there. And we got all the busted cabinets out. Ya might want to install some new ones. That can wait. But like I said, the pipework inside is what caught my eye."

"Just tell her. Before I do," Zigla said, prodding at him.

"Right, right," Glink said, beaming. "I was just so excited. The pipework was a Kwikbrew spout. Older one, but still works like a charm. The enchantment on those lasts an incredibly long time."

"No way!" Trinx squealed. "Seriously? I've always wanted one."

"That's beyond amazing," Quilka effused. "The one at the Tender is so handy. They can be expensive for homes. Whoever once owned this place must have done well for themselves. I wonder who it was?"

"Dunno, but I'm glad they moved on and left the place," Trinx quipped. "I'm pretty sure they aren't haunting the place. We didn't find any dead bodies. Goblin ones, at least. Just found some dead rats." Her nose wrinkled, and her fangs dug into her lips.

"Well, anyway," Zigla said, rolling her eyes at Trinx's tangent. "Zurt, Draz, and Vex finished the repairs upstairs, as you can see. You could mostly tell before, but now it's all in good shape. There's a bathroom on the third floor and one on the second floor as well. Third floor has one larger room and two smaller ones. Thought you two might want to claim two of the rooms up there, but there are still open rooms on the second floor, too."

"Yes," Trinx nodded. "Quilka and I have been talking about it this afternoon. We're going to take the large room on the third floor."

"You are?" Zigla asked, raising an eyebrow. "The two of you, then?"

"Yes," Quilka said with a wide grin as she grabbed Trinx's hand. "We are." Then she let out a melodious giggle.

"Thanks for fixing up our room, guys," Trinx called to Vex, Draz, and Zurt. "I think the big room had the most damage. At least from out here, it looks great."

"Oh, it did," Vex agreed. "Looks good inside, as well. Zurt did the hard parts. Draz and I just helped out hauling and holding stuff."

"Was a good project," Zurt said. "Not too hard, 'specially with the help. Guessin' if you two are takin' the big room, that date with Q is off the table."

"It never was on the table," Glink barked at him. "Already settled that."

Giggling, Trinx said, "Thank you, Zurt. I'm sure it will be a fine room. We'll try to find you someone who might be more interested in you."

Right about then, Trinx noticed two newcomers walking up the path to the house. "Gristle? What are you and Brizla doing here?"

"Evening, Luv," Gristle said, holding out a tray as he approached. "Heard about everything going on over here today. Brizla and I thought everyone could use a hearty meal. She's got a pot of fire lizard stew. Should be plenty for everyone. Brought these loaves of bread, too. Goes great with the stew. Don't worry 'bout the Tender. We're headed right back. Jix has it covered for the moment."

"Geez, Gris," Trinx said. "I can't believe you did this. It's way too much. But thank you. I'm sure everyone is hungry."

Zigla walked over to meet Brizla partway, holding her hands out to take the pot. "I can take that. It looks heavy."

"Not a problem," Brizla said, handing her the pot. "But thank you."

Quilka took the tray from Gristle. "Thanks, Gris. You really are softer than you let on. I'll be in tomorrow night for my shift."

Gristle waved his hand at her compliment after she freed it up by removing the tray. "Was nuthin', really. And ye better be in tomorrow night. Working the room alone is a lot to put on Jix. Speaking of, we'll head back now. Enjoy the meal."

Trinx and Quilka waved as the bartender and cook turned to walk the short distance back to the tavern. Zigla motioned for everyone to follow, then took the pot of stew in and placed it on the table that had been delivered earlier that afternoon. She had washed the dishes, so she set out the eclectic assortment of plates, bowls, and cutlery. Quilka set down the tray of bread and then took a seat.

Trinx encouraged everyone to sit and ladled out portions of stew. Quilka passed the tray of bread around so everyone could take a small loaf.

"Ma'am?" Snixil said, looking at Trinx. "Would it be okay if I made a small bowl for Nibbles?"

The raccoon was making circuits around the girl's chair, weaving in and out of the chair legs, his nose sniffing frantically.

"Of course," Trinx replied, stifling a laugh. "But only if you stop calling me ma'am."

Snixil sheepishly grabbed a bowl and spooned some stew in. Then, she pulled off a piece of her roll and placed it on top. She slipped it down under the table, and Nibbles grabbed it with his paws, taking it the rest of the way to the floor.

Trinx dipped a spoon in her bowl and stirred it. The stew had a thick tomato base with pieces of spicy green peppers and barley. She scooped some up, making sure to include a piece of the lizard meat. After blowing on it lightly, she slipped it into her mouth and savored the smokey flavor. The spice wasn't bad on the tongue but lingered pleasantly in the back of her throat.

"Brizla outdid herself on this stew," Trinx announced to the table. "I'll have to thank her again next time I'm in at the Tender. And thank you all. I really appreciate you giving your time, skills, and supplies to fix this house up. I'm going to throw a party to celebrate the opening of TQ House. You all have to come."

A chorus of *you're-welcomes, don't-worry-about-its,* and *anytime* clamored over one another. Small conversations then broke out among those in neighboring seats as they ate and laughed through dinner. Eventually, they finished their meal, and the chatter subsided. Those who were not living in the house said their goodbyes and drifted away.

Everyone left helped gather up the dishes and formed a brigade to wash, dry, and put away the clean items. Then, with Zigla's help, Trinx and Quilka brought their belongings up to the third floor. They put Trinx's old bed in one of the unoccupied rooms that still lacked furniture, and they set up the rest in the largest room.

"Before making your piles, maybe we can attempt to find a better way to organize your things?" Quilka asked as they started opening boxes.

"If you help me find a good place, maybe we can put some things in containers," Trinx agreed. "But I'll probably need at least one pile. Some stuff is just too hard to deal with if it isn't in a handy pile."

Once they had unpacked and set up enough of the room, they both agreed it had been too long a day to stay up much later. They each took turns getting ready in the bathroom, then reunited in the bedroom.

Trinx looked at the bed, then at Quilka. "So, that's where we'll be sleeping then," she said as reality caught up to her.

"Yup," Quilka said, looking quite pleased. "I mean, if you're ready."

Trinx looked into her eyes. "I'm ready. You are, and always have been, my favorite person. I love you."

"I love you," Quilka replied.

They climbed into the bed, held each other, and had a wonderful night together.

In the morning, Trinx woke before Quilka and slipped out of bed. She dressed quietly, then went downstairs to the kitchen. There, she found Zigla making a list while drinking some tea.

"What's that you're working on?"

"Oh? This?" Zigla said, then slid the parchment over. "Just a list of some staples we'll need to get. We have enough furniture and housewares for the time being. We can always use more, but we're in reasonable shape for now, I believe. The cupboards, though..." she trailed off and swept her arm around the room. "They're bare. We need food to cook meals. So, I thought I'd write down what came to me as far as the basic necessities."

"That makes a lot of sense," Trinx said, looking over the list. "Your list looks good, and you're right, we need food. I kinda forgot about that. I brought a little from my house, and so did Quilka. But neither of us has a fully stocked kitchen. Money is still tight, but I think Quilka and I can pool enough together to get some food to stock our pantry with the basics. I'll leave the money I have here. Maybe you can talk to Quilka about it when she wakes up?"

"Sure," Zigla said, nodding. "I can do that. Does that mean you're leaving then?"

"Sure am," Trinx confirmed. "I'm going to Distilled Magic. Brinta has been super generous, giving me time off for the house. They said I could take however many days I needed, but we did so much yesterday. I don't see any reason I can't work at least some of the day in the shop."

"Sounds like a plan then," Zigla said. "I'll work things out with Quilka once she is up. If you want to have that party, we'll also need some extra food and drink for that."

"Right! The party. We have to have a party," Trinx said. "See you later. Gonna head to the shop now."

When Trinx arrived at Distilled Magic, she pushed on the door, but it wouldn't budge. Confused, she knocked with three quick taps.

After a few moments, the door opened a crack, and Brinta peered out. "Oh! Good, it's you. I hoped you would come in today. Get in, quickly."

Trinx entered the shop, and the alchemist shut and re-locked the door. She immediately noticed she wasn't alone with Brinta. Over by the workstations stood a tall person wearing a hooded robe and a traveling cloak. The hood was large, obscuring their face in the shadows completely.

The alchemist walked toward the hooded person and waved for her to follow. She did so, wondering what in the world this secrecy was about.

"Sorry for the cloak-and-dagger treatment this morning." Brinta laughed at their own pun in the stranger's attire. "I didn't want any customers walking in on us when we were talking with our important guest."

The cloaked person pulled down their hood and revealed herself to be a human woman.

"You must be Trinx," the newcomer said. "I've heard quite a bit about you. It seems you have quite the knack for alchemy and a lot of novel ideas. I am an alchemist myself. My name is Elizabeth Vash."

"Vash?" she asked. "Just like Vash's Extreme Lashes. No, wait! You mean? You're *the* Vash? Who makes it?"

The human let out a tittering laugh and said, "Yes. That Vash. I make that product and many others. While I'm based in Ryefeld, I've achieved a wide distribution of my products across all the neighboring kingdoms. That's why I'm here, actually."

"Yes," Brinta jumped in. "She came to talk to me about EverSmooth. However, I told her we would need to send for you since you had the idea in the first place and came up with the key part of the solution."

"Oh?" she asked. "What about EverSmooth? You want to know how it's made? We can teach her that, right?"

"No," Vash said with a smile and a slight head shake. "I don't need you to teach me how it's made. The formulas are in the patent, after all. I've already made a sample batch and tested it out on some interested customers. No. What I want to talk about is a licensing, manufacturing, and distribution deal."

"This is a wonderful thing for us," Brinta added.

"Yes," the human continued. "This can be very lucrative for both of you. There was a time when I ran a small alchemy shop, and I know the issues with setting up any large-scale manufacturing and distribution. I like this product, though. I like it a lot."

Trinx pulled out her fidget toy to distract her fingers while she listened. This sounded important, and she didn't want to miss anything.

"Sorry, my hands get a mind of their own sometimes. Continue, please."

Vash said, "In addition to all the older women of any race, there also seems to be a very popular style among human males these days. They prefer to keep their chests smooth and free of hair. It's called elven style, and it's quite popular. The dwarves can't fathom it and give them quite the ribbing. However, that doesn't seem to stop its spread."

"But that's not even why I made it," Trinx said. "I made it for me and people like me." She paused, thinking before continuing. With a nod to herself, she said, "I'm a transgender woman. Without EverSmooth, I get really hairy. Or maybe not anymore. With our latest potion, I mean."

"Well," Vash said, looking her over appraisingly. "It looks like it works very well indeed, then! You look fabulous. What I listed were just the uses I knew would be a fit. But that's a valid use, too. We won't stop anyone who wants to buy it. Now let's talk about details on licensing."

Vash pulled out a scroll with a long contract that had runes that enforced it through magic.

"The standard patent process ensures that you receive a portion of every sale from the production and sale of your invention. However, there are limits to the quantity I can produce under the standard patent license. Even if there weren't, it wouldn't likely be financially viable at scale. This contract is a licensing agreement that grants me exclusive rights in the kingdoms where I currently operate, and non-exclusive rights in the rural unincorporated territories, with the exception of both of you. I've included an upfront payment for the exclusivity, and you'll receive monthly residuals from the sales. Please take your time to read through it."

Brinta explained to Trinx, "This means we'll get a fairly large payment upfront and then monthly payments based on the sales. This is huge. We wouldn't normally have access to these markets. However, we still get to sell it here in the warren, and we can even decide to open another shop outside the larger cities."

This was a lot for her to take in. She definitely wasn't ready to be negotiating contracts when she woke up this morning. A thought struck her.

"For the bit about our sales? We can do what we want, right? Like if we wanted to give discounts, or even give it away for free to some people. That would be okay under this contract?"

The human quirked an eyebrow. "Well, yes. Under this contract, you hold the rights within the unincorporated territories, anyway. You can use those as you wish, even giving the product away. However, I'd recommend you don't do too much of that. You'd be leaving money on the table."

"I just," she started. "I just want to make sure that if other transgender women want it, that they don't have to worry about it being too expensive."

"Oh, yes," Brinta said. "Don't worry about that. We'll make sure that's the case. That's a very thoughtful idea, Trinx."

Vash cradled her chin in her hand and looked off to the side for a moment. "You know, I think that's a good idea all around. It will make my company look good as well. I'll do something similar in the cities."

The alchemist and her apprentice looked over the contract together, pointing out various parts and chatting about the expected revenue streams. Finally, they nodded to each other, and Brinta said, "We like the looks of this. You have a deal."

Brinta pulled out the pen they used for patent applications, which enforced the contractual binding on signatures. They signed the contract first, then handed the pen to Trinx. She signed it and set the pen down.

"Now I'll countersign." With a flourish, Vash drew her signature. "There we go. It's official. The upfront payment is large, and I didn't want to carry it with me while traveling this far. You'll find the funds in your accounts shortly. I'll stop at the nearest banking outlet before I leave the warren."

Brinta extended a hand to shake and said, "Thank you for this opportunity. If any of our other inventions catch your eye, let us know. We can discuss similar deals with them."

The human shook their hand and pulled up her hood. She then left the shop, leaving the two alone.

They both let out a breath and looked at each other.

"I-I can't believe it," Trinx said. "Did you see the size of the initial figure for the exclusive? And that was for each of us!"

"I know!" the alchemist exclaimed. "It was all I could do to hold in my excitement. We probably should have tried negotiating. But I didn't want to wreck it. And Vash is known for fairness in the industry. Be careful. A lot of money can be dangerous."

"Don't worry," Trinx said. "I already know what to do. I'm going to use it to set up a trust for TQ House. That way, it will always have funds to stay open and provide a safe place."

"What a wonderful and generous idea," Brinta said with more warmth than they usually showed. "Speaking of TQ House, is everything coming along? I thought we'd have to send for you, but you surprised me by coming in today."

"It's great!" Trinx said enthusiastically. "Yesterday was amazing. We got so much help. I came in because I can work in the shop today. In fact, we're going to have a party to celebrate the opening of TQ House. You and your partners will have to come."

"We definitely will," Brinta agreed. "For now, since you are here, I could use your help. A shipment of inventory just came in. In fact, that's how Vash came to be here. She traveled with the merchant caravan that brought the alchemy supplies. I could use your help in the back."

"You got it," Trinx said. "Mind if I put on some music while I work?"

"That's fine," they said. "Just keep it in the back. There may not be too many customers today, but still best to treat this like a shop and not a nightclub."

"WAIT!" Trinx said, stopping dead in her tracks. "That's a great idea! I'm definitely going to do that. Thanks!"

"What?" Brinta asked, raising their brow. "I'm confused. I hope by *that*, you mean unpack the supplies. You just said you would."

"Oh. What?" she asked reflexively. "Oh, yeah. Of course, I'm going to unload stuff. I just said I would. That's not what I meant. I meant your idea. I'm going to do that."

"You're talking in circles, Trinx," Brinta said, smiling ruefully. "I didn't have an idea. I just said to keep the music in the back."

"No, silly. Your idea about the nightclub," Trinx said, looking as if it was all perfectly clear. "I can announce the shelter at Unity. Mungo said he'd help spread the word. People at the club might know people and can spread the word."

"Oh," Brinta said. "I understand now. That wasn't my idea. That was your idea. But regardless, I'm not sure it's a great plan. Your shelter is primarily for youth in need of a safe home, right? Mungo wouldn't be letting them into the club. Maybe folks might know of a few kids, but it's not worth putting up flyers. I'm sure Mungo will just whisper in the right ears."

"Fair point and a good call," Trinx said. "It was a spur-of-the-moment idea that I hadn't fully thought through. I could still make posters and put them up around town."

"That's a much better idea," Brinta said. "They'll be much

more likely to be seen by people that need a spot at TQ House."

"Perfect," Trinx said with a wide grin. "I'll make some flyers. I need some paper and colored ink. I'll be back soon." She moved toward the door to the shop.

"Hold on!" Brinta called. "You can't go make flyers. The inventory. Remember?"

"Oh, right? Right," she said. "Of course, the inventory. I was just going to the back room."

Trinx turned around again. This time, she walked to the supply room with a sheepish look on her face. She spent the next several hours unpacking crates, updating inventory tallies, and putting the ingredients on the shelves.

The time seemed to crawl by. Her mind wandered the entire time. More than once, she had to revise a tally to correct an error, backtracking several reagents to figure out where she had made the mistake. Finally, she finished, entered the shop proper, and gave Brinta the updated inventory records.

The alchemist flipped through them and said, "Thank you. This looks good. Assuming everything made it onto the shelves, you can work on your flyers."

"Yup," she said. "Everything should be on the shelves. In order even. I'll see you tomorrow!"

"One thought," they said. "If you know what you want on the flyers, you can likely hire a printing service to make you a stack of copies. There's a print shop to the west—four blocks from here."

"Great idea. I need to remember, we have money now," Trinx called, already walking out the door.

Chapter 31

TQ Open House

Trinx first went to the bank and found that Vash had deposited the licensing fee in her account, just like she said she would. She withdrew some for the printer and some extra for stocking the pantries at the house. After that, she walked to the area Brinta had mentioned and found the print shop. A sign above the door read: "Expeditious Printing." She entered and found two goblins at work.

They sat at small desks with a scroll and several pots of ink, each a different color. Behind them, larger tables held many sheets of parchment laid out in a grid. As they wrote on the scrolls in front of them, pens floating in the air scribbled on the parchments.

"One moment, please," one goblin called out. "Just need to finish this batch."

Trinx stood patiently. She watched in fascination as the floating pens copied everything the goblins wrote. When the goblin who had called out earlier finished, a cloud of fine-grained sand fell on the large worktable. Then, a bellows lowered from the ceiling and pumped twice, blowing away the sand and leaving the newly printed documents.

The goblin stood and came over to her. He said, "Good afternoon. How can I help you?"

"I'd like a flyer made," Trinx said. "Lots of copies. Maybe a hundred? Is that a good amount?"

The goblin snorted. "It might be a good amount. Depends on if the amount you need is a hundred. Hopefully, you know that answer, though."

"Oh," she said, putting a finger to her chin. "I guess that's just it. I don't know. I suppose I could always get more if it's not enough. Let's do one hundred."

"Excellent," he continued. "And what are we making a hundred of?"

"A flyer," she answered. "I know what I want it to say."

"Wonderful," he said. "Knowing that is even more important than the number. I would think anyway. Come to my station. You can dictate the message. We can look it over. Then, if it looks good, I'll add your job to the queue. Payment upfront, I'm afraid. Need to cover the material costs."

"No problem," she said. "I have some coin on me. How much?"

"For one hundred single-sheet flyers?" the printer asked more to himself than to Trinx. "That will be five silver."

Trinx counted out the coins and slid them over to him. "There you go."

"Thank you," the printer said as he slipped the coins into a pouch. "We can figure out the flyer, and then I'll get the production going."

"That sounds fair," Trinx agreed and followed him to the table.

"Are you ready to dictate the flyer, then?" he asked.

She nodded and said, "TQ House. Then skip down. Don't

write that part. I just mean, make a new line. Home for Youth. Skip down. LGBT Folks Welcome. Skip down. Upper West Side. Skip down. A Safe Place. That's it. Er, I mean, I'm done. Don't write anymore after the safe place part."

The goblin chuckled to himself and said, "I think I got your meaning. How's this look?" He picked up the parchment he had written on and showed it to her. The script flowed in a fancy-looking calligraphy. It read just how she meant it.

"Thank you," she said. "That's just what I meant. You're pretty good with that dictation stuff, huh?"

"I've been at it a while," he said with a snort. "I have a question for you now. If you'll hear it."

"Sure," she agreed.

"Is this your place, then?" he asked. "This TQ House? And it's all true what you have here?"

Nodding, she said, "Yes. We're just opening. It's over near The Arsonist's Tender. You know the area?"

"I do," he said. "Pretty sure I know the house you speak of. I think it sounds wonderful what you are doing. I'll slip this project ahead of the others in the queue. It won't take long, and the other orders aren't due until tomorrow."

"Wow," Trinx exclaimed. "Thanks. I'll just wait over here."

Standing against a wall, she watched as the magical quills crafted her flyers in batches. When they finished, the printer returned and handed her a stack of flyers. "Here you are. Thank you for the business."

"These look great. Thanks," Trinx said and left to return to her new home.

Back at TQ House, Trinx found it empty except for Zigla. The newly minted house manager stood up from the couch where she had been resting and followed Trinx into the kitchen.

"Let me make you some tea," Zigla said. "I'm still getting

used to it here and the extra people around. The kids ran off earlier. Not sure where, but I figure they have things to do. Keeping busy."

"I'm sure it's a change," Trinx said. "I hope it hasn't been too disruptive."

"No, no," Zigla assured her. "I'm coming into it well enough. I'm still not sure if I'm up for wandering around the warren at large yet, though. Quilka was a dear and went shopping for us. She brought back plenty of staples to build out our pantry. But she had to get to the Tender. I'm sure you'll see her later."

"That's going to be something to get used to," Trinx said. "But also very exciting. I get to see her every night...and morning." She added the last with a playful grin.

"You two seem fit for each other," Zigla agreed.

"I'll have to tell Quilka all over again later, but I have big news," Trinx said as she remembered what had transpired earlier.

"Let's hear it, then," Zigla encouraged and slid over a mug of tea.

"Brinta and I signed a contract to license EverSmooth!" Trinx blurted in her excitement. "We received a nice lump sum upfront, and there will be residual royalty payments. I'm using the money to set up a trust fund for TQ House. We'll always have plenty of money to run the house. In fact, we never talked about it yet, but if you are going to be the house manager, you need a salary."

"That is good news," Zigla chuckled. "I had faith you and Quilka could bring in money to run this place, but I imagined it would be tight based on what I've seen. This could definitely change that picture. And thank you for bringing up the salary. I knew you had a lot going on and knew you would bring it up eventually."

"The only reason I hadn't yet is I was still trying to figure out how much we could pay you," Trinx explained. "But with the house trust, we can make sure you have what you need."

Trinx then helped Zigla prepare dinner. They assumed the kids would show up at some point and would likely be hungry, which proved true. They all sat down to a simple meal of chili-spiced rice, black beans, and sauted peppers and onions, all wrapped in a flatbread. Zigla had been heavy-handed with the cumin, but it was delicious. Afterward, Trinx retired to her room to read until Quilka came home from the Tender.

Much later that evening, the door to the room opened, pulling Trinx from her dozing. She had drifted off while reading more about the various uses of magical beasts. She rubbed her eyes and saw Quilka trying to enter the room quietly.

"Sorry, Trinx. I was trying not to wake you," Quilka said. "But I'm glad you're awake. I've been looking forward to seeing you."

"Me, too!" Trinx said with a newfound burst of energy. It seemed Quilka's arrival had given her an extra boost. "I have big news."

"You do?" Quilka asked. "You have to tell me, then. Before anything else."

"Vash! You know Vash, right?" Trinx asked. "Well, obviously, you don't know her. I do now, though. I mean Vash from Vash's Extreme Lashes. She came to the shop."

"What!?" Quilka exclaimed. "Vash? In the shop? Why?"

"Oh, right," Trinx said. "That's what I was getting to. She came to make a deal. A deal with me and Brinta. And we did! We made the deal."

"What kind of deal?" Quilka asked, barely able to keep herself calm with Trinx's excitement trying to engulf her.

"It's for rights," she began. "Her company gets exclusive

rights to EverSmooth in the kingdoms. She also gets the rights in the rural lands, but Brinta and I have them, too. So, we end up competing some. But that's okay. It means we still get to do what we want with it. But the money. It's so much money."

"Are you serious?" Quilka asked.

"Yes. Dead serious," she said. "I already have the upfront part in the bank. Then we get monthly payments based on how much of it sells."

"That can solve so many issues," Quilka said with a relieved sigh. "I helped get food for the kitchen today. Thanks for leaving some money, by the way. But even after I added some, too, it took a lot to get everything Zigla said we needed."

"That's just it," Trinx said, nodding. "I'm setting up a trust fund for TQ House. We won't have any money issues. I'm still going to focus on alchemy though, and work at Distilled Magic. I have so much more to learn. Did I tell you she said I had a knack for alchemy? Vash, I mean?"

"Of course you do," her friend said. "Brinta clearly thinks so, too."

"I've been thinking," Trinx said. "With money not as tight, it would be nice to just practice alchemy. Do you think Gristle would hire Jix permanently? Is she doing an okay job? What would you think about that? Now that we live together, I'd get to see you all the time, even if I'm not working at the tavern."

"I think that's a good idea, Trinx," Quilka said with a reassuring smile. "I know you love alchemy, and working two jobs is a lot for you to juggle. Maybe you can take a nap after work at the shop so we can spend time together when I get home."

"That's a great idea," Trinx said. "I'll definitely do that."

They both got ready for bed and climbed in for some cuddling.

Over the next few days, everyone in the house worked their way into a routine. Trinx went back to the bank and set up the trust fund as she had planned. She hung posters up all around town based on where Snixil and Flek thought they'd most likely be seen. And she handed out invitations to the open house to everyone she knew.

The day of the open house arrived, and both Trinx and Quilka took the day off from work. In a surprising turn of events, Gristle actually closed the Arsonist's Tender so he, Brizla, and Jixnet could attend. Brizla and Zigla worked together in the kitchen to prepare a feast for the party. Snixil and Flek took on the decorating duties, while Nibbles helped by placing decorations in hard-to-reach spots—he had a talent for getting to places one wouldn't normally think were reachable.

As the day drew to a close and evening set in, friends and friends of friends began drifting into the house. Trinx mingled with the growing crowd, welcoming everyone and encouraging them to enjoy some food or drinks. Brizla arranged the food buffet-style, with salads, soups, roasts, and desserts. Gristle set up a small table as a bar with some ales and spirits—the cheaper ones, of course. Zigla created a tea station with pots of various teas and a tower of small cakes.

Everyone seemed to have a wonderful time, but as the evening continued to unfold, Trinx found herself over-whelmed. Everyone wanted her attention to ask her about her plans for the house or to thank her for everything she had done. She wasn't used to this much attention, and needing a break, she escaped up to her room on the third floor.

She sat on her bed, smoothing out the beautiful orange dress she had bought for the occasion. Her fingers needed more distraction, so she pulled out the wooden toy Zigla had given her so long ago. The beads still spun with ease, and the gentle clacking soothed her mind.

After a while, the door creaked open, and Quilka peeked

in. "I was wondering if you had come up here. Is everything okay?"

"Come in," Trinx said, placing her toy aside and patting the bed next to her. "Hop up. I could use a hug. It was getting to be a bit much for me down there."

Quilka crossed the room, hopped up on the bed, and wrapped an arm around her. "Sure, there are a lot of people, but you've been in crowds before. The tavern would get pretty busy sometimes. Plus, the crowds at the club are usually huge."

"It's not the number of people," Trinx explained. "They all want my attention. Everyone wants to talk to me like I'm the most important person in the room. But I'm not."

"Who says you're not?" Quilka asked. "You seem pretty darn important to me."

Trinx leaned into her. "Thanks. You're important to me, too. But that's not what I mean. It's just a lot of responsibility. They want to know my plans. They all thank me for what I've done. But I didn't even really do that much. Everyone else chipped in to help."

"You've done a lot more than you give yourself credit for," Quilka said, squeezing her tighter. "This house—this was all your idea. Sure, people helped, but they did so because they believe in you and what you can do. You chose this. You made this. Remember? You even said you had figured it out. You decided to make the change, and then you made it."

"That's true," Trinx said. "I did say that. I did make this change. I became the change. Just like Vorti told me to."

"See," Quilka said, giving her a jostling shake. "You are change. Everyone can tell. That's why they are so excited."

"Thanks, Q," Trinx said. "This is why I love you."

"I love you, too," Quilka said and kissed her forehead. "Now, let's go downstairs. I think you should give everyone a speech. Maybe then they won't all barrage you with the same questions."

Trinx and Quilka returned to the party downstairs. In classic Trinx style, she pulled out the whistle she had used on moving day and held it to her lips. Then she gave three sharp trills with it. This made her giggle, but she quickly composed herself as all heads turned her way.

"Thank you all for coming to celebrate the opening of TQ House."

A light round of applause rose from the crowd, then died down.

"Ever since Zigla helped me realize who I really was, I've wanted to change not only myself but life here in the warren as well. I'll admit now that I didn't always have the greatest ideas as I tried to find my path to accomplish that change."

A few chuckles rose in the crowd.

Trinx let them finish, then continued, "But with Brinta's help, I changed my body so that it better fit me, and others can now use those same methods if they choose. Or not. What matters is that they have a choice now. However, I realized that this wasn't enough. It was more about me than anyone else. I knew my alchemy work could help others, but really, it had been focused on what I personally wanted. During my time in the warren, I've met many people in situations similar to my own. I needed to change the entire situation. We shouldn't have to live like outcasts. That's why I opened TQ House. This is now a safe place for everyone in need of a welcoming home."

Everyone erupted in thundering claps and cheers.

Trinx looked over the crowd and felt like she was home.

Chapter 32

Epilogue

Over the next few weeks, the house gradually filled up. Flyers and word of mouth spread the news throughout the warren. Some newcomers to Chubug even moved in, and the news traveled to some of the closer settlements.

After only a month, nearly every bedroom in TQ House had at least one occupant, and some of the larger bedrooms had two or three. Zigla hired a cleaning staff who made sure the house stayed tidy. She loved cooking and prepared the food herself more often than not. The house was running smoothly, and the youth who lived there felt safe and made new friendships.

One morning, Trinx received a wax-sealed letter delivered by messenger.

Quilka asked, "What is it?"

"Don't know," she replied. "I have to open it."

She broke the seal and unfolded the parchment.

Trinx,

The High Council of Goblin Grandmas is holding a meeting this evening.

We request you appear before the council.

Location: Council Chambers
Date: Today

Sincerely,

Vorti, High Council of Goblin Grandmas

Trinx held out the parchment to Quilka. "Take a look. The council. They want to see me. Tonight. What do you think they want?"

"How would I know?" Q asked. "I'm sure everything will be okay. You should dress up, though. Make a good impression. That signature. That's Zigla's mother, right?"

"Yeah," Trinx said. "I told you about how we had tea. Maybe she changed her mind about helping? But I don't even want a youngling anymore. Heck, there are enough young folks at TQ House now. I don't need more responsibility." She laughed, fidgeting the fingers of her hands together.

That evening, she wore a black, long-sleeved dress that fell to her ankles. The dress had silver trim around the neckline and a double column of silver buttons up the back. Quilka had to help her button them up. She wore her nicest black pumps and a silver chain around her neck, accenting the trim on the dress.

When she arrived at the council chambers, a clerk took her name and reviewed the parchment. They escorted her in and announced her arrival to the council. After the council acknowledged her, the clerk left her facing a half-circle of chairs. She recognized Vorti from their tea together, and she had seen some of the other members from a distance. It struck her that some of the women did not look that old. She always assumed everyone on the council was ancient.

"Thank you for answering our summons, Trinx," Vorti said. "The council elected me spokeswoman this evening since we have sat together before. To be clear, I'm not the leader. We don't have such a position."

"Thank you for inviting me," Trinx replied deferentially. "Is there something I can do for the council? Or have I done something wrong?"

She fidgeted, her fingers twisting in knots. Her right foot found its way behind her left leg, propped up on the toes.

Vorti chuckled softly. "No. You have done nothing wrong. Quite the opposite, actually. It seems you have found that path of change we spoke about over tea. We admire the work you have done opening TQ House. The number of young folks who find it a safe place to live is quite an achievement."

She twisted her fingers together and blushed a deep purple. "Thank you. I've just been trying to help."

"Yes. We have seen that," Vorti continued. "And on a personal note, I appreciate what you have done for Zigla. We have called you here today, Trinx, to offer you a seat on the council."

"B-but. But," she stammered. "I'm not a grandma. I can't even have children, much less grandchildren. I think you made a mistake."

The entire council chuckled at that.

"We don't make mistakes," Vorti said. "We're the High Council. Granted, the official title is High Council of Goblin Grandmas, but that is simply by tradition. The council is made of women in the clan who show wisdom and compassion. Most are grandmothers, but not all."

Trinx stood silent, her mind racing to process what she heard. "I-I don't know what to say."

"Quite understandable," Vorti said. "You do not need to say anything at the moment. The invitation is open."

The councilwoman paused and then said, "You told me once that you wanted to join the council so that you might change goblin culture. However, the council does not change goblin culture."

Trinx fidgeted, but before she could say anything, Vorti continued, "The council invites into its membership those who *have* changed goblin culture. You had it backwards, Trinx. But we believe, based on your actions, that you figured it out. You are welcome here."

"Thank you," Trinx said with a small curtsy. "I accept, and you are right. I did figure out what you meant. I became the change I wanted. Now I hope to teach those who pass through TQ House that they, too, can change the warren and the world."

About the Author

Alex Peachy lives in the Pacific Northwest, and to stave off the cold and lack of sun, he writes cozy fantasy novels full of warmth, whimsy, and magic. The stories Alex creates explore identity, community, and personal growth themes. He shares his home with his wife, son, and their three adorable cats. His favorite cat considers Alex her human and often demands to be held. You can find him writing and sipping on a glass of good whisky in the evenings. Alex encourages you to take the time to slow down and relax. Grab a cozy book from Alex or another of your favorite authors and escape into a world of magic and adventure.

You can find Alex on the internet in a number of places:
AlexPeachy.com (Sign up for the newsletter)
tiktok.com/@inlightsyrup
instagram.com/in_light_syrup
bsky.app/profile/inlightsyrup.com
facebook.com/AuthorAlexPeachey

Join the discussion about Distilled Magic:
www.reddit.com/r/DistilledMagic
discord.gg/C8pbQPrFsa

If you enjoyed this book, please consider writing a review. Reviews are extremely important to indie authors like Alex.

Aberterrene Series

Distilled Magic
Social Sorcery

www.ingramcontent.com/pod-product-compliance
Lightning Source LLC
Chambersburg PA
CBHW061114310726

48974CB00002B/522